MAGUS

BOOK TWO OF THE ADVENT MAGE CYCLE

HONOR RACONTEUR

 RACONTEUR HOUSE

Published by Raconteur House
Murfreesboro, TN

MAGUS: Book Two of the Advent Mage Cycle

www.raconteurhouse.com

The Human Familiar
The Void Mage

GÆLDERCRÆFT FORCES

Call to Quarters

KINGMAKERS

Arrows of Change
Arrows of Promise
Arrows of Revolution

KINGSLAYER

Kingslayer
Sovran at War

SINGLE TITLES

Special Forces 01

The Midnight Quest

*upcoming

ACKNOWLEDGEMENTS

Many thanks to my family, as usual, for giving me their time and attention when I needed it—and silence when I needed that instead. Special thanks to Pam, for all of her wonderful input, and to Velvet, who got me unstuck after I spun my wheels helplessly for three weeks. I'd be lost without both of you. Thanks go as well to the usual suspects—Jen, Ken, Peggy and Dave. I'd peter out without your enthusiasm and thoughtful questions. And last, but never least, thanks go to my wonderful editors and critics: Katie, Jen, my father, Mike; and LaNelle. I don't know how the story would have looked without you. I'm blessed to have such wonderful friends.

On the edge of destiny, you must test your strength.

-William Avery Bishop

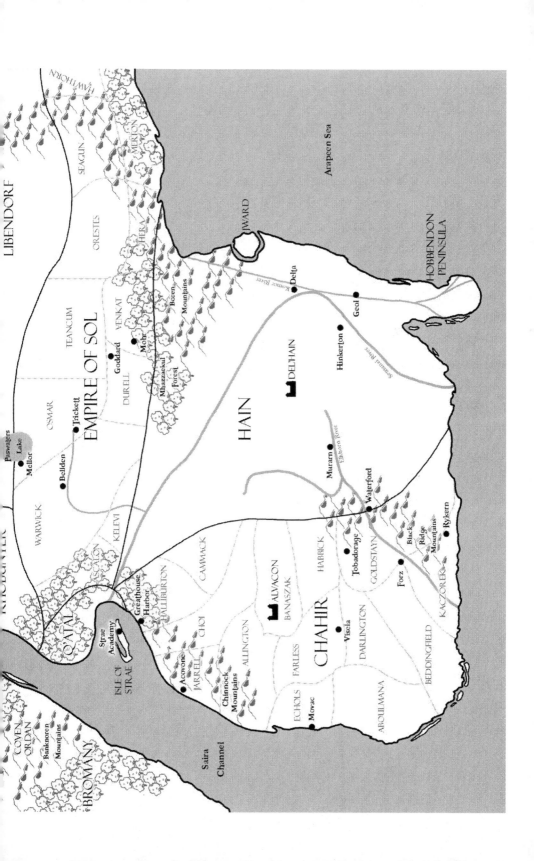

PROLOGUE

"What have you done?"

He didn't know how to answer that question. Slowly, his head turned as he took in everything around him. The caravan was in shambles—wagons overturned, trunks and boxes scattered around them, their contents spilled out over the ground. The horses still shifted about in panic, some of them tangling the reins in horrible knots. People were scattered everywhere, some standing, others leaning against the wagons in various positions. There were cries and moans from the wounded—and the terrible silence of the dead.

Finally his eyes traveled to the body lying at his feet. The bandit had probably been fairly young, but the hard life of thievery had put age into his face. It was in that slack face that he found an answer to the question.

"The only thing that I could do," he whispered.

"De Xiaolang," his uncle demanded with a voice thick with tears. "What have you done?"

De Xiaolang was not quite a man, being only eleven, but he would not duck away from the consequences of his actions. He knew that murder, even in self-defense, was the worst crime possible among the Q'atal. His people could not forgive the taking of a life. He knew that. He understood that. He just hadn't been able to stand aside when the bandits had descended on the caravan and started killing his family and friends. He had done the only thing that he could do—made the only choice that he could make—and picked up the bow he used for hunting. The bandits hadn't expected any of the Q'atalians to fight back, and after three of their company fell, they had broken and run in panic.

Drawing a deep breath into his lungs, he sought for the courage hidden somewhere deep within him to face what he knew was coming. He didn't feel like he had enough, but he turned to his uncle regardless. "De Shiolang, I will leave your house."

His uncle flinched in pain. "You are too young to put yourself in exile," he denied harshly.

"I will accept the consequences of my actions," De Xiaolang answered with quiet conviction. "You must accept this. Even if I could do it over, I would react the same way."

His uncle could do nothing. The law was clear on this, and there was no leniency. He nodded jerkily, face tight with pain.

Without a word more between them, Xiaolang gathered up his bag of clothing, put in a few items of food and a few other necessities, and rolled up some blankets together. His uncle wordlessly pushed a bag of money into his hand, embraced him hard, and then turned his back resolutely to his young nephew.

Xiaolang walked away from the caravan, each step separating him from his homeland. He didn't turn to look behind him, to take one last look.

He was afraid his courage would break if he did.

"Let me get this straight; a group of bandits attacked your caravan a few days ago, and you picked up a bow and killed three of them?"

Xiaolang could not blame the captain for his disbelief. If it hadn't happened to him, he'd have a hard time believing it himself. His people were notorious for being very reclusive. Q'atalians did not leave their homeland except for quick business trips. Period. De Xiaolang was the first one to be exiled in hundreds of years. In fact, their written history didn't go back far enough to record who the last person to be exiled was, or why. Rather than repeat himself, he simply nodded.

Captain Magavero sat back in his chair, studying the young boy in front of him with intense scrutiny. A patrol had stumbled across the young Q'atalian early that morning and had promptly escorted him to the nearest battalion headquarters, which happened to be Magavero's. Like all Q'atalians, this boy had thick blue-black hair, light blue eyes, and a thin build. He apparently spent a great deal of time out of doors, since his skin was nearly white, instead of the typical dusky blue that most Q'atalians had. Magavero had heard that the sun could bleach a Q'atalian's skin white; he just hadn't seen it until now.

He'd never heard of a Q'atalian hurting anyone, or one being exiled. There was something about the boy's expression, however, that made the captain believe him. No Q'atalian would voluntarily leave their country. Something drastic must have pushed the kid to leave, that much was certain.

"From what you tell me, it was clearly self-defense," Magavero finally stated. "Won't your authorities take that into consideration?"

"No."

The word was stated with such finality that Magavero couldn't bring up an argument against it. Letting out a low breath, he sat back up, leaning forward over his desk in order to bring himself closer to eye level with the boy. "All right. So what do you plan to do now?"

At this, the boy hesitated. "I understand that the Empire of Sol will take in people from different nationalities."

Magavero's eyebrows rose a little. What was the kid driving at? "Yes, we do."

"Does Ascalon accept such people into their military?"

Since each city-state in the Empire of Sol had slightly different rules and policies on how they dealt with their military, Magavero could see how it would be a valid question...or he could have, if it hadn't come from an eleven-year-old Q'atalian. "Look, maybe I'm jumping to some conclusions here," he said slowly, eyes narrowing, "but are you suggesting that you want to join the military?"

There was a single, affirmative nod.

Magavero reached up and rubbed his chin thoughtfully, a subtle way of picking his jaw up off the floor before he could catch any flies in it. "Killing in self-defense is one thing, but surely you don't want to actually join the military and become a soldier. I mean, there are other professions you would excel at, surely—"

De Xiaolang shook his head firmly, cutting the captain off. "I could not stand by and watch people be hurt before. I won't be able to do it in the future. I want to protect people. The military will teach me how to do that."

He couldn't fault him on his determination, that was for sure. Magavero eyed the kid thoughtfully. Empire of Sol was built on the back of its city-states, and most of those city-states were militaristic in nature. That being said, drafting an eleven-year-old into the military was a little much, even for them.

The captain hesitated, deliberating on the right course of action. To buy himself time to think he asked, "What is your name?"

De Xiaolang nearly answered, but at the last moment hesitated. He was exiled. He had no right to claim his clan anymore. It felt like he were twisting his heart, but he omitted his clan name. "Xiaolang."

Magavero looked into that determined face, the eyes older than they should have been, and found that he couldn't deny the kid. "You'll train under me first," he stated firmly. "And if you still want to be in the military by the time that you get old enough to enlist, I won't stop you."

Xiaolang gave him a small, grateful smile. "Understood...sir."

"I don't care how incredible the kid is, I'm not making any sixteen-year-old a captain!"

Capka sighed, wishing that he had been able to put this request for promotion to General Gibaldi instead of General Bellflower like he had wanted to. Gibaldi was much more open-minded about things. "Sir, respectfully, no one else in Ascalon can touch his scores, and he has the highest rate of success in the Empire. He is the best at intelligence, infiltration, and leadership. I've personally sparred with him and I lasted about fifteen seconds. He is the best we have. In all reality, we should have promoted him to captain last year." And they probably would have, if the administration hadn't strongly suggested that letting Xiaolang mature for another year was a good idea.

"He's too young for this sort of responsibility."

"No sir, he's not," Capka disagreed, with the strongest tone that he dared against a superior officer. "He's been team leader for the past year, and has excelled at it. I actually have a waiting list of men that want to be on his team that's longer than my arm."

Bellflower blinked at this. A waiting list to be on someone's team? That was...well, it was highly unusual, that was for certain! He hummed thoughtfully and settled his bulk more comfortably in his chair. "Capka, I'm just not comfortable giving someone that young such power."

"Then assign him a very strong, mature second in command," Capka suggested readily. He started silently praying that the general would see his viewpoint on this. "It would balance out his youth, but still give him the promotion that he deserves."

Bellflower hummed again, in a rather noncommittal tone. Capka was left to wait on pins and needles for long, agonizing minutes as the general thought it over.

"A permanent team," Bellflower finally stated.

Capka blinked. "Sir?"

"Give Xiaolang a permanent team of experienced people, and I'll promote him to captain."

Capka was a veteran colonel of Ascalon, a true son of the Empire of Sol, so he didn't grin like a loon as he wanted to, but it was a very near thing. "Yes sir!"

"And Capka."

Capka froze half out of his chair. He was suddenly afraid that this was too easy, and the general was about to add some sort of outlandish clause. "Yes, sir?"

"I won't promote the boy to major before he hits twenty, no matter how much you might plead or bargain with me, is that clear?"

A grin broke out over Capka's face. "Perfectly, sir."

NEW ALLIANCES

Sometimes he hated it when he was right.

King Guin of Hain stood looking at the large map of Chahir hanging on his study wall. He'd had it put there two months ago, just after coming home from the negotiations with Vonlorison. He had hoped that the new laws dealing with magic would take root in Chahir, but had been pessimistically aware that perhaps only half of the Doms in Chahir would actually do anything to enforce the new laws.

As it turned out, it wasn't even half. Perhaps a third of the provinces in Chahir were abiding by the new laws, no more.

There were still people coming in from Chahir, looking for sanctuary and training, but those people told of a hard and dangerous journey filled with dodging patrols and running from local law enforcement. What made the situation worse was that the provinces on the Chahir-Hain border were by far the worst offenders. Crossing the border was more a matter of luck than skill.

Guin found that he couldn't ignore the situation. He was always short on magicians, the need for their skills and knowledge always outweighing the people available. That alone would make him consider helping people out of Chahir, but it was more than that.

Killing someone just because of a talent they were born with was wrong. He knew that to the depth of his being, and he could not turn away from that knowledge or pretend that he had no right to interfere.

There was a knock at the door, and he turned away from the map, calling "Enter!"

Val Haben opened the door and his face was alight with a satisfied smile. "Sire, Captain Xiaolang of the Red Hand is here."

"Bring him in, please." Guin rubbed his hands together, a fierce feeling of anticipation tingling at the base of his spine. Considering how dangerous using magic was in Chahir, he hadn't thought it wise to send magicians in as rescue teams. A non-magical solution to this problem would be better. He had contacted Ascalon a week ago, asking for their best team in infiltration. He hadn't expected the Red Hand, but was absolutely delighted to have them. Even here, in Hain, the Red Hand team was famous for their abilities to infiltrate anywhere, and to recover anything...or anyone.

Guin smoothed his face out into more neutrally polite lines when he heard the approach of two sets of feet. Grinning like a demented goat with a new chew toy would hardly be dignified, after all.

The first one into the room was Val Haben, but close on his heels was a lithe young man wearing the black and red uniform of Ascalon. He was striking with thick black hair, pale skin, and sharply penetrating blue eyes.

Guin was an experienced politician, with years of practice in keeping his face straight, so he didn't gape. Much. He'd heard that the captain of the Red Hand was young, but he hadn't expected him to be around Garth's age! Reflex kicked in, and Guin was composed and in control once more. "Captain Xiaolang, thank you for responding so promptly."

"Not at all, Your Majesty." Captain Xiaolang flashed him a smile, one filled with easy humor and confidence.

"Please be seated." He used the few seconds that it took for his guest to sink into a comfortable armchair to give the captain a quick perusal. So young! And he was obviously not native to Ascalon. They were a darkly complexioned race, and this young man was too fair and by far too light of frame to belong to that people. Actually, Guin couldn't quite pin what nationality he was. (This didn't surprise him, as his intelligence officers hadn't been able to figure it out either.) That blue-black hair and brilliant blue eyes were almost Q'atalian, but the skin color was wrong. Besides, the idea was absurd. No Q'atalian would be a captain in any military; they were a very pacifist culture.

Before he could be caught staring, he sank into a nearby armchair. "May I offer you any refreshments?"

"I'm fine, but thank you." Xiaolang was relaxed in his seat, perfectly at ease and attentive.

"Very well, I'll get straight to the point." Guin took a breath, ready to launch into his prepared explanation, and then paused when a thought struck him. This man was reputed to be excellent at gathering information. Actually, Guin wouldn't be surprised if the captain already knew why he was here. "Captain Xiaolang, would I be mistaken if I said that you already know why you are here?"

Xiaolang's head cocked slightly to the side. "Did you call me here in order to hire my team to help rescue people with magical abilities out of Chahir?"

Guin felt the corners of his mouth twitch slightly as he suppressed a smile. "Indeed."

"Then no, Your Majesty, you are not mistaken."

"Dare I ask how you knew?"

Xiaolang gave an elegant shrug. "I have many sources of information. The political tension between Chahir and Hain over the treatment of magical people, and of course, your recent visit and the results of those negotiations were rather obvious. I simply inferred a number of things from that."

The man was certainly living up to his reputation. Guin nodded thoughtfully. "Then I needn't bore you with a full explanation. Most of the province lords in Chahir do not choose to enforce the new laws. Actually, some of them are actively hunting magically gifted people down. I cannot ignore the situation."

Xiaolang nodded in understanding. "How many people do you want retrieved?"

"All of them," Guin answered simply.

Those penetrating blue eyes widened slightly. "All of them?"

"Captain, I'm fully aware of how impossible this task seems," Guin admitted with a weary sigh. "After all, people with magical gifts are being born daily. People will become aware of their gifts at random moments. You might not find anyone one week, and find a hundred the next. It's a dangerous and very time-consuming task that I'm asking you to take on, and one without any end in sight. All I can promise you is that I'm not done with Chahir yet. I am still in close correspondence with Vonlorison, and still trying to sway him to do something to stop this atrocity. Eventually, I think he will enforce the laws that we agreed to two months ago. But this will take time. Captain." Guin leaned forward slightly in his seat, giving his words emphasis, "I know that this will keep you from your home for quite some time. Are you willing to do it?"

For a long moment, Xiaolang sat in silence, his eyes locked with

Guin's. "What fee are you offering?"

"Name your price," Guin retaliated.

Xiaolang's eyes flew wide, and then he started chuckling in genuine humor. "That is a dangerous thing to say to a mercenary captain, King Guin. It's almost a shame that I promised my reflection that I would be nice today, and not take shameless advantage of the situation." With a rueful sigh he shook his head. "The temptation is almost too much. No, Your Majesty, I shall charge you standard fee, plus traveling and living expenses since we shall be in Chahir for so long. Is that acceptable?"

Guin blinked. He had expected to pay far more than this; had steeled himself to pay his entire family fortune, actually. He had not expected this much generosity. "More than acceptable, Captain." He almost felt like bargaining for the captain, but restrained himself at the last moment. One didn't argue when handed a bargain. That would be foolish. "You shall have support as well."

Xiaolang looked intrigued. "Really? What support?"

"I have two people within my service that excel at finding people with magical abilities," Guin explained. "They can search for several miles around them, sometimes up to twenty miles. They will be at your disposal."

"That is a relief to hear," Xiaolang admitted with a wry smile. "I had been wondering about how to tell the magical people apart from anyone else. Rescuing people without knowing who to rescue would be a tricky business."

"I can imagine," Guin drawled. "When can your team get here?"

"They're here now," Xiaolang corrected. "They came with me. It was an easy trip down river, and they wanted a chance to play tourist. We can begin at any time."

Guin beamed, thoroughly caught up in a wave of enthusiasm. "Excellent! I shall call in the people that you'll work with. If you'll gather your team, Captain, we can meet here within an hour?"

"Perfectly acceptable, Your Majesty."

When Val Haben comes and gets me with that smile on his face,

I know it's time to quickly disappear somewhere. I probably would have, too, if he hadn't already had Chatta in tow. There was no way that I could leave my best friend in a lurch, which Haben knows and was probably counting on, which is why he got her first.

I wasn't sure which was worse, being manipulated, or knowing that I was being manipulated but unable to do anything about it.

As I followed Haben down the palace hallways, Chatta leaned in close and murmured, "Garth, do you know what this is about?"

"No idea," I answered quietly. "Do you?"

"I have a hunch," she admitted. "The last few people that came out of Chahir were in pretty bad condition. It infuriated Guin."

It had infuriated me, too, but I saw what she was getting at. "You think that he's going to do something about it, and we're part of it."

She nodded grimly.

Haben had obviously overhead us, because over his shoulder he said, "You're right."

Well, since he was confirming our suspicions, he might tell us something more. "Can you tell us anything else?"

"I'll let the king explain it," Haben said easily.

I would have persisted, but we were practically at Guin's study, so I let it rest. I'd get my answers soon enough.

Haben was apparently expected as he only gave a quick rap on the door before shoving it open and stepping inside. I followed him in, but stopped when I realized that there were five complete strangers in the room.

They all wore the black and red uniforms of an Ascalon soldier, from the Empire of Sol.

I blinked at them dumbly, exchanging a quick look of bemusement with Chatta. Well. This was something we hadn't expected.

"Good, we're all here." Guin was beaming, like a giddy child with hidden candy in his pockets. That expression made me want to run for the hills. "Chatta, Garth, this is Captain Xiaolang of the Red Hand."

I turned to see who he had indicated, and nearly swallowed my tongue in surprise. The man facing me couldn't have been much older than Chatta or me, and was obviously not Solian. I'm not sure precisely what I had been expecting as a captain. I just knew that whatever it was, he was on the other end of the spectrum.

"Captain Xiaolang," Guin continued, oblivious to my surprise, "This is Magus Rhebengarthen, and Witch L-Chattamoinita Delheart."

"Ainlie." He extended a hand in greeting, so I accepted it, hand clasping his forearm.

Then I nearly dropped it in surprise.

His eyes narrowed slightly, and the grip he had on my arm tightened. "You know what I am."

That wasn't true. I had no idea what he was; I just knew that he wasn't completely normal. He wasn't magical, precisely, but I was feeling something in him that was different, something…something that felt like the warmth of a lantern's light. "Chatta," I pleaded in a strained voice, "please tell me what I'm sensing from him."

My best friend hissed in a shocked breath. "He's Q'atalian!"

He's what?! My Jaunten blood poured knowledge into my head, but all of it was telling me that no Q'atalian would ever voluntarily be a soldier. I was more than surprised now, I was dumbfounded. Judging from the expression on my king's face, so was he.

"This is amazing," Xiaolang stated in growing enthusiasm. "I have no real magic in me, but you both can detect it? Well, your king has not exaggerated your abilities, certainly."

Finally it hit me what I was sensing in him. Q'atalians are empaths—his emphatic ability was close enough to magic that I could sense it. "No magic," I confirmed hoarsely, "but you're an empath."

"Indeed," he agreed with a brilliant smile. "And I can feel both of you very clearly. King Guin," he dropped my hand and turned to face Guin. "You have given me very good people to work with."

It took a second for Guin to get his mouth working again. "Two of my best," Guin acknowledged.

I blushed at hearing this, and when I took a peek at Chatta, I saw that she was just as embarrassed as I was.

Xiaolang was apparently amused at our reactions, but took pity and diverted the conversation away from the topic. "Let me introduce the rest of the Red Hand. This is Shield Garbracen, my First Lieutenant."

Shield was a stocky man with shockingly light hair and dark skin, but his manner was easy enough, the smile he gave us genuine. "Ain."

"Hazard Harewood, my Intelligence Officer," Xiaolang continued, indicating a bear of a man who was sprawled comfortably in a chair. Hazard only waved a hello and smiled, not offering a more verbal greeting, but something about him said that he was an easy person to get along with.

"Aletha Saboton, Infiltration Specialist and overall queen of sneaky and underhanded tactics." Xiaolang flashed the woman a teasing smile.

"One day, Captain, we're going to have a little 'discussion' on the way you introduce me," Aletha promised direly.

"I look forward to it," Xiaolang promised with a mischievous wink.

She frowned at him, but smiled when she greeted us. "Ainlie." It was almost odd to see a woman in uniform, especially one as darkly lovely as Aletha was, but she somehow fit into the group with ease. She certainly had no qualms about taking her captain to task.

"And last but never least, Eagle Sevar, who is our Language Specialist."

Eagle was tall, with bleached hair and golden brown eyes. In fluent Chahirese he turned to me and said, "De Evana."

I blinked at hearing this from a Solian, but responded out of sheer reflex. "De Evana. Evana anata te dame."

I could swear his ears perked slightly. "Are you from Tobadorage?"

My jaw dropped before I could catch it. "How did you know that?"

"Your accent," he explained enthusiastically. "Everyone from Tobadorage has a habit of stressing their a's. This is wonderful; you can coach us better on how to blend in than I can."

Xiaolang was nodding in agreement. "Very helpful, indeed. Having a Chahiran along will be very beneficial."

I foresaw a lot of language and cultural lessons in my future.

Guin cleared his throat slightly to catch our attention. "Garth, Chatta, I'm sure that I don't have to explain why the Red Hand is here. You've surely guessed by now, and what role you will be playing."

We both nodded. It was fairly obvious, really. The Red Hand had been called in to do the job that we couldn't—they were here to help get people out of Chahir. We were to help them find those people.

"I've set up several houses near the border to serve as way stations for you. Haben has a map with them marked. Garth, Chatta, I realize that this will be very time consuming. You have no other duties except to help the Red Hand."

"Understood, sire." I thought about this for a moment, and then added, "You get to tell Trev'nor."

Guin actually growled at me. "Garth, that is hardly fair."

I smiled at him sweetly. He could assign me impossible tasks, and I couldn't argue, but that also meant he got to explain to a five-year-old why his adopted brother wouldn't be around for the foreseeable future.

Guin growled again, muttering darkly under his breath, but nodded in resignation.

"Anything else, sire?" Chatta inquired politely. She was obviously amused, but better at not gloating than I was.

"No, I'm sure you need to prepare and notify your families. I'll have the Red Hand settled into the Ambassador Inn. You'll start tomorrow morning."

It was afternoon right now. He expected us to be ready by daylight tomorrow?

The man really was a workaholic.

We hadn't set a specific time for meeting the next morning, but Captain Xiaolang struck me as a morning person, so I arrived fairly early, just in case. As it turned out, it was a good thing I did.

I entered the common room of the inn to find Captain Xiaolang already at a table, eating a very large breakfast with pleasurable enthusiasm. He looked up as I came in and waved me over with a friendly smile.

"Good morning," he greeted.

"Good morning." I slung the two saddlebags in my hands into the seat next to me before sitting at the table.

"You're quite early," the captain noted after taking a quick sip from his cup.

"I wasn't quite sure what time I should be here," I answered honestly. "So I decided to come early just in case. Chatta hasn't come yet, then?"

"No, you're the first I've seen this morning," he replied. "Would you like to join me?"

"I've already eaten, but thank you." Not as well as he was, though. I wished I had waited now.

"Forgive me if I seem nosy, but I must ask a few questions. You and Witch Delheart seem like close friends. Are you accustomed to working together?"

"Very much so," I confirmed. "We're often paired together on projects. Actually, we were in school together, and trained under some of the same teachers."

"Good, then you're aware of each other's capabilities and reactions." Satisfied, he popped a piece of bread in his mouth.

"I should warn you that we both have companions." I felt it only fair to tell him about this now. Didi warranted a lot of warning, after all. "I'm not sure if they've been mentioned or not."

"You mean your nreesce, Night, and Witch Delheart's meuritta, Didi?"

I managed to catch my jaw before it could crash land into the table. "Er, you've been told, then."

"No, but I am an information specialist. It's my job to know everything."

If that were true, then why did he need to ask me if Chatta and I were used to working with each other? "Really."

He heard the doubting tone in my voice and started laughing. "Actually, Val Haben thought to warn me about them. Where is Night? I was given the impression that he followed you everywhere."

"He went to make sure Chatta was on her way," I admitted. The captain's laugh was so infectious that I found myself smiling back at him without really meaning to. "She's not known to be coordinated in the mornings. He figured she might need some help."

"Kind of him," Xiaolang noted. "Magus, you don't strike me as a formal person. Are you?"

"Not in the least," I assured him. "Call me Garth, please."

"Very well. You can drop the 'Captain' as well. We're going to be working together a long time, so we might as well start out as friends."

I nodded in agreement. This was a man, I had the feeling, that would make an excellent friend. I had no qualms about accepting such an offer of friendship.

Someone stumbled down the stairs at that point, approaching the table in a slightly unsteady shuffle. It took a moment for me to put name together with face, but I finally remembered. Hazard Harewood. Apparently, he was not a morning person either.

Hazard stopped at the table, dropping heavily into a chair. I'd never seen the walking dead before, or anything of that nature, but Hazard was doing a very good impression of one. Xiaolang didn't say a word, just handed him a mug filled with steaming tea. He indicated to me to not say anything, so I stayed quiet, and watched as the big man drained the mug dry.

It was like someone opened the storm shutters—he went from being bleary eyed and unfocused, to awake and alert. "Morning, Cap'n."

"Good morning, Hazard," Xiaolang returned with a twinkle in his eyes. "Welcome back to the land of the living."

"Oh ha-ha," Hazard returned. His hands were already moving, filling a plate of food for himself. "Good morning, Magus."

"Garth," I corrected him. "I'm not a formal person. And a good morning to you, as well."

"Call me Hazard, then," the Solian replied cheerfully. "Where's the beautiful witch?"

"On her way," I responded confidently, although I wasn't entirely sure if that were the case or not.

"Where's the rest of the team?" Xiaolang countered.

"Shield was making groaning noises, so I'm pretty sure he's up and moving," Hazard reported while putting away food at an alarming rate. "Aletha was shaking Eagle awake last I saw."

Xiaolang shook his head in exasperation. "How late did Eagle stay up studying?"

"I dunno, Cap'n, but when I went to sleep around one this morning, he was still at it."

"Eagle hasn't actually spoken Chahirese in a year or so," Xiaolang explained to me. "He's been studying it ever since we heard about this mission, but he doesn't feel that he's comfortable enough to pass as a native anymore. Do me a favor and spend some time coaching him, otherwise I'll have to take his books away from him."

"I'll work with him as we ride west," I assured him. "Actually, I'll work with all of you as we ride."

"Good idea," Xiaolang approved.

Aletha was the next to descend, followed closely by Shield. They were more awake than Hazard had been, so I ventured a friendly good morning, and received one in return.

"And how is Eagle?" Xiaolang inquired of Aletha.

"Blood shot and wet from the waist up," Aletha reported with rolled eyes. "I had to douse him with cold water to get any sort of reaction. Captain, take his books away, otherwise he'll be like this all the way to Chahir."

"Garth will work with him," Xiaolang promised her. "That should distract him from the books."

I had been keeping an eye on the door, so I saw Chatta when she came in. She wasn't entirely awake yet, judging by the dull look in her eyes, but she was moving all right. I moved my saddlebags so she could have a place to sit.

Didi wasn't awake at all, but draped across Chatta's shoulders, like some sort of woman's fur stole.

"Morning," she greeted as she sank into a seat.

"Not 'good morning'?" I teased.

"No, because there's nothing good about mornings," she growled back at me.

"Diii," Didi muttered in dark agreement. Oh, so he was awake? Well, sort of.

Night nudged the door open and came in, looking bright eyed and bushy tailed, as usual. "Good morning."

Everyone at the table but Chatta and I jumped, whipping around to stare at him. A bemused smile quirked the corners of my mouth as I took in this extreme reaction. "Xiaolang, I thought Haben told you about Night?"

Xiaolang managed to get his mouth working again. "He failed to mention he was a telepath."

That was so typical of Haben. "Ah. Well, he is. He's also a Breaker—if he hits anything with both hooves at the same time, whatever he hits will break."

"That's handy," Hazard noted. "Ain, Night. I'm Hazard Harewood."

"A pleasure, Hazard."

Belatedly, I finished the introductions. There were polite greetings, and I could tell by the way that Night studied Xiaolang that he was intrigued by the man. I had filled him in the night before while doing some very quick packing, so he knew what the captain was. He was being studied in return by everyone at the table. Night didn't seem to mind, probably sensing that it was because they were curious about him as well.

Eagle finally made his appearance, looking very sleep deprived. By mutual consent, no one talked to him until he had downed three cups of tea. Once he looked semi-intelligent again, Xiaolang gave him a pointed look and a droll, "Good morning, Eagle."

"Er...morning, Captain." The blond wore a very sheepish expression.

"Do I have to take your books away from you?"

Eagle flushed and ducked his head. "Sorry, sir. I've just forgotten a lot, and to be really prepared for going into Chahir—"

Xiaolang raised a hand, stopping him. "Eagle, stop, I'm not upset. But leave your books packed, all right? Magus Rhebengarthen has promised to work with all of us as we travel. He's a better way of reviewing Chahirese than your books, anyway."

Eagle shot me a grateful look. "You don't mind, Magus?"

"Garth," I corrected. "And no, it will be my pleasure."

"Thanks," Eagle responded happily. The look he gave his captain included him in that thank you.

"Good," Xiaolang stated with satisfaction. "Then eat, I don't want to hear any hungry stomachs later. Garth, only Eagle has ever actually set foot in Chahir. What can you tell us about the country?"

"It's colder than Hain," I answered promptly. "With it approaching fall like it is, we'll need heavy coats and gloves. And hats. Hats are very popular in Chahir."

"It'll help to cover our hair as well," Aletha noted. "Eagle and Shield won't have a problem, being blonds, but the rest of us won't blend in as well."

"There are a few brunettes that crop up from time to time," I ruminated thoughtfully as I looked over the group. "Xiaolang could pass, with his fair skin, but you and Hazard won't have a prayer. You're just too dark."

"I can do something about that," Chatta offered in a questioning tone.

Xiaolang leaned forward so he could see around me, and look directly at her. "Oh? In what way?"

"There are potions that can turn a person's skin and hair into different colors," she informed him. "They only last about twelve hours, but I can make them look Chahiran." She paused suddenly and gave me a concerned look. "Will they be able to detect that?"

"I'm not sure," I said slowly.

"Witch Delheart, you're speaking cryptically," Xiaolang complained.

"Chatta," she corrected him with a slight smile. "I'm not a formal person either. But in answer, Chahir has ways of detecting when magic is used."

"Which is how they hunt down magical people," Aletha said in sudden understanding.

I nodded in grim acknowledgement. "The only time I triggered the alarms, it was something very minor. Those alarms are very sensitive. Still, I'm not sure if potions would be enough to give you away. Potions are not active magic, not really. There's no build up of power when you use them, which is what I think actually sets those alarms off."

"But you're not sure," Xiaolang stated, his eyes searching mine.

"No," I was forced to admit. "That part of the process, how they detect magic, has always been a closely guarded secret. I'm not precisely sure how they do it."

"If we're to have a prayer of success, we better figure it out," Shield noted.

"Hazard," Xiaolang commanded quietly. "That will be your task."

Hazard nodded once. "Understood, sir."

"I'll help you with that," Chatta volunteered. "I have ways of detecting magic too."

He blinked, but smiled in pleasure. "I appreciate that, Chatta."

"She's better at it than I am," I told him. "But if I can help, I'll be pleased to do so." With sadistic cheer, I added, "And I'll be more than pleased to help destroy their detection system, whatever it is."

The look in Hazard's eyes said he understood why, but he didn't say anything, just nodded.

"What else, Garth?" Xiaolang prompted.

"Chahir is rather flat, for the most part," I answered after a beat. "The south has some mountains and forests, but most of it is grassland or farmland of some sort. It makes it difficult to hide, and difficult to cross." That was the voice of experience. It had been nerve-wracking covering the distance between Tobadorage and the Black Ridge Mountains. I had been sure someone would spot me and chase me down. "Each province is like a state unto itself, with its own culture and rules. The small villages are especially wary of strangers. I only visited a few, usually when I went to see relatives, and I was under suspicion the entire time. Even though people knew who I was."

"Paranoid villagers," Shield drawled with a roll of his eyes. "I hate dealing with paranoid villagers."

I agreed with him. It made our job harder. "If you do get questioned, or stopped for any reason, the safest thing to do is say that you're a mapmaker."

"Mapmaker?" Hazard repeated dubiously.

Eagle was the only one that nodded, apparently knowing what I was referring to. "Yes, of course! Brilliant, Garth." Seeing his teammate's confusion, he leapt into an explanation. "You see, all the provinces' lords—Doms, they're called—are in constant conflict with their neighbors about where their borders actually are. The government has gotten tired of their arguments, as they usually lead to blood feuds. They've hired a number of people to go in when requested, and measure out the full lay of the province. But they always hire foreigners, or people from across the country, so that the mapmaker isn't partial to one dom or another."

"So," Xiaolang said in understanding, "they actually expect the foreigner to be a mapmaker. Good cover story. Everyone, buy the necessary supplies to draw maps with and carry it with you. I want us to be able to back our stories up."

"There's not much else I can tell you now," I said while rubbing the tips of my fingers together thoughtfully. "I'll coach you on customs and language as we go. One important thing to keep in mind, however, is this—do not touch people unless you can't help it."

Eagle nearly choked on his tea. "Ye gods, I nearly forgot about that! It's a huge culture taboo they have."

"Not a taboo, it's just really rude," I denied. "Touching someone casually means that you are very close to them. Unless the other person will be injured or something if you don't touch them, then avoid it as much as possible."

"That includes handshakes," Chatta added dryly. I gave her a wry smile, as she had been through this speech before, three months ago. The no-touching rule had been a hard one for her to get used to, as she was a rather physically demonstrative person. "Bow when you meet someone."

"Somehow," Xiaolang noted sardonically, "I get the feeling that this mission is going to get very interesting."

After breakfast, we did some last minute shopping, mostly for those map making supplies. Chatta was by far the most comfortable person about shopping in Del'Hain, so I went with her to pick up the supplies. We rendezvoused in the stable yard Inn with the Red Hand at the Ambassador.

Have you ever come face to face with something that you believed to be a legend, or a myth? I took a long look at the creature in front of me and had a hard time convincing myself that my eyes weren't lying to me.

Dragoo.

I could not believe it. There was an actual dragoo standing not ten feet away from me!

Chatta saw what I did and stumbled to a halt, gasping. "That's a dragoo!"

Eagle was saddling a horse nearby and obviously overheard her, because he turned around to comment, "Yes, it is. Didn't you know? All captains in the Empire ride dragoos as a sign of their rank."

Actually, I hadn't known that. The Jaunten didn't exactly deal much with Solians, so my information about them was sketchy.

I hadn't seen more than a textbook illustration, but this dragoo at least seemed to match what I had studied. He was roughly fifteen feet long, from head to tail, and covered in thick black scales. His head was elongated, similar in shape to a dragon's head, only slimmer and without all of the ridges. His body was long, but slim, with four feet ending in razor sharp claws. He stood nearly as high as a horse, although his back was lower to the ground.

Unlike all of the descriptions, he was not acting ferocious, but was currently pressed up against Xiaolang's chest and whining pitifully.

"Will you quit?" Xiaolang demanded in obvious exasperation. "If you eat anymore, you'll be sick later, you know you will."

"Bacon," the dragoo mourned in pitiful tones.

"You had three pounds of bacon, Hayate!" Xiaolang responded, running one hand roughly through his hair. "That's more than enough, now quit."

The dragoo pouted—and believe me, on a creature with long fangs, a pout was a very alarming expression—and pulled away from his captain.

Xiaolang, now that he wasn't distracted by his dragoo, saw that we had arrived and waved us closer. "Garth, Chatta, this is my dragoo, Hayate. I already introduced him to Night."

I had to wonder about Night's reaction to meeting Hayate, but I could ask him later.

Before I could respond, Hayate's head snapped around, his amber eyes fixating on Didi. He gave a low hum, and a long, forked tongue licking his lips appreciatively.

Didi took one look at that hungry expression and shrieked in alarm. He rapidly scrambled behind Chatta's head and attempted to burrow himself under her cloak.

"Hayate!" Xiaolang snapped out sharply. "You will not eat the meuritta."

"Nekon," Hayate said dreamily.

"No, it is not a nekon, it is a meuritta," Xiaolang explained firmly. "Meurittas are not something you can eat. Especially this meuritta. Understand?"

Hayate grumbled in dark dissatisfaction.

"Sorry," Xiaolang apologized to Chatta. "It's just that there are cat-like creatures in Libendorf, and dragoos are used to thinking of nekons as food. Didi looks rather similar to a nekon, aside from the wings and tail, so Hayate thinks he's a snack. But you needn't worry, Hayate is very well trained, and he knows better than to countermand my orders."

Chatta nodded dubiously. She was still trying to reach behind her and extract the meuritta, but he had thoroughly burrowed into her hood and wasn't budging. "All the same, I think it's a good idea to keep him well fed."

"Wise idea," Xiaolang muttered to himself. Clearing his throat, he changed subjects. "Now, I assume that you've got all of the necessary supplies?"

"Everything," I assured him.

"Good, let's pack that up and we'll move out."

It took a few minutes to get everything stowed and everyone mounted, and then we followed Xiaolang out of the yard. It was truly odd to see him riding the dragoo. The saddle that he used was completely compact, folding the rider up so that he rested completely on the dragoo's back, and the gait was more of a side-to-side motion, like how a cat would move. It made me sea sick just looking at it. However, he seemed to be very fast—his movement appeared slow and effortless, but he was keeping up with everyone else just fine.

Didi still clung to Chatta's neck and stared at Hayate in wide-eyed fear. I felt sorry for him; it couldn't be comfortable traveling with something that thought you were a nice after dinner snack.

Night and I were apparently thinking along the same lines, because my nreesce tilted his head slightly and said, "Didi, if you need to, you can come to me for protection, all right?"

The meuritta's ears perked and he stopped cringing for a moment. "Di?"

"I don't think he'll do anything, not with his captain saying he can't, but I'll let you ride me if he's scaring you."

Didi chattered happily, and while I didn't speak meuritta, he seemed to be accepting the offer. After that he settled down some. Chatta gave Night a smile of pure gratitude, which made him prance a little in pride.

We'd barely cleared the city's limits when Eagle came up to ride beside me.

"So Garth, explain the difference between imashite and doimashite. They're both used to say 'you're welcome' but is one more formal than the other? As far as I can tell, they're used interchangeably."

I looked at that attentive, curious expression and knew that this conversation was going to take a while.

RAPPORT

We really should have seen this coming.

After riding most of the day, we'd found a nice clearing off the road and settled in for the night. Chatta and I were in the habit of erecting personal barriers around ourselves as we slept, as much for protection from bandits, as from Didi's pranks.

We just hadn't considered protecting everyone else the same way.

I woke up that morning to Chatta's voice growling, "—the most impossible creature! I should never have let you spend so much time with Trev'nor."

Hmmm. That didn't sound good. I dragged my eyelids open and turned until I could see my friend. She held Didi up by his waist, and was scolding him ferociously. She seemed fine, though, so I was a little confused as to what Didi had done until I looked over and saw Aletha.

The beautiful Solian officer was sporting not one, not two, but three Tonkowacon braids in her dark hair. Didi had put his grubby little hands on some ribbons somehow, and given Aletha one braid to signify that she was an adult, another to signify that she was in the military, and the last to indicate that she was an officer in that military.

I groaned as the situation became clear, and dropped back to my bedroll. "Not again."

"He does this often, then?" Xiaolang inquired dryly.

"Not often, but he has done it before," I said. I looked around the group as I responded, seeing if Didi had tampered with anyone else, but apparently their hair had been too short for him to braid anything into it. Luckily for them! With a groan I rolled out of my bedroll and up to my feet. "He has a friend that is Tonkowacon, and taught him how to do all the braids."

"Ah, I thought they looked familiar." Xiaolang studied the scene with amusement.

"Since this has happened before, you know how to get them out, right?" Aletha asked me plaintively while gently tugging on one of the braids in her hair.

I looked at the situation, thinking it over. Aletha had no magic in her whatsoever, so the solution that we had tried with Kartal all those months ago would actually work with her. "You can't untie those braids, but we can cut them out and Chatta will grow your hair out to the right length again."

She blinked. "You can do that with magic?"

"I can't," I confessed with an easy shrug. "But she can."

"Ah yes, we need to talk about that." Xiaolang had been pouring himself a cup of water from a canteen, but at this statement he looked up at me. "What precisely is the difference between a mage and a witch? I know that she needs some sort of tool to focus her magic, but are there other differences?"

"Many." I unstrapped a dagger from my saddlebags and set about cutting the braids out of Aletha's hair as I answered him. "A mage's power is very different in nature than a witch's. Everything has latent energy in it, and she can tap into all of that energy and change things according to her will. My power is more focused. I can only tap into the latent power of the earth itself."

Our conversation was garnering everyone's interest, and it was Shield that said the obvious. "So if its not dirt or stone, you can't do anything with it?"

"For the most part, yes, that's precisely right. There are a few exceptions, of course. I can use magical devices made by someone else. I can alter plants some, as they are a part of the earth. And I can sense people, especially magical people, at quite some distance." The last braid fell free and I stepped back. "There, done."

Chatta came forward and pointed her wand at Aletha's head. "Hold still. Grow."

The hair grew quickly, reaching shoulder length within seconds. Chatta stopped it there and looked at her handiwork critically. "Does that look right to you?"

I thought it was perfectly the right length. "Looks fine."

"Good." Dropping her wand, she smiled sheepishly at Aletha. "I am sorry about this. I'll put him in a special barrier from now on, so he can't work any mischief at night."

"I think we'll all appreciate that," Aletha noted wryly.

Chatta didn't refute the statement, just smiled. "One thing Garth didn't mention," she turned to look at Xiaolang, "is that we can both erect different types of barriers. We can shield against power, weapons, and even weather. Those shields can be tied to a building, or they can be mobile, and move as we move."

"They'll set off the alarms in Chahir, of course," I added. "But if we do need protection of some sort, you should know that we have the ability."

The captain listened attentively. "Is it draining?" Xiaolang asked. "How long can you sustain them?"

I shared a look with Chatta. "Um, that depends?" I offered tentatively.

"I can hold mine for hours without it becoming a strain," Chatta answered with a thoughtful look at me. "Wards on a building take a life of their own—we don't have to sustain them, and they last as long as the building does. Garth's shields…hmmm."

"I've never tired of holding my shields," I answered slowly as I thought the situation through. "But I've never had to hold mine for more than a day or so at a time."

Xiaolang nodded, but kept pressing the point. "But how long do you think you can hold them? A guess is fine. I just need to have an idea of your capabilities."

"I doubt he'll ever grow tired." Chatta was looking at me thoughtfully. "Your shields are powered by the earth's power, right?"

I nodded in confirmation. "I could hold them indefinitely, assuming that I'm not injured or knocked unconscious, of course."

"Interesting," Shield noted quietly as he studied both of us with solemn eyes. "Brute strength and subtle power, eh?"

"To sum it all up in a pretty package, yes," I answered easily.

"While we're on this topic," Shield continued with a quick glance at his captain, "are you able to defend yourselves without magic?"

"It's part of our training," Chatta answered with an emphatic nod. "We actually go through weapons training at school. I'm not really good at hand to hand combat, I lean more towards archery."

"She's a very good marksman, though." I grinned at her when she blushed and shot me a look. "I use a bon'a'lon."

I got a few blank looks at that, so I snatched my bon'a'lon up from where it had been resting near my abandoned bedroll. I took three steps away from everyone—hitting someone accidentally with this weapon would be a bad thing—and hit the release spell.

In sheer instinctive reaction, every Red Hand member reached for their own weapons when the bon'a'lon snapped out to its full extension. Then they realized what they had done and slowly took their hands away again.

"Now that," Hazard noted with a growing smile, "is impressive."

"Captain," Shield had a pleading expression on his face, "can I have one?"

"I doubt it will work without a mage's power to back it up," Xiaolang drawled, his eyes cutting over to me for confirmation.

"It does take magic to open and close it," I replied to that silent query. Shield's face fell, and I couldn't help but try to console him a little. "Chatta might think of a way to make it work, though."

"Perhaps," she agreed, running an absent finger along her chin. "Let me think on it a while."

"You needn't spend much time on that," Xiaolang advised. "He has more than enough toys." Shield pouted, but his captain ignored the expression with the ease of long practice. "For now, let's pack up and get back on the road. I want to reach the Elkhorn River by tonight."

Once we arrived at the Elkhorn River, Xiaolang hired a boat to take us toward Chahir. Since it was a faster and easier way to travel, none of us argued with him.

The only times I'd ever traveled by river, I'd slept most of the way. It was a different experience to be on a riverboat while awake, especially with such…diverse traveling companions, shall we say.

Night was currently in the front of the boat, dozing under the warm suns. Didi was curled up on his back, sound asleep (which we were all grateful for). The interesting one, though, was Hayate. He'd lasted about a minute under the suns' warm rays, and then he sprawled out comfortably next to Night and toppled straight into dreamland. If he weren't such an obviously reptilian creature, I could swear that he was part cat.

It hadn't taken everyone long to find their own spots and get comfortable. Chatta and Eagle were bent over the same book, probably studying Chahirese. Again. They couldn't seem to stay away from the language for more than five minutes. Shield was going over all of his weapons and polishing them. I doubted that was necessary; it was more like busy work, I think. Hazard had curled up next to Hayate, his head pillowed on the dragoo's side, peacefully snoozing.

"Garth, may I borrow you for a moment?" Xiaolang called.

And Xiaolang, being the responsible person that he was, was going over a map of Chahir, for the hundredth time. I was used to being consulted over that map by now. With an internal sigh, I weaved my way around sleeping bodies and coils of rope. He had made a niche for himself on the top of a water barrel, his map weighted down with two daggers so that the wind wouldn't carry it away.

I was amused to note that he had his mapmaking supplies out, the pens and paper especially, and were using them. "You're actually going to use them?"

"It would look suspicious if I were carrying tools around that had never been used," he responded.

Good point.

"Now, out of the fourteen provinces in Chahir, there are four that are supposed to be either neutral or in favor of Guin's laws: Cammack, Farless, Habbick, and Jarrell. Val Haben's report suggests that Echols province is indifferent, but I wouldn't push my luck while in that territory. What can you tell me about these four?"

I looked at the map with dismay. The neutral provinces were scattered all over the country, which was both good and bad. One was far north, near the Empire of Sol; one was to the far west, along the coastline; two of them were adjacent near the middle of the country. These four provided something of a safe haven, but still, traveling between them was going to very dangerous and very nerve-wracking. I took a deep breath, and thought about them. "Jarrell was where the Jaunten originated, actually."

Xiaolang perked up at this. "Really? Are you sure?"

"Very sure," I replied. I studied his expression, but I could tell by the way that he was watching me that he had no idea what I was. "Something else we forgot to mention, apparently. Xiaolang, I am a Jaunten."

He blinked. "I thought that was against the rules."

"Not against the rules, but highly discouraged," I corrected with a wry shrug. "I was changed by a man trying to save my life. It's a long story, I'll tell you later. But I have Jaunten knowledge. Trust me, that's where we came from originally. Tolerance for magic was very low in those days by the government, but the province people themselves didn't seem to care one way or another. I doubt that attitude has changed much."

"Fascinating," he murmured with a thoughtful look at me. "What is it like, having generations' worth of knowledge in your head?"

"It was really odd, at first." Relaxing against the side of the boat, I tried to put it into words. "All of it is pure knowledge, you know. There's no memories attached with it. It's very strange to know something, and yet have no memory affiliated with it, no experience to back it up with. You get used to it after a while, though. I think the most disturbing part of the whole experience was having my hair change to white."

"White?" he parroted in surprise. "That's not your natural hair color?"

"No, I was born blond, about the same shade as Eagle, actually. The shock of the Jaunten blood changing my body turned my hair white." I tugged at a lock of said hair ruefully. "Dying it back doesn't work, so I've learned to live with it. When I turn fifty, people will stop giving me odd looks, or so I hope."

He gave a noncommittal "hmmm" and let the subject drop. "So Jarrell will be fairly friendly. What about the other three?"

"Cammack is not a very wealthy province. I doubt they have the resources to chase people all over the place. Farless…is hard to explain. The dom of that province has a half-brother who is dom over a neighboring province, Darlington. If his brother is for something, he'll be against it, just out of spite."

"So neutral, but not precisely in our favor," Xiaolang muttered. He was making small notations on a writing pad as I spoke.

"That's my interpretation on it," I replied honestly, lifting both hands in a sort of helpless gesture. "But I'm not a political expert. Now Habbick is a different matter entirely. They do a great deal of trading with Hain, mostly for medicines and tools. They'll even buy potions, and call them medicine on the tax forms. We'll have a genuine welcome there."

Xiaolang nodded in acknowledgement even as his hand sped across the paper. "Elkhorn River will take us into Goldstayn Province.

That's where you're from, isn't it?"

I nodded shortly. "If we do have to go into Torbadorage, it would be best if I waited outside of the city. My family was fairly well known."

"Ah. Something for me to keep in mind, then." Finished writing, he looked up at me. His voice was gentle when he spoke. "Garth, this won't be easy."

"I know," I replied quietly. "Xiaolang, I would have given anything to have had help getting out of Chahir. Realizing that you have magic is a terrifying experience in some ways, and it's only worse when you're Chahiran. I can't turn my back on these people; not knowing what it feels like, not knowing how desperately you wish that there was someone, anyone, to help you."

"I know," he whispered. And by the look in his eyes, I knew that he really did know. He'd been in a similar situation before; he knew precisely what I was talking about.

I wanted to ask how he knew. I wanted to know why a Q'atalian was an Ascalon captain. There was just so much remembered pain in his eyes, that I couldn't ask those questions, and re-open old wounds. If he ever felt comfortable enough to share his story, I would be honored to listen, but I wouldn't pry. It wasn't my right to do so. So I only said, "Yes, I think you do."

His smile conveyed silent gratitude for not pushing it any further. "What do you need in order to scry for magical people?"

"Quiet and a few moments of concentration," I answered simply. "Chatta needs a clear reflection, like a mirror or a bowl of water. Our skills are fairly equal in this area. Chatta is more precise over distance than I am, but I can reach a little farther than she can—we balance out each other's weaknesses."

"So you can search the furthest distance, but are a little vague, and Chatta can't reach quite as far, but can find the person even from a distance?"

I couldn't do anything but nod. "Basically, yes. Give her the right tools, and she can almost double her range."

"But that will set off all of those magical alarms," he guessed.

"Pretty much. Limited scrying with just a reflection takes practically no power." I left it at that, and let him come to his own conclusions.

"Hm. Then I guess our method of scrying is rather obvious. As soon as we come close to the Black Ridge Mountains, start searching, please. We might as well start looking right in front of us."

It sounded like a request, but that was an order, so I nodded. Xiaolang was my friend, but he was also captain and leader of this group, so I'd better form the habit of obeying him now.

We landed in Waterford, a small river town built on the banks of the Elkhorn River, some two days later. Hayate drew some attention, being dragoo, and so did Didi, but when they saw the black and red uniforms of the Red Hand, most people shrugged it off and turned away. Apparently Solian soldiers weren't uncommon here. That would change after this town, however. Xiaolang and I had already talked about the right clothes to put his people in so they would blend in better.

I had been periodically scanning for any signs of magic since Xiaolang ordered me to, but I hadn't picked up on anyone. I'd half-hoped that I would find someone, just to give us a direction to go, but now we were going to have to start out blind. None of us were really comfortable with that.

We went to a nearby inn for lunch and to discuss options. Xiaolang had the serving girl take us to a back room for privacy. We weren't in a very friendly province, and it would be wise to keep a low profile here.

Once the food was served, we all sat down. There was thick beef stew and flat bread, which looked very appetizing, so I dug in immediately. It took me a second to realize that everyone was staring in confusion at the bread.

"Garth, what is this?" Chatta pointed to the bread.

"Flat bread," I answered, tearing off a chunk. "It goes great with soup."

Xiaolang was more adventurous than everyone else, and tore off a piece of bread, dipping it into his stew and taking a bite. After a moment of consideration, he nodded approvingly. "This is good."

Everyone else followed his example, some more hesitantly than others, and I smiled when they all agreed that it was fairly good.

Chatta started laughing at this point, shaking her head in amusement. "Now I know how you felt that first morning in school,

Garth. It must have been odd to not have recognized any of the food."

"Oh, I recognized it fine," I reminded her cheerfully. "Jaunten knowledge told me what it was—I just didn't know how it tasted. There's a difference."

"A big difference," Hazard agreed.

Xiaolang paused in eating, giving me an intense scrutiny. "The difference between knowledge and experience, eh?"

"Precisely."

We were all starving, so the conversation stalled there while we fed our faces. Aletha, being the fastest eater, finished first, and was idly mopping up a bit of gravy with the last piece of her bread. "So where do we head now, Captain?"

He looked at me when he answered. "North, I think. Most of the people who have made it to Hain came from the south. I haven't heard much about the north, and it makes me wonder how many people are hiding up there."

I concurred. I thought there was a better chance of finding people up north too. "Are we going to follow the border up?"

"I'd like to stick close to the border for now, at least until we are comfortable working with each other." He looked at each person around the table, drawing our attention to him. "You are all good at what you do, experts in your field, but we are not accustomed to working with each other just yet. Completing our mission is going to be difficult enough, and if something does go wrong, I don't want us to be far from the border—and safety, if it comes to that."

I thought that wise, and agreed to it.

"For now, we'll head north toward Beddingfield Province."

BEDDINGFIELD

Late afternoon of the next day, we skirted the Black Ridge Mountains, traveling along a somewhat well-beaten path. A recent downpour had turned the ground into mud, and waterlogged the forest. The road—if you could call it that—meandered in between the trees, which meant that we had a lot of branches over our heads. Wet branches that dripped. Oh fun.

I had been searching the area around us for any signs of magic, not detecting anything all day, so when I finally did feel someone, I froze.

Then I realized they were practically on top of us, and I nearly fell out of my saddle.

How did they sneak up on me?!

I twisted around, searching frantically, trying to spot the person that I knew was there, hiding somewhere among the foliage.

Xiaolang turned in his saddle, manner alert. "Garth?"

"There's someone nearby, someone with magic," I answered distractedly.

"How close?" Xiaolang demanded.

"Close," I answered shortly. I still couldn't see them, but I could feel them. Wizard, would've been my guess, maybe a witch. I couldn't always tell gender while scrying, just power.

"And powerful, apparently," Chatta inputted as she joined me in searching the woods around us. "Itherwise Garth would have felt them sooner than this."

I nodded in confirmation. "He's shielding himself, somehow."

Aletha snorted in amusement. "Here we are, spending all of this time looking for someone, and they find us. Now that's ironic."

"Captain?" Shield searched the woods like the rest of us, being very careful to not make any aggressive movements. His hands were spread out to rest on his thighs, well away from any of the weapons resting on his belt. "How do you want to handle this?"

Xiaolang turned Hayate about, moving closer to us. He reined in right next to Chatta, keeping his eyes on our surroundings as he spoke. "Chatta," he said quietly, "you're the least threatening of us, in appearance at least. Try making some friendly overtures."

"All right," she agreed. Swinging down from her mare, she walked a few steps off the road, closer to the woods. "My name is Chatta Delheart," she called in a clear voice. "I'm a witch from Hain. Won't you come down and talk to me?"

A few taut moments ticked by, and then I saw him—a short, lithe figure that was carefully making his way down. He stopped some fifteen feet away, remaining an obscure shadow. "If you're a witch, then what is he?"

I could tell by the voice that the person was young, and definitely male. What was he doing out here, in the middle of nowhere?

Chatta indicated where I was still sitting on Night. "Do you mean Garth?"

"Yeah, him."

"He's a mage," she answered without any inflection.

There was a weighty pause, as if the boy was thinking that revelation over. "What's a witch and a mage doing in Chahir? And with a group of soldiers?"

"Looking for magically gifted Chahirans to take back to Hain," Chatta called back cheerfully. "How about it? We'll help you get across the border and into Del'Hain so that you can be properly trained."

There was pregnant silence, but apparently the boy decided to trust us, because he moved forward again. It took a moment for him to weave his way through the trees, but he finally came into view, stopping only a few feet away from Chatta.

This close, I could see that the boy was very powerful, and very gifted. He'd give Kartal some fierce competition that was for sure. Untrained as he was, he was still managing to shield most of his power—and wear something of a glamour, as well. On the surface, he looked clean, well dressed, well fed.

Chatta gave a sharp hiss when he stepped into view, a sound that I echoed.

The glamour didn't fool me or Chatta.

We could see that the boy was filthy, his legs and arms covered in bruises and scratches. He was rail thin, dressed in clothes that were little better than rags. His skin and hair was so dirty and matted that I had no idea what his normal coloring was, only that he had grey eyes.

Chatta took one look at him and went into Mother Hen Mode.

I'd seen my friend do this before. She can turn on so much charm that a poisonous snake would feel ashamed of itself for attacking her. When she gives that particular smile to men, most of them melt like so much ice in the noonday sun. This poor kid didn't stand a chance of resisting her.

"I'm so glad you came down so that I can properly meet you," she beamed with convincing sincerity. "And what is your name?"

"Reschkeenen," he replied almost shyly. "Are you really a witch?"

"Really," she assured him. As proof, she slid her wand out of her sleeve and extended it to him. "Feel it," she encouraged. "You're a wizard; you should be able to feel the magic in my wand."

Very hesitantly he reached out, only touching the tip of the wand with his fingers. His eyes went wide with wonder as he felt the magic, and the grip that he had on her wand tightened for a moment. "There really is magic in there," he whispered. "Can you do something?"

"A demonstration you mean?" At this she hesitated, looking at Xiaolang.

He shook his head. "That's not wise I'm afraid, Master Reschkeenen. We're not in a friendly providence, and I don't wish to attract attention from the authorities."

The boy looked a little disappointed, until Chatta slid an arm around his shoulders and smiled brilliantly at him. Under the force of that charm, any disappointment he felt vaporized.

All right, I admit it, I was a little jealous that she was being so charming and familiar with him. But I'm an adult, I could handle it.

Chatta introduced him to everyone, and then offered to let him ride with her. I think it was the idea of staying in close proximity with the beautiful witch that decided the boy, because he didn't hesitate to come with us. I watched as he snuggled up against her back, smiling in contentment.

"Garth, there's steam coming out of your ears," Night informed me drolly.

I ground my jealousy under a mental heel and strove to not let my pettiness show. Trying to show Night that I wasn't jealous, I uncapped my leather canteen and handed it to the boy. "I'm sure you're thirsty, it's a warm day." And it was, for Chahir.

He took the canteen eagerly, with a muttered thank you, and drained it dry.

Chatta and I exchanged looks while he was distracted. She knew as well as I what condition the boy was in. The glamour that he wore, however, said that we would have to be careful in how we offered help. He had too much pride to let us see how bad his condition really was— he certainly wouldn't let us treat him like a charity case.

I thought about it for a moment, and then when I had an idea of the right thing to say, I caught his attention. "Reschkeenen, I'm not sure if you know this or not, but magical users eat more than most people, because using magic is so draining on us." Which was true. Mostly. "I'm sure this is an unnecessary question, but are you hungry?"

"It's important that you always eat when you can," Chatta added quickly, backing me up. "We've brought extra food with us just for that reason."

I knew he had to be starving, so was a little impressed with his control when he nonchalantly shrugged. "I could eat something, I guess."

"Good," Chatta approved. "Garth, dig out that sweet bread I brought from home."

I knew what she was referring to. Chatta loved this particular pastry that was filled with strawberry jam and covered in powdered sugar. It traveled fairly well, so whenever we had to go anywhere, she inevitably bought some for travel food. I leaned close to her saddlebags and dug the food out, then handed it Reschkeenen.

He didn't wolf it down, as I'd expected him to, but still he ate so quickly that within a minute there was nothing but crumbs left. The taut pain of hunger faded some from his face. He was no longer starving, but still hungry.

"That was quite good, thanks," Reschkeenen said with a cheerful smile.

"You're very welcome," Chatta responded with a smile over her shoulder.

I wanted to stuff some more food into the kid, as I was sure he needed it, but wasn't sure what to do next to get him to eat some more without putting his back up.

Xiaolang caught my eye and waved me forward. Reluctantly, I urged Night into a fast walk until we were abreast of the captain, and then settled into a pace that matched Hayate's.

"That boy is not in as good a condition as appearance suggests," Xiaolang observed in a quiet undertone.

I looked at him in surprise, and then felt like smacking my head for being an idiot. Of course Xiaolang would sense that something was wrong, he was an empath. If the boy's condition didn't say something to him, Chatta's reaction and mine would have tipped him off. "Yes. He's wearing a glamour."

"I thought so." Thoughtfully, he glanced back. "He has great pride, that one."

"Yes," I concurred. "But he's starving, and we need to feed him as much as possible."

"And give him a bath, as well. Hmmm." Xiaolang looked ahead, as if he could look through the multitude of trees and see the land ahead. "If memory serves, we'll come across a small town in a few hours."

It took me a minute to remember the town's name. "Sutton, I think."

Xiaolang nodded in confirmation. "We'll stop there for the night. I'll set Aletha and Chatta on the boy. They'll make sure that he's properly taken care of."

Aletha was rather like Chatta in that way—she had a lethal amount of charm, and no qualms about using it to get her way. The poor kid really didn't stand a chance with both girls ganging up on him.

Xiaolang interrupted my musings with another low question. "More importantly, is he going to attract attention while—actually, what is he doing precisely?"

"Glamour and shielding," I answered with an absent look over my shoulder. "I'm actually impressed he's learned how to do that. Most wizards can't do anything without some tool of focus—this boy must have incredible willpower."

"It's probably that willpower that's kept him alive this long," Xiaolang observed. Something was off about his expression, but his face cleared before I could discern what. "Anyway, back to my original question. This glamour and shield that he's wearing, will that set off the alarms?"

"It could," I admitted. "He's shielding so strongly that I doubt it, though. I barely felt him, even when I was practically right on top of him."

"Hm," he responded absently. "Still, I want to persuade him to not use any magic, not until he is safely out of Chahir. It's much safer that way. I'd rather not take any chances."

I thought it was very wise to take precautions, but I still wasn't sure on how to convince our young wizard to see our point of view.

"Once we reach Lovett, we'll take the highway north. That road comes very close to the border at one point—we'll separate there, and I'll have Shield and Aletha get him to a safe house."

I knew enough of the geography to know what he was talking about. "That's still a good day's trip."

"I know, but I don't wish to separate prematurely. Many things can still go wrong, and I want to keep us in a cohesive group as long as possible."

It seemed like a good plan to me, but then, sneaking people out of hostile countries wasn't my specialty. "You're the expert," I shrugged.

Xiaolang frowned a little in thought, head cocked. "Garth, how does shielding work, exactly? You and Chatta aren't shielding, are you?"

"No, we aren't," I confirmed. "There's no reason to, because we're not using magic at all. You see, shields come in various styles for us. Some we can use to repel weapons, others to protect us against backlashes of magic—and then there's the kind that helps us to remain unnoticed. It's not really a shield, in the strictest sense of the word. It's more like we're projecting a thick spell around us so that we completely blend in with our surroundings."

Xiaolang was following this explanation carefully. "Camouflage."

"Actually, that's an excellent word for it." I thought about it for another moment, then shrugged off-handedly. "Anyway, that's probably why no one else has found him either. They literally didn't see him."

"You saw him," Xiaolang pointed out. His tone and expression were almost completely neutral when he said this.

"I felt him," I corrected. "I can't see magic. And even then I was practically on top of the boy before I felt that anything was off. I think his shield must have slipped for a moment, because even though he's right behind me, I can't feel him now."

"Hm." A moment passed while Xiaolang considered this. "But can you do something similar?"

"It's not easy for me, but I can do it for short periods of time."
That sort of shield fell on the subtle magic border, and I had to really
concentrate in order to be able to hold it. "Chatta is much better at it
than I am."

"Can it cover whole groups of people?"

Ah. I was beginning to see what he was driving at. "I can't. Chatta
can."

Xiaolang cast a thoughtful glance over his shoulder toward the
smiling witch. "Good to know. Now, in the more immediate sense,
how do we convince the boy to drop that glamour of his?"

Good question. I graciously waved him back toward Reschkeenen.
"I leave that to your incredible diplomatic skills."

The captain gave me a dirty look. "Thanks, Garth. Your confidence
is underwhelming."

I gave him a mock innocent smile—and then wisely moved out of
hearing range, before he could think of a way to get revenge.

I was going to kill him.

Slowly.

With a very dull spoon.

"Jealousy is unbecoming," Night informed me with a smugly
superior look.

I growled back at him. Everything had been fine when we settled
into a decent inn for the night. I'd zipped out to a nearby merchant's
stand and bought some better clothing for Reschkeenen, came back
and ate some dinner, and then thought I should probably deliver the
new clothes before our young wizard got out of his bath.

That was where the trouble began.

I found Reschkeenen in Chatta's and Aletha's room, wrapped up
in fluffy towels, ensconced on the bed, and being practically hand fed
by both women. Convincing the boy to drop his glamour had revealed
just how thin he was. His skin was mottled in bruises and cuts. The
sight had made both women start coddling him like mother cats with
a new kitten. That I didn't mind—the boy obviously needed some
attention.

What I minded was how he was responding.

Reschkeenen was somewhere around fourteen years old, which meant he should be more than capable of taking care of himself. Right now, however, he was downplaying his capabilities, and flirting shamelessly with both women in order to keep their attention on him.

I hadn't stayed long in that room—I was afraid I might give into my impulses and beat some common sense into the kid—so I'd quickly retreated to the stables. Being in Chahir, as we were, no one could know that Night was a nreece. Advertising his true nature would be like painting a target on our backs, so he had to play the part of a normal stallion while we were around people. I'd expected him to pitch an absolute fit when Xiaolang had told him that, but Night had only grumbled a little before sighing and giving in. We had indeed come a long way. A year ago, I would have had a major temper tantrum on my hands.

So, I'd gone to talk with my nreesce and cool down some. I'd ranted a bit, telling him about the situation, and he had listened to me patiently as he crunched on a carrot.

Of course, as soon as I was done, he had immediately started laughing himself silly.

"Garth, seriously. He's a fourteen-year-old boy that's been running scared for weeks," Night chided with obvious patience. "Having two beautiful women suddenly rescue him and then pamper him must be a fantasy come true. Any other male would react the same way."

I know. That didn't mean that I liked it.

"They're both sensible women—"

"They sure aren't acting that way," I grumbled under my breath.

Night gave me a severe look and continued as if I hadn't interrupted. "—and I'm sure that they're not going to let it get out of hand. Besides, it's only for another two days or so. Then he'll be sent to the nearest safe house."

That was actually a cheerful thought. Surely I could put up with this ridiculous behavior for another two days. I had some control of myself, after all. "Yes, you're right."

"I usually am."

"Don't push it," I advised him dryly. "Do you need anything?"

"No, I'm quite comfortable. I'll miss sleeping with you, though."

"I won't," I teased him, already edging out of the stall. "You snore something awful."

He took a playful nip at me, which I dodged. Grinning, I ran for safety before he could catch me.

"Brat."

"Good night, Night!" I caroled back with an impish smile.

"May your bed have many crawling visitors."

I snickered. "You too, my four-legged friend."

Two days, can, under the wrong circumstances, seem like an eternity.

"—that's so sweet of you to say, Keen."

Hearing Reschkeenen's given name out of Aletha's mouth, I winced. Keen had wasted no time in giving both women the right to call him by his given name. A privilege, I noted, that he had not extended to the rest of us.

"But it's really true, Aletha. I've never seen a soldier as beautiful as you are—"

Hearing that sly flattery behind me, I had to restrain the urge to turn around, grab the kid by the throat, and start shaking. If that flattery had been sincere, fine. But it wasn't, and hearing him gushing along these lines for a whole day was driving me up the wall.

And despite what Night might think, it wasn't because I was jealous. It was just disturbing to listen to. I knew this for a fact, because I wasn't the only one reacting like this. Shield was right there with me. So was Eagle.

Hazard thought it hilarious at first, but his amused expression was turning slowly darker with every passing mile. I was betting that he'd join us in being irritated soon.

The only people that could accept this calmly, so far, were Xiaolang and Night. Night, because he thought the drama around him was highly entertaining. I wasn't sure what Xiaolang thought of the situation. So far he just watched everyone with a thoughtful look, like his mind was a thousand miles away.

Actually, that might have been the case. Xiaolang spent a lot of time thinking. He was constantly tweaking or re-evaluating his plans, and often studying the map of Chahir he carried around.

Of course, right now he was probably wondering who it was safe to send Keen off with. The original plan had been to send Shield and Aletha off to deliver Keen to a nearby safe house, but Shield was ready to strangle Keen at this point. It was only because of the boy's age that he wasn't already "missing."

I didn't envy Xiaolang trying to make that decision. No one he sent would really be safe, except Aletha and Chatta. And even they might be tired of the boy's antics in another day or so.

"Might" being the key word. I hadn't seen any signs of that yet.

Eagle came up to ride beside me, doubtless to avoid being near Keen any longer. He looked rather, well, murderously frustrated. "I hope the next person we rescue is a girl."

Actually, I wasn't sure if the situation would change all that much if we had rescued a girl instead of a boy. There were some pretty good looking men in this group. The roles would be switched, certainly, but history was bound to repeat itself.

I didn't feel it was wise to point that out to Eagle at that moment; maybe later, when he's had a chance to cool down. So instead I uttered a neutral, "Hmmm."

"Garth, I hope you don't mind my asking…" Something in his voice caught my attention and I looked at him closely. He really did look rather hesitant, visibly unsure if he should continue with his train of thought. "They say that you are the most powerful mage in all of Hain."

I blinked. I had heard no such rumor. "Well, I was the first mage discovered—"

"I'm not referring to that," Eagle corrected with a quick shake of the head. "I know how they call you the Advent Mage. But according to the information we gathered prior to this assignment, you are the most powerful magician in all of Hain."

This was definitely news to me. I blinked at him stupidly. "Ah. Well…um…I didn't know that. Did you bring this up for a reason?"

Eagle gave a nervous glance to the back of Xiaolang's head, who was riding a few feet in front of us. I cast a glance in the same direction. Whatever it was that Eagle wanted to talk to me about, he obviously didn't want Xiaolang to overhear. "Can you put some kind of a protective barrier around a whole country?" he blurted out.

I stared at him like he had sprouted another head. Where was this coming from? I could tell from his expression that he was serious, and that he was desperate to know the answer.

I wasn't sure if I could give him one, though.

"Honestly, Eagle, I've never tried," I admitted slowly. I was thinking it over, trying to judge from past experiences whether it would be possible or not.

"You should be able to," Night informed me. He turned his head slightly so that he could give me a thoughtful look. "Other Earth Mages in the past have been able to do it. Of course, they normally had a little help, like another mage assisting with the effort. With any large project, it takes a lot of power and control."

Sometimes Night's knowledge of magic—and of my own abilities, for that matter—was much better than mine. It was the benefit of being Jaunten, and knowing everything that his mother had known. And considering that Advent Eve had been the mount to a powerful Earth Mage, she'd known quite a bit about a mage's abilities. I was definitely intrigued by this information.

"Really? Hmmm." I quirked an eyebrow at Eagle, who looked very excited. "What country do you want me to put a barrier around, anyway?"

With another nervous look at Xiaolang's head he answered quietly, "Q'atal."

Q'atal? My eyes drifted to Xiaolang's back, and I stared at him thoughtfully as I considered everything I knew. Xiaolang was Q'atalian. Q'atalians were notorious for not leaving their country unless absolutely necessary. I had always assumed that something very drastic had pushed the captain out of his homeland, although I still had no idea what. Most exiles weren't fond of their homeland once they were kicked out. Eagle's question to me, however, indicated that Xiaolang might still care about his country.

But why a barrier?

My voice lowered automatically to match Eagle's quiet tone. "Why would Q'atal need a barrier?"

"Q'atal is a pacifist country, you know that, right?" I nodded quickly. That was common knowledge. "Did you know that it is illegal to kill someone there—under any circumstances? Even self-defense?"

That I hadn't known. "That's a little…extreme, isn't it? I mean, a person should be able to defend themselves."

Eagle's smile was wry. "Believe me, I agree with you. Still, that's the law there. If you break it, you're exiled. End of discussion. And it's because of that law that Q'atal is getting raided so badly."

"Raided?" I repeated, feeling like a knot was twisting low in my stomach.

"Raided," Eagle confirmed with a dark frown. "The bandits know that no Q'atalian would fight back, not facing the sentence of exile. So it's easy pickings. They wait until there's a caravan of goods heading out for the market. Then they scamper into Q'atal, ambush the caravan, and scurry out again before anyone can catch them." Eagle's forehead furrowed, expression as black as a thundercloud. "They don't dare get in too deep. The Empire of Sol has a contract with Q'atal—we'll protect them if they'll come to our markets first to sell their goods. Still, we can't afford to constantly patrol those borders. Sometimes we miss bandits, and they're able to get in and out before we even knew they existed."

This wasn't painting a pretty picture in my head. I could see in my mind's eye exactly what he was describing. "So you want me to put a barrier around Q'atal, to protect the inhabitants."

"You can do that, right?" There was a trace of desperate hope in his voice. "Make a barrier that will only let Q'atalians in and out?"

"Yes, I can do that. Whether or not I can make a barrier large enough to go around a whole country? That I'm not sure about."

"You can do it," Night assured me again. "You'll be exhausted afterwards, but it's within your ability."

I was only marginally reassured by this. My idea of exhausted and Night's idea of exhausted might be two completely different things, after all.

"We'll be perfectly willing to pay you to do it," Eagle put in quickly. I think he knew by my expression that I was considering it. "The whole team is behind this."

"Except your captain," I pointed out. Eagle was being too furtive for me to believe otherwise.

"No, no," Eagle corrected hastily. "He'll agree to it. It's just, well, we don't like to bring up Q'atal around the captain. He's always quiet—" Eagle looked away, eyes falling to his hands on the reins, "—and sad, after he's reminded of Q'atal."

I probably shouldn't have pushed it any farther than that, but I was dying of curiosity. A Q'atalian soldier was one of the greatest oxymorons in the universe; you couldn't leave a mystery like that alone. "Do you know why he left?"

Eagle nodded glumly. "The bare bones, anyway. That's all anyone knows, since he refuses to tell the whole story. His family are merchants, dealing in several things that trade well in the Empire. They were bringing everything in for the spring market—"

I felt the blood drain from my face, because I just knew what he was going to say next.

"—but the caravan was attacked by bandits before they could fully cross the border." Eagle's eyes were dark and unreadable when he looked up into my face. "The captain fought back, and killed three of them before they broke and retreated."

I spoke through frozen lips. "How old?"

"How old was he, you mean? Eleven."

Eleven years old. Great ancient magic. To be faced with that kind of horror at eleven; to be forced to choose between obeying what you were taught, or watching your family being slaughtered in front of your eyes, knowing that you might be next—I wasn't sure I could have done it.

"He came directly to us, after his family was safe," Eagle continued without prompting. "He came to us and asked that we let him sign up in the military. That was the best decision the Ascalon Commanders ever made. He's the best captain we've ever had in recorded history." Eagle let out a heavy sigh. "But you can see why it's painful for him to be reminded of home."

Yes, I could understand that all too well.

I wanted to help. Hearing that story, it was impossible not to. "I'm not sure that I'll be able to do what you have in mind, whatever Night says to the contrary," I warned Eagle. "But if I can't do an actual barrier, we'll think of something else."

Eagle gave me a smile so bright that it put the sun to shame. "Are you serious?!"

"Very much so," I assured him. After a year, nearly, of working magic for towns and villages, I had a handle on the politics involved when working magic. Still, I had a feeling that convincing a government to let me put up a protective barrier might be far beyond what I'd done before. And it would probably take a while, too. Still, I didn't imagine that the Q'atal government would argue too much with this plan. Not when it meant protecting their citizens. "We'll need to confer with the government before I can do anything." I was pretty sure he knew this, but felt it was safer to mention it now just in case.

Eagle was already ahead of me. "Oh, it has been. Not you, precisely, but one of the things we were tasked with was to find out the exact abilities of magic and see if there was any way to protect Q'atal. The Q'atalians are for anything that will protect them without killing anyone else."

So I had groundwork laid for me already. Good. "Maybe when we get up to the top of Chahir, we can take a quick detour?" I suggested. "It's only, what, a half day's travel by boat?"

"If we cut across the Dorrough Gulf," Eagle agreed. He nearly rubbed his hands together in glee.

I couldn't help but be caught up a little in his enthusiasm. Still, I had to be practical. "We're going to have to warn Xiaolang of our intentions before we do any detours."

Eagle laughed ruefully. "I know, believe me, I know. And I better do it soon—the captain hates surprises."

Considering his occupation, I didn't blame him.

JAILBREAK

Finally, finally, the day ended. We made camp a little off the road in a shallow depression surrounded on all sides by prickly trees. It was a fairly good campsite considering that there was a shallow stream nearby, and we were shielded from view.

The highlight of the day, in my opinion, was when Keen curled up and went to sleep. I liked the kid much better unconscious. After all, he didn't talk in his sleep.

The heavy mood lifted as soon as he started snoring, and for the first time that day, every man in the group relaxed.

Night was nice enough to curl up on his side so that I could lean against him. It was the only warmth I had available, since Hayate was hogging the fire.

During the course of the day the temperature had slowly started to drop. For Chahir, we were still in the tail end of summer. For Hain, it was like an early onset of fall weather, and the wind had a definite nip to it. Hayate, as a desert creature, felt the cold far before any of us did and had reacted like any other reptile would.

He went straight for the only heat source in sight.

Hayate was literally wrapped around the fire, his head resting on the tip of his tail. He was like this organic fire-ring or something. We'd had to cook while leaning over him, because no matter what Xiaolang said, we couldn't get the dragoo to budge one inch. He was warm (or at least, one side of him was) and he was going to stay warm, thank you very much.

I was staring at him in bemusement, wondering how he was going to react when winter really set in, when Xiaolang sat down next to me. "Funny sight, isn't it?"

I nodded, mouth quirking into a smile. It really was a funny sight to see this supposedly dangerous creature huddling around a fire like a newborn kitten. "Maybe we can get Chatta to attach an untraceable heat charm to a blanket," I suggested thoughtfully. "I bet she knows one. That will keep him warmer than the fire does."

"And give us access to all that heat he's hogging as well," Xiaolang said dryly. "I'll speak with her about it."

A gust of chilly wind raced over my skin, and I shivered involuntarily. The past year spent in Hain had apparently thinned my blood. I wasn't really used to the cold anymore either.

"Thank you, Garth."

Those quietly spoken words were completely unexpected. I turned to look at him, confused. I hadn't done anything recently to earn his gratitude. Xiaolang was looking straight ahead of him, eyes blind to his surroundings.

When he didn't elaborate, I ventured, "For what?"

"For putting a protective barrier around Q'atal."

Hmmm. Either Eagle had told him at some point, or he'd apparently overhead enough of the conversation to know what I'd agreed to. "I haven't done anything yet," I felt obliged to point out.

He finally looked at me, expression more at peace than I'd ever seen. "I know. But you said that you would, and I know that you will do it."

I waved away his thanks, since it was completely unnecessary. "You're helping me with my country, Xiaolang. I think it's only fair that I help you with yours."

"It's funny, isn't it? That two exiles like us are returning to our homelands in order to help protect them."

I hadn't thought if it that way, but when he said that, it made me think. He was right—there was a lot of irony in what we were doing. A soft chuckle bubbled out of my mouth. "It is rather ironic, isn't it?"

"Try very ironic," he corrected with a chuckle of his own. "At least Q'atal's problem is easier to solve than Chahir's."

I winced in agreement. Chahir's problems (because there was definitely more than one) were infinitely more complex than Q'atal's. Unfortunately.

Xiaolang changed the subject without warning. "We're splitting up tomorrow, somewhere around noon. Aletha and Shield will take Reschkeenen into Hain."

I didn't say anything, but I had to wonder if that was wise. Shield's patience with Keen had noticeably evaporated earlier this morning.

Xiaolang must have read my concern because he said, in reassurance, "Shield would never harm the boy. Gag him, perhaps, but never more than that. I trust that between the two of them, they'll get Keen away safely."

Actually, gagging wasn't a bad idea. Why hadn't I considered that before?

Oh, right, because Chatta would never let me hear the end of it. Busted buckets, I knew there was a catch somewhere. There was always a catch. "And after we've split up? Do you have a specific destination in mind?"

Xiaolang shook his head. "That will be entirely up to you. I assume that you haven't felt anyone recently, as you haven't said anything."

"You assume correctly." I wished I could say otherwise. I was straining my senses out as far as I could, but so far, nothing.

"We are out in the middle of nowhere," Xiaolang pointed out in a reassuring tone. "I didn't expect you to find anyone out here. Tomorrow afternoon, however, keep a sharp eye out. We'll be getting closer to cities then."

I nodded in confirmation.

"For now," Xiaolang's face gathered into determined lines, "I suppose I need to convince my dragoo that he has no right to hog the fire."

As he got up, I silently wished him luck. He was definitely going to need it.

Keen barely survived long enough to eat lunch the next day. For a few hours, his life expectancy was very short indeed. Fortunately, most of us knew that if we could just put up with him for a few hours more, he'd soon be gone forever.

All of us except for Shield, of course. Shield had another two days, perhaps three, to deal with the boy. From his dark expression, he definitely was considering the pros and cons of gags.

Chatta had to say a proper good-bye to Keen before he left—this involved a great many hugs and admonishments to be good—which I managed to largely ignore. Then, thankfully, Shield dragged Keen off, Aletha following along.

As soon as Keen was out of sight, Eagle caught my eye and did a sharp tossing gesture over one shoulder—a silent Chahiran gesture meaning that we'd left the troublemaker behind us. I grinned and nodded in agreement. Yes, the troublemaker was definitely gone.

I was glad that Eagle had used that silent gesture (which Chatta wouldn't get) when she said, "I'm going to miss that boy."

I couldn't respond (politely) without lying through my teeth, so I settled for a neutral "Hmmm." Eagle and I looked at each other, and rolled our eyes. Great magic, but were we glad that boy was gone!

The rest of the day passed slowly as we continued traveling north, winding our way out of the mountains and into flat grassland. Didi took to the air and spent most of that afternoon as a scout for us. From his very lofty perch in the sky, he looked like some sort of bird of prey, instead of a meuritta. I had to wonder if he was warmer up there than we were down here—the wind over the grass had a definite nip to it.

It wasn't until late that evening that I started having problems searching. We were nearing a fair sized town with a respectable population. Searching for people out in the countryside was easy—trying to find a specific person in a city? Not so easy. There were just so many different auras to shift through; I was developing a headache trying to keep them separate.

Chatta pulled up beside me, frowning slightly. "Garth?"

"We're approaching a town." She knew as well as I did what a trial it was to do any sort of scrying on a sizeable population.

"Oh," she said in understanding. "We'll have to stay the night there anyway; I'll help you search then."

Xiaolang must have heard us, because he dropped back to ride on my other side. "Is there a problem?"

"We're approaching a town," I explained.

"Ashton," Xiaolang agreed.

What, did he have the map memorized now? I ignored that and kept going. "It's harder to search in towns."

A thoughtful expression dropped over his face. "Really. Why?"

"Because the people keep moving, for one," Chatta answered with a rueful shrug.

"And because there's too many of them in one place, for another,"

I added. "It's hard to keep them separate, sometimes."

"That's his problem," Chatta denied with a pointed look at me. "Because he feels magic instead of sees it, it's harder for him to separate one kind of aura from another. I see it, so it's obvious for me. It's just difficult when the people you're looking at keep moving."

Xiaolang looked like he was trying to be patient, but was having to work at it. "And why didn't either of you mention this before?"

I blinked at him. "Sure I did—on the boat, coming into Chahir."

Xiaolang immediately shook his head, still radiating exaggerated patience. "Garth, you told me that your reach was a little farther than Chatta's, but her precision was better than yours. That's it. I never heard a word about this searching business being more complicated in cities."

I ran the memory of that conversation back through my head and realized that he was right. I hadn't mentioned that. Oops. "Er...sorry?"

Chatta gave me a pointed look. "Obviously I should not leave any explanations of our abilities to you."

"You know I'm not good at talking," I returned with a pointed look of my own.

"You spent a year traveling all over Hain, talking with tons of people. I had expected that your verbal skills improved," she replied with a roll of the eyes.

"Sixteen years didn't do the trick," I observed dryly. "Why would another year make a difference?"

Chatta, being Chatta, did what she always does when she's losing an argument—she sinks to insults. "Winner of an obtusity contest."

I, not to be outdone, had to respond accordingly. "Vertically challenged pipsqueak."

"Noodle-legged weasel!"

My legs were not noodles! Nor was I a weasel, for that matter. "Mother of a fat, drunken pig."

"Flea bitten imbecile."

"Do they do this often?" Xiaolang inquired politely of Night.

"Only when they have no way of defending their view in an argument. Entertaining, isn't it?" Night drawled with a slight snicker.

"Very," Xiaolang assured him. He looked up with feigned surprise at us. "Oh don't stop now, you were doing splendidly."

"He's taking all of the fun out of this," I complained to Chatta.

Chatta, by this point, was laughing. "I know. Still, it is rather immature of us, isn't it?"

It really was. But I still liked doing it. "Fun, though," I replied.

She was nodding in agreement, a smile dancing in her eyes. "Is this more or less mature than our lint wars?"

"Oh, I think it's more mature," I assured her.

"Lint wars?" Xiaolang repeated with obvious curiosity.

"Whenever we're stuck in boring meetings," Chatta answered, her lips twitching up into a smile, "we sit next to each other and try to put all of the lint on our robes on the other person's robes."

"Not with magic, of course, but with just our hands," I added. "We're sure to get out of control if we use magic."

"We get out of control with just hands," Chatta said under her breath. I still heard her, though.

Xiaolang was trying to keep a straight face, but his eyes danced madly. "Somehow, I can't imagine that the people in those meetings with you are ever bored."

"We do our best to keep the people around us awake," I answered with (false) modesty.

"I bet you do." The Ascalon captain lost his control, a chuckle breaking free. "But back to the situation at hand. Will we need to stay longer in cities?"

"If we can just stay overnight there, I think we can search it within a few hours, between the two of us." I glanced at Chatta as I said this, making sure that she agreed with me. She nodded as I talked, so I kept going. "Of course, this isn't a real city, more like a town. The larger the city, the more time we'll need."

This didn't seem to bother Xiaolang. He just gave a thoughtful hum. "Very well. I'll keep that in mind in the future. For now, let your mind rest. We'll search when we get to Ashton." He paused, eyeing both of us suspiciously. "Is there anything else that you've forgotten to mention?"

My mind was a blank. I couldn't think of anything else.

"I can't think of anything," Chatta stated slowly. "Sorry, Xiaolang, it's just that we're used to our magic—we don't think twice about what we can or can't do, we just do it."

She was unfortunately right—we took our own abilities for granted, most of the time. I only thought about them when I was trying to explain to someone else what magic did. "I think we've mentioned all the important parts to you, though."

Chatta abruptly snapped her fingers. "Earth Path."

My eyes widened in realization. She was right—I hadn't mentioned that. Double oops. "Busted buckets, you're right. I forgot about that completely." Turning back to Xiaolang, I started to quickly fill him in. "An Earth Mage is able to drop into the ground, and travel underneath the surface. I can even take people with me, without any risk to them."

Xiaolang's jaw dropped so far I could swear that it bounced off the pommel of his saddle. "You can go into the ground and travel?"

I gave a single nod of confirmation. "It's very fast to do it that way, and much safer than normal means of travel, in my opinion. The only downside is that anyone who is claustrophobic hates it."

"I hate it, and I'm not afraid of dark spaces," Night muttered defensively.

I wisely decided not to comment on that. "Anyway, if we're ever in a tight spot, or if you need me to drop someone off across the border quickly, then I can travel the Earth Path and do it. But be warned, it would really trigger the alarms."

Xiaolang didn't remain stunned for long, and by the end of my explanation, he was rubbing his chin thoughtfully. "Despite that, this is a very handy ability. We might very well use it in the future. Does it cost a lot of power, on your part?"

I shook my head. "Whatever power I lose, I gain twice as much by being in the earth."

"Because the earth is your power source," Xiaolang murmured in understanding. "Hmm. Very well, that's something else for me to keep in mind. Is there anything else?"

I looked at Chatta, to see if she could think of anything more, but she was already shaking her head. "I can't think of anything."

"Nor I," I admitted.

Xiaolang didn't look like he trusted that answer. I guess I couldn't blame him. "Sleep on it, and we'll talk about it again tomorrow," he advised. "While the two of you are searching the town tonight, I'm sending Eagle and Hazard out for provisions. Give them a list of anything that you want."

Chatta apparently had several things that she wanted, as she immediately turned and went back to talk to Hazard.

"Garth?"

"Yes, Night."

"For your sake, I hope the next person we find isn't a boy."

I groaned at the very thought. "That makes two of us."

We didn't find a boy next.

We found three girls.

Once we reached Ashton, we'd eaten a hearty supper in the taproom, then scattered in different directions. Chatta and I had gone upstairs to start searching the city. I hadn't been at it for more than twenty minutes when I stumbled across the nearest prison—and the occupants of that prison.

"Chatta," I urgently grabbed her attention. "The prison has three inmates that are magical."

"Where?"

"Just north of us," I answered.

She immediately shifted her focus, and within moments saw what I had felt. "Three girls," she whispered in dawning horror.

I had suspected they were girls—I could sometimes feel gender in power, although not often—but hearing her confirm that made me sick to my stomach. I hated the idea of anyone in prison, much less young women. "We've got to get them out of there," I said in rising panic. I was already rolling off the bed, heading for the door.

Chatta was right behind me. "I'll get Eagle and Hazard, you tell Xiaolang. Meet us in the stables in five minutes."

A thought occurred and I shook my head. "We need to switch," I disagreed, already out the door and going down the stairs. "You know what the inside of the prison looks like, you go find Xiaolang. I'll get the other two." Xiaolang would need all the time he could get to plan a breakout.

Chatta's eyes lit up as she saw my point, but she didn't do anything more than nod sharply before she disappeared out of sight, moving quickly toward the back of the inn.

As it turned out, I found Hazard and Eagle on the street. They were weighted down with several packages—food and the like—but apparently were done with the shopping, as they were heading back toward the inn. I waited until I was close to them before speaking, not wanting anyone to overhear. The streets were fairly empty at this time of night, but it never hurt to be cautious. "We found three more."

They both stopped dead, eyes flaring wide in surprise. It was Eagle that asked the obvious. "Where?"

"Local prison. Chatta's telling Xiaolang now."

They didn't ask another question, just started for the inn again, their pace so quick that they were nearly running. We made a brief detour past our rooms, long enough to throw everything inside, then I led the way to the stable yard.

The small yard was empty, filled with nothing but shadows and a pile of hay. I almost turned back toward the inn, thinking that I had somehow passed Chatta and Xiaolang, when I saw a flicker of movement near the stable door. Looking harder, I realized that it was Chatta, and she was waving me forward. It was so dark I could barely see her.

I wasn't inclined to stay disgruntled at the darkness for long—it might come in handy later.

I crossed the stable yard with Hazard and Eagle close on my heels. Chatta moved out of the doorway, giving us room to enter the small stable.

Xiaolang was bent over a bowl filled with clear water. From the glimpse I gave it, I saw that Chatta had done another scrying of the prison, apparently so that Xiaolang could see for himself what the interior was like.

Smart girl.

Xiaolang gestured us closer, gaze not moving from the water. "Garth."

I obeyed the terse summons and went directly to his side. He was pointing at the image in the bowl, and I followed the direction of his finger. There were three girls in a small, dank cell, their ages ranging from about fourteen to seventeen. They were cold, a little dirty, and huddled together as if trying to find some comfort. From what I could see of their features, I guessed them to be sisters—they looked remarkably similar to each other.

"The collars around their necks," Xiaolang asked with quiet anger, "what does that mean?"

All three girls wore a loose collar around their necks. I growled when I saw the color of those collars. Black. "They're marked for death."

Everyone hissed in surprise around me. I looked up to meet Xiaolang's eyes, giving him the rest of the information that he needed.

"The policy is that once a person is marked for execution, they're dead within a day. We don't have a lot of time."

Xiaolang nodded curtly, his eyes already turning toward his men. "Eagle, get everything packed back up and saddle the horses. Meet us at the back gates of the town. Chatta, help him. Be prepared to leave in a hurry." Without pausing to see if he was obeyed, he turned to Hazard. "I trust you have your lock picks?"

"Of course."

Chatta was nearly at the door when she heard this and turned back. "I'd let Didi deal with the locks, while you deal with the people," she advised.

Xiaolang blinked at her. "Didi?"

"I'll explain," I told her, "you go pack."

She nodded in agreement, disappearing from sight.

"There's no lock in the world that a meuritta can't pick. He'll get us in, in record time."

We had been throwing so many magical and strange talents at Xiaolang that he didn't even blink at this one. "Get him."

I darted to the back of the stable where Night was. Didi was also required to hide when we entered any kind of town as he was obviously a magical creature, and would give us away if spotted. He normally hid with Night when we did stop at an inn. "Didi?"

He was curled up in the straw next to Night, but at my call his eyes snapped open and he lifted his head, curious. "Di?"

"I need you," I told him, extending an arm to pick him up. "I need you to pick a lock for me."

His ears perked at this. Didi loves it when we tell him he can pick a lock—he probably thinks of it as permission to misbehave. He scampered into my arms, curling a paw and his tail around my arm for balance. "Di!"

I couldn't help but smile a little at his enthusiasm. He could certainly be an adorable little creature, when he put his mind to it. "There's a prison near here with three young women in a cell," I told him, carrying him to where Xiaolang and Hazard were. "I need you to pick the lock to their cell and free them."

Didi nodded fervently, obviously relishing the idea that he would be able to play the part of the hero, for once.

"I might need you to unlock the door to the prison itself, too," I continued thoughtfully. I wasn't sure if the prison doors would be locked or not, this time of night. "We'll have to see when we get there, all right?"

He nodded again, eyes shining, whiskers bristling.

Xiaolang had been conferring with Hazard, but keeping an eye on my conversation with Didi as well. He looked up, studying the meuritta with bemusement. "He's intelligent enough to understand you, isn't he?"

I felt almost proud of my furry, mischief loving friend when I answered, "Yes, he is."

Of course that intelligence was usually used to think up pranks, but we weren't going to go into that.

"Hm." I could almost see the wheels turn in Xiaolang's head as he filed that bit of information away. I had the feeling that Didi was going to have an active role in future rescues. "Didi, I want you to fly ahead of us and look at the back door to the prison. That door isn't guarded, but from what Chatta showed me I think it's locked. See if you can unlock it for us."

Didi straightened, obviously trying to look serious and dependable. He couldn't quite pull it off—he just looked adorably earnest—but the effort was sincere. He nodded firmly.

"Do you need a lock pick?"

Didi cocked his head in question.

"I've never seen him use one," I told Xiaolang. I thought about it, but I'd never seen a tool of any sort in Didi's hands. "I'm not sure he'd know what to do with one."

Hazard plucked a thin metal file out of a pocket and showed it to Didi. "This is what I use to open locks with."

Didi took it with both hands, turning it this way and that as he examined it. Apparently he liked it because he gave a happy chitter.

"I think he'd like to borrow it," I translated dryly.

"I guessed that," Hazard replied just as dryly.

Chatta appeared in that moment, carrying several saddlebags and two packages in her hands. I handed Didi over to Hazard so that I could help her before she dropped something.

"Chatta, come show Didi the prison so he knows what he's looking for," Xiaolang ordered.

I took over saddling and tying the bags on as Chatta did another scrying for Didi's sake. By the time that I had Night and Chatta's mare saddled Didi was already gone.

The next few minutes were a flurry of activity as we all prepared to leave. Xiaolang outlined a quick plan for us which could be summed up in a few words: break the girls out, ride hard north, don't get caught.

An easy enough plan in theory. I just wasn't sure if we could manage it.

By the time we were all saddled and ready to go, the plan had been refined a little. Chatta and I were to wait by the back door, ready to load the girls on the horses and hightail it out of town. Xiaolang, Hazard, and Eagle would enter the prison itself and get the girls out.

We were as quiet as possible as we traveled the short distance to the prison. They'd built it near the center of town, and it was entirely constructed of thick grey stone—all in all, it was a dreary building. I would have hated it even without knowing of its more sinister purpose.

Xiaolang led us toward the back entrance, hidden from the main street. We had to travel down a short, narrow alley in order to reach the back door. With four horses and a dragoo, it quickly became crowded in the narrow confines of the alleyway.

Didi waited patiently for us on the roof. He flew down once he saw us, then proudly pointed at the door, chittering softly.

"It's open?" Xiaolang guessed. He was becoming better at interpreting meuritta body language.

Didi nodded fervently.

"Excellent work," the captain praised quietly. Didi preened. "Now, I'm going to crack that door open and let you through. Go directly to the cell and open that door, please. How long will you need?"

"About five seconds," Chatta inputted wryly.

Xiaolang gave her a swift nod of thanks, his attention still on Didi. "I'll give you cover to get that lock undone. As soon as it's free wave at Hazard or Eagle, and then come back out here and join Chatta, all right?"

Didi went back to being the serious hero, and he nodded somberly.

I was silently impressed as I watched the three men gather at the back door. They never looked at each other or said a word, but they moved as one unit. It was obvious from watching them that they had worked with each other for a long time. That level of comfort couldn't exist otherwise.

My nerves were taut with tension as they crept through the door. They left it open a few inches, just enough for me to see a sliver of hallway.

"Can you see anything?" Chatta whispered to me.

"A wood floor and three cell doors," I answered just as quietly.

She pondered that for a moment. "That's not very helpful."

"I didn't think so either."

From inside, there was a sudden shout of alarm, then several thuds.

"I think they were just discovered," Chatta muttered in dark humor.

Didi flew out the door, almost diving into Chatta's arms. She caught him with the ease of long practice. "Did you get the door open?"

Didi nodded fervently, eyes still on the back door, as if he were expecting to be followed.

He wasn't wrong. Not two seconds later, Eagle appeared, shoving the door roughly open. He was urging three young women to hurry—unnecessarily, I might add. They were already sprinting outside.

I caught the first girl out by her wrist, towing her toward Night. Her hands were handcuffed together at the wrist, and I knew she'd have difficulty climbing up on Night while tied up like that. Picking her up by the waist, I lifted her up onto Night's back with a single heave of effort. She gave a slight squeak at the sudden motion, but grabbed at the horn readily enough with both hands to catch her balance.

I turned back to help the other two, only to find that Chatta already had one up on her mare, and Eagle the other on his stallion. There was nothing more for us to do here. I climbed up behind the girl, and didn't even pretend that I needed to have the reins in my hands. "Night, get us out of here."

"Hold tight," he ordered grimly. He reared slightly in order to turn quickly in the enclosed space of the alleyway, and then he was sprinting madly.

When Night decides to move, he moves. I'd never seen him run this fast. The brat'd been holding out on me.

I could tell the girl in front of me was afraid we were on a runaway horse, so for her peace of mind, I picked the reins up. But I didn't give Night any direction. He knew where to go. I was more focused on the people behind me. Chatta was right on my heels, as was Eagle—I didn't see Hazard or Xiaolang yet, and I wasn't pleased about that.

What was holding them up?

We rounded a corner, and I was forced to look ahead or become so unbalanced that I would fall off. I didn't fancy crashing on the cobblestone streets, so I decided I better pay attention to where Night was going.

The streets were dark and deserted, so we thankfully didn't have to worry about dodging people. It took five nerve-wracking minutes to get clear of the town, and then we were on a flat road that was barely illuminated by moonlight.

I dared another glance over my shoulder, and was relieved that at some point Xiaolang and Hazard had joined us. They were catching up quickly, and there was no one in pursuit behind them.

It looked like we had done it.

Hayate was amazingly quick—he managed to catch up to us within a few minutes, despite the fact that Night hadn't slowed down his mad sprint. Over the sound of the pounding hooves, Xiaolang called out, "Chatta, can you put a shield over us?"

Chatta looked like she wanted to smack herself in the forehead for being an idiot. "Yes." She erected a quick shield, hiding the entire group from sight. As soon as it was up, Xiaolang motioned for us all to slow down.

"There's no point in wearing ourselves out if no one can see us," he observed aloud. "Now, let's get some introductions done. I am Captain Xiaolang of the Red Hand." Since he was closest to me, he was directing his words to the young woman sitting in front of me. "Whom do I have the pleasure of addressing?"

"I am Rheiveraan," she answered shyly. She was the youngest of the group—at least, I thought so. She was certainly the smallest of the three girls. "That's my sister Rheijennaan," she pointed to the young woman riding with Chatta, "and my other sister Rheinellaan."

All of those hours that Eagle and I had spent teaching Xiaolang proper Chahiran customs hadn't gone to waste. The captain made the polite response without hesitation. "Thank you for the gift of your name. Allow me to introduce the rest of your rescuers. Behind you is Magus Rhebengarthen."

She twisted abruptly to stare up at me, jaw dropping slightly. "Magus?" she parroted in disbelief.

I was so used to this response, I didn't do anything more than shrug. "I was the first mage found in over two hundred years, Rheiveraan, but I can assure you, I'm not the only mage out there."

Xiaolang continued as if we hadn't interrupted him. "Riding with your sister Rheijennaan is Witch L-Chattamoinita Delheart."

It was Rheijennaan's turn to twist around in surprise. She was too surprised to say anything coherent, however.

"Eagle Sevar is riding with Rheinellaan, and last but not least, Hazard Harewood."

In the silence of the night, Rheinellaan's voice carried easily. "Why did you rescue us?"

"It's our task," Xiaolang answered. "The King of Hain has ordered us to find every magically gifted person in Chahir, and send them to Hain."

"Then," Rheiveraan whispered in front of me, "we're going to Hain?"

"Yes," I answered gently. "You'll receive training there. You won't have to worry about your safety again, Rheiveraan."

Silent tears slipped down her cheeks, but she wiped at them quickly. "Thank you."

"Didi," Xiaolang summoned the meuritta with a brief wave of his hand. Didi, being the attention hog that he was, instantly responded and flew to hover around Xiaolang's head. "Scout ahead of us and see if you can't find a good place to camp for the night. Make it at least another two miles farther from the city."

Didi was still high from his successful role of hero; he chattered back in cheerful tones then rapidly flew forward along the road.

"What," Rheijennaan demanded with awe in her voice, "was that?"

Chatta started to explain about meurittas, and then about dragoos, and finally about Night—which made Rheiveraan start in surprise when she realized that she was riding a magical creature. As Chatta explained, she zapped the manacles off the girls' wrists. They fell to the ground with a clatter. I let her words become background noise as I turned my attention to other things.

We wouldn't be able to travel far with the girls. We simply didn't have the supplies for three extra people. Xiaolang, being the prepared person that he was, had bought extra bedding and food in case we picked up another person. But no one had expected that we would pick up three people at the same time.

Xiaolang and I must think alike. He shifted in closer to me and said in Hainish, "We won't be able to travel far doubled up like this."

"I know," I responded. From the thoughtful expression on his face, I knew that he had already thought of something. "What's the plan?"

"We'll come close to Habbick tomorrow morning," Xiaolang

mused, as if he were thinking the process out loud. "You said that they are very tolerant of magic."

I began to see where he was going. "Yes, I did. You want me to take them across?"

"By that earth-traveling method you have," Xiaolang confirmed, happy that I was following his train of thought. "It won't take long to take them over to Hain, will it?"

"Not long," I agreed. I tried to estimate how long it would take because Xiaolang liked having a time frame to work in. "Perhaps an hour, altogether. I'd like to properly introduce the girls to whoever is in charge."

"Instead of dropping them off like a litter of kittens?" Xiaolang drawled, the corners of his eyes crinkling up in sardonic amusement.

"Precisely." I gave him a brief grin.

Hazard had urged his horse into a brief trot so that he could fall in on my other side. "So what's the plan?" he asked—in Hainish, apparently realizing that we didn't want the girls to really overhear us just yet.

Xiaolang filled him in, ending with, "Garth assures me that this shouldn't take more than an hour or so."

Hazard's eyebrows rose sharply, kissing his hairline. "I'm suitably impressed. An hour instead of a three day trip on horseback?"

I had no good response to this, so I only shrugged.

"So what do we have, anyway?" Hazard asked with genuine curiosity. "Three witches?"

Actually, until he asked, I hadn't even thought to check. I focused my power, feeling the three we had rescued. Rheiveraan was definitely a witch. I indicated her with a nod of my head. "Witch."

Hazard inclined his head to the group riding behind us. "And the other two?"

Turning my head slightly, I looked behind me. "Rheinellaan is a witch as well. Rheijennaan is—" It finally penetrated what I was sensing, and the words dried up in my mouth.

Xiaolang was studying me closely. "Garth?"

I had to swallow—twice—before I could get my mouth to work. "Rheijennaan is a mage."

I was bracketed by twin looks of jaw-dropped surprise.

"What kind?" Xiaolang demanded hoarsely.

"That I'm not sure of," I admitted slowly. "She's not a Life Mage, and she's not an Earth Mage. She feels different."

"A completely new kind of mage…" Hazard breathed, staring at Rheijennaan like a man would look at some rare work of art. "How can we find out what kind she is?"

If we had one of those triangle devices, that would tell us. Since we didn't have one, however, there was only one other option. "We talk to her."

Hazard's reaction turned comically blank. "What?"

I gestured for him to be silent for a moment then I called to Chatta, "I need to ask Rheijennaan a question."

Xiaolang maneuvered farther away so that Chatta could come in closer to me. As she approached, I silently indicated the Chahiran riding in front of her. Chatta nodded, indicating that she knew she was riding with a mage.

Chatta knew more about magic than I did—the benefits of growing up in a magical culture—so she might recognize what I couldn't. So I carefully mouthed the words "What kind?"

She gave me a bewildered shrug.

Busted buckets, she didn't know either. That meant we had to flounder through it, somehow. We couldn't just leave a mage alone until we got them to the school, like we could a witch or wizard. A mage's power didn't require a tool of focus to work, and because of that mages were more prone to have magical accidents. We had to know what kind of mage she was, just so we knew how to properly shield her power.

I was hoping that Chatta would question her, as she was better with people. However, she was looking expectantly at me, like I should be asking the questions. Apparently, because I was the mage, I would know the right questions to ask. At least Chatta thought so. With a sigh, I turned to Rheijennaan.

"Rheijennaan," I asked as gently as I knew how, "did you have anything strange that happened around you? Things that only could be done by magic?"

She bit her lip, eyeing me nervously. Still, she nodded.

"It's all right," I assured her deliberately smiling to put her at ease. "We all have magical accidents in the beginning. Once you learn how to control your magic, you won't have to worry about that. Can you tell me what happened?"

"I-I could sharpen Da's sword just by looking at it," she whispered.

"And the iron work on the front gate always changed when I touched it."

Metal? Warning bells started clanging in my head. "Was it only metal?"

"Sometimes the fire would flare up around me…" she licked her lips, shifting a little in agitation. "And I could heat up the water by putting my hand in it, sometimes."

"Elemental Mage," Chatta breathed.

Rheijennaan jerked around to stare at her, nearly upsetting her seat on the horse and falling off. I grabbed her arm, catching her until she was steady again. I didn't think she even really noticed.

"I'm what?" she demanded with wide eyes.

"An Elemental Mage," I told her with a calm voice. "You are a mage that has control over all five elements; air, water, earth, metal, fire. Judging from what you said, you have an affinity for metal and perhaps fire."

Wonder and anxiety battled across her face. "And my sisters?"

"They are both witches," Chatta answered. Without prompting, she started an explanation of what the differences were between witches and mages. I admit I wasn't paying a lot of attention to her. I was wondering instead why the majority of mages that we had seen so far had been from Chahir. The sole exception was Trev'nor, and while discovered in Hain, he wasn't from Hain. My guess would be that he was Chahiran as well, because he had the look of my countrymen.

Why didn't Hain have any mages?

POWER

It was an easy process to zip over to Hain, drop off the girls, and then zip back again. I was pleasantly surprised at the safe house established by Guin. This one was a rather large, two story building that still smelled of new paint and sawdust. Actually, the size of the house rather unnerved me—Guin didn't honestly expect for us to find enough people to fill this huge house. Did he?

An elderly couple was in charge, the matron being a witch with a kind smile and sharp eye for detail. I felt no qualm leaving the girls in her capable hands.

The whole trip took roughly an hour or so. I made it alone, as Night wasn't about to stay in the earth that long. He said, when I asked if he wanted to come with me, "No one can attack you while traveling. I think this trip you can do alone." I was a little surprised by this answer, actually. It was the first time that Night had ever voluntarily let me out of his reach. I wasn't sure whether to be pleased by this show of independence or disturbed.

Right before I left the safe house, I was given a very interesting piece of news. Someone in Jarrell—apparently the dom of that province, or perhaps the warlord—had sent a message to Guin. There was some sort of magical person loose in Jarrell, and he was setting buildings on fire. The dom was perfectly willing to let him leave the country, but wasn't too keen on letting this person stay and continue torching things. Hainian assistance was urgently requested.

I couldn't quite believe my ears. Someone was going around setting magical fires in Jarrell? And apparently they were quite crafty about it, if the Dom of Jarrell thought it necessary to call in experts. I didn't like the sound of that at all. My return trip to Habbick, where everyone was waiting for me, was much quicker. I went as fast as I dared. Xiaolang needed to be told about this immediately.

When I arrived, I was pleasantly surprised to see Aletha and Shield had caught back up with us. Before I had left, camp had been made in a small clearing off the road. They were both sitting by the campfire.

Aletha came to her feet as I rose out of the earth, head cocking to one side. "They weren't kidding; you really did come back in an hour. That was a quick trip, Garth."

"One of the reasons why I like traveling that way," I agreed. I wasn't paying a lot of attention to her, my eyes darting around the clearing in search of Xiaolang. At first I didn't see him because he was partially hidden from my view. Just as I was about to ask where he was he rose from behind Hayate's crouched form.

"So, how was it?" the captain asked me.

"Fine. I have news." His eyes sharpened. "There's a young man loose in Jarrell that's setting things magically on fire. The dom of that province has requested help from Hain."

The entire group stared at me. I shrugged with palms splayed. "I don't have much more information than that. The message was passed along to me when I dropped the girls off."

"I see," Xiaolang murmured. "Well then. Let's go to Jarrell."

It took two days of hard riding to get to Jarrell providence. As soon as we crossed the border we all breathed a little sigh of relief. This providence, at least, didn't really mind magic. We wouldn't have to hide our purpose or identities here. Didi, for the first time in weeks, dared to fly just above our heads within plain sight. I stopped acting like I was guiding Night, and just tied the reins loosely to the pommel of the saddle.

I constantly searched around me, but I didn't feel anything magical. The message passed on to me had been noticeably short on details. We knew that the magical arsonist was loose in Jarrell, but that was a very wide area to cover. We weren't sure exactly where to go once we hit the border. It was nearing noon when I gave up searching.

"Xiaolang!" I called.

He twisted in the saddle at my hail. "What?"

"I think we'd better stop and let Chatta search. As it is, we might be heading in the wrong direction."

He nodded in agreement. "Chatta?"

"This hopefully won't take long," she assured him. "But it's close to lunch anyway. Why don't we stop and eat while I look?"

All of the men in the group instantly praised her for such thoughtfulness. Food was always a good idea.

We found a nice clear area near the road where we could dismount and stretch out a little. I pitched in and helped Aletha cook lunch. This was not a matter of charity on my part, but a matter of survival. I'd quickly learned on this trip to not let Hazard or Shield anywhere near the cooking utensils. They could make sandwiches. That was it. Anything else was hazardous to one's health. I didn't even trust them to heat things up properly.

Lunch was happily consumed and the dishes grudgingly washed before Chatta found anything. She made a sound of victory, effectively capturing all of our attention. I darted over to her side, Xiaolang right behind me.

"What?" I asked eagerly, peering over her shoulder and into the small scrying bowl she was holding. I didn't know why I bothered as I wouldn't be able to discern much. I couldn't see magic, after all. But the image in the water, as it turned out, wasn't of a person. There was a scene of charcoal and black stone, instead. Judging from the small wisps of smoke the building had burned down very recently.

"Well, I haven't found the man, but this building was definitely burned by magic," Chatta explained. "He's in this area."

"Good enough for now," Xiaolang declared. "Where are we going?"

"Northwest."

Xiaolang gave a sharp circular gesture. "Load it up, people. Let's move."

By twilight, we'd found the smoking building.

Actually, that was the least of what we found.

The air was thick with soot and smoke, rising high into the sky and serving as our beacon. As we crested a hill and came into full sight, it was immediately clear that a good half of the city was engulfed in flames. Acovone was a very metropolitan city built with sturdy brick and granite buildings. I knew it to be a major center for trade, as it was close to the coast and near the border of the Empire of Sol. I felt bile rise in my throat as I took in the damage already done. Even from a distance it was hideous to look upon.

I didn't wait for Xiaolang's order, I just tapped Night's flanks and bolted down the hill for the city. There was little I could do about the damage already done, but there was a great deal I could do about stopping further damage from happening.

I had to find that rogue magician.

The whole team was on my heels, I could hear the thundering of their mounts' hooves behind me, but I paid them no attention. I had my senses stretched to the max, but it was hard to find him. Cities are difficult to search, even on a good day, and today was hardly that.

"Can you find him?" Night asked, slowing slightly as we reached the main gates of the city. I snatched at the saddlehorn when he abruptly side stepped to avoid knocking a hysterical woman over.

"No," I growled in frustration. I scanned the road in front of us, trying to find an opening we could slip through, but it was impossible. There were hundreds of people rushing toward us, trying to escape the city and its wall of flames, and they pushed against us in their panic. "There's too many people milling around, I can't pinpoint him!"

"We need to find another way into the city," Night gave a toss of his head, dancing in place. "I can't get through, not without hurting people."

We were at a complete standstill, unable to move against the flow of traffic. Growling out a curse, I reached for the ground deep beneath our feet and built a bridge that arched out over the crowd and over the city wall. Night let out a yelp.

"Garth, warn me!" he snapped.

"Go!" I ordered impatiently. I'd probably owe him a jar of peanut butter later as an apology for my brusqueness, but I'd handle that moment later.

Night bolted up my makeshift ramp, and judging from the sound of hooves behind me, we weren't alone in our ascent. My bridge touched the top of the city walls, which was fortunately wide enough to hold several horses, although it was a bit crowded. The scene that met my eyes as I cleared the final obstruction made my chest constrict. There were people of every possible age and occupation running, jostling each other, carrying children or bundles in their arms. Dozens of people were passing buckets of water from one to the other, fighting a losing battle with the fire.

I twisted in the saddle until I found Chatta. "Help me!" I ordered desperately. "I can't find him in this mess!"

She nodded curt understanding, raising her wand and conjuring a large, round mirror. As she started scrying the city, I closed my eyes and focused more intently than I'd ever had in my life. Where was he? I started with the people directly in front of me and fanned out from there. With the aura of people came other signals—heavy collisions as buildings collapsed and sank roughly to the earth's surface, rapid footsteps from thousands of people as they ran in every conceivable direction.

Where, where, where…he has to be here somewhere.

"That way!" Chatta abruptly cried, pointing off to the northeast. "He's in what looks like the main market area."

"Garth, let us down," Xiaolang ordered. "We'll help put out the flames."

I took the ground I'd used to build the bridge to here and reshaped it into a new bridge that led to the street below. Miraculously, there was a small corner near the gatekeeper's house that was free of people and gave us room to descend.

Night leapt onto the bridge without pause and handled the steep angle of it at a dead run. I had to angle myself almost flat against his back to keep my balance, legs wrapped tight around his barrel and fingers knotted around his mane. When he landed, I was thrown forward, the horn lodged into my sternum with an unpleasant jolt. His hooves had barely touched cobblestone when he spun and headed in the direction had Chatta pointed to. I grimly held on.

We didn't make quick progress simply because of the people we had to dodge. Three different times Night barely avoided trampling some poor man. It wasn't just the people, however, but also the fire we had to contend with. Buildings were succumbing to the fire as we passed them, slowly collapsing in on themselves and sending out errant sparks and support beams that toppled into our path. It made us cautious, nervy about entering new streets or getting close to any of the buildings. We were down to a slow canter and impatient with our progress.

Chatta cast quick shields that hovered over our heads, protecting us from anything falling. It didn't do anything to deflect the sparks that singed our hair and clothes, or the thick soot that seemed to hover in the air. We were barely two streets away from the wall and I could already feel it clinging to my skin and leaving an aftertaste in my mouth.

Time clicked away in the back of my mind, and I was hyperaware that for every second more it took for us to get to him, the magician caused just that much more destruction. Night lowered his head and started using it as a battering ram, forcing people to give way and let us through. Chatta stayed close on our heels, following the trail that Night blazed.

We finally reached a main street that led directly to the market. I didn't need Chatta's mirror to see him now.

He was in front of me.

The whole street was lined with vendors' stalls, small wooden constructions with colorful roofs and banners that were burning earnestly. Merchants ran around with buckets in their hands, frantically trying to put the flames out. It didn't stop me from getting a good look at the magician.

He just walked along, hands gesturing wildly, flames shooting out of his palms and hitting buildings at random. When I was closer, within twenty or so feet of him, I could see his mouth moving, but I couldn't hear the words. The noise was too thick for me to discern anything.

Ten feet away, it struck me that he was young, probably two years younger than me. His clothes were plastered with sweat, emphasizing his whipcord build. He kept running his hands over his fair hair, making it stand up in different directions, and there was a manic smile on his face that spoke of unholy glee at the destruction he was causing.

When he lifted his hands again, I instinctively grabbed a chunk of cobblestone and threw it up around him, blocking his attack.

He stumbled to a halt, looking at the rock in confusion. In the moment he was distracted, I slid quickly off Night's back and ordered over my shoulder, "You and Chatta get the people out of here!"

Night bobbed his head sharply and turned toward the nearest

group that were working desperately to recover bolts of fabric before it could become nothing more than char.

There were perhaps fifty or sixty people in my immediate vicinity and that was a concern I didn't need. I'd never fought with another magician in confined conditions before, but I knew how destructive it could be, and I didn't want other people being caught up in it. This battle would be far worse than anything I'd experienced before for one simple reason: he was a Fire Mage.

His eyes left the crumbled cobblestone at his feet and he looked up at me with oddly unconcerned eyes. The smile was gone from his face now, but the lack of emotion was somehow more disconcerting. "Did you throw that?"

I nodded in short confirmation.

"What are you?" he asked with childlike curiosity.

"I am Rhebengarthen, Earth Mage." As I spoke, I lifted my shields up around me, as strong as I could make them. My power was building, poised for attack. I didn't trust this strange attitude of his one bit.

"Earth Mage..." he repeated thoughtfully, head canted to the side as he considered me from head to toe. "What am I?"

"A Fire Mage," I answered neutrally.

"Fire Mage? Is that why I like to destroy things?"

"No," I refuted harshly. "Fire Mages have always been the ones with the most control, the most discipline. Your magic cannot be blamed for your delight in destruction."

A cruel smile teased at the corners of his mouth. "I wonder what it would be like to destroy you?"

I had no time to garner a response to that. He lifted both hands, palms facing me, and screamed, "Fire Inferno!"

The flames he shot at me were hot enough to melt steel, large enough to incinerate a full grown stallion instantly. I didn't flinch, simply held his eyes as his fire washed over my shields without noticeable effect. As the attack faded, he stared at me in disbelief.

Did he really think himself invincible? My hands clenched at my side, nails digging into my palms, as I raised up my own attack. I gathered cobblestone, any loose bricks or stones from destroyed buildings, and threw everything at him.

He threw up another wave of hot flame, the force of it knocking back my attack. "You didn't say a spell!" he yelled at me in accusation, as if by not saying anything I was somehow cheating.

I wasn't about to explain to him that as a mage, I didn't use spells. His habit of saying things as he attacked would help me defend against him. Instead, I gathered up more stone and attacked again, this time as a feint. While he deflected my airborne attack, I tried to suck him into the cobblestones beneath his feet as I'd done with a group of city guardsmen so many months ago.

Swearing viciously, he aimed a concentrated burst of flame toward his feet, melting the stone enough to where he could pull free. He didn't emerge unscathed from this, as his clothes were clearly scorched, but he wasn't trapped, and the victorious smirk he gave me gloried in that fact.

I ground my teeth together in frustration. Alright, these types of attacks wouldn't work. What else could I do? I threw more stone at him to simply buy another moment to think.

From the side, a torrential wave of water came out of thin air and hit the Fire Mage square in the chest. He went down and rolled, back on his feet as quick as a cat.

I risked a quick glance to the side, even though I knew that the water could have come from only one possible person. Chatta met my eyes and gave me a reassuring nod. "They're all clear!"

At least I didn't have to worry about the people, then, although I didn't like the idea that she and Night were joining the battle. Night, get clear, I thought to him firmly. You can't protect yourself from flame.

"I'm well back," he reassured me. "Focus on him."

Flame burst up around the mage, whirling around him like a dust devil, and the expression in his eyes was that of a madman. "Two of you," he rasped out, teeth bared. "I won't deal with two of you!"

I instinctively knew what he was going to do in the next second, and despite the intense heat pressing in around me, my blood ran cold. "Chatta, shield!"

Even as she raised them, he cast his attack, the flame so hot that it was nearly white. It hit her shields full force but unlike mine, her shields couldn't withstand that kind of attack. The shields shattered on impact, the force of it throwing Chatta back.

My own defense of a stone wall was a split second too late, only protecting her from the main onslaught. It also blocked her from my sight, so that the image of her falling was emblazoned in the front of my mind.

With a snarl of rage, the Fire Mage produced more fire, the flames leaping up high around him. I prayed Chatta was alright and dove back into the fray. To do otherwise would kill both me and her. I had to stop him. At any cost, I had to stop him.

"Chatta?!" There was raw panic in Night's voice.

A hammer of fire struck my shields, forcing me back a step. I barely felt it. My mind was focused on Night's cry. I'd never heard him sound like that, not once. His panic froze my heart for I knew what it meant.

Rage, hot and quick, dug in with barbed tendrils. Under my feet, the ground trembled in reaction, every loose brick and piece of stone rising in the air to gather around me. I was past thinking, past strategy. I wanted him dead.

With absolutely no finesse, I reached into the earth and tore it asunder under the mage's feet. The cobblestone let out a tortured groan as I wrenched it apart. The ground shook under my feet in violent tremors as the surface of the world shifted. A fissure spread rapidly, starting from under the mage's feet, extending a mile in both directions. Buildings started to slowly topple, collapsing completely as the bedrock supporting them was suddenly yanked away. The mage screamed as he abruptly dropped into the ground, the sound of his voice cutting off seconds later.

I spared him not another moment's thought as I quickly scrambled around all of the potholes and strewn wreckage to Chatta. She laid unconscious, limbs sprawled. Night was already hovering over her, anxiously nudging her face with his nose. She never twitched.

I skidded to a halt next to her side, anxiously laying my hand against her chest. When I felt it rise and fall with shallow breaths, I closed my eyes and uttered a quick prayer of thanks. She wasn't dead. "Night, call for help."

"I already did. Xiaolang is coming."

He'd better be bringing a doctor with him.

I didn't dare move her, as I had no idea what kind of injury she might have sustained. She was a good three or four feet away from where she had been standing, which said that she had been knocked quite some distance. I did anxiously feel around her, checking for any open wounds, but didn't find any blood. Her hair was singed around her face, and there were light burns along her forearms, but I saw no signs of any major injuries.

"Garth!"

I snapped my head up and around. Xiaolang was just inside the entrance to the market, Hayate slowing to a lope. The dragoo had barely stopped before his master had thrown himself off and to the ground. "Chatta?" the captain inquired anxiously.

"I think she's just unconscious, but I can't tell," I replied in frustration. Why couldn't I have had at least one Jaunten doctor ancestor?

Xiaolang nudged Night away so he could kneel next to her, doing the same anxious check that I had just done. He lifted her head very carefully, fingers combing through her head and around her skull. "I feel a significant bump, but nothing more than that. Her brain is emoting properly. She'll be fine."

I let out a breath I hadn't realized I was holding. Thank the Guardians....

Xiaolang looked up and scanned the area around me, a frown gathering on his face. "Garth, where's the magician? I thought you were battling him here."

I bared my teeth in a feral smile. "He's underground."

Those penetrating blue eyes locked with mine and I knew that I didn't have to say another word. He could feel quite clearly the rage still simmering within me. "Let him up," he ordered softly.

I didn't want to. I wanted that man safely dead, well away from the people he had tried to take from me.

"Garth," Xiaolang reproved.

Shifting, I lifted Chatta as I rose to my feet. I kept one eye on her as I turned to watch Xiaolang. There was no sound coming from the mage, but I didn't need it to know exactly where he was. It would be so easy to just let the earth merge back together, keeping him forever trapped underground. So terribly easily. If I were not perfectly in control of my magic, I could do exactly that without even meaning to.

The ground was still trembling, inching closer as if echoing my thoughts. Xiaolang grabbed my shoulder with a firm grip, and with his touch, my rage was divorced from me. I blinked at him in shock, reeling at the sudden loss of that overwhelming emotion.

"Garth," his voice deeper, firmer than his usual tone, "let him up."

I felt numb, detached except for a projection of serenity from Xiaolang. Without that rage dictating my magic, it was easy to obey his command. With a deep breath, I turned to face the fissure and focused, breaking off the piece of earth the mage was lying on and raising it to the surface.

He had definitely been battered by his fall. I noted in an analytical fashion that a number of scrapes and gashes covered his skin. His right arm hung limply at his side, bone poking through, and his knee was at such an angle that it must be broken as well.

When solid earth was beneath him once again, Xiaolang released me, and with it his control. My emotions slammed back into me and it took a few moments before I came to grips with them again.

Without looking away from him I requested, "Xiaolang, get the sealing amulets from Chatta's saddlebags. At least four."

"I'll fetch them," Night volunteered. He scampered away in the next moment, treading carefully to avoid tripping. He trotted back with the saddlebags clenched between his teeth. "Here."

"Where are the sealing amulets?" Xiaolang asked.

I shifted around a bit and pulled up a handful, all loosely tied together by their cords. "The blue disks are sealing ones."

Xiaolang took them from me, deftly undoing the knot and taking four of them. "Can I put these on him?"

"Of course," I answered, stealing a peek at the still captive mage over my shoulder. "They'll become active as soon as they are in contact with him."

"Good." Xiaolang didn't say anything more, but the look he gave me said that he wasn't going to let me near that mage again anytime soon.

That was probably wise.

Xiaolang approached the huddled man and slid the amulets over his head. A petty part of me was viciously satisfied to see the mage sobbing hysterically, gulping in deep breaths. When he noticed me, he stared in frank terror.

Xiaolang kept a tight grip on the mage as he turned to me and said, "The Dom of Jarrell found me earlier. We're all to use an inn over on the main street. Why don't you leave Chatta and this idiot with me. We'll take care of her. You need to stay here."

"I should go with her," I protested.

Xiaolang looked me square in the eye, repeating firmly, "Stay here."

I looked down at the woman in my arms. I knew that he would take care of her. That wasn't something I needed to worry about. It was just my protective instincts were insisting I shouldn't let go of her.

A part of me recognized that Xiaolang was right. I shouldn't be near the mage while my control was still so tenuous. After a brief internal struggle, I forced myself to nod.

"Fine."

It takes a lot for me to lose my temper. Maybe that's why it takes a long time for me to cool down again. Usually when I am truly angry about something, I either take a long walk, or go wrestle with one of my brothers.

This time, I put all of my energy into fixing the city around me.

Destruction was everywhere. I started with the courtyard that I had battled the Fire Mage in, since most of the damage done there was my fault. The fissure especially took a lot to fix, as I had to put the buildings back together that had slid into the crack. I winced the entire time I repaired it. The whole thing was messy and a very sloppy display of power. With every mend I made, the more embarrassed I was that I had lost control.

I'd been far too enraged to care about a clean capture.

Aside from the massive hole in the ground, the main structures of the buildings, and the holes in the cobblestone, there wasn't much else I could fix. I could do little about the wooden buildings, as I just didn't have the spare energy to tackle the problem. Wood is not one of my best elements and it always takes more focus and energy on my part to build anything out of it. Reconstructing a single building would have done me in, so I chose to ignore the wood and set up the framework for the stone or brick structures.

With Chatta still unconscious, it was all up to me to do the repairs, but that might have been a good thing. By the time that I was done, it was well past dawn, and I was so exhausted that I didn't have the energy to be angry anymore.

When the last repair had been made, I dropped heavily onto the ground, leaning my weight against a building. Sweat poured down my face, stinging my eyes, so I swiped at my skin with a dirty shirtsleeve. The coolness of the brick against my back felt marvelous, and I let my eyes fall closed as I enjoyed the sensation.

"I think that's everything," Night observed.

"I hope so," I groaned weakly. "I'm all out of energy."

"Yes, so I see." He sounded more amused than tired, the brat. "If you can climb onto my back, I'll take you to the inn."

Just the thought of standing was too much for me. "Give me a moment," I pleaded.

"Magus?"

I didn't recognize the voice. During the course of the night, I had met quite a few people as I went around fixing the city. Some of them were noticeably nervous in my presence, but most of them were just grateful that I was helping. I opened my eyes and let my head flop to the right so I could look at who was calling me.

If I had possessed the energy, I would have scrambled to my feet.

The Dom of Jarrell stood next to me. His attire was enough to tell me who he was, the formal dark suit having his family crest embroidered on the right breast. He looked to be in his early forties, although that could have been because of the soot emphasizing every tired line around his mouth and eyes. He was filthy as I was, from his sandy blond hair down to his scuffed boots. In his hands were two cups, one of which he held out to me.

"Thank you," I said in heartfelt gratitude, taking the cup and draining it one long gulp. Then I let out a happy sigh. Never had plain water tasted so good.

The dom came to sit next to me, letting out a tired groan as he put his back to the building. "You've done excellent work," he commented with a small smile. "More than I would have asked of you. Thank you."

I was too tired to think of some sort of eloquent response. I settled for a simple, "You're welcome."

"Captain Xiaolang assures me that the mage responsible for this is under tight security." A question lingered in his light blue eyes.

I wasn't sure where this statement was going, so I just nodded.

"What will happen to him when he is taken into Hain?"

Ah, that was what he wanted to know. "He will be stripped of his magic."

The dom blinked, surprised. "That's possible?"

"It takes a full circle of people to do it, but yes, it is."

He thought about that for a long moment, turning it over in his head. Finally he nodded. "Good. We were never properly introduced. I am Overlyten, Dom of Jarrell."

"Rhebengarthen; thank you for the gift of your name." I gave him a half-bow, which was as polite as I was going to get in this position.

Overlyten grinned, an expression that made me overlook the lines of fatigue around his eyes and mouth, and the layers of dirt and sweat. Looking at that brilliant smile, I felt his sincerity. "Welcome to Jarrell, Rhebengarthen. Well met. Well met, indeed."

THE BEST LAID PLANS

Night made good on his promise and dragged my sorry carcass to the inn. My body ached all over, so exhausted that every muscle felt strained. Still, crawling straight to a bed barely crossed my mind. I wanted to see Chatta first.

Xiaolang must have been on the lookout for me, for I'd barely dismounted in the stable yard when he appeared from the inn's backdoor. He looked me over from head to toe, a slight smile tugging at his mouth. "I'd say you were busy last night."

I braced myself against Night with my forearm, afraid that if I didn't, I'd just pitch to the ground face first. "I went around the city and fixed all the damage I could. Chatta?"

"She was seen by a doctor, and he agreed she'd be fine," Xiaolang assured me, stepping from the doorway. "She took several potions that hastened her healing process. Right now she's resting and waiting for you."

So. I let out a deep breath. "Am I allowed inside now?"

"Yes," he answered, smile going crooked, "although I think I'd better help you, considering how unsteady you are. I think you overdid it, Garth."

I didn't have a good response to that.

"Night, Shield is in the stable at the moment," Xiaolang directed with a nod toward the cramped building. "He'll help you get all of the tack off."

"Sounds heavenly," Night responded with a sigh. With a last look at me, he walked off.

Xiaolang grabbed me by both elbows and started frog marching me toward the inn. I was tired enough to appreciate the help instead of feeling uneasy about it.

I felt like I needed to say something to him. Working all of last night had put things into perspective for me. I'd been given enough time to think about what if's. The answers had unnerved me thoroughly. Last night I had resented Xiaolang's interference. This morning I felt very differently about it. "Xiaolang? Thanks."

I think he knew I wasn't really thanking him for his help right now. "You're welcome," he replied softly.

My brain was a bit sluggish, so it took a few seconds for me to think of the obvious question. "Does Chatta…know?"

"I told her the basics of what happened," he answered calmly. "Garth, there's no reason for you to feel either panicked or guilty about the events of last night. In your position, I'd probably have killed him."

I put my hand against the doorjamb, pausing before entering the inn, so that I could turn and look him in the eyes. His gaze was steady on mine, without any judgment. He would have killed the mage? But… "You stopped me from doing that."

"You're not a killer. We're different in that regard. Carrying his death with you would have been too heavy of a burden." He gave me a wry, pointed look. "Just look at how you feel from injuring him."

Empaths, I tell you. There are moments when it's unnerving to be around them. The fact that he was right on every count was too much for me to take in at the moment, so I let it drop. Tomorrow. I'd think about it all tomorrow.

I lowered my hand and continued into the inn.

Fortunately for my shaking legs, the rooms given to us were on the main floor, so I didn't have to navigate any stairs. Xiaolang steered me down the hallway and to the one open door. He released me as soon as I entered the room, waiting just outside.

Chatta was on a narrow bed, propped up against the headboard, rooting through her saddlebags. At my entrance, she looked up, face lighting up in absolute relief. "Garth."

I barely took two steps before she flung herself off the bed and fitted her arms around my waist in a tight hug. I returned the embrace just as fiercely. No matter how many assurances I was given, it was only now that I felt truly reassured.

"You're filthy," she said against my shoulder before pulling back a few inches to look up into my face. "And your magical core is far too low. What have you been doing?"

"I was fixing the city. Well, what I could fix," I amended.

Her brow furrowed in acute displeasure. "You overdid it. Didn't it occur to you to rest and tackle some of it later?"

"I had a lot of anger to work off," I answered quietly.

Those dark eyes went wide in understanding. "Oh. Um, you look calm now?"

Her reaction was amusing for some reason. "Nah, I'm just too tired to be angry right now. I'll make a go of it again later."

That had her rolling her eyes. "That is so typical of you. I would ask you more questions, but judging from the way you're swaying, you desperately need sleep. We'll talk about it later, alright?"

I nodded gratefully, not really in the mood to rehash everything now.

Xiaolang took this as his cue to draw me back out of the room, guiding me to the right room. I fell into the bed he pointed me to, not even bothering to take my boots off or attempt to clean up any. I don't think my head even touched the pillow before darkness reached up and sucked me under.

The Arsonist Mage (as I was beginning to think of him) was called Remcarparoden.

Dom Overlyten filled me in a bit on his background. Apparently three months ago his powers had started to awaken, and when that happened, his family promptly abandoned him. Unfortunately, that wasn't an atypical reaction in Chahir. However, it was only about two weeks later that Jarrell received word about the change of policy dealing with magic. Overlyten himself sent out a proclamation saying that he intended to abide by the new rules. He also said that if anyone confessed to their new abilities, they would receive enough money to make the trip to Del'Hain.

Not a month passed after that generous offer before Remcarparoden started randomly torching buildings.

I gritted my teeth. When I had discovered my magical talents, there had been no hint of mercy in my providence. Granted, my family was supportive, but I still had a whole country out for my life.

Remcarparoden had it much better than I'd had, and he'd still gone bonkers. That was the hardest part for me to forgive him for. A year and a half ago, I would have given my eye teeth to have switched places with him.

He was a noticeably different man this morning. With his power sealed, and a group of people keeping a close watch on him, he'd lost his arrogance. Now he was just a teenager who was scared, worried, and abnormally quiet.

I think there was a general consensus in the group—I was never left alone with Remcarparoden. I wouldn't have murdered the kid, as I was past my protective rage of last night, but I was still pretty upset with him. Xiaolang sensed that. He kept as much of an eye on me as he did on the kid.

I babysat our new mage as I finished breakfast. I didn't feel entirely comfortable letting the kid out of my sight, seals or no seals. The three of us—Remcarparoden, Xiaolang, and I—were seated around a table in the inn's taproom. Remcarparoden was too nervous to eat—he kept shooting me anxious looks out of the corner of his eye—and was playing with his food. Xiaolang had already finished, and was focused instead on his ever handy map of Chahir spread out on the table. I knew by watching the captain what he was doing.

Unfortunately, Remcarparoden had changed our plans. Because Jarrell was on the Chahiran border and near to Q'atal, the original idea had been to deal with the situation here and then continue up to Q'atal. Aletha and Shield were to take whoever it was we found over into Hain while we continued north to Q'atal so I could put a protective barrier up around it. But it was too dangerous to stick with that plan—if, by some miracle, Remcarparoden managed to break his way out of the seals, Aletha and Shield wouldn't be able to stop him. They wouldn't even realize something was going wrong until he hit them with a fireball.

For safety's sake, someone magical had to go with Remcarparoden, and deliver him to Del'Hain.

And it couldn't be me.

There were two reasons for this; one, if the shielding amulets started to fail, I couldn't fix them. My power can only augment or use such devices—it can't create or repair. If the amulets did stop working, the only thing I could do was to subdue Remcarparoden again. Two, I needed to go to Q'atal. The more time that I spent down here in

Chahir, the more that country was left open for attack. It made no sense for me to go into Hain.

Problem was, I wasn't feeling sensible.

"I'm sending Chatta back to Hain with the young Fire Mage," Xiaolang announced with a wary eye on me.

I stiffened, biting back on an instinctive protest.

I think he saw from my face how I felt about this; or maybe he just felt the turmoil of emotions swirling in me, I don't know. Somehow, he knew. "You don't like the idea."

"No," I choked the word out of a dry mouth. I didn't like the idea. At all.

"You don't think she can handle him?"

That wasn't the reason. He was wearing so many seals that mage power or not, Chatta could handle him. I slowly shook my head. "No. She can keep him under control."

"You have to give me a valid reason, Garth," Xiaolang stated gently, "or I can't justify sending you instead. We're too close to the Q'talian border."

I couldn't think of anything. The truth was Chatta was perfectly capable of taking care of herself. There was no good reason for me to be reacting like this. Actually, it was me that got into the scrapes—and her that usually had to pull my fat out of the fire. I looked away, rubbing in agitation at the back of my neck.

"I can't give you one, Xiaolang. I just don't like having her out of my sight, not when she's so close to him."

Xiaolang opened his mouth to respond, but paused. His eyes darted over to Remcarparoden—who was intensely watching this conversation—and he visibly changed whatever he was going to say to something else. "Your concern and love for her does you credit, Garth, but in this case your fears are not necessary."

I couldn't look at him. Burying my face in both hands, I spoke my words to the table instead. "I don't want her out of my sight, Xiaolang. That's no reflection on her abilities—she's better at surviving on her own than I am. I just…"

"Feel protective of her," Xiaolang completed with complete understanding. "I know, Garth. What you're feeling is so strong it nearly bowls me over. I just wasn't sure if you realized what you're feeling."

I did know, all too well.

"I'm sending her over with Shield and Aletha. They are very strong fighters, so whatever happens, they'll be able to protect her."

I looked up at Remcarparoden, and I tried to look as menacing as possible. Judging from the expression on his face, I succeeded. He looked ready to bolt. "If you dare to give Chatta any trouble on the trip to Del'Hain," I informed him with a menacing growl, "you'll be dead before you know it. Mage or not, you'll still die if someone puts a foot of cold steel through your heart. I'll make sure that both Aletha and Shield realize this before you leave."

"You w-won't really k-kill me, will you?" he stammered out, looking truly alarmed.

"You've already proven to be dangerous and uncontrollable with your power," I answered quietly. I could see the blood drain from his face as my words sank in. "You're not the first mage that we've found, Remcarparoden. We have no reason to keep you."

Let the kid chew on that for a while.

Xiaolang gave me this look that suggested he wasn't entirely pleased with my scare tactics. I didn't really care if he approved or not; if this kept Chatta a little safer on the trip, then I considered myself well justified. Still, I knew better than to push it any further. I'd probably intimidated the kid enough anyway.

So I pushed away from the table, and strode outside into the bright sunshine.

For northern Chahir, it was a gorgeous day. There was hardly a cloud in the sky, and the breeze was so slight that it almost felt like summer. When I walked onto the inn's yard, I found Hayate curled up in a patch of sunlight, blissfully sunbathing. Poor dragoo—this was probably the first time he'd been truly warm since entering Chahir.

Night and Didi were lazily stretched out near Hayate, also dozing in the sun. Night opened one eye when I approached, but when I didn't say anything, he let if fall closed again. My, he was feeling lazy, wasn't he?

As I'd suspected, I found everyone else in the stables. Chatta, Aletha, and Shield were already packing for the trip to Del'Hain. They were supposed to leave in an hour. I caught Shield's eye and summoned him with a brief gesture. He cast a quick glance at the girls, to make sure they weren't paying attention to him, and then quietly came to me.

"Problem?" he asked softly.

"Not really," I responded. I kept my voice low, not wanting Chatta to hear. If she knew that I was taking precautions like this, she'd probably be a little miffed at me. My friend was a highly independent woman, after all. "Just a warning. If you see Remcarparoden acting strangely, or you think he might attack, don't hesitate to act. Magic or not, we're all vulnerable to weapons."

The light dawned, and he nodded in complete understanding. "Understood. I'll pass that onto Aletha. Anything else?"

"I think I've scared the kid enough to where he'll be docile the entire trip, but keep an eye on him anyway? Those amulets weren't really meant to work on a mage." Especially a mage that would be fighting against them.

"Ah, I was wondering why you were still a little nervous…" Shield's eyes were far too knowing, which made me wonder if he'd already spoken to Xiaolang about this.

"If they start failing, Chatta will see it," I assured him. For the most part, I believed my own words. There was only a small part of me that worried. "I'm just being overly cautious."

"The kid's already proven to be a loose screw, I think caution is a good thing in this case." Shield clapped me on the shoulder, his smile confident. "Don't worry, all right?"

That was harder to do than he realized, but I nodded anyway.

It was difficult to see them go, but I trusted that they would make it there and back safely. I had Chatta swear before she left that if they had any problems, she would contact me. With the Earth Path open to me, I could reach her side within minutes. She dutifully promised, hugged me, and then they left for Del'Hain.

The rest our group prepared to leave as well. There was no reason for us to stay, after all. I had done all that I could to help rebuild the city. Chatta had done some work as well before leaving, making any repairs that I hadn't been able to do. The citizens of the city had been very thankful, and had repaid our efforts by paying for food and board while we stayed.

I had just strapped the last saddlebag onto Night's back when a man stumbled around the stable door, a little flushed. I didn't recognize him, but he was dressed in the black and silver livery of the dom house.

"Magus!" the man panted out, a little flushed and breathless from running. "Dom Overlyten requests to speak with you before you leave."

He wanted to talk to me? Why? "That's fine. Where is he?"

"He's waiting inside the inn, Magus."

I turned to look at Xiaolang. He looked confused as well, but amiably gestured me to follow the servant.

Well, it looked like we would be delayed a bit. I followed the (still breathless) servant back inside the inn. Overlyten was seated at one of the tables, but at my entrance he stood to greet me. He looked more like a dom now, with his clothes clean and pressed, and without any streaks of sweat and soot on his skin. He was genuinely pleased when I walked into the room. "Magus! Good, you're still here. I was afraid I might have missed you."

"You almost did," I replied. For some reason, Overlyten reminded me of King Guin. He had the same expression on his face that Guin did when he was thinking up new projects for me to do. That look made me just a little nervous. "Did you need something, my lord?"

"Actually, I'm not quite sure how to put this." He rubbed a hand against his chin, studying me carefully. "Magus, how are you at unraveling old legends?"

LIVING LEGENDS

Overlyten had a talent for spinning a tale. He called Xiaolang, Eagle, and Hazard inside and then arranged us so that we sat in a half-circle around him. Satisfied with his captive audience, he started in a low, almost hypnotic voice.

"The Magic War began slowly, at first. It wasn't even considered a war in the beginning, just a disagreement. People began to argue heatedly, and the arguments became duels. And then the duels began to be battles…

"Certain magicians retreated to places that could be better defended. Jarrell Castle was one such place."

Xiaolang shot me a sharp, enquiring look, silently asking if I had known this. I shrugged helplessly in response. The Jaunten had appeared twenty-five years after the Magic War. I had practically no knowledge about the Magic War itself.

Overlyten's eyes narrowed slightly, taking note of our silent exchange, but he didn't stop his narration. "For the most part, magicians fought magicians, and the civilians did their best to stay out of the way. However, there was one man in this province that dared to fight against the magicians, even though he had no magical abilities of his own. His name was Riicshaden."

I blinked, sure that I hadn't heard him right. "He had no magical abilities, but he fought against them?"

"You said yourself that magicians are only mortal," Xiaolang pointed out to me. "You're just as fallible to weapons as the rest of us."

"Yes, I know, but do you know how hard that would be?" I objected, still genuinely surprised. "Those fancy shields of ours aren't just for magic, Xiaolang. We shield against weapons, too."

"And if you take a witch or wizard's wand away?" Overlyten enquired. He was amused at my reaction, and delighted that we were so involved in the story.

The realization started to sink in. "You mean this man found a way to disarm them?"

Overlyten nodded, like a proud teacher to a student. "Precisely. He was quick to realize that most witches or wizards couldn't defend themselves if they were without wands or crystals. And so he developed several strategies to do just that. Before the Magic War started, he had been an excellent soldier. He went into intensive training, honing his skills and refining his techniques until it was literally impossible to touch him. No one could match his speed, or his quick reactions."

"He outran their aim…" Hazard breathed in realization.

"Of course," Xiaolang murmured. His eyes were alight with admiration. "No matter how strong or deadly the weapon, it doesn't do any good if you can't hit the target."

Overlyten flashed him a feral smile. "You are exactly right, Captain Xiaolang. This man set a precedent—he was quickly promoted to a captain in the Jarrell Castle Guard, and given men to train. His people became nearly as good as he was, and there weren't many magicians that were a match for them. Because of him, this was the one castle in all of Chahir that was relatively untouched during the war." His voice fell to a sad murmur, "Until the last battle…"

This story sounded like it had a tragic ending, and like any child, I was put out at the prospect. I liked happy endings.

"Shortly before the order was given for all magicians to leave for the Isle of Strae, there was an intense battle at the castle. The fighting was intense and fierce. Captain Riicshaden led his men in the fight, and many people were saved because of their efforts. However, the battle took its toll. During the course of the battle, the captain was shoved off the top of a battlement and fell fifteen feet onto stone."

I winced, my body giving sympathetic twinges. I'd once fallen about four feet and broken a leg in the process. I could imagine what a fifteen-foot fall—onto solid stone, no less—would do to a body.

"Captain Riicshaden was gravely injured. Most of the major bones in his body were broken, and he was bleeding internally. The battle was such that they could not take the time necessary to heal him, even though there were two witches present that were capable of the task. In desperation, they came up with another plan. The witches put several healing charms on his body, meant to slowly heal his injuries, and an Earth Mage—" Overlyten looked straight into my face as he said this "—encased him in a special crystal meant to sustain his life."

"…I'm sorry," I croaked out, "what?" I could not have been more astonished if he had announced that the Earth Mage had turned the sun into a pink parasol. With ruffles.

Overlyten, I thought, had said that line in a deadpanned way just to get this sort of reaction from me. He was enjoying my discomposure far too much. "He encased him in a magical crystal, a crystal that kept him alive while the healing charms had a chance to work."

"And then…what?" Eagle prompted, completely engrossed in the story.

"And then every magician was ordered to the Isle of Strae, and never came back," Overlyten replied, splaying his palms in a helpless shrug.

The full implication of this statement hit me like a bolt of lightning. I nearly fell out of my chair. "You mean this captain of yours is still in there?!"

"Yes." Overlyten leaned forward, intense and pleading. "Magus Rhebengarthen—please get him out."

I simply couldn't believe what I was seeing.

Deep within the bowels of the castle, within a dark room that had never seen sunlight, was the most ancient magical craftsmanship that I had ever laid eyes on. The crystal was a good eight feet long, standing upright, and was thick enough to where it would have taken two men to reach around the width of it. There, suspended inside that perfectly clear crystal, was a man. He was as still as death, and if not for my magical sense telling me otherwise, I would have thought he was.

"Magus, meet Captain Riicshaden," Overlyten said softly.

Riicshaden wasn't the large, bulky warrior that I had envisioned. He was of a normal height and slim build. The muscles that I could see on his arms spoke of strength, but more built for speed and endurance than anything else. He was still in the black and silver uniform of Jarrell, ripped and bloodstained from battle. They apparently hadn't even taken time to change him into clean clothing.

"Is he still alive?" Overlyten enquired hesitantly.

My eyes never left the crystal. "Yes."

"Rain and drought," he whispered in amazement. "Can you free him?"

Maybe? "I hope so," I answered honestly. "Allow me to study it, please."

"Of course, of course." He backed away a few paces, supposedly to give me room to work.

I strove to ignore my audience, turning my mind to the problem at hand. Night was still outside the castle, as we hadn't known how to get him down the very narrow staircase without destroying said staircase. I described what I was seeing to him, ending with, Any Jaunten knowledge you want to share?

"I think my mother heard about this, but she never saw it. I don't know more than you do."

That's helpful, Night. Thanks. My mental "voice" dripped with sarcasm.

"You're the all-powerful Advent Mage, you figure it out."

Now that was low.

"Stop stalling."

I sighed, wondering what I had done to deserve such abuse. He was right, though. I was stalling. I felt completely out of my depth, and I was deathly afraid of making a mistake and accidentally killing the captain. It would be really pathetic if Riicshaden had managed to live for the past two hundred years, and then I killed him trying to get him out of the bloody crystal.

That would hardly do wonders for my reputation.

"Garth?" there was an odd tone to Night's voice.

Yes?

"Captain Riicshaden is talking to me."

My jaw hit the floor so fast it bounced on the stone tile. "WHAT?!"

"Magus?" Overlyten exclaimed in alarm.

I was too flabbergasted to say anything to him. What do you mean, he's talking to you?

"Just that. I checked to see if he was awake or not, and he responded. He's requested that you get him out, even if it kills him. He says that he's tired of being trapped in there."

I felt the blood drain rapidly out of my face, leaving me cold and shaken. Great ancient magic, he was aware in that bloody thing?

Overlyten was not a patient man. When I didn't respond, he reached out and grabbed my shoulders, nearly shaking me. "Magus, what's wrong?!"

"He's awake," I whispered.

The dom froze, as if he were a statue. "He's what?" The question was dangerously calm.

"He's awake. He requested that I get him out, even if it kills him." What must it be like, to spend two centuries so thoroughly trapped that you couldn't even twitch a muscle? That must have been maddening. I would have gone insane.

My fears suddenly didn't matter. I had to get him out. And I had to do it now. I nearly shoved Overlyten out of the way, intent on my purpose. I put both hands against the crystal's surface, feeling the warm texture against my skin. How to do this?

The crystal itself was nothing remarkable, but made like every other crystal in existence. It was the power imbued in it that made things interesting. Earth power was there in abundance, which wasn't surprising, considering who had made it. That power was tied to a ley line—which was unusual, but again, not unexpected. The mage's spells would not have lasted this long without some help. There were healing spells put into the crystal as well. I'd seen similar spells, so I recognized the feel of it. It confirmed what I had been told.

I wasn't sure if that spell would complicate extracting the captain or not. Chatta would know, but she wasn't here. I'd have to guess, and under the circumstances, guessing wrong was very hazardous.

Taking a mental step back, I thought about it logically. The healing spell on that crystal was nearly gone, so Riicshaden was probably completely healed. At least, after two hundred years, I should hope he was completely healed. It was safe to remove him from the crystal in that sense. But how to extract him?

I examined the crystal again, carefully feeling out every nuance. A half-formed idea started swirling around in my brain. I almost dismissed it as ludicrous, but the more I thought about it, the more plausible it seemed.

"My lord?"

Overlyten appeared at my side like a puppy expecting a treat. "Yes?"

"Be ready to catch him."

He lit up, as excited as any child during a celebration. "You can do it?"

"I think so. Just be ready to catch him, if he falls your direction."

"Right." He scooted over a foot, arms spread in preparation.

I said a quick prayer that this would work, then I made myself focus. Crystal, in essence, was rock that was so compressed by heat and pressure that it turned into this sheer, transparent material. In theory, all I had to was put it under a different kind of heat and pressure, and it would melt again. The problem was controlling that heat and pressure so that I didn't bake the poor man trapped inside.

I started from the top, working my way down, influencing the stone to melt. Rivers of liquid rock flowed down to the floor, like wax would from a candle. This was a very nerve-wracking process. Was I hurting him? I had no way to tell, and didn't want to lose my focus by talking to Night. Just melting the rock, however, without taking any precautions was too dangerous. But what to do...?

I almost froze when an idea plopped into my head. Busted brass buckets that just might work!

No, forget that, it would work. Riicshaden didn't deserve my doubts right now.

Because this was a construction of an Earth Mage, I found it easy to manipulate it. I braced my feet, and placed the palms of my hands firmly against the facets of the crystal. I concentrated on the face of the battered warrior trapped inside, and imagined I was holding him in my arms instead of the crystal. I blocked out everything else around me; I became the crystal, holding his body in a protective embrace and keeping him alive. When I was satisfied that my focus would hold, I slowly extended a shield around the both of us.

Yes...yes, it worked! He had a shield around him now protecting him from heat and magic.

Still, I was worried that the process was taking too long. I sped it up, and soon Riicshaden's head was clear. Within seconds, his torso was free, then his knees.

It was at that point that he toppled forward. Overlyten leapt forward to catch him, supporting the body until he was completely clear. Then I reached out, pulling his feet free of the crystal and helping Overlyten carry him a few feet away. No one wanted to stay around melted rock, not when it was hot enough to scorch skin. Once he was completely free, I dropped the shield.

I was about to suggest taking him upstairs when Riicshaden's eyes opened, and he looked at me. They were bright with unshed tears. "Thank you, Magus."

I grasped his shoulder, squeezing gently. "My pleasure, Captain. Welcome back."

Riicshaden wouldn't hear of staying indoors. After being cooped up in a dark room for two hundred years, I didn't blame him. I carried him up the staircase myself, and out into the main courtyard. By the time we stopped, I was very grateful he wasn't the large man I had been picturing—I was winded as it was. Being a blacksmith's son, I wasn't any stranger to carrying heavy objects. I think it was climbing up three stories of very steep stairs that got me.

When we were finally in the open, I settled us both on a stone bench that was under the shade of a tree, only partially exposed to the sunlight. We were attracting a lot of attention, just sitting there, but Overlyten was taking care of it. He drew his people away, and I had no doubt that he was already telling the story.

Riicshaden wasn't very strong because of his long confinement, so I kept a supportive arm around his back to keep him upright. He lifted his face to the suns, eyes closed, and I think that if he had been capable of it, he would have purred in contentment.

"I've missed sunlight," he whispered.

The curiosity was eating at me. I just had to ask. "Were you really awake all that time?"

"Most of the time, I slept," he admitted. "Whatever spells were put on the crystal encouraged me to do that. But I woke up whenever people came into the room. I heard their voices."

If he had remained sleeping most of the time, I could understand why he was still sane. Awake for two hundred years would not have kept one's sanity intact.

After another moment of sheer enjoyment, he lowered his head enough to talk to me. "Your nreesce, Night, is a very nice fellow. He was telling me all sorts of stories to keep me distracted while you worked. I'd like to thank him."

"Of course. I'm sure he'd like to meet you in person as well." A suspicion entered my mind and I asked hesitantly, "What stories?"

Riicshaden's smile turned far too innocent. "Oh, minor things really. He told a great many of his early days with you."

I groaned. That brat! He loves embarrassing me.

The captain started laughing. "It's not that bad, I promise. He really does love you, I could tell. You're good friends."

"He's one of the best friends that I have," I admitted. Sourly, I added, "Although there are days when I'll swear just the opposite."

That set him into chuckling again. "I like you, Magus. Do you mind if we drop the formalities?"

"Not at all," I assured him. "Call me Garth."

"And I'm Shad, thank you for the gift of your name."

"There you are!" Xiaolang appeared from behind us, Night at his heels. "Night said that you'd done it. Welcome back, Captain."

Since I knew everyone, I did the introductions. "Shad, this is Captain Xiaolang of the Red Hand Squadron, and Night. Night, Xiaolang, Captain Riicshaden."

Xiaolang and Shad exchanged polite bows, and then Shad lifted a hand and placed it against Night's nose. "I'm glad to meet you in person, Night."

Night pressed into that palm, tail flicking happily. "Me too. How are you feeling?"

"A little tired, but I don't want to go inside," Shad admitted.

"I don't blame you." Turning his head to me, he flicked both ears thoughtfully. "I think he needs to eat, Garth, don't you?"

"Not a bad idea," I concurred. "Shad?"

He was already nodding, perking up slightly in excitement. "That's something else I've really missed. Food," he sighed dreamily. "Can I have beef stew, some steak pie, apple crisps and a big tankard of mulled apple cider? Oh, and some hot biscuits with butter and jam on them."

Either he was really hungry after two hundred years, or the man had a hollow leg. "I think you better start out easy first. The beef stew is probably the best food to eat."

"Kill joy," he grumbled.

Shad had his beef stew, and was finally convinced to rest, after a lot of persuasive arguing. Even with all of the healing spells on that crystal, being trapped like that for so long had taken a toll on his body. It would take time for him to build his strength up again.

Xiaolang and I settled in a room near Shad's. Overlyten had insisted that we stay in the castle, and close to Shad, just in case something went wrong. I don't know what he expected me to do if something did go wrong. I wasn't exactly a healer, after all. But maybe he thought that because I was a mage, I could do anything.

Yeah, that was probably it.

I wasn't going to turn down free lodging for the night, however. And I did want to stay near Shad. He needed someone to watch his back. The entire providence, it seemed, wanted to catch a glimpse of the revived captain. It was proving challenging to keep people away long enough for Shad to sleep.

The room I was in now was large, comfortable, and obviously meant for guests. There were two over-stuffed beds on either side of the room, with rich canopies hanging over them. I threw myself onto one of them, wriggled around comfortably, and prepared to doze off.

"Garth?"

I mentally groaned. I wasn't in any mood to talk to Xiaolang. "Yes?" I answered reluctantly.

"I think we should take Shad with us."

Huh? Okay, this sounded somewhat important. Maybe I'd better pay attention. I opened my eyes so I could look at him. He was sitting on the edge of the bed, idly rubbing his hands together. "Why?"

His eyes never left his hands, still slowly moving against each other. "He's not...comfortable here. Not anymore."

And Xiaolang would know. "Has he said anything?"

"No," he denied with a brief shake of the head. "I just sense uneasiness from him. He was well-known before, during the war, but now his fame is overwhelming. He'll never be able to live here comfortably, Garth. He's just too famous."

I thought of all those times I had run into someone that knew me only as the Advent Mage, and immediately understood what Xiaolang meant. People with hero-worship were never any fun to deal with. "Then I can understand why he wants to leave. But why do you want to take him with us?"

"A few reasons," Xiaolang answered slowly, as if he were having difficulty putting his thoughts into words. "One, he can teach my team and me how to actually fight against magic."

That was a valid point all by itself.

Xiaolang wasn't done, apparently, because he kept going. "Two, I'd feel better having one more Chahiran on the team. There are times when we'll need to infiltrate an area, and right now only you and Eagle have a prayer of blending in. It would be better if you had one more person with you, just to watch your back."

Two valid points. I nodded to show that I was agreeing with him, and to encourage him to continue.

"The last reason is more selfless," Xiaolang admitted. He smiled ruefully. "Shad is far more comfortable with us than with anyone else here. Part of it is because we're not treating him like some sort of warrior-angel descended from the heavens, but I think part of it is because of what we are."

"A soldier and a mage," I said in dawning realization.

"Before being sealed up in that crystal, that was the people that he was around the most—magicians and soldiers. We understand him in ways that no one else can, Garth, and vice versa. I think if we offer the invitation to join us, he'll jump at it."

Stated that way, I could see Xiaolang's point. "I agree. I wouldn't mind having him along," I added. "It's nerve wracking enough bumbling around in enemy territory with only seven people. Another person would make me feel a little better."

"You and me both," Xiaolang muttered under his breath.

"Will you ask him in the morning?"

Xiaolang bent a perplexed look on me. "Why do you think I should ask?"

"It will come better from you." I couldn't offer a reason for that, it was just a hunch I had. "Because you're both soldiers."

"Your logic is a little shaky, Garth, but I'll ask him." Shaking his head, he finally rolled comfortably into the bed. "Where's Night?"

"He volunteered to keep watch over Shad tonight." It had surprised me how quickly Night and Shad had become friends. That actually had something to do with how I felt about the captain. Night was an excellent judge of people. Every person that he's liked on sight like this inevitably became a very good friend.

"Good, someone needs to keep the rabid fans at bay." With a large yawn, Xiaolang flopped onto his belly. Three seconds later, he was snoring loud enough to wake the dead.

I yawned myself, closed my eyes, and let the mattress swallow me whole.

"Can't I get up now?" Shad whined pitifully. His puppy eyes in my direction would put any dog to shame.

"Can you stand up by yourself?" I replied dryly.

"Er…"

"Then no, you can't."

"Spoilsport." Shad slumped, actually pouting. He was still in bed this morning, because obviously his body hadn't miraculously recovered overnight. I hadn't expected it to.

Obviously he had.

"But I'm bored!"

Just as obviously, he didn't deal well with confinement. Most active people didn't, but still, he was driving me up the wall. If I didn't find some way of distracting him soon, I was going to strangle him. "What if I move you outside?" I suggested out of sheer desperation.

"Okay!" He lit up in an expectant smile.

I subdued a put upon sigh, and helped him get out of the bed. Shad could—sort of—stand now, he was just very wobbly. And his legs tended to give out from underneath him at random moments. He put one arm around my shoulders for support, I wrapped an arm around his waist, and then we shuffled our way outside.

It was thankfully a short distance to the outside courtyard. Still, I was glad to put him down on a bench. Shad gave me a quick smile of thanks then he turned his face up to the suns. He still hadn't gotten enough sunlight, and was outside every chance he got.

"There you two are!" Xiaolang walked up, faintly amused to see us outside already. "You're going to burn if you keep this up, Shad. Your skin isn't used to sunlight right now."

"So I look like a lobster for a few days, who cares?" he retorted flippantly. "The sooner I burn, the sooner I'll tan."

"You'll burn, and then peel, and then you'll have to start the process all over again," Xiaolang corrected. "And we care because we'll have to hear you whine the entire time you're burned."

Shad turned the full force of his puppy eyes onto Xiaolang. I felt vaguely justified when the Ascalon Captain caved. At least I wasn't the only one here with a soft touch.

"It's your skin," Xiaolang sighed in resignation. "Anyway, I tracked you down for a reason." He took a seat on the other end of Shad, effectively capturing his audience's attention. "Shad, has anyone explained why it took two hundred years to free you from the crystal?"

I'd learned in the day that I'd known him that Shad was a fairly happy-go-lucky person. So it was strange when he became solemn and pensive. "No, no one has. Why?"

"I think it's perhaps best if Garth answers that question, considering who he is."

"Who he is?" Shad parroted in confusion. He twisted so that he could look at me. "Who are you, besides the obvious?"

"I am the first mage born since the Magic War," I answered softly.

"It is for this reason that he is called the Advent Mage," Xiaolang added just as softly.

Shad was so stunned that you could have knocked him over with a feather. "The first…since…" he swallowed hard, and started over. "But why?! There's always been mages! Not a lot, I'll grant you, but there's always been at least a dozen running around."

"I think we better start at the beginning," Xiaolang observed. "Garth, you know the history better than I do. Why don't you tell him the full tale?"

And so I did. I started with the order for all magicians to remove to the Isle of Strae, and then spoke of the effect that the war had on Chahir. I told of the Jaunten, and how they were chased out of the country. There had been no magic in this country, at least none that we were aware of, until I had shown up in Del'Hain. I gave him a brief summary of the agreement Guin had with Vonlorisen, and why such an agreement was necessary.

By the time I was finished, Shad looked sick to his stomach. It took several tries before he could manage a coherent response. "I can't believe it…. I know that magic did a lot to hurt us during the war but it did so much good as well. For them to just throw that power away..." he shook his head, incredulous.

"Maybe you can tell us what started the war?" Xiaolang asked in genuine curiosity.

I think that questioned startled Shad just as much as anything I had said. He jerked around so quickly that he nearly lost his balance on the bench. "You don't know?!"

"A lot of history and knowledge was lost during the war," I explained quickly. "You won't believe how much. They weren't even really able to train me—it was mostly trial and error. They could barely tell me what kind of mage I was."

"Great good Guardians! What kind of insanity is this?" he demanded in sheer disbelief. He shook his head, visibly pulling himself together before answering. "There was this great contention in the magic community. There were some that held that the more powerful magicians needed to be regulated more. I don't understand the finer details, as I'm no magician myself, but the gist of it was that they wanted to put some kind of power limitations on people."

I went stock still as the full implications of what he was telling me sank in. "Mages. They wanted to control how much power a mage could draw."

"Them, and any wizard or witch deemed too powerful," Shad acknowledged. "There were others, mostly the mages, that argued against it. They said it was hard enough to do their job as it was, they didn't need any power restrictions to make it even harder."

"Would it?" Xiaolang asked me quietly.

"Very much so," I answered shortly. Idiocy. The people back then were absolutely insane to think that would work. "Think about this, Xiaolang. The only time that I'm ever called in is when a witch's or wizard's power isn't enough to do the job. How could I do anything effectively if my power is limited to 'normal' levels?"

"That's the same argument they were using," Shad stated bleakly. "Much good it did them. They started to get into really heated arguments about it, and then fights started breaking out. Before we knew it, we had a total war on our hands, and no way of protecting the civilians. Some of the more compassionate magicians went around putting up wards around the cities and castles, to help protect people, but that didn't do much good if the fight started inside the wards. It was a bloody mess," he concluded grimly. "Still, to banish all magic..."

that's too extreme."

"Especially now that more of our countrymen are being born with magic," I agreed. "But that's one of the reasons why I'm here—to help those people into Hain."

"And that brings me to the original question I wanted to ask." Xiaolang was intent, eyes locked with Shad's. "Will you go with us?"

Shad froze, sheer surprise keeping him in place. "You want me to go with you?"

"We could use your expertise," Xiaolang admitted with a charming smile. "And we could certainly use another person. We're only doing this impossible job with seven people as it is."

"Nine if you include a mischievous meuritta and a prankster-loving nreesce," I inputted drolly.

Xiaolang's lips twitched but he continued as if I hadn't interrupted. "If the stories are true, Shad, you're an incredible fighter that knows how to combat magicians and win. I need that knowledge. You're also Chahiran, so you have a better chance of infiltrating than my own people do. I can do this job without you but it would be much easier with you."

Shad seriously considered that for about a millisecond. Then he lit up in a smile that was eerily similar to Didi's when he was about to do something he shouldn't, but was going to enjoy doing anyway. "So basically, we're going to sneak all around Chahir under Vonlorisen's nose, steal people, smuggle them into Hain, and not get caught doing it."

"That's about the size of it," Xiaolang agreed. He smiled too, a reflection of the expression on Shad's face.

"Sounds like fun to me! I do love the impossible missions; it keeps me on my toes. So when do we start?"

"Soon," Xiaolang promised. "We have one more thing to do before we get back to what we were assigned to do." He extended a hand, which Shad clasped firmly. A little kernel of worry, that I hadn't even realized was there, eased when Xiaolang said, "Welcome to the team, Riicshaden."

Q'ATAL

It was a fifteen mile stretch from the top of Chahir to Q'atal. At least, it was if you went by boat and crossed the gulf to get there. If you went by land, it was a good three hundred miles, filled with flat grassland, impossible mountains, rocky shorelines, and bandit infested forests.

We chose to go by boat.

Shad still wasn't up to full strength yet, but three days out of the crystal had done a lot to restore him. He was capable of walking on his own for short stretches of time, and his balance was much better. We had all debated on leaving him here to recuperate, and picking him up later, but in the end decided that might be a bad idea. There would be no one to fend off his rabid fans since we were all leaving. And besides, it was an easy trip. He could rest in the boat, and again in Q'atal. It wasn't like anyone but I would be working when we got up there, after all.

There was just one hitch in these plans.

I couldn't get Xiaolang on the boat.

He kept offering all sorts of excuses to put off boarding. At first I didn't realize there was a problem, but after the third excuse in fifteen minutes, it became obvious that something was going on.

The shipyard in Jarrell was a very busy place, filled with cargo, people, shipping equipment of all sorts, and vendors. I had to duck around and in between all of it in order to reach Hazard's side. He stood there watching his captain and chuckling to himself.

I turned to see what Hazard was laughing about, but nothing struck me as funny. Xiaolang was arguing with the captain of the ship about something, one hand waving emphatically to emphasis his point.

The captain—a large man with a protruding belly and a drooping mustache—was arguing back just as vehemently. Even in this din of noise, I could hear his voice, if not the words. "What's so funny?"

"The cap'n," Hazard answered, voice rich with humor.

"You've lost me, Hazard."

"Ah, that's right, you wouldn't know, would you?" The question was apparently rhetorical, as he didn't pause for my reply. "On riverboats, he does all right, because he's so close to the shore. He figures he can make it, if he tries hard enough, and latches onto something floatable. But here, across the gulf..." Hazard shook his head again, nearly laughing all over again. "Captain Xiaolang of the Red Hand," Hazard gestured grandly, smirking. "Youngest captain in Ascalon history. Perfect soldier. Sinks like a hammer."

Ahhhh. That was the problem! "Doesn't he realize that we can't possibly drown?" I demanded in exasperation.

Hazard blinked at me, clueless. "What do you mean?"

"Hazard, think about this," I chided. "I'm an Earth Mage. The ship is made out of wood. Even if we did spring some kind of serious leak, I could make the wood grow and patch it up again. Or, if we were somehow tossed out of the ship, I could raise a patch of the sea floor so that we'd have something to stand on. As long as he's in my company, he can't drown."

Hazard's mouth opened, closed, and then he hummed thoughtfully. "You know, I never thought about it like that. Garth, I'm so glad you're with us."

I gave him a mocking bow in acknowledgement. "Thank you. Now grab your captain and let's go. We're wasting time."

"Right."

Despite my many assurances to Xiaolang that he could not drown while he was with me, he still kept a nervous eye on the open sea around us. Just watching him started to make me a little nervous. I felt like picking up a clue-bat and hitting him over the head with it a few times.

All of us were on the foredeck of the boat, well out of the sailors' way. I chose to move over to the right side where Shad was sitting before I gave into temptation and said something to Xiaolang. He gave me an understanding smile as I approached.

"Getting on your nerves?"

"I know there are just some things that people can't help, but he's making me nervous," I growled.

"I understand," Shad assured me ruefully. "Why do you think I'm sitting over here? How much longer should this trip take, anyway?"

Jaunten knowledge came to the rescue, and with only a brief glance at the (barely visible) shoreline, I was able to answer the question. "About an hour, perhaps two."

"Thank gods, goddesses, saints, angels, sprites, and little pink elephants!" he exclaimed.

I snorted, amused at the expression. "I haven't heard someone say that in the longest time. Not since my grandfather died."

"Hey now! No cracks about my age, you young whippersnapper!"

I started laughing at the mock-serious frown on his face.

"Show some respect for your elders," Shad continued severely. He sounded so much like a crotchety old man that I lost it, my laughter completely uncontrollable. I was laughing so hard that it got him started, and in no time, we were hanging off each other and laughing like loons.

That, of course, got Hazard's attention, and he had to know what we were laughing about so hard. I tried to explain, but every time I got half way through the sentence, I'd remember what I was explaining, and start chortling all over again.

"Obviously I'm not going to get anything sensible out of you two," Hazard noted. He was grinning, apparently amused at our being amused. "Well, at least someone is having fun on this trip."

I pointed an accusing finger at Shad. "He started it!"

"I did not!" Shad protested, grinning broadly. "You started making wisecracks about my age!"

"I was just making an innocent observation!" I protested.

Hazard, hoping to get an explanation, pounced on that. "What observation?"

"Shad said something that I haven't heard since my grandfather passed on."

"Now isn't that a remark on my age?" Shad demanded. "Isn't that cruel? Here I am, a poor old man, and he's commenting on my age."

"Shad, if you're a poor old man, then I'm at death's door," Hazard retorted. "You were what, twenty? When you were put into the crystal, I mean."

"About twenty-three," Shad admitted.

Hazard nodded, as if that didn't surprise him. "I'm thirty, so you have no room to talk."

"But you know," Shad had an impish light in his eyes that I didn't trust at all, "out of all of us, Garth looks the oldest."

"Because of the white hair," Hazard agreed. "You're what, Garth, twenty-eight or so?"

I blinked at this. "You're way off, Hazard. I'm seventeen."

The silence that followed my statement was so absolute that it would make a graveyard at midnight seem lively. They both stared at me so incredulously that I almost felt like defending my age.

"Seventeen?!" they gasped, nearly in stereo.

I tugged a strand of my hair into view, peering at it thoughtfully. It was long enough now to hang just past my shoulder blades, and I was thankful that Chatta had chosen such a good hair-clasp for me. That much hair would surely get in my way. "Does it really make me look that much older?"

Shad nodded vigorously. "It really does."

"I wish I could dye it back," I muttered in resignation.

"Dye doesn't hold?" Hazard studied my hair curiously.

"Not at all." I smoothed my hair back into position, determined not to let it bother me. "As Chatta pointed out, when magic changes something, it's difficult to change it back." I thought about it a bit longer, before something occurred to me. "Actually, I guess it's a good thing that I look so much older. Most people would be a little nervous about a teenage mage."

"There is that," Hazard agreed. "Actually, I might have been a little nervous when we first met if I'd known your real age. This side effect is probably a good thing, Garth."

"Probably." I'd still be relieved when I hit fifty, though.

Xiaolang carefully inched his way towards us, an eye on the sea the entire time. "Garth, tell me we're close."

I sighed. If we made it to Q'atal without me strangling Xiaolang, it would be a miracle of holy proportions.

Xiaolang was much better once he had his feet on solid ground again. He looked like some sort of crab as he scrambled down the gangway, but he definitely regained his confidence once he was away from the ship and the sea.

Some Jaunten ancestor of mine must have been this far north at least once, because I had an idea of where I was. Q'atal didn't actually extend its borders all the way to the shoreline—there was a Solian city port that hugged the rugged coastline. We had to go another mile inland before we actually reached Q'atal.

Our Ascalon Captain was his usual commanding self, and started giving us directions once we were completely unloaded. "Hazard, you and Shad go find us an inn somewhere. Take Hayate with you."

I noted that neither Night nor I were mentioned in these orders. "What about us?"

"We need to go report into the City Council and get an idea of where to go," Xiaolang responded. His forehead furrowed slightly as he thought. "I'm not sure how much groundwork has been laid for this. I know that my superiors talked to the Remcar-ol and reached some sort of an agreement that they would accept help, but I'm a little shaky on the details. We need to talk to someone who knows what's going on."

That made perfect sense to me.

"If it's all the same to you, I'll go with them." Night was rather irritable, like a grizzly just waking up from a long winter nap.

This was so far outside of Night's normal behavior that I gave him a worried once-over. "Are you all right?"

"If you must know, I feel a little queasy."

Shad choked, trying to stifle his laughter behind one hand. "Are you suggesting that you got seasick?"

Night raised his head, and with great dignity, refused to answer him.

Poor Night. I very carefully didn't smile. "Go on, then. I'll stick with Xiaolang and get an idea of where we are supposed to go next."

The group left with Night grumbling about how he wanted nothing more than cool water and shade. I watched him in bemusement. I didn't know that horses could get seasick. Or maybe Night was an exception to the rule?

Xiaolang seemed perfectly comfortable with the city, as he struck off confidently through the streets without asking for directions first. I had to scramble to keep up with him. For a short person, he walked really fast.

"Xiaolang!"

The Q'atalian pivoted about, turning toward that hail. His face lit up in a sincere smile, and one hand waved in greeting. "Magavero!"

A tall man in the black and red uniform of Ascalon rapidly approached us. He was lean, with brown hair greying at the temples, dark eyes, and skin leathered from too much sun. But the smile on his face was just as delighted as Xiaolang's, which wiped years from his looks. As I watched, he grabbed the younger man in a fierce hug, lifting Xiaolang's feet from the ground. Judging from Xiaolang's reaction, he didn't mind—the greeting was returned with equal force.

"Burn my eyes, boy, but I'm glad to see you." Magavero finally let Xiaolang go, but he only retreated a foot or so, eyeing the captain thoughtfully. "What are you doing up here?"

"Nice to see you as well, sir. And I might very well ask you the same question," Xiaolang parried.

Magavero's face fell slightly, becoming more professional. "Border patrol," he answered in slightly clipped tones. "There've been more raids, Xiaolang."

Xiaolang didn't say anything, simply nodded in curt understanding; his dark expression stated quite plainly how he felt.

I didn't like seeing that expression on my friend's face. I came to stand beside him, putting a comforting hand on his shoulder. His head turned sharply, looking at me. "I best get to work, then," I said quietly.

As I'd had hoped, his anger and grief fell away, and a smile chased its way across his face. "Indeed. Forgive me, I'm forgetting my manners. Magavero, this is Magus Rhebengarthen of the Jaunten." With sadistic cheer he added, "You'd probably know him better as the Advent Mage."

Magavero had been faintly surprised at the word "Magus" but at my ludicrous title, his eyes nearly fell out of their sockets.

I gave Xiaolang a dirty look. "You just had to say it, didn't you?"

"But of course!" he sing-songed brightly. "What's the use of having friends if I can't torment them?"

I silently swore to myself that I'd pay him back for this later.

"Garth, this is Major Kin Magavero," Xiaolang continued the introductions, ignoring my dark scowl and the major's discomposure. "He was my mentor before I joined the military, and a good friend."

Remembering at the last second that Solian's greet each other by touching palms, I lifted my hand in greeting. "Ainlie."

Magavero touched his palm to mine, his hand rough with sword calluses. "Ainlie, Magus."

"Garth," I corrected him with a smile. "I'm not a formal person."

The major blinked, but thawed noticeably. "Understood, I'm not a formal person either, usually. Now I'm truly curious, why are you here?"

"Garth thinks that he can put a protective barrier around Q'atal," Xiaolang answered. He looked like the cat that knew how to open the canary cage.

Actually, it was Night that thought I could do this, not me. But I wasn't going to argue. There'd be no point.

Magavero stared at me like a man waiting for the punch line of a joke. "A barrier? Around a whole country?"

"The key word in that statement," I told him dryly, "was the word think. I'm not sure if I can do this or not. Earth Mages in the past were able to do it, however, so I think it's feasible." I had been doing a great deal of practicing with barriers ever since that fiasco with Chatta trying to do building wards. I had a better grasp on how to do it now. It helped when I put up barriers around natural earth, instead of something manmade—like buildings.

After a stunned moment, Magavero got his mouth working properly again. "Is this difficult magic?"

"Is the sky blue?" I drawled.

The major's face cracked into a grin. "I'll take that as a yes. Can we do anything to help you?"

"I need some information," I admitted. "Are all of the Q'atalian people in the country right now?"

He stopped and thought about that for a moment, one finger idly tracing the bottom of his chin. "There's one caravan out that I know of. I think that's it, but I could be wrong."

"Double check," I ordered him. "It's imperative that every Q'atalian be in the country when the barrier goes up."

"Garth, I think you'd better explain," Xiaolang advised.

"I was heading toward the wharf for lunch," Magavero eyed us both thoughtfully. "Why don't you join me? You can explain everything while we eat."

Food sounded like a wonderful idea. I nodded without any hesitation.

Magavero must've been a frequent visitor to the city, because he weaved his way around the traffic and cramped streets as comfortably as any native. He led us to this little hole in the wall café that I would've passed right by without noticing. They didn't even have menus. As it turned out, menus weren't needed. A waitress came out, plopped three glasses in front of us, and then sauntered back to the kitchen. In moments she was back with a huge platter mounded over with hot biscuits, freshly fried fish, and golden crisps.

My mouth watered at the aroma alone.

Needless to say, no one said anything until we had demolished about half the contents of that platter. Once our hunger was for the most part satisfied, we slowed down enough to actually talk to each other.

"So how does this barrier of yours work?" Magavero asked me after a long gulp from his cup.

"It's linked to the power of the earth." At his blank look, I realized that I would need to backtrack a little. "The earth has its own power, and it's very potent. There are lines, ley lines we call them, of that power that weaves its way all through it. What I'm going to do is set up the barrier so that it connects with several ley lines. That way it will never run out of power."

Magavero looked suitably impressed. "And why do all the Q'atalians have to be in the country?"

"It's part of how barrier magic works," I answered with a shrug. "When I put the barrier up, I have to tell the magic who to recognize. As I don't know these people, the easiest way to do this is to say that only those inside of it are recognized. Anyone outside of that barrier will be automatically repelled."

His face drew down into a concerned frown. "They will be able to leave the country, right?"

I hastily tried to erase the assumption he had just jumped to. "Of course, they can leave and return after the barrier is up. No problem. It's just when I first put the barrier up that they all need to be inside. The magic will recognize them that way."

Relieved, his frown eased and he sat back in his seat. "Good, good.

How long will this take?"

"I have no idea," I was forced to admit. "A day? Two? I might have to put the barrier up in sections, and then put a final spell on it to make it a cohesive shield. I'm not sure."

"We also need to know how much the Remcar-ol have been told," Xiaolang added, "and if there was any agreement made."

"I just spoke with the Remcar-ol," Magavero stated. "Actually, that's why I'm still in the city. They had one of those 'feelings' that something was going to happen soon." This last sentence was said with a certain amount of exasperation.

I held up a hand, stopping him. "Before you continue, clarify for me. Who exactly is the Remcar-ol?"

"Think of them as a sort of council for Q'atal," Xiaolang advised. "Only they have a great deal more power and influence over my countrymen than any council does over other countries." He thought about it another moment, then shook his head. "Although, even that description doesn't do them justice. They're more like our parents than anything. Every citizen in Q'atal is referred to as 'their children' and they literally mean that."

Interesting. I had assumed that it was something of that sort, but in cases like this, it was never a good idea to assume anything. "And the feeling that Magavero is talking about?"

Xiaolang was slower to answer this question. He looked visibly reluctant to say anything at all. "My people are known as more than just empaths. We sometimes…have a bit of precognition…"

I could tell by his expression that people had scoffed at this before. I kept my voice level and patient when I replied. "Xiaolang, keep in mind who you're speaking to. Magic comes in many forms, and personally, I think people only acknowledge a small part of it."

He relaxed, and a sheepish smile grew on his face. "I should have known that's how you'd respond. I've never seen you condemn an idea outright."

"I've seen too much that's unexpected, or downright unusual." I shrugged. "All right, so the Remcar-ol had something of a hunch that we were coming. And?"

"And they sent for me," Magavero continued. "I've been in town for about a day now. They wouldn't really talk to me—they just said to wait." Sardonically, he added, "Apparently they were waiting on someone."

"I think the wait is over," I drawled. "Well, if they're expecting us, we shouldn't keep them waiting. Where do we go?"

"Into Q'atal," Magavero answered simply.

I wasn't sure what I expected Q'atal to look like. All I knew was that the reality was completely different than any mental picture I would have come up with.

It was intuitively obvious when we crossed the border. We went from relatively flat coastline to this deep forest that looked and felt so ancient that I wouldn't have been surprised if it had existed when the world was newly created. There were these huge, primeval trees that stretched up to seemingly touch the sky, shading everything below them. I felt very tiny and insignificant in comparison. I think Night did too—he kept eyeing his surroundings as if he were waiting for something to reach out and bite him.

"The Forest of Antiquity," Xiaolang murmured.

That was a very appropriate name. Too appropriate, perhaps. To distract myself, I decided I might as well ask Xiaolang a few questions. "Xiaolang, you said that the Remcar-ol is more like parents than a council. Can you explain that a bit more?"

"There are only eight hundred Q'atalians," Xiaolang answered quietly.

My jaw dropped in sheer surprise. "Eight hundred?!" That's it?!

"We're not a large nation, by any means. We never have been. Because of that, the Remcar-ol has always been more hands-on with us. They come to check on us, give advice, support us in whatever we are doing—just like your parents would."

Busted buckets, I hadn't expected anything like this. "How many are in the Remcar-ol?"

"The number changes. There's usually more than five, never more than twelve. When..." he looked away, uneasy, "...when I left, there was eight."

I could almost feel his pain, and carefully changed the subject. "So if they're more like parents than anything, are they formal?"

"Not really. You shouldn't have a problem." The smile was back on his face, and he looked almost amused for some reason. "You're normally quite polite."

I didn't know how to respond to that, so I shrugged and stayed silent.

"Don't worry about this much. Magavero talks with the Remcar-ol on a regular basis. He'll keep you from making any serious mistakes." Even as he spoke, his eyes darted about in a nervous study of the forest, and he kept shifting on Hayate's back. "Garth. I'm not sure if I should go any further than this."

It took me a moment to understand what he meant. He'd put himself into exile, true, but Xiaolang had still broken the rules. He was still considered exiled by his country. I could understand his hesitation in getting too close to the border. "If you think that you should stay here," I answered gently, "then stay. Just tell us which direction to go."

He gave me a grateful smile. "Thank you. Don't worry about finding them—they'll find you."

Somehow, that wasn't reassuring. I nodded anyway, and led our small party deeper into the forest. I didn't look back, but I could feel Xiaolang watching us as we disappeared into the trees.

Shad urged his horse up so that he could ride next to me. "Is Xiaolang staying behind for a reason?"

Ah, right! He didn't know. I lowered my voice and told him a brief version of Xiaolang's history. Shad's eyes grew progressively darker as the story was related. By the time I was done, he was holding his reins in a white knuckled grip. "I don't think I care much for that law. It's stupid."

Considering Shad's background, I had expected that response. "I agree. But we're not the ones that made the rules."

"Hmph."

Apparently that rationale hadn't appeased him one iota.

Ah well.

We broke free of the tree line before I could think of something else to say to Shad. The view that met my eyes wiped all thought from my head.

Great…ancient…magic…

There was a valley in front of us, full of lush green grass, sparkly rivers, and huge trees. It glowed like some precious gem, and took my breath away with its beauty. If ever there was a place that could be described as heaven on earth, it was here.

Night stumbled to a halt, apparently just as captivated by the view as I was. "This place is gorgeous!"

I nodded dumbly, my tongue still too tied to speak.

It took me a few seconds before I started to notice details. There were houses in the valley, built out of native stone or wood in such a way that they almost blended in with the massive trees. I hadn't even noticed them at first, and probably wouldn't have, if not for the smoke rising out of a few chimneys.

It was out of one of these buildings that a group of four people emerged from. They looked like Xiaolang, but at the same time, they didn't. Their skin was a dusky blue, hair black as midnight, and hanging well past their waists in elaborate braids. The three men were in long tunics of light grey with elaborate embroidery work all along the collar and sleeves. The woman was in a dress of the same color, with similar embroidery. Looking at them, I didn't have to be told that they were of the Remcar-ol. With the power and confidence they displayed, I knew.

We all dismounted as they approached, coming a little forward to meet them.

Magavero sidled up next to me and muttered in a low tone, "In Q'atal, they greet each other by pressing their hand to your heart. You're supposed to do the same thing to return the greeting."

"Thank you for mentioning that now," I replied fervently. I hated messing up on the introductions.

His face stretched in a brief grin, and then he turned to everyone else, repeating the instruction. He barely finished before the Remcar-ol were in front of us.

It was the woman that spoke first, gliding forward to rest her hand against my chest. I could feel the power in her through that touch, the same power that I had felt in Xiaolang, all those weeks ago. "We have been waiting for you, Magus. I am An Meiling of the Remcar-ol."

I carefully returned the greeting, my hand resting more on her collarbone than on her chest, for obvious reasons. "I am Magus Rhebengarthen. Thank you for the gift of your name, An Meiling."

She blinked at this greeting, her hand slowly falling to her side. "A Chahiran mage? Vonlorisen must have had an absolute conniption when you showed up!"

It was my turn to blink at this unexpected statement. It was so off from what I had expected her to say I couldn't stop a rueful laugh from escaping. "I don't think he was far from it," I admitted. I turned and gestured to Night. "This is my nreesce, Night."

She went to him, pressing her hand against his chest. "Greetings, Night."

Night, being the affectionate creature he was, rubbed his cheek against hers. "Greetings, An Meiling. I am pleased to meet you."

"And I, you," she assured him. She continued down the line, greeting everyone else. I basically tuned her out, as I was greeting her three companions. There was an elderly gentleman by the name of Li Shen who reminded me strongly of Professor O'danne. He looked like a model grandfather, especially when he gave that crinkly smile of his. Yu Tung was tall and somewhat imposing in stature, but he reminded me so much of a grown up version of Trev'nor that I couldn't take him seriously. He had the same irrepressible curiosity and energy as my adopted brother did.

The last member was An Quon—probably some relation to An Meiling, considering they shared the same clan name—and it was he that struck me as the real leader of the group. He had the same mantel of authority and power on him that I saw in Shad, or Xiaolang, or Magavero. He greeted me just as properly as everyone else had, but he paused after he removed his hand from my chest.

"Was not our son with you?"

For a moment his question didn't make any sense. Then it made entirely too much sense. I froze as intuition flashed, telling me what he really meant. "You mean Xiaolang."

"De Xiaolang," he corrected me, and there was real worry on his face. "Our missing son. Wasn't he with you?"

Hope rose in me so hard and fast that I almost choked on it. Was Xiaolang wrong? Was there a chance that he could return home? "He stopped at the border," I answered carefully. "He did not feel that he had the right to come any farther."

An Quon acted as if I had slapped him. "No…" he choked out.

An Meiling rushed toward him, catching his arm and shaking him. "Do not make assumptions," she chided him. "I have said before that we have ignored this too long. We gave the child too much time, and it has done too much damage. I'm not waiting any longer." She abruptly turned to me. There was so much determination and anger in her eyes, I felt like ducking for cover. "Magus Rhebengarthen, you will take us to our missing son."

I didn't dare disobey that order. I wasn't sure what the consequences were for refusing, but I was sure they wouldn't be good. "Yes ma'am! Um, the quickest way is to take you by the Earth Path," I offered hesitantly.

"Then that is what we will do." She gestured to the other two men, and they promptly scurried over to stand beside her. I watched this and thought, Yup. I know who's really in charge.

I glanced at Night, quirking an eyebrow in question. "Do you want to wait or go with?"

"Wait," he said firmly.

"I thought as much. Back in a few minutes." Despite the way the Remcar-ol was impatiently clustered around me, I thought it prudent to give them a few words of warning. I didn't fancy the idea of dealing with any panic attacks. "To travel the Earth Path, I'll wrap us up in a cocoon of magic, and then descend into the earth under our feet." There were a few anxious looks at this, so I added the necessary assurances. "This is completely safe, and much faster than normal travel. We'll be there before you know it."

"We trust you, Magus," An Meiling declared, still determined.

Li Shen and Yu Tung stared at the back of her head like she was crazy, but they didn't say anything to contradict her. Well, they'd had their chance to back out. It was too late now. I wrapped us in magic, and dropped us all into the ground.

Xiaolang couldn't have been more than a mile away. It took only a few seconds to reach him, barely time for anyone to react. I popped up again, more focused on not getting tangled up in the roots of any trees than on my passengers. Because of that, I missed Xiaolang's initial reaction to our arrival.

But I didn't miss the expression of absolute joy on An Meiling's face. With quick strides she passed me, and I turned to see where she was going.

Xiaolang was standing beside Hayate, eyes as big as saucers. He looked like he wanted to say something, but his mouth wasn't cooperating. His jaw flapped like a landed fish.

An Meiling didn't give him a chance to pull his scattered wits together. She framed his face with both hands, pulling him down a little to her level. Despite the fact that Xiaolang was surely twice as strong as this petite woman, he docilely allowed the maneuver.

"I have had enough of this nonsense. You will come home, De Xiaolang."

His eyes closed in pain. "I broke the law, An Meiling."

"You protected your family," she corrected sharply. "Did you think we would judge you harshly for that? Nonsense, boy! I will not hear any contradictions. You will come home." Now, her tone added.

Li Shen went to their sides, affectionately cupping the back of Xiaolang's head. "We've missed you, child."

A single tear traced its way down Xiaolang's cheek. "So have I," he whispered huskily. As I watched, all of the sadness and pain just melted from his face and fell away. What replaced it was a joy so pure, so immense, it was nearly blinding. A smile broke out on my face seeing it.

Yu Tung and An Quon joined them, bracketing Xiaolang on all sides. I wasn't sure what passed between them, but I knew that I felt uncomfortable watching it. Somehow, that moment seemed too private for me to witness.

I turned away to give them some privacy. And since I had nothing better to do, I decided to take a look at the earth under my feet. I had sensed a great deal of power when we were traveling the Earth Path. Strangely enough, I thought I sensed enormous power in the trees as well. Now, it's true that plants have their own innate power, but it's not terribly strong. Not by itself, at least. If it grows on a ley line, that changes matters. I went to the nearest tree and placed a hand on it, closing my eyes so that I could better focus on what my senses were telling me.

It just about knocked me flat.

I could not believe the sheer amount of power in a single tree! I knew that it was a big tree, but still! Were all of the trees like this, or was this one sitting right on a ley line?

Someone's hand descended on my shoulder. I jumped, startled, and whirled around. Xiaolang was watching me through narrow eyes. "Garth, what are you doing?"

"Checking something," I answered. I still felt like my head was reeling and I wasn't even touching the tree anymore.

"You look…drunk…" he said slowly, eyes searching my face.

"I feel a little drunk," I replied with a dazed smile. "Whew. You would not believe how much power is in this tree."

"You're punch-drunk from being touchy-feely with a tree?"

I grimaced. "It sounds ridiculous when you put it that way."

"Garth, it will sound ridiculous regardless of how I phrase it."

I hated to admit it, but he had a point.

"We're ready to go back into Q'atal," he informed me. A mischievous twinkle lit his eyes. "And I think we should leave before you get so giddy that you start going around and hugging the trees or something."

I had this childish urge to stick my tongue out at him. I wasn't so far gone as to do that, however. I manfully glared at him instead.

Xiaolang ignored me and beckoned Hayate with a wave of his hand. "Come on, Hayate. We're going into Q'atal."

Hayate eyed him distrustfully. "Go in earth?"

"Yes, we're going by the Earth Path. It's faster that way."

Hayate shook his head adamantly, the reins jingling at the rapid motion. "No."

Xiaolang growled in exasperation. "Why not?"

"Night not like it. I not like it."

"You haven't even tried it!" Xiaolang retorted, flinging his hands up in the air.

"Not like it," Hayate insisted stubbornly.

"You like caves," Xiaolang pointed out persuasively. "Going by the Earth Path is like going into a cave."

That made the dragoo pause for a moment. "Like caves?"

"Yes, it's just like going into a nice, warm cave."

I thought that was a bit much, as Xiaolang had never traveled by Earth Path either. How would he know what it was like? Still, if this argument worked, I wasn't protesting.

Hayate didn't look like he entirely bought this story, but he sidled up next to the group regardless. Before any other issues could be raised, I gathered everyone up and took them back to where we had left the rest of the group. I had the presence of mind to turn slightly as I brought us to the surface, so that I could see Xiaolang's face.

I wasn't disappointed.

For the first time in seven years, Xiaolang was seeing his homeland again. I couldn't begin to describe all the emotions on his face. I recognized joy, relief, and a sense of belonging; it was only now, as I watched it play over his face, that I realized that peace had been missing.

His eyes sought mine, the only other person here who could fully comprehend what he was experiencing in this moment. I smiled as he did, and said the words that he obviously so wanted to hear. "Welcome home, De Xiaolang. Welcome home."

SURPRISES

Chatta was never so glad to see Del'Hain in her life.

It had been a long, long week. Once she'd had Remcarparoden safely in tow, she, Aletha, and Shield had ridden hard for the capital. She'd kept a weather eye on the young mage as they traveled, but he stayed very quiet and very subdued the entire trip. Chatta had a hunch that this submissive attitude was somehow brought about by Garth. She'd seen him talk to Shield, and shortly afterwards, Shield had taken Aletha aside to have a quiet conversation. Both Ascalon soldiers had acted very differently toward Remcarparoden ever since then. Maybe Chatta was just being paranoid.

But she wouldn't bet on it.

It was a definite relief to enter the city walls. All Chatta needed to do was deliver Remcarparoden to the Trasdee Evondit Orra, explain everything, and then she was home free. Well, she should probably go and talk to Guin and give him a more formal report. And going to see her father while she was in town was probably a good idea as well (in the interest of staying on said parent's good side).

They went to the Academy of All Magic first, as it was the only building in Del'Hain that could hold a captured mage. One would have thought a circus had invaded the school because it was so crowded with people and curious nreesces. Granted, the Academy was always chaotic to some degree, but this was more of an uproar than usual, which was confusing to Chatta. Judging from the amount of people in the main courtyard, no one was in class. Had she forgotten some holiday?

"Chatta!"

She turned, looking for the person calling her. Kartal was moving toward her in long strides, relief written all over his face. She regarded him with justified confusion. Never in their acquaintance had Kartal been relieved to see her. She stopped, turning so that she could keep one eye on Remcarparoden, and the other on Kartal as he approached.

As soon as Kartal was within hearing distance, he started talking. "I'm so glad to see someone from Garth's team. But what are you doing in Del'Hain?"

Chatta jerked a thumb at the mage standing next to her. "Delivering him."

Kartal took a long look at Remcarparoden, and his scrutiny was thorough enough to make the young mage shift uncomfortably. "That's a Fire Mage."

"One that has proven incapable of handling his power," Chatta informed him flatly. When Kartal stiffened in alarm, she smiled humorlessly. "It's a long story. I'll fill you in later. For now, I need to get him to a holding room, and call an emergency Council session. What's all the ruckus about?"

A truly sadistic smile grew on Kartal's face. That expression thoroughly alarmed Chatta—she braced herself, trying to prepare for whatever Kartal was about to throw at her. "I'm so glad you asked. Three mages from Bromany showed up yesterday."

"Three mages from Bromany," Chatta repeated. Her tone indicated that she was trying to do some elaborate formula in her head using those four words, only it wasn't computing.

"It gets better," Kartal assured her. His smile was nearly diabolical. "They're the descendents of the surviving mages from the Magic War."

Chatta stared at him, speechless. Was he joking?

Aletha interrupted at his point, nearly spluttering. "Now wait a minute; I thought that no one survived the last battle of the Magic War."

"That's what we all assumed," Kartal corrected. He was truly getting a kick out of their reactions, bouncing happily on the balls of his feet. "No one came back from the Isle of Strae, so we thought they must have killed each other off. But no one went and investigated that, either. The Remnant Mages—"

"Remnant?" Shield questioned, highly curious.

"That's what they call themselves," Kartal explained, a trifle impatiently. "The Remnant. Anyway, these mages claim that there were a few mages and witches that survived that last battle, but they chose not to return to Chahir. They went to Bromany instead, and established a colony there."

"Claimed?" Chatta pounced on that word like a cat on a trapped mouse. "You don't believe them?"

Kartal spread his hands in a neutral shrug. "Guin tells me that they brought proof with them, and he doesn't doubt their story. I just haven't seen it for myself. Anyway, back to my original point. The Remnant Mages have come here specifically to talk to the mages. They really want to talk to Garth, because he was the first one out of Chahir. We've been trying to figure out a way to contact you."

"That's why you're glad to see me," Chatta surmised. Her head still spun madly—mages? Remnant? Bromany?! That was across the ocean! Fortunately, her mouth came up with an intelligent response without much input from her brain. "Well, I guess our timing is good, then."

"Very good," Kartal approved. "Especially considering that they were going to send me to hunt you down."

"I'm so glad that I've saved you some extra work," Chatta drawled.

"So am I," Kartal agreed, deliberately disregarding her sarcasm. "I'm overworked as it is. I wish Garth would get back here; they keep shifting his duties over to me. It's a pain."

That was so like Kartal that Chatta just ignored it. "So where are these Remnant Mages now?"

"Talking with the Trasdee Evondit Orra, I imagine. Let's get this Fire Mage of yours in proper lock up, and I'll take you to them."

Chatta nodded. "Good idea. Shield, Aletha? Can you go to Guin and update him on what's happened? I think I'd better go talk with the Trasdee Evondit Orra first."

They both nodded in understanding. "No problem," Aletha assured her. "We'll see you later?"

She had been fantasizing about a long hot bath, but with this new situation, that wish was going up like so much smoke. "Much later, probably," Chatta sighed ruefully.

The Remnant Mages were not at all what Chatta had pictured.

Bromanans were known as a very expansive, loud, physically affectionate culture. They were into every type of business imaginable, and didn't think twice about traveling all over the known world to expand their business. Chatta had expected the Remnant Mages to be rather like a Bromanan, considering that they grew up on that continent.

They weren't.

In fact, she couldn't place them in any single culture at all.

Her first look at them was necessarily brief, because they were in the Council Room with the rest of the Trasdee Evondit Orra. To avoid being rude, Chatta had to properly greet the rest of the Council first. Still, she got quite the eyeful as she entered the room. There were three of them, as Kartal had mentioned; two men and a woman. The woman was in a deep red coat that fit her snugly, flaring out at the hips. The two men were dressed in a similar coat, but they were in different colors—deep blue and white, respectively. Chatta had a suspicion that the colors signified something.

"Witch Delheart, we are pleased to see you," En-Nelle of Tain said, perfectly sincere—perhaps even relieved. "Allow me to introduce our long-lost comrades."

Chatta personally thought that statement was a bit much, but held her tongue.

"This is Magus Tyvendor, Air Mage from Coven Ordan."

Tyvendor was a large man, not so much in height as in stature. He was solid, like an ancient oak tree, with wildly curling brown hair. The only soft part of him was his light blue eyes and childlike smile.

"Magus Hay-el D'Auch," En-Nelle continued, "Life Mage from Coven Ordan."

Hay-el D'Auch was a woman that could only be described as striking. Her dark hair and wide black eyes were set in a face too angular to be labeled as pretty, but something about her made her looks attractive instead of plain. The smile she gave Chatta was genuine, and perhaps a touch curious.

"And Magus Terran Far'Auchmage, Water Mage of Coven Ordan," En-Nelle finished with a triumphant smile. Chatta had no doubt that En-Nelle was silently plotting on how to get control of these three mages.

Terran Far'Auchmage was as fair as the other two were dark, aside from his dark eyes. In fact, with his slim build and fair coloring, he could almost pass for Chahiran.

Almost in perfect unison, the Remnant Mages bowed slightly, hands spread out to the side. "We seek the balance."

Chatta, after a startled beat, translated that, roughly, as how do you do?

"Mages, this is Witch L-Chattamoinita Delheart."

Chatta had spent so much time in Chahir recently that she gave them a polite bow without thinking about it. "A pleasure to meet you."

With the proper introductions out of the way, En-Nelle turned eagerly toward Chatta. "Is Magus Rhebengarthen with you?"

"No, he is in Q'atal," Chatta answered.

En-Nelle blinked, obviously confused. "Q'atal? Not Chahir?"

"The Q'atalians asked that he take a brief detour and help them with something," she explained. "He should be there by now." Chatta wasn't about to be sidetracked, and launched into the more important matter first. "I came to deliver a rogue mage. I put to the Council that this mage must have his power stripped from him."

As she had expected, there were immediate protests from all corners. Chatta wasn't about to try to shout them down—for one thing, she didn't possess the necessary lung power—and just stared at them, waiting for them to settle again.

"I would like to hear the reasoning behind this request," Tyvendor announced. His deep voice rumbled through the room like approaching thunder, silencing people instantly.

Chatta liked this calm, reasonable response, and chose to direct her reply to him. She had spent most of the ride here thinking about how she would explain this, and so the words came easily to her now. It took several minutes before she was done explaining exactly what Remcarparoden had done in Jarrell, and when she was finished, the room was as still as any wake.

"That is grave, indeed," Doss finally stated, breaking the silence. "You are quite correct, Chatta. We must strip this young mage of his powers."

"Surely the boy can be taught," En-Nelle protested, hands flapping in agitation. "I mean, consider his history…where he was…"

"Every other mage that we have discovered has a similar history or worse," Chatta snapped back. Sometimes she was just ready to strangle this woman. "None of them have ever abused their powers. Besides, this boy went crazy after the new laws were put into place. He had even less of a reason to burn the city than all of the other mages that we have rescued!"

O'danne actually applauded her. "Well said, my dear, well said. No, Nellie, we shan't play with fire—no pun intended, of course. A full circle must be called."

"I quite agree," BycLewsh stated, in a deceptively mild manner.

En-Nelle knew when she was outnumbered, and grumpily subsided. But she definitely wasn't happy about it.

"A full circle won't be necessary," Hay-el D'Auch announced. "We will be pleased to assist you in this matter."

"Very pleased," Terran Far'Auchmage agreed darkly. "People who abuse their powers anger us. Where is this Fire Mage?"

Chatta wanted results, and she frankly didn't care who did the deed, so she answered quickly. "I put him in a holding room in the basement of this building. A wizard is watching him now." Kartal had thought it prudent to keep an eye on Remcarparoden—neither of them had been sure if the building's wards, as old as they were, could really contain a mage. He had surprised her by offering to babysit while she went up and talked to the Council.

"If you would show us the way?" Tyvendor asked her politely. "After we are done with that, I would like to talk with you about several matters."

You and me both, Chatta thought. "Certainly, Magus."

A half an hour.

Three mages had done in a half-hour what it would have taken a full circle—fifteen people—a whole day to do.

Was she ever so glad that these mages were on her side!

She wasn't sure how they did it, as she had been outside the room while they worked, but she certainly knew when the job was complete. Remcarparoden, when he realized his magic was gone forever, started sobbing hysterically. Chatta had half-expected this reaction, but even with his screams echoing in the hallway, she felt no pity for him. He had brought this entirely on himself.

They didn't even look tired when they came out of the room, just unhappy.

"It is done," Hay-el D'Auch assured Chatta. "Now, we would like to speak with you."

"Let's choose a more comfortable place to talk," Chatta suggested. She, for one, was looking forward to a nice, soft chair.

There were no protests to her suggestion, so she led them to some of the more private study rooms in the building. They were meant for students, but normally remained vacant because of their small size. However, there were enough chairs to comfortably seat four people, which made them perfect for Chatta's purpose.

She found a vacant room on the second try, and ushered everyone inside. It was with deep satisfaction that she sank into a faded, overstuffed armchair, relaxing for the first time in days.

"You look tired," Hay-el surprised her by commenting.

"It was a long trip," Chatta admitted. "And a little nerve-wracking. We weren't sure if the amulets would contain a mage's power."

"By 'we' I assume you mean you and the Advent Mage?" Tyvendor inquired.

"Yes." Chatta paused, but decided she might as well be frank with him. "Just as a warning, when you meet Garth, don't call him the Advent Mage to his face. He hates that title."

The three exchanged puzzled glances. "We were given the impression that he was a man of great power and reputation," Terran commented, his eyes studying her carefully. "Is this in error?"

Chatta couldn't help but smile. "His reputation doesn't match reality at all," she laughed, shaking her head ruefully. Chatta was more aware of how Garth was perceived than her quiet friend was. Garth was under the impression that everyone viewed him as some sort of demi-god of tremendous power. And that was true, to a point. What he wasn't aware of was the rest of his reputation.

"Perhaps you can tell us just how much of his reputation is off course?" Hay-el suggested. "And what your relationship is with him?"

That seemed perfectly reasonable to Chatta. "Certainly. I'm Garth's best friend. We went through part of our schooling together, and we are usually paired up on projects. I've known him almost two years now. As for how much of his reputation is right..." She started ticking points off on her fingers. "It's true that he's insanely strong, but he isn't egotistical about it. He really did turn a coastal city into an island, but he didn't just bounce up and go slay a dragon afterwards. It took him a while to recover." She paused, trying to think of all the rumors she had heard. "He really is a Jaunten, and he really does have white hair. He really has saved about twenty people from Chahir, but he had a lot of help doing that, too. Have I missed anything?"

A wicked smile darted over Hay-el's face. "Is he secretly engaged to you?"

Chatta blinked, briefly stunned. "Um. Haven't heard that one. No, we aren't. Actually, our relationship isn't like that at all. We really are friends…" she trailed off, cocking her head to one side. "Was there truly a rumor about us?"

"Several," Terran drawled in open amusement. "Guin's keeping your real purpose in Chahir secret, so all the public knows is that you and Magus Rhebengarthen have been off somewhere for two months now. Some people think your father refused to give the magus permission to marry you, so you two eloped."

That was so different from reality that Chatta nearly fell out of her chair laughing. It took several deep breaths before she felt like she could talk coherently again. "Oh dear. I've got to tell him that when I get back." She giggled again when she pictured what his reaction would be. "He'll be completely dumbfounded." She was sure that Garth would have a good chuckle, after he reattached his jaw and put his eyes back in their sockets. Maybe she could buy a fake engagement ring to tease him with…hmmm, now there was a thought.

"So what is he really like?" Tyvendor leaned forward slightly, eyes bright with interest.

Chatta softened, a gentle smile tugging at her lips. "Kind. Patient. Quiet. He's the type of person that will help you, no matter what the cost is to him. And he has no tolerance for people who abuse their power, or deliberately hurt others." Memories flashed in the back of her head, of times when he had leapt to someone's defense. "He is the kindest and best of men."

"You love him a great deal," Terran observed quietly.

"Yes, I do," she agreed without hesitation. "It's not difficult—even his enemies eventually learn to respect him. That's the kind of person he is. Perhaps you can tell me why you're asking me these questions?" Chatta figured it was about time to turn the tables.

"How much have you been told about us?" Hay-el countered.

"The basics," Chatta responded carefully. "You are descendents from the magicians that survived the last battle on the Isle of Strae.

Your ancestors settled in a colony on Bromany soil. You've come here to speak with the mages, Garth in particular. Perhaps you could give me more detail?"

"Tyvendor, you tell her," Terran ordered with an expansive wave of his hand. "You're the best storyteller out of us."

Tyvendor rolled his eyes. "You're only saying that because you don't want to do it." With a dark look at his friend, he began anyway. "Our ancestors didn't actually fight in that last battle. They went to the Isle of Strae as ordered, but they had no desire to fight with comrades or friends. They chose to leave instead.

"One of them was a Water Mage, and it was he that gathered everyone up, and traveled along the Water Path through the Stagway Ocean to Bromany. There were eight of them, and several dozen children.

"They went straight to the Bromanan government and offered them a deal. In return for land of their own, they would work for the government for one year. The offer was accepted with alacrity. A year later, they were given a huge valley in the BankNoren of Ordan."

Chatta stiffened in her chair. She'd heard of the BankNoren of Ordan. It was a huge mountain range that had played a part in the protection and defeat of several armies in the history of Bromany. In recent times, it was a famous place for bandits and the like to hang out. "But isn't that a dangerous place?"

"For normal people." Tyvendor flashed a smile that was as feral as any wolf's. "For us, it was merely a…challenge. Anyway, for the past two hundred years we, the Remnant, have lived there and cultivated the land as we wished. It is now a city in its own right. We call it Coven Ordan.

"Five years ago, one of our wizards began to carefully keep watch over Chahir. He had a feeling that magic would again live in that land. Then two years ago, we were all surprised when he reported that a mage had awakened. We went looking for him, of course, but we couldn't find him again in Chahir after that first sighting."

Reality hit Chatta about who he must have seen, and she whispered breathlessly, "Garth…"

"Yes, it must have been him," Tyvendor acknowledged. "We have spoken with King Guin, and the timeline fits too neatly for it to be anyone else. That is one reason why we wish to speak with him. Over the past two years, we all kept a closer eye on Chahir, and we saw more and more magicians awaken. But they never stayed in the same place long. We kept losing them, which was quite frustrating. Three weeks ago, it was decided that we couldn't continue to just sit and watch. Hay-el, Terran, and I decided to come over and see for ourselves just what was going on. We approached King Vonlorisen first, but…" his face gathered in a fierce frown. "That man was not helpful."

"I can imagine so," Chatta sympathized. "He probably threw an absolute tantrum that three foreign mages showed up at his palace."

"Tantrum is a good word," Hay-el growled darkly.

"While he was ranting, he mentioned something about King Guin, so we came to Del'Hain," Tyvendor continued. "King Guin was much more helpful explaining what was going on. He was genuinely glad to see us, too. He explained how he needed help training all of the mages that were being discovered, so we decided to come here to the Academy and help out until we could find a way to contact the Advent—er, I mean, Rhebengarthen. Two days later, you show up." Tyvendor smiled, relaxing back into his seat. "Now you know everything. You said he was in Q'atal now. Doing what?"

"The Q'atalian borders keep getting overrun with bandits," Chatta explained. "A lot of their people keep getting hurt. They asked that Garth come up and put a barrier around the country."

One would think, judging from the frozen horror on their faces, that Chatta had just suggested setting the Academy on fire.

"He's setting up a barrier around a whole country?!" Terran demanded. "ALONE?!"

"Garth is the only trained mage we have," Chatta pointed out, confused about their reactions.

"Your king just finished telling me two days ago that no one here could really train the mages!" Hay-el retorted. "So how is your mage trained?"

"Experimentation, mostly," Chatta muttered. "He was given some guidance, and a rough idea of what he was capable of from the little bit of history that survived the Magic War. He just kind of took it from there. Experience has helped hone his control."

"That's not proper training!" Tyvendor protested. "And barrier magic is the most difficult magic of all!"

Chatta abruptly lost her temper. "What do you expect us to do?" she snapped at him. "No one here can help Garth! No one, do you hear me?! We've tried! I've personally tried, and passed out from the attempt! If you're so worried about him making a mistake, then you go help him!"

"Excellent idea," Hay-el declared firmly. "Tyvendor, you'll be able to get there faster than us. Take Witch Delheart with you, and fly there as quickly as possible."

"If we're lucky, he hasn't started yet." Terran scrubbed his face with the palms of his hands.

Chatta privately thought it was probably too late to help Garth. He'd had more than enough time to get up to Q'atal and set to work by now. The deed was probably already done. But she didn't say any of this out loud. She had a feeling that her protests would have fallen on deaf ears.

BARRIERS

I was beginning to understand why no one wanted to leave Q'atal. It really was a wonderful place to live.

It wasn't just the beauty of the land that made me say that, although that was certainly a factor. I'd never seen prettier country than this. More than my surroundings, it was the Q'atalians that truly influenced my opinion.

I'd never, as long as I'd known Xiaolang, heard him say one harsh word to someone. He could tease a body to murder, but he'd never been unkind to anyone. I thought that was just how Xiaolang was— until I discovered that his entire culture is like that.

Maybe it's because they are all empaths, or maybe it's for some other reason entirely; all I knew was that they were the most peaceful, loving people I'd ever met. I found myself acting with more patience and tolerance than I thought possible, just because of their influence.

It would have been entirely too easy to become distracted by the people, and forget my true purpose here entirely. I didn't intend to become lazy, however, and on our second day in Q'atal I got up early.

I had work to do.

The entire team had been put into this large building in the center of the city. I thought it was normally a hall, or some sort of formal meeting room, but it had been made over for our use. Someone had placed several mattresses and chairs and tables in there for us. In the center of the room was a large fireplace, which kept the place warm during the cool nights. Hayate, to my lack of surprise, was snuggled up in front of the fire. I looked around as I rolled out of bed, checking on everyone. They had given Night a huge mattress next to mine. He was still out, snoring like a wounded banshee. Everyone else was asleep as well, the one exception being Xiaolang. That didn't surprise me. The captain was very much a morning person.

Since I wasn't a morning person, it took some time and effort on my part to get moving. I stumbled into some clean clothes, splashed water on my face, and headed outside.

I was barely two steps out the door when someone spotted me.

"Garth! You're up quite early." De Lien summoned me with a wave of her hand, a gentle smile on her face. "Come eat breakfast with my family."

I'd met De Lien—and the rest of Xiaolang's family—yesterday, and had liked her. That feeling went up a notch when she offered to feed me. "If I'm not imposing…"

"Nonsense, child, you are quite welcome here. Now come, I left a pot on the stove, and I don't want it to burn."

I didn't either, so I hurried to join her. The De family had this huge house that they all lived in, which fortunately wasn't far from where I had stayed the night. It was only one story, but it sprawled out into every conceivable direction. I had the feeling that additions were just added on as the family grew.

De Lien ushered me in through the front door and into a bedlam of noise and confusion. The house was laid out so that the front door would dump people right into the dining room. At the moment, the table was crowded with people ranging in age from infancy to tottering old men. De Lien gestured me silently toward the table and then scurried around the corner, presumably to the kitchen before her pot of food could burn.

In the midst of this madness was Xiaolang, sitting at the table with a little girl snuggled in against his side. He looked up as I came in, smiling in greeting. "Good morning! Now this is rare, I never see you up this early."

"I have a lot of work to do," I responded with a shrug. "I figured I should get an early start." I didn't get a chance to say anything else before I was tackled on both sides. I stumbled back a little at the impact, looking down sharply to see what had hit me. Two pairs of big blue eyes stared up at me innocently.

"De Shin, De Chan, stop that," Xiaolang ordered in exasperation. "You'll make him uncomfortable."

Actually, I didn't really mind. The twin boys were barely three years old and cute little rascals. They had followed me around all day yesterday before their mother had carted them off to bed. Apparently they were intent on following me today, too.

I bent and gathered them up in each arm—which made them giggle and squirm—and made my way to the table. As soon as I was seated, they glued themselves to my sides. Again, I didn't really mind, although I began to wonder how I was supposed to eat when I couldn't easily move my arms.

"Boys!" a grandfatherly man to my right reproved. "You must give the magus a little breathing room."

This didn't get much of a response, aside from twin stubborn looks.

Xiaolang sighed as he watched this. "Sorry, Garth. They're too young to understand."

So was I, apparently, because that statement didn't make any sense to me. "Understand what?"

He blinked, studying me thoughtfully for a moment. "Ah, you probably don't know, do you? I don't think I ever said much about it. Remember that first time that we met? I told King Guin that you and Chatta were excellent people."

I vaguely remembered him saying something to that effect. "Yes. And?"

"Good people, to an empath, feel like a warm summer day," he explained. "It's very pleasant to be around people of good character. This feeling is especially enhanced if that person is some sort of magician."

I was beginning to see. "So to the twins, I feel good?"

De Lien appeared from somewhere behind me, chuckling. "You feel good to all of us, Magus. But we're better at restraining ourselves."

I was grateful for that, as it would be embarrassing to have Q'atalians ambushing me all day.

"De Shin, De Chan," De Lien's voice was soft, but there was a firm tone to it, "you must let the magus eat. You may sit next to him, but only if you behave."

That had the desired effect, and both twins reluctantly sat back a little. To reward them, I ruffled both of their heads a little. That put a smile back on their faces.

"Good," De Lien stated in satisfaction. "Now everyone, let us eat."

I didn't recognize any of the food, but everything I tried was really good. Xiaolang must have realized that, because he grinned at me.

"Feel a little lost, Garth?"

"More like I'm repeating history," I sighed.

"Repeating history? Ah, right, I remember. When you went to Hain for training. I bet the first few months in Hain were a challenge for your taste buds."

I cleaned up the last bite on my plate, feeling full and content. "I wish Hain would adopt Q'atalian food for breakfast. Yours is much better."

"What a lovely compliment," a young woman at the table (her name escaped me) declared.

"It's the honest truth," I assured her. "Everything Hainians like to eat for breakfast is either crunchy or bitter. I've never understood why." That was why I was grateful that my family was settled in Del'Hain. I showed up at my parent's house for breakfast with religious regularity.

"So what exactly are your plans for today?" Xiaolang inquired.

"I need to do a thorough study of the land," I responded, mapping out a strategy in my head as I responded. "Judging from the little that I've seen, you have quite a few ley lines running all through this country."

"That's good?" Xiaolang guessed.

"Very good," I assured him. "It means that whatever barrier I put up will have power to draw on. It will last a long time. My main worry is that the ley lines won't be in the right place for me to connect a barrier with them. That's what I'll try to confirm today."

"Do you need anything?"

I thought about that for a moment. "Time. Quiet. Chatta."

Xiaolang nearly choked on the water he was drinking. "Er…in that particular order?"

"I'll take them as I get them." I could just see that he was jumping to the wrong conclusion (probably several of them all at once) and decided that I better straighten him out. "Scrying always gives me the devil of a headache. Chatta's very good at mixing up a potion that gets rid of them. I didn't think to snitch a vial from her before she left, which is one reason why I wish she were here right now."

He was still giving me an odd look, but the only thing he said was, "You'll have to settle for the more conventional Q'atalian medicine. You'll be following the border, won't you?"

"I won't need to go anywhere," I corrected. "I can sit right here and do a scrying of the whole country. It's not that big of an area, after all. I just need some time to do it."

"Take it in easy forays," Xiaolang advised. "I don't want you to keel over. For one thing, without Chatta here, we'd have no idea how to help you."

"I'll behave," I promised, raising a hand in mock-solemn oath.

I found this nice, deserted shady spot to do my scrying in. It was remote, quiet, and had a nice thick patch of grass nearby where Night could graze while waiting for me. I settled in comfortably, closed my eyes, and put my mind into the earth.

After two years (nearly) of doing this, I'd gotten better at scrying. And while it was never easy, it was at least easier. I was confident that it wouldn't take long, or be terribly taxing to do a scrying of Q'atal.

Wrong.

I could not believe the sheer amount of ley lines in this place! Most areas, from my experience, had perhaps two or three ley lines within a twenty mile radius. That was normal. Q'atal had so many ley lines that it resembled a ball of tangled yarn. One played with by a rambunctious kitten, no less! This was just ridiculous. There was enough power here to blow my mind. Literally.

After that first hour of study, I began to realize that I didn't have the problem I thought I had. Originally, I was afraid that I wouldn't have enough power for a barrier, or the ley lines would be in the wrong location. Now I was afraid that I had too much power. If I didn't handle this right, and tapped into the wrong ley line, I could very well overload myself. I wasn't entirely sure what the consequences would be for that, but I was absolutely certain that they would be bad. I had this worry that I would go up in flames like a stack of kindling.

I took a breather, relaxing back on the grass with my eyes closed. Not having the power to sustain a barrier obviously wasn't an issue. But exactly how should I approach this?

"Garth?"

I was too lazy to really respond. "Hmmm?"

"Are you all right? You look…a little spacey." Night shifted so he could nudge me in the side with his nose.

"There's a lot of power under us," I informed him, absently patting him on the nose. "I think I got a little high looking at it all."

"So you'll have enough power for a barrier?"

Too much, but I didn't say that, as I didn't want to worry him. "Yes. I just have to figure out how to tap into it right. And I think I'd better talk with the Remcar-ol."

"Why?"

"Well, I don't want to put up a barrier that only Q'atalians can go through. What if they make friends with someone, or marry someone outside the country? They'd have no way of entering. I think I should make at least one opening for people. I'm just not sure where to put it."

"That's a good idea," Night agreed. "Scratch right between my eyes, would you? There's an itch there that's driving me crazy."

I obligingly scratched, still thinking. Yes, a regular "doorway" would be a good idea, I think. Was there any other aspect that I overlooked?

"Hey, Garth!"

Shad? I twisted around until I could see him. He was walking up the slope in a steady stride, and despite the fact that he had just hiked a half mile to reach me, he didn't look at all winded. His stamina had really improved over the past few days. I was pleased to see this.

"Something wrong?" I called to him.

"No, just thought you might want to know. The last Q'atalian caravan has come home. They're ready for you to put the barrier up."

That'd be fine, if I knew how to do it.

I rolled up to my feet, still feeling a little tingly. Why was scrying so difficult on the body? Well, it would pass. "I need to speak with the Remcar-ol first. I have some questions that need to be answered."

Shad had reached me by this point, and he was giving that same concerned look that Night was. "Are you all right, Garth?"

"Do I still look a little spacey?" I asked dryly.

"Er…a little."

And that was from just looking at the ley lines. I couldn't imagine how it'd feel to actually touch them. "I'm fine. Let's go."

The look Shad gave me said he didn't believe me. "And after you get your answers? Are you going to try and put the barrier up today?"

"Why not?" Wasn't like it would be any easier waiting a day.

The general consensus of the Remcar-ol was that a doorway in the barrier was a good idea. They requested that the doorway face Ascalon, as most of their trading was done with that country. With that piece of information, I went back to my remote spot and did another scrying.

After a full afternoon of studying the problem, I reached the conclusion that I would have to treat this barrier like I would any barrier.

It had to come up all at once.

It just wouldn't work if I tried to raise it in sections, and then magically glue it altogether. There would be too many areas that would be weaker than the rest, and with enough time and patience, those weak points could be exploited. No, I would have to raise the barrier as a whole. I groaned at the thought, because I just knew how this would make me feel. I could do barriers—pure earth barriers, at least—but it was never easy magic for me. Actually, I'd rather turn Jward into an island all over again than put a barrier up around Q'atal. It would be far easier.

I went back to the main part of the town, looking for Xiaolang. I found him wrestling with some of his younger cousins—they had him currently pinned to the ground—with an elderly woman watching on in fond amusement. At my approach, he looked up. "Garth! Are you done for the day?"

I shook my head. "I'm putting the barrier up. I just wanted to double check that everyone was in the country."

Xiaolang quickly rolled to his feet, children dangling off of him and squealing in surprise at his quick movement. "You're putting it up today? You said this was difficult magic! And the day is nearly gone."

"It's very difficult magic, but it won't take long to do," I answered. "It just takes a lot of energy. Is everyone inside the country?"

He was slow to answer, eyes locked with mine. "Yes."

"Good." I turned away, looking for a good place to land. I had no doubt that once the barrier was up I was going to collapse on the spot. I wanted to land on something soft when that happened.

There was a nice pile of sand nearby, meant for the younger children to play in. Sand shouldn't be too bad. I edged closer to it, trying to not make it obvious what I was doing. If anyone had an inkling of how hard this would be for me, I was sure that they would protest and argue. Loudly.

Satisfied that I was within range, I took a deep breath to steady myself. Here goes.

Closing my eyes, I tapped into the three ley lines that I deemed necessary for the barrier. Let me just say this—I would not have been surprised if energy had started shooting out of my fingertips. My nerves sang with power, and it was so intense that it was almost painful. I gasped at the shock of it, realizing that I just couldn't hold this kind of power in check for long. I had to put up that barrier.

Now.

I didn't put up barriers like anyone else would. My power just worked too differently. I didn't sing an incantation, say a spell, or anything of that nature. What I did was mentally envision the barrier that I wanted, and willed the power at my fingertips to do my bidding.

Mentally picturing a barrier was the easy part—molding power to fit that vision? Not so easy. It took a lot of fine control on my part, and I had to keep a firm grip on the ley lines while working.

I lose all track of time when doing magic like this. I couldn't tell you how long I was at it before my heart started to pound in my ears, and black spots started swimming in front of my eyes. I was gasping for breath, feeling my muscles began to shake under the strain. I couldn't take much more of this. The barrier was almost up…the shape almost completed…I just had to last…a bit…longer…

The barrier snapped together and began working with an almost audible hum. Or maybe the humming was the sound of my blood rushing south. With the last of my strength I looked up. There was a dome of dark green over my head—the barrier was up. Darkness was encroaching on my vision, and the last thing I knew was that the ground reached up and smacked me.

Something soft and cool was stroking the hair away from my face in a soothing manner. The sensation was so pleasant that I smiled and tried to lean into it. Hmmm. Chatta…

"Garth?" a gentle voice asked from nearby. "Are you awake?"

My mouth felt glued together, it was so dry. I pried it open and croaked, "Chatta?"

"Yes, I'm here."

She was actually here? I wasn't hallucinating? Needing to verify that with my own eyes, I pried open an eyelid. No, she really was there, leaning over me and watching with obvious concern. "You overdid it again, didn't you?"

"Had to do it all at once," I muttered vaguely. I fumbled around until I found her other hand, and put it against my face. Her skin felt blessedly cool against my heated skin.

"You feel a little feverish," she fretted.

I did feel a bit warm. My body wasn't too happy with the events of the past couple of hours. I wasn't thrilled about it either. The next time someone asked me to do something like this, the answer was going to be no.

Another voice I had never heard piped up. "Is he awake?"

I felt Chatta shift next to me on the bed, turning to talk to whoever had just entered. "Tyvendor, he's running a fever. I've never seen him so low like this. Is there something we can do?"

"He just needs rest. And a lot of water; magic like that can drain you." There was a hint of awe in his voice when he spoke again. "You weren't kidding, Chatta, when you said he was incredibly strong. I've checked that barrier from top to bottom, and it's completely impenetrable, even for a mage. I thought something like this was just a legend. I never imagined he could actually do it!"

Okay, now I was really curious. Who was this man? He didn't feel like a normal person, or a wizard. Twinges started hammering in my temples, and I stopped trying to figure out what he was. My brain was too sore for me to carry that investigation any further.

"I told you not to worry about him," Chatta replied tartly. "Experience is a good teacher. Give me that glass, will you?" her voice gentled again, and the hand stroking my hair paused. "Garth, can you sit up a little? I think you need to drink some water."

Water? That was a wonderful idea. I struggled to sit up a little—this was difficult, as my muscles were as cooperative as wet noodles—so that I could drink something. Chatta shifted around until she could put a shoulder behind mine, giving me some support, then steadied a glass against my lips. I drained the cup in one long draw and sighed in satisfaction once it was gone.

I wanted to ask questions, about the barrier, about the man in the room, about how Chatta had come up to Q'atal so quickly to be here. I didn't get a chance to utter one word before I sank back into comforting darkness.

The next time I woke up, the world was a much friendlier place. For one thing, my headache was nearly gone. For another, I didn't feel like death warmed over. My body was a little stiff, probably from lying still for so long, and my stomach was so empty it grumbled plaintively, but other than that I felt fine.

I shifted my head around, getting my bearings. I was back in the main hall, but the room was empty, all the beds made. Well, not quite empty. Night was taking a nap on the bed next to mine.

Slowly, I sat up, feeling stiff and a little uncoordinated. Had it all been a dream, then? Had Chatta really been here, and that other man I didn't know?

"Di!"

Didi? I looked around until I spotted him. He was sitting up in the rafters, peering down at me with ears quivering. When he realized I saw him, he dropped straight down onto my bed, bouncing a little at the impact. "Di!" he proclaimed, smiling.

Apparently everyone enjoys bouncing on the bed. I smiled back at him. "You enjoyed that, didn't you?"

He nodded vigorously.

"If you're here, I suppose Chatta's here as well?"

"Di," Didi agreed. He held up a little paw, indicating for me to stay put, then scampered across the room and out the door.

I assumed that he was going to fetch Chatta, so I obediently stayed put. There was a glass of water next to my bed, and I gratefully quaffed it down while I waited. As soon as I saw Chatta and figured out what was going on, I was going for a bath and food—not necessarily in that order.

Chatta appeared in the doorway, skidding to a halt when she saw me. "Garth! Finally, you're awake!" Without pause she flew the rest of the way, nearly bowling me over with an exuberant hug.

I put a hand quickly behind me as a brace so I wouldn't get knocked over, returning the hug with my free arm. She smelled like sunshine and flowers, a heady combination that filled my head. I smiled as I held her, enjoying the solid warmth of her pressed close. For a moment I just relaxed, letting my questions wait. "I thought I dreamed you," I murmured into her hair.

"You've been asleep nearly two days," she mumbled into my shoulder. "You woke up once yesterday afternoon, long enough for me to get some water down you, and then you went right back to sleep. I've never seen you so exhausted!"

Well, there was a good reason for that. I've never been that exhausted. I decided it might be wise to not say that out loud. "So how did you get up here so fast?" I asked instead. "I wasn't expecting you for another four or five days, at least."

She sat back a little, enough to see my face. There was a very disturbingly impish light in her eyes. "I hitched a ride with an Air Mage from Bromany."

My jaw hit the ground so hard it probably left a dent. "WHAT?!"

"You look like a beached whale," she giggled.

"Chatta, stop teasing me and explain!" I requested plaintively.

I listened with rapt attention as she filled me in on the past few days. What she was telling me was incredible—a whole colony of magicians on Bromany soil, who were descendents of people who escaped the Isle of Strae? Three mages in particular that came over to Chahir, and then Hain, in order to meet the new mages being born? There was one point to all of this that I couldn't let pass unchallenged. "Why do they want to meet me in particular?"

"Because you're the first mage they saw awaken," she answered promptly. "I think that your reputation has something to do with it too. You wouldn't believe the rumors that are spreading around the capital right now."

Actually, I probably would. People have very vivid imaginations, and for some reason, they keep inflicting their ideas on me. "So they want to meet the man behind the myth?"

"In part," she agreed. That impish light was back in her eyes. "Speaking of rumors…you're going to have to make an honest woman out of me."

I had absolutely no idea what she was talking about. "Eh?"

"One of the rumors going around right now is that Da wouldn't give you permission to marry me, so we eloped. That's why no one has seen us for the past few months."

She said this with such a straight face that I had a hard time believing that she was serious. When it finally hit me that she was serious, I just groaned. "Those people have obviously never met our parents. I wouldn't dare elope with you, my mother would scalp me. She's always wanted to do a big wedding for all of her kids."

"Mine too." Chatta was trying not to laugh, but it was obvious that she was enjoying this rumor. "I've been thinking about buying some fake wedding ring, and showing it off to our families when we get back."

I groaned again, louder. "Are you trying to get me killed? Besides, your father would know I couldn't—" too late I realized I was saying and snapped my mouth shut.

Chatta's amusement faded, replaced by growing suspicion. "Garth? Why would my father know you couldn't elope with me?"

I eyed her warily. I knew that look. I was in hot water, and only a lot of fast talking was going to save me. "Er, well, we kind of had a talk one night."

Her eyes narrowed. "What talk?"

Busted buckets, I had hoped her father had mentioned this to her... apparently the coward had left that up to me. "Um, well, apparently he had heard rumors about us as well. He was rather concerned about you traveling around with me alone..." I took a peek at her expression, and immediately wished I hadn't. She looked on the verge of exploding.

"And just what did you say to that?" she growled.

"That you would have hexed me if I tried something on you," I replied quickly. "We both know you can take care of yourself, it was just the situation he didn't like."

That mollified her some, and she settled a little. "That couldn't have been the entire discussion; I know my father better than that."

Rats. Why did she have to be so sharp? I winced, resigning myself to the inevitable. "I, er, sort of promised him that I would be on my best behavior."

"I want the promise you gave him word for word," she ordered in a flat voice.

Great magic, I really was in trouble. Chatta hated it when she thought that someone was patronizing her, and having anyone sworn to protect her was a form of patronizing, to her mind. I longingly eyed the door, but even if I made a run for it, she'd catch me. With a sinking heart, I repeated it. "On my blood, on my honor, and by the name of my family, I swear to you that my life will be forfeit before I allow any harm to befall her. Sven Delheart, father to L-Chattamoinita Delheart, will you accept this oath for your daughter's protection."

She froze, staring at me with a horrified expression. "You honestly swore to my father that you would sacrifice your life for mine?!"

I re-evaluated the idea of running for the door, but her grip on me was too tight to escape. I gingerly nodded.

"Garth! WHY WOULD YOU DO SUCH A THING?!"

Owwww! That was my eardrum. Cringing, I tried to hastily explain. "It's the traditional oath of protection in Chahir! It's the oath that we use when we're traveling alone with a woman, so that her family doesn't have to worry about her."

"That's still insane!" she snapped back.

"Chatta, I would never hurt you," I pointed out impatiently. "I don't need to worry about it."

"And if I'm hurt in front of you, and you're not able to help me for whatever reason? What then?" she demanded.

Then…well then, I was in trouble.

My face must have said something to that effect, because she nodded in dark satisfaction. "That's what I thought."

I took a deep breath, forcing myself to be calm and patient. "Chatta, that oath didn't change anything."

"Oh?" she challenged archly.

"Do you honestly think that I could ever stand by and just watch you be hurt?" Her expression changed, becoming pensive. "I would do everything in my power to protect you, you should know that. The oath I swore was only for your father's peace of mind."

She fell silent, thinking that over. "Yes…I guess I do know that." Her eyes cut to my face, eyes narrowed. "And you realize that feeling goes both ways?"

"Of course," I readily agreed.

"So I just got mad at you for no good reason?"

I smiled, but wisely didn't say anything.

She blew out an irritated breath. "All right, I'll drop it. So my father knows that you'd never marry me without permission. Does your family know about this oath?"

"I never told them," I said easily. "Guin did, though."

"Then there's no way for me to tease them with a fake wedding ring," she lamented.

She was still on that? "No, probably not."

"You're taking all the fun out of this, Garth."

I rolled my eyes. "Your father did that, not me. Now that you're satisfied, can I have breakfast?"

"Lunch," she corrected. "It's past noon."

I didn't care what meal of the day it was, I just wanted food. "Lunch, then."

MAGES

I'd gotten a chance to have that bath, and into some clean clothes. De Lien fussed around me like my own mother, keeping people at bay long enough for me to get cleaned up. Then she practically dragged me into her kitchen, intent on shoving food down me (not that I was complaining). I had just sat down to eat a late lunch when the magus came in.

Magus Tyvendor wasn't exactly what I was expecting. For one thing, he looked more like a blacksmith than a mage. His large, solid build and slightly ruddy skin probably had something to do with that impression. And his eyes were penetrating, so much so that I felt like he was examining my soul when he looked at me. That was hardly a comfortable sensation.

He bowed slightly in greeting, hands splayed out to either side. "Tyvendor, Air Mage from Coven Ordan. We seek the balance."

I gave him a half-bow from my seat. "Rhebengarthen, Earth Mage of Hain. Thank you for the gift of your name."

"Do you mind if I join you, Magus?" he asked politely.

"Not at all, please do." My curiosity was eating at me, but my stomach was threatening to revolt if I didn't feed it soon. I compromised by taking a quick bite while the magus sat down, then asking a question. "Chatta's told me your history, and a little about your purpose here. Why are you so interested in the magical politics of this continent?"

"We've always considered Hain and Chahir to be home," Tyvendor answered slowly. By the way that he was watching me, I gathered that he hadn't been expecting that question. At least, not yet. "Some of us would like to return and live here."

"Why have you waited until now?" I really wanted the answer to this question. Why had they waited until mages appeared again?

"Actually, your awakening was a catalyst," Tyvendor admitted. "We've been toying with the idea of returning home for generations now, but we didn't feel it wise to do so. Bromany demands a great deal of our time and talents—we didn't want to alert Chahir or Hain to our presence, and have them do the same thing. No one wants to be caught in the middle of a tug of war."

I understood what he meant perfectly.

"When mages began to appear again, we thought it safe enough to announce ourselves. Neither Chahir nor Hain could demand our services when they already had mages of their own." He grimaced. "Or so we thought. We were naïve—we had no idea what the situation would really be over here."

"I'm glad you came," I told him honestly. "We can use the help."

"So your king told me, although you seem to have adjusted to your magic quite well." Those light blue eyes were sharp and appraising. "This barrier that you erected over Q'atal is very impressive."

I squirmed a bit, uncomfortable under this praise. "I had a lot of power to draw from—that helped."

"You had a lot of power to draw from, which probably made the whole situation harder to manage," Tyvendor corrected in dry amusement. "Don't tell me otherwise. I know better."

De Lien turned around sharply. She had been doing something at the kitchen sink, but was obviously listening. I didn't need to look at her face to know that her suspicions were aroused. I carefully side-stepped the issue. "So it's sound, then? I haven't had a chance to check my work."

"Perfectly sound. I went over it thoroughly. That doorway you created was a particular stroke of genius. I didn't know you could leave a hole like that in a barrier without the whole thing coming down on your head. How did you manage that?"

"It's the trees," I explained after swallowing another bite. The food was really good, but I wasn't giving it the attention it deserved. I was too caught up in the conversation. "This forest has been around for a very long time. It's soaked up the energy of the ley lines under it. I was able to anchor the barrier in two specific trees, building the barrier up around it."

His eyes narrowed thoughtfully. "Would that make the trees the keystone? That's dangerous, you know. What if someone tries to chop down those trees?"

"They'll get the shock of their life," I answered, chuckling at the mental image that had popped up in my head. I could just picture some poor sod trying to chop down that tree with an axe—and getting blown out of his boots in the process. "Those two trees are sheer power—just touching them will make your hair stand on end. Trust me, you can't cut them down."

He gave a noncommittal "Hmmm."

"Garth, aren't you finished yet?" Night stuck his head into the doorway.

"Will you be patient?" I replied in exasperation. "I've barely been up an hour! And I'm starving."

"Everyone keeps asking me questions about you. I'm tired of repeating myself," he complained.

"Is this your nreesce?" Tyvendor stared at Night with a strange expression on his face.

I found it odd that in the past two days he hadn't met Night yet. "Yes, this is Night. You two haven't met?"

"I'm afraid I was too distracted studying the barrier to get more than names," Tyvendor apologized.

"Then let me do the introductions." I waved a hand between them. "Night, this is Magus Tyvendor, Air Mage from Coven Ordan. Tyvendor, this is my nreesce, Night."

"Pleasure, Magus." Night was returning Tyvendor's scrutiny like for like.

"I hope you don't think this impertinent, Night, but who was your mother?"

"Advent Eve."

Tyvendor went rock still, and he made a strangled sound like a duck choking on a cracker. "Are...you her only son?"

Night exchanged a glance with me—why was he asking this?—but answered. "Yes, I am."

"Trivoxor," Tyvendor breathed shakily.

My fork dropped out of my nerveless fingers, clattering to the plate. "How did you know that?" I demanded sharply. Only four people knew of Night's true name—including Night and me—and there was no way that either Professor O'danne or Professor Bryer would tell Tyvendor this information.

Tyvendor had to swallow twice before he could get words to come out of his mouth. "There is a prophecy, from before the Magic War. It…mentions him."

I looked to Night to see his reaction. My brain was too stunned to think up a rational response. My nreesce looked just as pole-axed. I wanted to demand answers, but didn't feel comfortable doing so with De Lien in the room. Not that I didn't like her, but—this was not a secret that should get out.

She must have sensed this. De Lien left the sink, patting me on the shoulder as she passed me. "I think you need some privacy."

I smiled at her gratefully, only relaxing when the kitchen door was shut. Then I turned back to Tyvendor, pinning him in place with my eyes. "What do you know of the prophecy?"

He licked dry lips, a little nervously. For some reason, he was staring back at me like I had just sprouted a second head. "You've read it?"

"Yes." I didn't feel like elaborating any further.

"A great deal of knowledge has been lost in Hain. Let me recite it, just to make sure we're talking about the same thing."

I thought that a sensible idea, and nodded for him to continue.

With a deep breath, Tyvendor recited calmly, "The Mother shall give birth, and her son will be named Trivoxor. Blood shall be mixed with his coming; strangers shall seek him. A Rider shall be chosen. Great power shall be his, and all shall know his name. When Trivoxor has chosen a Rider, the Balance will be restored. The son will be named Trivoxor and blood will be mixed with his coming."

I felt a cold shiver run up and down my spine. What he had recited was word perfect for the prophecy I had read, nearly two years ago, except for that one sentence.

"Repeat the last part," Night requested. To my mental ears, he sounded a little…disturbed.

"When Trivoxor has chosen a Rider, the Balance will be restored. The son will be named Trivoxor and blood will be mixed with his coming."

"Garth…that's not the prophecy you read to me."

"It's a little different," I agreed. "Tyvendor, the part about the Balance being restored when Trivoxor has chosen a Rider…where did that come from?"

"It was in the original texts that came with my ancestors," he answered with a helpless shrug. "You have a different version?"

"Yours was nearly word perfect, except that sentence." And that sentence was giving me the creeps.

"The Seer who gave the prophecy was one of my ancestors," Tyvendor said this while keeping a careful eye on both of our faces. "I believe it to be the most accurate version."

That wasn't the answer that I wanted to hear.

"That was another reason that we came here," Tyvendor continued, when it was obvious neither Night nor I would say anything more. "We knew that Advent Eve had to be very old, if she were still alive. We wanted to find her son, and figure out if he had chosen a Rider or not."

"And if he had?" I kept the question neutral.

"Then we were certainly going to keep tabs on them both." Tyvendor met my eyes levelly. "Can you blame us, considering the nature of that prophecy?"

"No," I sighed heavily. "I can't." After a moment of thought, I added, "Can you tell me what it means?"

Tyvendor snorted, amused. "The wonderful part about prophecies is that they can be interpreted a millions ways, and only hindsight will tell you what they really mean."

That was unfortunately true.

There was an unexpected side effect to the barrier that I hadn't foreseen. I knew that the Q'atalians could pass in and out of the barrier with ease, of course. I'd designed it that way on purpose. What I hadn't known was that they could feel it when they passed through. More, that apparently it felt oddly pleasant to do so.

After my late lunch with Tyvendor and Night, I went out to see for myself what my handiwork looked like. The first thing I saw was a group of children, ranging from perhaps three-years-old to thirteen, all jumping back and forth through the barrier and squealing with delight.

"They've been doing that since yesterday," Night said at my elbow. "Apparently, it never gets old."

"They can feel it?" Most non-magical people couldn't feel magic at all, unless it was in vast quantities.

"I think it's because of their empathy. They certainly feel something when they pass through."

I found that very interesting.

With eyes and magical sense, I took a better look at the barrier. It was a huge dome overhead, transparent for the most part. If you looked at it in the shadows of the trees, you sometimes caught a hint of green in the barrier. I tested it in a few places, but Tyvendor was right. The barrier was perfectly sound.

"Garth!"

I turned, looking behind me. Shad was approaching at a quick lope, but he was smiling slightly, so I doubted that he was looking for me because there was some sort of emergency. It took him only a few moments to catch up to me, and he stopped, not even breathing hard.

"Xiaolang wants to leave tomorrow morning," he informed me.

I blinked. "So soon?" I'd expected him to want to stay longer, all things considered.

"We've already been here five days," Shad reminded me. "And we weren't supposed to come up here to begin with. I think Xiaolang is feeling like he's neglecting his duty to Chahir."

Knowing Xiaolang, that was probably exactly what he was thinking. "Hmmm. Well, all right."

Without any transition, he changed subjects. "Did you say something to Chatta?"

Apparently while I was sleeping, Shad had met Chatta. I wasn't surprised by this, as Shad had proven to be a true people person. I didn't know why he was asking me that question however, and eyed him sideways. "Why?"

"Because she keeps muttering darkly to herself. She wasn't doing that until you woke up." Shad had both eyebrows arched, expectantly waiting for my response.

Curse his observant hide. "I gave her father an Oath of Protection. She just found out about it."

Shad whistled softly. "I haven't known her long, but she strikes me as the independent type."

"Why do you think I kept it to myself for so long?" I grumbled.

Night snickered, not even bothering to hide his amusement. "She didn't take it well, did she?"

"I got yelled at," I admitted darkly. It was a miracle he'd slept through it.

"It probably wouldn't have been as bad if she hadn't been caught in that mage battle of yours recently."

Drats, I hadn't thought of that. That experience probably was making things worse.

"What mage battle?" Shad had his ears perked, nearly bouncing with curiosity.

I let Night tell him the story, as I didn't wish to relive that experience, even in my head. The first time had been bad enough. I was more focused on what Shad had said. Chatta was still upset about the oath? I couldn't do much about that, as there were only two ways to be absolved of that oath. Either her father could release me, or I died. That was it.

I sighed ruefully. And here I thought I'd been so clever giving that oath. I didn't regret doing it, by any means, but it had sure put me into a sticky situation with my friend.

Shad clapped me on the shoulder, bringing me back into the present. "You do get into the most remarkable trouble, Garth."

"It's a gift."

He laughed, eyes sparkling madly. "Well, she'll forgive you. Eventually. In the meantime, do you want to spar with me?"

"Are you up to it?" I asked in concern. He had been entrapped in a crystal a bare week ago.

A wicked grin crossed his face. "I'll prove it to you."

Twenty minutes later, I dropped to the grass, thanking any god, goddess, demi-god, or guardian that came to mind that the day's sparring was done. Shad wasn't really more advanced than I was (although he knew more dirty tricks than I did)—the man was just too bloody fast! The brief amount of time I sparred against him had told me plainly that he was MUCH better. Considering that he was supposedly "convalescing," that was just humiliating.

"Not bad, Garth," Shad congratulated me.

"Shad, do me a favor."

"…What, tote you inside?"

"No." I cracked open an eye to glare at him. "At least pretend to be breathing hard."

Bright laughter spilled out of his mouth. "Next time, I promise."

"Thank you. Being whooped by you is bad enough, but you're not even out of breath! It's…ridiculous!"

"So do you agree that I'm better?" he enquired sweetly.

I cracked open an eye to glare at him. "I'll agree that you carry your age well, old man."

He tsked me cheerfully. "You shouldn't say that, Garth, because this 'old man' ran rings around you."

I wanted to retaliate, I really did, but he was right, and we both knew it.

Shad sighed mournfully. "I suppose I'm going to have to train with Xiaolang to get any real competition."

"I can always fight you as a mage," I offered with a beatific smile. "That should keep you hopping."

He eyed me suspiciously. "I'll pass, thanks."

"Now, Shad, don't be like that," I said condescendingly. "I won't hurt you. Much."

"Yes, it's that 'much' that concerns me. I like having all my limbs attached."

"Are you two done beating up on each other for the day?" Chatta stood a few feet away, a glass in each hand. My eyes focused on that water, throat aching and parched.

"Is one of those for me?" I asked eagerly.

"It certainly is."

I was up and at her side in two seconds flat, guzzling down ice cool water with relief. Ahhhh. That was so good. I handed the glass back to her with a smile. "Thanks."

"You're quite welcome," she responded as she handed the other glass to Shad.

Shad gulped his down just as quickly before handing it back. "Thanks, Beautiful."

Chatta didn't even blink at this endearment. "Anytime, Cezza."

A frown gathered on my face as I looked between them. Beautiful? Cezza? Why was she calling him a sweetie? What was going on here? Did something happen while I was out those two days?

"I came to fetch you," Chatta informed me. "Tyvendor wants a word before he returns to Del'Hain."

"He's going back already?" I asked in surprise. I'd barely gotten a good conversation in with him.

"I think he's worried about leaving his two friends with all the work," she admitted. "Anyway, he's in the main hall."

I really wanted to dig into this beautiful and cezza thing, but now obviously wasn't the time. I made a mental note to investigate later.

Tyvendor was indeed waiting in the hall for me. I was barely within hearing distance when he started talking to me. "Magus, I need to leave soon. I've gotten a message from Del'Hain, and my friends there are a little out of their depth with something. They need my help. I'd like to talk to you more, however. Is there any way that you can come to Del'Hain soon?"

"I can't promise that," I refuted with a helpless shrug. "I'm caught up in my own project in Chahir. But I can promise you that I'll speak to Xiaolang about it, and see if we can't find a day, or at least a few hours, for me to pop back over and have that conversation."

He looked faintly relieved at this. "That's all I ask," he assured me.

There were still a lot of questions that I wanted to ask him as well, so I fervently hoped that I might be able to return to Del'Hain soon.

POSSIBILITIES

It was…difficult to be back in Chahir. I'd gone from Q'atal—one of the most loving and beautiful places in this world—to one of the most paranoid, and I definitely felt the difference.

I especially missed the good food and soft beds.

Not to mention a roof over our heads.

Tonight was our second night back in Chahir, and we were outside of Jarrell's territory, which unfortunately meant we were back to hiding. Xiaolang hadn't liked the look of the last town that we had passed—something about the enclosed look of the walls and the hyper-paranoia of the people struck him as wrong—so we were camping out of doors. It was unseasonably cold, even for fall, so we all huddled in warm cloaks and jackets. Hayate, as usual, was curled around the fire, hogging its heat.

Also as usual, Night and I were curled up together in order to keep each other warm.

It was chilly enough that even Didi, with all his fur, was feeling it. He had snuggled his way in between Night's folded legs, and was snoozing peacefully. I made a mental note on that one. A cold meuritta was a good meuritta.

Shad, without any warning, slid his way under the blanket Night and I shared, sitting close enough to where he was pressed against my side. "This is much warmer," he sighed happily. "Does the dragoo usually hog the fire like this?"

"He has no cold tolerance," I groaned. "I keep forgetting to have Chatta attach some sort of untraceable heating charm to a blanket for him."

"I'll remember for you," he volunteered in a drawl.

I grinned, but didn't respond. With Shad here under the blanket, we were getting much warmer. Not precisely warm enough to be comfortable, but pretty close.

"Garth."

Shad sounded somewhat serious, which was disconcerting. He was hardly ever serious. I looked at him, arching an eyebrow in silent question.

"Xiaolang and I have been talking about this. You said that the mages in Bromany could see Chahir because of a huge scrying pool they have, right?"

"That's what they told Chatta and me," I agreed. Where was he going with this?

"I never understood how magic worked," he said slowly, like he was thinking something through out loud. "I know the limitations, and some of the possibilities, but I never understood the mechanics, y'know? But I remember being told once, before the war started, that the Chahiran magicians had a way of seeing the entire country. That way they could keep an eye on everyone, and respond faster if some situation arose."

Theories started spinning madly in my head, and I stiffened as I realized what he was getting at. "You think there are scrying pools in Chahir?"

"At least, there were," he amended quietly. "I'm not sure if they would have survived the purging that went on after the war was over."

I shook my head quickly, disagreeing with what he was saying. "No, they kept things that could detect magic. I had one used on me about five months ago, in Tobadorage. What you're saying makes sense. It could explain why people are sometimes caught, and why others manage to slip over the border undetected. If you're depending on a person, or even a group of people, to scry an entire country, things are going to slip through the cracks."

"But can the scrying pools even be used by normal people?" he asked. His forehead furrowed a little as he thought it through. "It takes magic to use, doesn't it?"

"Small, portable scrying pools have to be used by a witch or wizard." That part I was sure on. "But a permanent pool? If it was powered by a ley line, it might be possible for it to be used by anyone."

"You don't sound sure of that," he pointed out.

"I'm not," I admitted. "But I have an expert handy. Chatta!"

She had been talking to Hayate, apparently trying to convince him to move a little (I wished her luck on that one) but at my hail, she straightened and looked up. "What?"

"Come here, we have a question."

It only took her about three strides to reach us, and as her eyes took in our arrangement, they narrowed speculatively. "You guys look cozy."

"Come join us," I invited.

She didn't even pause to think about that one. I barely had the blanket up before she was burrowing under it. As typical for Chatta, she decided that I was a comfortable pillow, and without any hesitation she snuggled in next to me. I didn't mind her head on my shoulder, but the icy hands on my chest were definitely a problem. I hissed at the touch. "Chatta, your hands are freezing!" I complained.

She had the absolute gall to giggle. "Sorry." Her hands didn't deviate an inch, but they were definitely warming. I sighed, and let her use me as her personal heater.

Resigned, I wrapped an arm around her waist, watching her with one eye as she squirmed around, getting completely comfortable.

Shad tapped a finger against my arm to get my attention. As soon as he had it, he inclined his head toward the woman so comfortably situated in the crook of my arm and then gave me an elaborate look.

I realized that by Chahiran standards, we looked very intimate, but my relationship with Chatta had always been like this. Still, I didn't want him to leap to any conclusions and muttered lowly in Chahirese, "Not what you think."

"You read minds now?" he muttered back, amused.

"Will you two stop talking in whispers?" Chatta requested in irritation. "I can't understand what you're saying. Now, what was your question?"

Shad repeated his theory about the scrying pools. I half expected for Chatta to shoot the idea down, but she didn't. "That's actually plausible," she concurred slowly, staring absently at the fire and snoozing dragoo. "Anyone can use a permanent pool, if they know how. And it would certainly explain quite a bit. Like why all of the people that made it over came from large cities."

My ears perked at that. "All the Chahiran magicians that made it across are from cities? I didn't realize that."

"I hadn't noticed it either," she admitted. "It was Xiaolang that pointed it out to me. He thought it an odd coincidence at the time. But if this theory about the scrying pools is true…"

"…Then it isn't a coincidence," I finished for her thoughtfully. "And if that is true, then using magic in this country isn't always dangerous."

"If you knew that no one was looking in your direction," she corrected.

"Oh, I know," I assured her hastily. "I'm just saying that we might have some leeway, especially in cities."

"The enemy has a blind spot," Shad agreed, backing me up. "That's always a handy thing to know."

"If only there was some way to prove it…" she trailed off.

"Until we do, this is only conjecture." I thought we were right, though. It made too much sense.

When I woke up the next morning, my right arm was killing me. It was all pins and needles. I stifled a groan, opening my eyes and looking around for the cause of this agony, only to stop short when I realized the reason.

Um…how had this happened?

I was still half-reclining against Night's side, as I had been last night. Shad was gone, but Chatta was still curled up against me, her head pillowed on my shoulder. I cast my mind back on last night, but the last thing I remembered was talking to her and Shad. I must have fallen asleep at some point.

From this angle, I couldn't see much of her face, just the crown of her head and the tip of her nose. Judging from the deep, even breathing, she was still asleep. That was very much a good thing. I wasn't sure how to react just now. Huddling under the same blanket to get warm was one thing, but sleeping in my arms all night? That was something else entirely. I felt like I had crossed a line, even if it was completely innocent and we hadn't done anything.

Lifting my head completely, I looked around the camp. Nearly everyone else was up, aside from Hazard. I wasn't surprised by this. Hazard was never really awake early in the morning. I was uncomfortable to note that everyone was shooting these amused glances in my—our—direction; looks that said That's so sweet.

Busted buckets.

I didn't even bother trying to deny anything at this point. It would only have made the situation worse.

I carefully untangled myself from Chatta, slipping free. The cold morning air was unpleasant, but it definitely helped me to wake up. Chatta grumbled when I moved, shifting so that she was closer to Night. Her eyes never opened.

As soon as I was free, Shad appeared from thin air. Without saying a word, he grabbed me by the arm and promptly dragged me away from camp.

"Shad, what are you doing?" I protested, stumbling along in his wake.

When we were a few feet away from everyone, out of hearing, he finally let go, whirling around to face me. The expression on his face was tight, with worry or irritation, I wasn't sure which. "Garth, what do you think you are doing?"

I sighed. Apparently this was going to be a Meaningful Conversation. "Be more specific," I requested, stifling a yawn.

"With Chatta," he clarified shortly.

I didn't quite know what to say to that. For one thing, I wasn't precisely sure what it was that I was being accused of. I'd discovered with people that if you just look at them, without saying anything, they usually keep talking in order to prompt a response. I just stood there and watched him, eyes level and noncommittal, waiting.

Shad continued, as predicted, irritated and uncomfortable. "Garth, I know that Hainian culture is more open, all right? And Chatta is more affectionate than most. And I know that you two have been through a lot together, and you're close, but do you realize what that looked like?"

"Yes," I said shortly, hoping he'd drop it. He wasn't the only one feeling a little uncomfortable. And while I knew that his intentions were good, I didn't like being questioned about my decisions like this.

"And do you realize the side-effects?" he persisted.

Now he had completely lost me. "I didn't break any rules," I pointed out, a bit more sharply than I intended. My head started to pound, probably from the effort of being coherent and alert at this insanely early hour of the morning. Dealing with emotionally charged conversations like this, before I'd had breakfast, was a bad idea. I made a mental note to not do it again in the future.

Shad stopped short, just staring at me for a long moment. "You really have no idea, do you?" he murmured, almost as if he were talking to himself. "Garth, do you realize the reputation that you have in Del'Hain?"

"The Advent Mage reputation?" I admit it, I was fishing.

"No, your personal reputation."

It was official. He'd lost me. I just shook my head helplessly.

"Gorgeous was filling me in while we were waiting for you to wake up."

I blinked at this. "Gorgeous?"

"Aletha," he clarified impatiently. "Focus, Garth."

I was! I couldn't help it if he'd confused me with nicknames.

Shad wasn't waiting for me to mentally catch up, and kept right on going. "She told me that you have quite the reputation in Del'Hain among the women. Apparently you are considered one of the most eligible bachelors in Hain."

My jaw hit the ground so hard it made a dent in it. "Are you serious?!"

Shad rolled his eyes expansively. "How can any person be this oblivious?"

"Shad, I'm never in Del'Hain for any length of time; day old bread is around longer than I am!" I protested. I felt like someone had tilted the world on me, and then started shaking it at random angles. "How am I supposed to know what rumors are going around about me? And how did they come up with this opinion anyway?!"

"Garth, you're not thinking about this," he informed me with forced patience. "You're a mage, the first in two centuries. You have the ear and confidence of the king. You are accepted by the Delheart family, which Gorgeous informs me is a very prominent figure in Hainian politics."

They were?

"And you're helping to actually shape the foreign policy of Hain when it comes to dealings with Chahir. You're a handsome, unique, powerful, influential man, Garth. Of course women are going to be interested in and attracted to you!"

You know, when he put it like that, I felt stupid for not realizing it sooner. "All right," I said slowly. "I have a reputation in Hain. What does that have to do with me and Chatta?"

"There are a lot of rumors about the two of you."

I nodded in understanding. Those rumors, at least, I'd heard something about.

Shad's next statement was said very slowly, as if he were carefully weighing each word before it left his mouth. "It would be very dangerous to encourage those rumors, even by a seemingly innocent occurrence. People adore jumping to conclusions, it's their favorite sport."

My temper, a little strained already by this well-intended interrogation, snapped like a dry twig. "Shad, what do you want me to say?" I demanded in a low growl. "You know that I'd never hurt her, she means more to me than my own life. You are fully aware that I've sworn an oath to that effect. And you also know that I don't dance attendance on other people's opinion of me!"

"I also know that you're oblivious!" he growled right back at me, like a wounded tiger. "Garth, seriously, do you realize what it looks like from an outsider's perspective? You two are physically comfortable with each other. I'm not talking about just last night, although that certainly illustrates what I'm talking about. You were comfortable enough to just drift off to sleep with her in your arms. You're just constantly in each other's personal space; sometimes it's hard to tell where one of you starts and one of you ends."

I opened my mouth to protest this (how, I didn't know, because he was right in many ways) but he didn't pause, just ran right over me.

"But it's more than that!" Shad was really getting into his subject now, and growing a little louder with each sentence, like he was gathering momentum and energy as he laid out his argument. "You're just in perfect harmony with each other. And yes, I realize that you're close friends, but you're even finishing each other's sentences, all right? Half the time you don't bother to talk at all! You're just doing some sort of silent straight line communication that the rest of the world can't hear. And I've never seen someone so unflinchingly protective as you are! It's not just when she's in danger, it's all the time. You always have at least one eye on her to make sure she's safe and comfortable." Heaving out a breath like a heavy stone, he demanded again, "Garth, do you realize what this looks like?"

I had my mouth open, supposedly ready for some sort of retort, but the words had all dried up. I hadn't really been doing all of that... had I? I mean, some of it made sense just because we were friends, and had spent a lot of time together.

But some of it wasn't so easily explained or rationalized.

I was still mentally scrambling for a response when Xiaolang drifted up to join us. He had this small, enigmatic smile playing on his lips. I expected for him to start in on me, too, but he barely gave me a glance. His eyes were zeroed in on Shad. When he spoke, it was soft and calming and final. "Shad, it's all right."

Shad's eyes nearly fell out of his head. "Are you serious? But Xiaolang, can't you see—"

"Better than you, my friend." There was confidence in Xiaolang's face, and wisdom. Looking at him, it was obvious that he knew something that we didn't. Shad snapped his mouth shut, staring back in bewilderment and growing suspicion.

Then those unfathomable eyes of Xiaolang's turned in my direction, and his enigmatic smile grew a notch wider. "Indeed, I do know what's going on much better than you."

The way he said that made cold chills run up and down my spine. Empaths were scary people, sometimes. I was torn between asking what it was that he knew…and burying my head in the sand.

Xiaolang clapped me on the shoulder, leaning in close to murmur, "Think about what Shad said, Garth. Not as an accusation, but as an observation."

I stared at him, bewildered. And yet there was a part of me, small, and always hushed, that knew exactly what Xiaolang knew. I just hadn't wanted to admit it—had forced myself, in fact, to not think about it at all. EVER.

In sheer reflex I tried to bury it again, shove it to the very back of my head where I wouldn't have to acknowledge it. Xiaolang's hand on my shoulder tightened in warning. "Garth," he reprimanded quietly. "You owe yourself more than that. You owe her more than that."

I couldn't take it. I simply couldn't stand there, looking at the knowing expression on Xiaolang's face, or the growing suspicion and enlightenment on Shad's. I spun on my heel, almost jerking free of the restraining hand on my arm.

"I need breakfast," I said shortly, as an excuse for me to flee.

Behind me, I could hear Shad whisper to Xiaolang, "What do you know that I don't?"

I didn't hear Xiaolang's response—for that matter, I didn't want to hear his response. I had been given about as much as I could handle for one morning. I wasn't sure if I could take any more.

As I came back into camp, my eyes met Night's. He watched me calmly, as if he knew exactly what was going through my head.

And he probably did.

I tensed, still on edge with the last conversation, and not particularly ready to rehash it with someone else.

"Relax," he assured me. "I won't gang up on you, too."

I felt sheepish for even thinking he would. Night could tease a body to murder, but he wasn't cruel about it. I thought back carefully, *Sorry. I guess you were listening in?*

"Yes, I heard the conversation."

His mental voice was neutral, but there was this slight vibration of amusement in it. I almost didn't ask the question because I wasn't really in the mood to talk about this subject anymore, but I couldn't restrain myself. *Is Shad...right?*

"Actually, what he said was rather mild."

That wasn't the tiniest bit comforting.

I went back to hunting up breakfast. Food was much safer.

Later that morning, on the road, we filled our illustrious captain in on the discussion from last night. Xiaolang was very interested in our theory about the scrying pools. Of course, he asked the one question that none of us really had a good answer to. "So how do we find them, if they really exist?"

Chatta and I shared a look, but we were pretty much stumped. Neither of us had been able to come up with an answer, and we'd been thinking about this all morning.

"Beautiful, you said that Bromany has a very large scrying pool. It's how they knew mages were appearing here in Chahir," Shad mused aloud.

"Right," Chatta agreed. Realization exploded over her face. "Of course! If they can find people across such a great distance, then finding all the scrying pools will be a piece of cake!"

I felt like smacking myself in the forehead for not thinking of that sooner. How was it that I always missed the obvious solutions?

Xiaolang was excited by this prospect. He twisted in his saddle to see me better, eyes bright with eagerness. "Do you think they'd let us borrow their pool for a bit?"

"Let?" I repeated wryly. "I think they'll be jumping for joy to have us visit for a few days. Do you want to do this now?"

"Can you take the whole group at once?"

Apparently I was going to make it into Del'Hain sooner than I thought. "Is the sky blue?"

"I'll take that as a yes," Xiaolang responded dryly. "All right, Magus, take us down."

"Do we have to?" Night protested in a plaintive voice.

I rolled my eyes. "You'll survive, Night."

"I get peanut butter for this," he grumbled.

I patted him on the neck, humoring him. "A whole jar," I promised. And then I took us down.

I wasn't sure how to describe being on the Earth Path. Obviously, there wasn't much of a view. I found it comforting and energizing—most of the time. The one exception was when I was in Q'atal. I was too worried about tree roots and tangling with ley lines to relax much. Not many people really shared my view though.

Out of the group, only Night, Chatta, Didi, Xiaolang and Hayate had been with me when I traveled this method. It was completely new for everyone else. I knew within the first minute who was going to like it and who wasn't. Aletha watched her surroundings with wide eyes, like she would bolt for the surface if she could only figure out how. Shield would have poked at the magic cocoon we were in, I think, just to figure it out, if he weren't afraid of the consequences. Eagle took one good look around, but when nothing dire happened, he leaned back in the saddle and started rummaging around, bringing a book out to read.

Xiaolang wasn't disturbed by any of this, so his mind was on more practical matters. "Garth, how long will it take to reach the capital?"

"Two hours?" I held up a hand, tilting it back and forth. "That's a rough estimation on my part."

"Can we get there faster?" Aletha asked in a thin voice.

I took a good look at her, and realized that she was so pale, a ghost would look healthier. I doubted that she would last the whole two hours without becoming sick or panicked. "I'll pick up the pace. If I double this speed, it will only take about an hour. Can you last that long?"

She was visibly relieved, and nodded. "Yes."

"What effects will that have on you?" Xiaolang asked in concern.

"This isn't dangerous," I assured him. "It just requires more focus. Traveling this way isn't even tiring for me."

Reassured, he nodded.

"Don't anyone distract me," I requested of the group in general. "I have to concentrate on what I'm doing, or we'll get tangled up in a ley line, or fall into an underground lake."

There were several alarmed looks, and people abruptly went quiet. "I'm not that distractible," I muttered in exasperation, but let it lie. They'd loosen up a little as time passed and nothing went wrong.

I was sure everyone with me was bored out of their minds by the time we arrived in Del'Hain. Time passed quite quickly for me, simply because my mind was focused and I had a task at hand. It seemed like mere minutes to me. I took us up in the palace's gardens, as it was usually clear of people and gave us enough room to arrive.

I didn't think about the reaction our arrival would generate. Not until I heard the screams of panic, at any rate.

People were scattering in all directions, tripping over everything and everyone, scrambling to get out of the area. I watched them with a wince, just knowing that someone was going to lecture me about this.

Chatta must have come to the conclusion I did, because she said, "Ooops."

Resigned, I nodded in agreement. "I didn't think this would terrify them…"

"It is sort of alarming to watch you pop out of the ground like this," she said slowly, eyes narrowing. "But not that alarming. I think they're scaredy cats."

"Well, it has been a while since they've seen the powers of an Earth Mage," I rationalized. I didn't know why I felt like I had to defend these people, I just did. Sometimes I'm too nice for my own good.

Xiaolang, as usual, was focused on business. "Where would King Guin be at this time of day?"

I turned toward him, head cocking slightly as I tried to discern his thought process. "You think we should update him first before going and seeing the mages?"

"Kings like being kept informed," he told me with an amused curve to his mouth. "They're finicky that way."

He had a definite point. "I think Guin will be in his study at this time of day," I ventured, looking to Chatta for support. She knew his habits better than I did.

Chatta's forehead furrowed. "Hmmm, maybe. If not, there should be someone in that area that can tell us where he is."

Xiaolang nodded, but his eyes were on his team. "Go ahead and stable the horses, and clean up some. I think this will take a couple of hours."

"A bath sounds heavenly," Aletha sighed.

I gave her a sympathetic look. Poor woman had barely arrived in Chahir from Del'Hain—she hadn't gotten that handy lift from Tyvendor like Chatta had—when we'd met up with her and Shield again. They hadn't had the luxurious break that the rest of us had.

"Go on," Xiaolang encouraged them. "I'll track you down when we have everything sorted out."

He didn't have to tell them again. They disappeared with alacrity, talking about hot baths, good food, and naps as they went. Hayate trailed after them, pleading for bacon in a pitiful voice.

"I'm going for a bath as well," Night informed me. "And then I'd better visit Trev'nor; otherwise we'll all be in the doghouse."

"Excellent plan," I approved whole-heartedly. My adopted brother, if he thought he was being neglected, could make a stone feel sorry for him. I didn't look forward to any impending guilt trips. "Take him to see my parents," I suggested. "You might get Mom to feed you some peanut butter while you're there."

Night visibly brightened at this idea. "I will," he declared as he sauntered off.

It took us about twenty minutes to hunt down Guin, as he wasn't in any of the places that we expected him to be. We finally tracked him down in the kitchen, of all places; when we entered, he looked up with a slightly guilty expression, three cookies balanced in one hand and a tall glass of milk in the other.

I was amused to see a king acting like a guilty five-year-old, and couldn't help but tease a little. "Let me guess. Your wife has you on another diet."

"She won't let me have any sugar!" he said plaintively. He even sounded like a five-year-old. "She said I've been gaining weight," he added indignantly.

"And of course Queen Chaelane is wrong," Chatta drawled, voice heavy with amusement.

Guin drew himself up, haughty and authoritative. "Garth, Chatta, I forbid both of you to mention this to her."

"Wouldn't dream of it, sire," I managed to say with a straight face. I didn't say the obvious, which was that we hardly needed to tattle—his expanding waistline would do that eventually. It would soon be very obvious that he was cheating on the side.

"Why are you here, anyway?" Guin asked, growing suspicion and alarm spreading over his face. "Nothing's wrong, I hope?"

"Nothing of the sort," Xiaolang hastened to assure him. "Actually, we think we know how Chahir is finding all of the magicians. But we need to talk to the Coven Ordan mages in order to prove our theory."

"Really?" Guin took a bite out of his cookie in an almost absent manner. "What's the theory?"

It didn't take long to fill him in on the details—barely long enough for him to eat a cookie—and by the end of the explanation, he was nodding thoughtfully. "That's actually quite plausible. Under the circumstances, I believe that proving this either right or wrong will take temporary precedence. This is very vital information. Garth, Captain Xiaolang, Chatta—your new assignment is to figure this out. Do whatever you need to in order to make sure, one way or the other. After that, go back to your original task."

I had pretty much expected that reaction and nodded. "Understood, sire. Are the mages still at the Academy?"

"They're supposed to be."

"Then we'll go there," Chatta said decisively. "Unless there's anything else that you need to tell us, sire?"

"Not a thing," he said dismissively. "Just keep quiet about my snack."

Fortunately for us, the mages were indeed where they were supposed to be. I was introduced to Hay-el D'Auch and Terran Far-Auchmage, who were delighted to meet me. As first impressions went, they seemed like pretty good people.

It didn't take us long to fill all three people in on our theory, and to relay our request to borrow their scrying pool for a bit.

"We'd be delighted to have you," Terran assured us sincerely. "I'm afraid Hay-el and Tyvendor are a little busy here at the school, but I can take you. When do you want to leave?"

"As soon as possible," Xiaolang answered.

"Hmmm. How about tomorrow morning?" Terran offered. "I'm pretty sure I can be ready by then."

"That will be fine," Xiaolang assured him. "We'll meet you here, in the main courtyard."

"All right." Terran hesitated, eyes going to me, but he didn't say anything more than that. "I'll see you later." With a last bow, he scampered back into the school.

I glanced up at the sky, realizing that I had the better part of the day still left. "Xiaolang, do you mind if I stay with my family tonight?"

"Not at all," he assured me. "Chatta, you can visit your family as well, if you wish."

"Thank you, I shall." She flashed us both a smile before sauntering off.

I was thinking better of my request, and decided I should revise it. "Actually, why don't you and the team come home with me? My parents have enough room, and they'd love to meet all of you."

Xiaolang hesitated, although I could tell that he was very curious. "Are you sure? You haven't even checked with them about this."

I waved this concern away. "My mother loves company. You'll see. Unless you want the time to prepare for going to Bromany?"

"I'm not sure what I could possibly do to prepare for that," Xiaolang admitted ruefully. "I would be pleased to go with you, Garth."

"Good." I smiled, happy to have gotten my way. "Then let's go get the rest of the team."

"I'll get the team, you go warn your mother," he corrected me.

All in all…probably not a bad idea.

MORE SURPRISES

No surprise to me, my parents were delighted to have the team visit. My mother ran about getting beds together for everyone, and calling orders to Kaydan to make sure that dinner wasn't burning. Somehow we all congregated around the kitchen table. This had always been a gathering place for my family. Even moving into a different country hadn't changed that.

My father sat at the head of the table, regaling everyone with the tale of how I'd rescued Asla and her boy, Aral. He had everyone completely enthralled but me. After all, I'd been there. I pretty much ignored him. Instead, I turned my attention to the house.

When I'd first brought my parents to Del'Hain, I made good on my promise and replaced everything that they had lost. The first order of business was buying them a house. It was in the middle of a new subdivision in Del'Hain, a tidy two-story with a small front and backyard. It was perfect for my parents, as it allowed my father enough room to work, and my mother the close proximity to all of the markets. It also had enough room for my brothers, sister, and my adopted sister, niece and nephew—Asla, her daughter Hela, and son Aral. I'd hoped to see them on this trip, but apparently they were across the city visiting with friends. The family had been slowly settling in, and by now, it almost looked like they had always been here. I was pleased to see how much progress had been made in making this a home.

From upstairs, there came the sound of running feet. I tracked it by ear as the stairs started echoing with rapid thumps. It didn't take much thought on my part to figure out who it was. There was only one person that ran like that.

I twisted in my chair, half-rising to catch the whelp before he knocked me over. From the base of the stairs, a tussle-headed blond boy shot in my direction. "Garth!"

I caught him by the waist, swinging him up into the air. "Trev'nor, you rapscallion!"

"You're here! You're here!" he cheered, leaning down to strangle me with an exuberant hug.

"Trev, I can't breathe!" I complained, faking a strangled voice.

He giggled, as I knew he would, and relaxed his grip. "Night brought me here ages ago, what were you doing?" In his face was a severe reproach, as only a child could do.

"I had to talk with someone," I told him. "And I had to get my other friends for you to meet."

He blinked then tilted his body to look around me. Apparently it had escaped his immediate attention that I wasn't alone at the table. He was awkward to hold at that angle, so I set him on his feet. "Trev'nor, this is De Xiaolang. The pretty lady over there is Aletha, the big hairy man is Hazard—" Hazard gave me a dirty look. I gave him a cocky grin in return, "—the one next to Hazard is Eagle, and then we have Shad, and last but never least, Shield. Everyone, this is my adopted brother, Trev'nor."

There were smiles and hellos around the table. Trev'nor watched them all with wide eyes, but the person he stared at most was Xiaolang. Remembering the first time I met Xiaolang, I had a hunch why he couldn't stop staring. I leaned in close to his ear and murmured, "What color is he, Trev'nor?"

"Blue," Trev'nor answered slowly. "A deep blue."

"He's Q'atalian. Do you know what that is?"

Trev'nor jerked around to stare up at me. "It's the people up above Chahir; the ones with blue skin." With a quick look in the captain's direction, Trev'nor whispered doubtfully, "He doesn't have blue skin."

Trev'nor was trying to be quiet, but he hadn't caught the hang of whispering yet. He was just a bit too loud. Xiaolang obviously heard, because he was grinning.

"No, my visible skin isn't blue, is it?" He left the chair so that he could kneel in front of Trev'nor. He unbuttoned the first two buttons of his shirt, pulling the white fabric aside to show skin usually protected from the suns. I was surprised to see that the skin was the same dusky blue that I had seen on most Q'atalians. "For my people, being exposed to the suns bleaches our skin. Rather like a backwards tan," he offered.

Trev'nor stared at the different skin tones in fascination. "Wow." After a moment, Trev'nor seemed to remember his earlier question. "But why do you glow blue?"

Xiaolang blinked. "I glow?"

"Unlike myself, Trev'nor can see magic," I explained. "To him, different sorts of magic have different colors. Chatta, for example, is white. I'm brown with edges of green."

"And you're blue," Trev'nor told Xiaolang in bewilderment. "Are you a magician, too?"

Xiaolang looked a little surprised at this. "No, I'm an empath."

"Empaths are magical?" Trev'nor looked to me for the answer.

"Sort of." He gave me a grimace at the uncertain response. I shrugged helplessly. "I know it's weird. I wouldn't think we could detect it, but apparently empathy has just enough magic to it that we can see it, or feel it."

From the look on Trev'nor's face, he was definitely going to think about this later. And probably ask everyone in the world the question again, to see if he couldn't get a better answer.

Shaking my head, I let it drop. "So where is Night?"

"He's out back taking a nap," my father answered.

Figured. How come he always got a nap when I didn't? It was unfair, I tell you.

"Garth," my mother called from upstairs. "Can I have your help?"

"Coming!" I called back. I set Trev'nor in my chair before taking the stairs two at a time. There had been a hint of strain in my mother's voice, which indicated that she had herself in a predicament.

I stuck my head into the first bedroom, but she wasn't there, so I tried the second. Sure enough, she had somehow managed to back herself into a corner with the bed at an odd angle. Shaking my head in fond amusement, I moved the bed aside so she could get out.

"Just put it against that far wall," she instructed.

"Yes, ma'am." The bed was a small, narrow twin that was easy to move. A single heave on my part put it flush against the wall.

"That's so unfair," she sighed while watching me. "I struggled with that thing for ten minutes."

I grinned at her, but knew better than to make a sarcastic comment. I'd get smacked for my efforts. "Anything else you need me to move?"

"No, I have enough beds set up for everyone now." She paused, questions forming on her face. "Garth, the friends you've brought here seem like very good people."

I nodded in confirmation. They were good people. I wasn't sure where she was going with this, so stayed quiet and waited.

"I've been worried about you," she whispered. "What you are doing is so very dangerous. I've been proud as well, of course, because what you're doing is saving people. It's just been hard for me to trust you to absolute strangers like this."

I wrapped an arm around her shoulders, hugging her close to my side. It felt a little odd, because I was a whole head taller than her; I felt like I, the child, was offering comfort to her, the mother. "Why do you think I brought them here?" I asked her gently. "I wanted you to see with your own eyes what kind of people I'm working with."

She sighed, hugging me back and burying her face in my shoulder. "You always were the most thoughtful of my children." After a pause she ventured, "You all look like good friends."

"We are. Actually, I think we're more like comrades-in-arms." I thought about that some more, testing the concept carefully and finding that if anything, it lacked the depth of what I felt for the people downstairs. "They are people that I trust absolutely."

"You don't do anything by halfway measures," she confirmed, lifting her face to smile up at me. "Even as a child you were like that. If you were friends with someone, then you were as close as possible to them."

I shrugged, silently agreeing with her.

"Well, let's go down and get supper on the table." With a last squeeze around my waist, she let go and headed downstairs.

Dinner that night was a riot. Shad, being Shad, couldn't leave anything alone and teased everyone mercilessly. My family rose to the challenge and gave as good as they got. I was thankful neither Xajen nor Braeden were home—if they had been, it would have gotten completely out of hand. Naturally, with Shad and my parents going at it, everyone else had to join in as well. There were some real zingers flying around the table. My face was sore by the end of the night from smiling and laughing so much.

I went out after dinner to make sure that Night was taken care of. He was snuggled into the small stable, sound asleep. I stood watching him for a moment, surprised to see that he actually fit in there. Night had grown to be a gangly stallion, tall and with a large bone structure; recently, however, he'd started filling out. I was grateful that my Tonkowacon friend Small Rider wasn't around to see this recent development. If he ever saw how well Night developed, I'd really have a fight on my hands!

I turned back to go to the house, and hopefully a soft bed. I was three feet away from the stable when I realized I wasn't alone out here. On the back porch, watching me, was Xiaolang. I couldn't see his face well in the fading light, but he had the air of a man who had something on his mind. I lengthened my stride, crossing to him in a few quick steps.

Even when I was standing next to him, however, there was a long moment of silence before he chose to speak. "I've often wondered, since I met you, what kind of family you came from. Meeting them like this," he cast a glance behind him, toward the house, "has answered a lot of questions for me."

That statement was certainly open ended. "Good or bad?"

"Good," he assured me with a soft chuckle. "All of its good."

I had the feeling that he wasn't going to go any more into the subject. I was very curious to know what questions he'd had, and what answers he'd apparently gathered here, but knew that it would be easier to spin the world on my pinky than to get Xiaolang to change his mind about something. I'd weasel it out of him later. Hopefully.

"I can see why you fit in with my family so well," Xiaolang declared with a smile lightening his face. "Your family is very similar in some ways. I haven't laughed this much since I left home."

I agreed with this with a vehement nod. "We are very similar in some ways."

The door opened and a small, reluctant face peered around the wood. "Garth, Mommy Jaylan says you have to take me home now," Trev'nor informed me with a desolate sigh.

I bent down and scooped him up. This wasn't as easy as it used to be—he'd definitely been growing while I was away. "It is getting pretty late, kiddo."

"Can't I stay the night?" Trev'nor bent his most pitiful, no-one-loves-me look on me, the one guaranteed to get his way.

And, as usual, I caved. "Well, we'll need to send a message to your parents to tell them we're keeping you."

"YES!" he bounced in my arms, face splitting in a wide grin. "Can I sleep with you, too?"

A part of my mind irreverently wondered if he still kicked in his sleep. But I couldn't deny the kid—it might be months before I got to see him again, and I knew how much he missed me. "Sure, why not?" I capitulated. "But you need to go get something for me. There's a mirror broach in my saddlebag."

"The talking one," he stated in recognition.

"That's the one," I confirmed.

"I'll get it!" he squirmed down, running almost before his feet managed to hit the floor.

"Doesn't the kid ever move at a normal walk?" I muttered to myself. I was vaguely jealous of having that much energy. Why is it squandered on children, when adults need it so much more?

"That boy thinks the world of you," Xiaolang murmured. "And…" he visibly hesitated, slanting a questioning look at me from the corner of his eye.

"And…?" I encouraged him. Xiaolang rarely hesitated in his speech. When he wanted to say something, he said it. I'd only seen him this hesitant once before, and that was when he'd told me that his people sometimes had a bit of precognition.

"He'll be very important in the future," Xiaolang murmured. "I'm not sure how to put this…" he paused, mouth rummaging for words. "Something will change very soon, Garth. Someone will be discovered who will change everything. When that happens, you need to trust Trev'nor like he trusts you. Much will be lost otherwise."

I could not have been more stunned if he announced that the sky would be green tomorrow instead of blue. Where had this come from? "I don't suppose that you could be more specific?"

"I wish I could," Xiaolang muttered in frustration. "Let me put it this way. Certain people have more…more…weight to them than other people. It…no, that won't work." He paused, thinking about it some more. "All right, try to imagine this. You worked with your father as a blacksmith, so you should be able to understand this. You use certain hammers for different work, right? Because one hammer isn't necessarily strong enough to do certain jobs, but other hammers are. Right?"

I understood entirely what he meant. You didn't use a normal carpenter's hammer to forge a sword, but another hammer entirely. "Right."

"You have that kind of weight to you. I can tell by looking at you that you are a hammer meant for certain tasks."

That made sense. My eyes went wide as what he was telling me started to sink in. "And Trev'nor?"

"Almost as heavy as you. And, well, in the immediate sense almost heavier."

"Any idea what he's meant to do?" I was grasping at straws now.

Xiaolang shook his head, frustrated. "Precognition isn't my strong point. I'm lucky to get snatches."

"Rats," I groaned.

"The one part of this that I'm firm on is that it has to do with a little boy that we'll take out of Chahir, and that somehow Trev'nor needs to meet that boy." Xiaolang's head tilted a little, eyes going blind as he focused on something that I couldn't see. "And you need to make sure that they meet."

"Well, that gives me something to go off of." I frowned to myself, thinking. "Will you recognize the boy when you see him?"

"Yes." Xiaolang was absolutely certain of this.

"Good enough," I decided. "We'll take the rest of it as it comes."

"Practical advice," Xiaolang agreed.

Trev'nor scampered back toward me, sounding like a herd of deer. "Garth, here it is!"

I looked, really looked, at Trev'nor as he handed me the mirror broach. Trev'nor had always been special, a child prodigy in a life that had no child prodigies. My head swam with questions after Xiaolang's revelation. Who was the boy we were to rescue, and why was Trev'nor so important for that boy?

Trev'nor gave me an uncertain look. "That is the right one, isn't it?"

I blinked back into the here and now and smiled at him. "Yes, it's the right one. Sorry, I was thinking." Shaking my head at myself, I grazed the mirror with a touch of power. "Chatta?"

There was a moment of silence and then a concerned voice came through. "Garth? Is something wrong?"

"No, not at all." Trev'nor and I shared a smile. "Just wondering if you could pass along a message for me."

We met at the Academy bright and early the next morning. Mom, being Mom, woke up early enough to cook a huge breakfast for all of us. By the time I dragged everyone out of the house, Shad had charmed my youngest sister, and was swearing up and down that he was going to adopt my mother as his. Neither Mom nor Kaydan minded, naturally. They found his antics charming.

Charming. Ha!

For revenge, I decided I would make him cook for the next week. That'd teach him to mind his manners.

Terran didn't say much—he apparently wasn't much of a morning person—just gathered us all up close to him. Then he nodded to me. "Magus, if you would take us to the Chahir coastline?"

I nodded in understanding, wrapped us all up in magic, and took us down to the Earth Path.

It was a quiet trip, for various reasons. Most of us were still a little asleep on our feet, some of us—like poor Aletha—were very uneasy being underground like this. After about a half hour of traveling, Terran maneuvered until he was standing next to me.

"I'm told that you weren't really trained in your abilities," he commented. It sounded idle, but the look in his eyes was very curious.

"I was given as much guidance as they could," I answered, shrugging. "The rest I either figured out, Night told me, or I found hints in history books."

"Ah yes," he cast a glance at the nreesce at my shoulder. "You would have inherited a great deal of knowledge from your mother, wouldn't you?"

"Not as much as I wish, sometimes. She didn't pay a lot of attention to how things were done. So I can tell Garth that it's possible, but he has to figure out how to do it." Night flicked his ears, slightly irritated.

"It's been an interesting learning experience," I agreed ruefully. "Do you have Earth Mages over in Coven Ordan?"

"Three," Terran answered with a growing smile. "And they will all want to meet you."

Somehow, that didn't sound reassuring. I eyed him suspiciously, wondering what he wasn't telling me.

"I assume that you can't move through water?" Terran continued, changing subjects without warning.

"Er, not really." I rubbed my chin idly, thinking about it. "I'm not really that good with water. It's not one of my elements."

"Fortunately I'm quite good with it." Terran flashed me a bright, cheerful smile, which was slightly sarcastic. After all, he was the Water Mage. "Just bring me to the water, and I can take over from there."

"All right," I agreed easily.

Little did I know....

I brought us up on the very edge of the Chahiran coastline. We took a bit of a breather, stretching out and walking about for a few minutes. Then Terran called us together, wrapped us up in magic, and dropped us into the water.

It'd always puzzled me that people found traveling the Earth Path disturbing. I was in complete control—nothing could possibly harm them. And it was safer, and far faster, than any conventional way of travel. There were people that were claustrophobic, of course, but it seemed to bother everyone on some level. I could never understand why.

I understood now.

I completely understood.

And boy did I wish I didn't!

Nothing Terran was doing could excuse my nervousness. The ride was perfectly smooth, the water completely repelled and molded by Terran's magic. He was absolutely in control.

That didn't change that I would give my eye teeth to be on solid land again.

"Garth?" Chatta was frowning, watching me with concern. "Are you all right?"

I resisted the urge to start openly fidgeting. "Chatta, you know how I always dismissed your fears whenever we traveled by Earth Path?"

"Yes..." she said cautiously.

"I'm sorry." My voice was hoarse but very earnest. "I'm truly sorry. I understand completely now. This is unnerving."

"Ah," she murmured in understanding. Sympathetically, she patted my arm, and while that was sincere, there was a smirk on her face, too. "You can see it from my point of view, now?"

"Completely," I groaned.

"There isn't an Earth Mage in existence that feels comfortable traveling in water like this," Terran declared over his shoulder. "I thought you knew that?"

"Terran, don't assume I know anything," I retorted acidly.

Terran, the rat fink, laughed. I think he forgot to mention it on purpose…in fact, I was nearly sure of it.

I spent the next hour doing anything to keep my mind off of where I was, to limited success. I actually reverted to taking the braid out of Night's hair and completely redoing it. Trev'nor had taught me a more simplistic and sturdy braiding pattern, and I used that while putting the seal back into Night's hair. Out of habit, I put a barrier spell back on. You never knew with Didi—sometimes he just couldn't let an opportunity pass him by.

Then, with nothing else constructive to do, I fell to fidgeting. Everyone watched me in amusement and with a bit of perverse satisfaction. I ignored the urge to stick my tongue out at them, like a frustrated child.

We could not get there fast enough to suit me.

When I'd pictured Coven Ordan in my head, I had a certain idea in mind—probably a small town, buried up high in the mountains. Considering how many magicians lived there, I was sure that there would be some pretty fantastic architecture to it.

My imagination didn't even compare to reality.

There, in front of my astonished eyes, was a floating city!

I didn't know you could do that with magic!

It was of a fair size, probably about the size of Geol. I was standing on the top of the mountain, and could look straight across into the city gates. From what I could see at this distance, it was a beautiful place, filled with rich plant life and spectacular buildings.

I just couldn't wrap my mind around the fact that it was suspended over the valley floor, hovering so that it was level with the tops of the mountains around it. How by the stars had they managed this?

"What do you think of the place, Garth?" Terran inquired politely. There was a hint of mischief brewing in his eyes.

"I've never seen anything like it," I answered honestly. Everything that I knew of magic defied what was in front of my eyes, actually. I was feeling a lot of power—some of it very old—underneath the city. That didn't surprise me, but it didn't give me a good idea of what was going on either. Although there was something about it that felt very familiar...

Even Didi was quiet and filled with awe, and that took some doing. What truly puzzled me was that I couldn't see any bridges connecting the floating city to the mountain ranges around it. Did they all use some sort of flying spell? But the mages wouldn't necessarily be able to do that...this was confusing.

"How are you doing that?" Chatta asked frankly.

"Garth can tell you." Terran shot me a challenging look.

I waved a hand, negating this idea. "I have no idea. There is a very strong residue of earth magic, that's about all I can say."

His smirk faded a little. "Can't you see it?"

"I can't see magic," I explained patiently. "I can only feel it."

"And even though I can see magic, I can't begin to tell you how you're making a city float," Chatta added tartly. "There's a very strong glamour spell under the city, which I'm sure you know, so I can't see anything. You've had your fun, Terran. Now explain!"

Terran shot her a look, but dutifully explained. "Actually, the city isn't really floating. We built up a huge pillar of earth under it, raising it off the floor. The glamour spell is to keep anyone from seeing that support. Oh, and there's also misdirection spells to make it hard to look at, and impossible to actually touch."

Now that made a lot more sense! "Clever," I said in true admiration. "It keeps all of those pesky bandits away, doesn't it?"

"It certainly does," Terran agreed brightly. "Not to mention anyone else that wants to borrow our talents." He waved a hand, and a bridge suddenly appeared, starting from where we stood and ending on the edge of the city. "Well, shall we go across?"

COVEN ORDAN

The bridge ended at the main street, or what I assumed to be the main street, of the city. A huge fountain sprawled in the center of the courtyard, jets of multi-colored water shooting out of it at random. It was quite pretty and very distracting; my eyes kept coming back to it unconsciously. All around the fountain were benches, large trees, and pots of flowers. Lining the courtyard were buildings—shops of various sorts, from bakeries to clothing stores. The architecture was a little different than I'd expected—it was like they were blending several different styles, with Hainian brick and Chahiran doorways, and some sort of slanted roof that I'd never seen before. Bromanian, maybe?

And then there were the people. Here it was obvious that they were mixing cultures—I saw every possible fashion of clothing being worn. As we arrived, people slowly stopped in their tracks, watching us with avid curiosity. I paused as well, waiting for some cue from Terran on where we were supposed to go. He, however, seemed to be waiting for our response.

"It's a beautiful place," Aletha observed quietly. "How much of it was made of magic?"

"All of it," I answered slowly. At least, that's what if felt like.

"You're not far wrong," Terran admitted.

"Terran!" A young woman separated from the crowd, running toward us. Her hair was a thick, rich mahogany, flying in every direction as she ran. She wore a simple black dress that gave no indication of what she was—but from the feel of her, I'd guess her to be an Elemental Mage.

Terran lit up at her appearance, walking forward quickly to meet her. He grabbed her when she was within range, swinging her up into a bear hug. "Liza! I swear you've grown again."

She sighed happily, a large smile growing on her face. "I have! Two inches!"

"Good grief, girl, no man wants a wife taller than him! Stop your growing, now."

"That's not true," she protested, pouting.

"Actually, it isn't," I agreed. Partly to tweak Terran's nose, I admit.

She turned bright blue eyes on me, wide with hope and curiosity. "You like tall women?"

"Considering how short I am, my lady, it's rather inevitable," I drawled.

Shad started snickering. "Too true!"

"You have no room to talk, Cezza," Chatta observed. "You're barely taller than he is."

"All of those vegetables my mother forced me to eat didn't do an ounce of good," he mourned. "I feel betrayed."

Liza giggled. "I like these people, Terran. Some of them glow, too. Who are they?"

"Liza, this is Magus Rhebengarthen of Hain and his nreesce Night, Witch L-Chattamoinita Delheart also of Hain, Captain Riicshaden of Chahir, and the Red Hand Squadron of Ascalon; Captain De Xiaolang, Lieutenant Shield Garbracen, Hazard Harewood, Aletha Saboton, and Eagle Sevar. Everyone, this is my sister Eliza."

She dropped out of her brother's arms in order to greet us with a proper bow. "We seek the balance."

"They've come to borrow the pool," Terran continued. "Where's Raile?"

"Here." Another man melted from the crowd, tall, with a hawkish look to him. He was fairer in coloring than anyone else I had seen so far, looking far more Chahiran than expected. He also looked ancient, and I wouldn't have been surprised if he had actually been alive during the Magic War. His clothing gave no indication of what status he might hold, being a solid grey. However, I felt power from him—the power of a very gifted wizard. "Welcome home, Terran," he said, a sound of warmth in his gravelly voice.

Terran moved to meet him, clasping one of Raile's hands. There was a great deal of fondness in his face. "Raile. How are you?"

"Old!" Raile responded with a broken chuckle. "But I'm still moving, which is a blessing. So." Faded blue eyes focused on me with such intensity that I would not have been surprised if he could see the back of my head. "Magus Rhebengarthen, we've been looking for you."

"So I understand, sir."

He nodded, as if this didn't surprise him. "I am Raile Blackover, wizard and unofficial governor of this city."

"Unofficial my left eyeball," Terran snorted. "If you say jump, we start hopping."

Raile ignored that and kept right on speaking. "I am glad you've come here. There are things you need to know. Follow me, and we'll sit down somewhere comfortable."

After that wild ride through the ocean, I was more than happy about the idea of sitting down. "By all means."

"I'll tell Mom that you're home," Eliza told her brother. With a nod toward us, she scampered away.

Raile turned, walking further into the city, all of us trudging after him. He was not a fast walker—frankly I was surprised he could still move—so we had a great deal of time to observe our surroundings and talk.

"This is a fantastic place," Xiaolang observed to me. "Garth, could you do something like this?"   .

"Parts of it," I admitted. "The basic structures of the buildings, the roads, fountains, things like that. But the finer details I'd have to leave to someone else."

"Chatta?" he guessed.

"She could do most of it."

"The metalwork would be difficult," she observed. "I'd definitely want the help of an Elemental Mage or two."

"I'd imagine that it would still take a while, though," I ventured thoughtfully. Buildings didn't come together overnight, magic or no magic.

"Oh, it took a while all right," Raile chuckled. "In fact, we're still building. We have to make room for the children, as they come."

"Don't take this question the wrong way," Eagle said hesitantly, "but are all of the children born here magical?"

"Most of them. There are a few exceptions," Terran admitted.

"Magic is largely genetic," I explained tonelessly. "If there is someone in your family with magic—your parents, for instance— odds are at least one child will have magic as well."

Sick understanding filled Eagle's eyes. "Which is why Chahir normally executes the entire family if one of the children has magic?"

I nodded, unable to give a more vocal answer.

"That isn't always the case, of course." Raile gave me an unfathomable look. "Sometimes magic will skip whole generations. Rhebengarthen, you are the only magician in your family?"

"Yes."

"Does anyone in your family line have magic?"

"Our family records only go back as far as the Magic War," I replied with a helpless shrug. "Tobadorage—the city where my family lived—was burned to the ground at that time. We lost all of our history in that fire."

"I suspect that was to your good fortune." Raile had an odd smile on his face, not quite happy, but not displeased. "The Rheben family is one very rich with magic. At one time, they were advisors and teachers to the nobility."

I stopped dead in my tracks, stunned by what I was hearing. "Are you serious?"

"Quite serious. My wife was a Rheben, you know. A very powerful Earth Mage, as you are. In fact, you have two living relatives right here in this city. Why did you think we were looking for you, boy?"

My knees wanted to give out on me. It had never occurred to me to wonder if there was magic in my family. Occasionally, there were children born into families with no history of magic in their blood whatsoever. Since no one in my family had been born a magician since the Magic War, I assumed myself to be one of those people.

"Who?" I whispered hoarsely. "Who was it out of my family that went to the Isle of Strae?"

"I don't rightly remember her name," Raile admitted. "But we'll go to Sallah's and Aral's house—Sallah is a Rheben, you see—and they can tell you. Actually, we'll need to go there anyway. Its Aral's brother, Don, that's been using the pool to search Chahir. I imagine you want to talk to him."

"Yes, we do," Xiaolang declared.

"Thought as much." Raile nodded to himself, continuing along the road.

"Garth?" Chatta was watching me closely. "You look like someone just knocked the wind out of you."

"It certainly feels that way," I murmured. Relatives? Here?

The rest of the trip passed in a daze for me. I was so caught up in trying to imagine how so much information in my family had been lost that I couldn't begin to tell you much about my surroundings. I knew that magic was a dangerous and forbidden topic in Chahir while I was growing up, but we still heard fairytales about it. We still heard stories, now and again, and knew of the history of the Magic War. So why hadn't it been passed down, orally at least, that the Rheben family had magic in them? That was pretty crucial information!

Night nudged me in the back when we turned off the road, bringing me back into the present. I blinked, switching mental gears, and realized that we were in front of a beautifully kept two-story house. It was largely made of wood and brick, with a wide wrap-around porch on the lowest level. With it being in the heart of the city like this, there wasn't much yard, but I could feel the magic in this place.

Earth Mages lived here.

Raile knocked out a quick rap on the wood before he opened the door. "You're being invaded, Sallah!"

"Come right in, Raile!" a woman's voice called back. There was the sound of quick footsteps coming from the back of the house, as if she were hurrying to the front door.

Raile waved everyone inside. I held back a little, looking at the doorway. It was so narrow, I wasn't sure Night would fit. "Night?"

"I don't think I'll fit in there," he said doubtfully.

"Think skinny thoughts," I suggested with a sadistic smile. I told him he'd been gaining weight!

He shot me a dirty look. "Don't forget, I know where you sleep."

"You say that like I should be afraid."

"You should be. After all, you're a deep sleeper."

You know, that was a definite point. I started to worry about myself. "Maybe you should stay out here?"

"Their grass is a little tall. I'll cut it back for them," he offered virtuously.

I shook my head in exasperation. The brat never stopped eating. You'd think he was a pig, instead of a horse.

"Garth!" Shad called in amusement. "Get in here!"

I left Night to his "mowing" and ducked inside. Everyone was already settled in chairs or on couches, and apparently already been introduced. Standing near the center of the room was a lovely woman in a simple blue dress, slightly rounded out with child. Her hair was dark, but her skin was so light that she could pass for Chahiran.

Raile, from his comfortable chair, cleared his throat. "Sallah, this is Rhebengarthen. Magus, your distant cousin, Sallah Bender, formerly Rhebensallahan."

Sallah had a hand over her mouth, eyes wide. "Great magic, it really is you!"

Before I knew what hit me, I had my arms full of pregnant woman. Sallah was laughing and crying at the same time, arms around my neck.

Nonplussed, I caught her at the waist and steadied her before we both toppled over. Part of me was glad to finally see this woman I had heard about, another magician in the family—but part of me was a little uncomfortable being ambushed like that.

She must have sensed that, because she backed off a little. "I'm sorry, I'm just so glad to actually see you! Don showed us two years ago when you arrived, but then we lost you completely, and we couldn't find you again, and we've all been so worried and frustrated."

"I went into Hain," I explained.

"We assumed as much," she confided, expression lightening. "We did catch it when you came back to Tobadorage, and took your family out. Now that was a sight! I never thought to use stone like that before."

Shad, being the brat he is, straightened in his chair and asked, "Now what's this? I haven't heard this story."

"Don stored it in a crystal; we can show it to you later."

I groaned. That was exactly what I didn't want to hear.

"Crystal?" Shield repeated in confusion.

"Magicians can store knowledge or memories in crystals, so that other people can see them," Chatta explained. She too, was very excited and curious. "I've heard this story before, but I'd like to see it too."

I looked at her woefully. Did she have to encourage this?

Sallah couldn't take her eyes off of me for long. "We were so surprised to see you—to finally have another mage in the family. For so long, it's just been us!"

"I never expected it," I admitted. "All of the family history was lost—I was never told anything about the Rhebens being a magical family."

"We'll have a marvelous time filling you in," she laughed. "And I can have a copy made of the family history book so you can take it back with you."

I nodded gratefully. "Please? My parents are going to want every detail."

"I'm sure," she murmured in complete understanding. "I'm delighted to have everyone else here, too. We've been watching all of you—" she turned so that she could see everyone in the room "—and have been cheering you on from here as you rescued people. We also have some information for you, as well. Another Elemental Mage has appeared on the Chahiran coast. Don marked down his location so that you could collect him."

We all perked up at that. "I'd appreciate it if he could show me where on the map," Xiaolang said firmly. "Is this person in immediate danger?"

"It didn't look like it," she refuted thoughtfully. "He's usually by himself in the mountains. Still...he's so young. Perhaps eight or nine years old. I hate leaving him where he is for much longer."

Xiaolang and I exchanged glances. We hadn't planned on staying here for more than a day or so. But that might be too much time. "Wait or go?" I asked him.

"...Wait," he finally determined. "We'll trust her judgment in this. One day shouldn't hurt."

"Sallah, where is Don?" Raile asked her mildly.

She blinked, realization dawning on her face. "Oh, shoot! He's in his workshop. Wait, I'll go get him."

I didn't like the idea of a pregnant woman running around alone, so I followed her out the front door. "Night, will you go with Sallah?"

He raised his head from the grass, looking at her curiously. "Your cousin, correct?"

Sallah stopped dead when she saw him, mouth hanging. "Y-you're—"

I felt like smacking myself in the forehead. Of course, they hadn't been introduced yet. "Sorry. Sallah this is my nreesce, Night. Night, my cousin Sallah Bender."

Night lifted one hoof and ducked his head, his version of a bow. "A pleasure, Sallah."

She bowed back, arms spread. "We seek the balance." The look she shot me was surprised and a little...uneasy, perhaps? I couldn't decide what that look meant. "You are very young to be trusted with a nreesce, cousin."

I rubbed the back of my head ruefully. "Um, actually, I was there when he was born. He adopted me as his Rider when he was five minutes old." When I thought back on that night, I groaned. "I'd barely been in school for a day when it happened!"

The odd look on her face grew more intense. "How do you get into all of these strange situations?"

Night had the gall to snicker. "He has a gift for finding trouble."

I had this childish urge to stick my tongue out at him. "See if I feed you peanut butter anymore."

He gave a disdainful toss of the head, dismissing the threat. "Where are we going, Sallah?"

She blinked, whatever thought she had been entertaining vanishing from her mind. "Oh, just down the street. I need to get my brother-in-law." With a smile at me, she scampered down to the street, Night trailing at her heels.

I was watching them walk side by side when Terran came up from behind, coming to lean against the railing. "Rhebengarthen, I should warn you that I'm going to reveal who Night truly is."

I shot him a look from the corner of my eye. "Is that strictly necessary?"

"Yes." There was no compromise in his tone.

"Why?"

"For one thing, it means that we can stop searching for you."

It was a valid point, so I couldn't argue against it. Unfortunately.

"No one knows, do they?" he murmured, eyes trained on my face. "About who he really is—or who you really are."

"Two people know, aside from us," I answered quietly.

"Your friend Chatta, I assume?"

"No," I reluctantly admitted.

"No?" he repeated in surprise. "I felt sure…"

"I barely knew Chatta when Night adopted me," I explained uneasily. "I wasn't sure who to trust with the whole truth at that point. Besides…one of the last things that Advent Eve said to me was his name, and who could be trusted with that name. I just…" I blew out a breath, frustrated that I couldn't find the right words to explain this. "I just feel that secret and sacred should go hand in hand."

For a long moment Terran mulled that over. Then his eyes lightened, crinkling at the corners. "Trivoxor did well when he chose his Rider."

I flushed slightly, shifting under that regard, not knowing exactly how to respond.

"But your secret isn't going to remain that way much longer." He spread his hands in a rueful gesture. "Prepare yourself, eh?"

"I think we're both experienced enough now to handle it." Hopefully. After all the hype that's been attached to us, with my ridiculous reputation, this couldn't be more than one more drop in the bucket, right?

Somehow, that thought didn't quell the sense of impending doom looming in the back of my mind.

"Didi! Quit!"

I groaned. Now what had he done? I ducked back inside the house, looking for a small, winged creature that was soon to be on the Endangered Species list. Sure enough, he had found some elaborate afghan with bright patterns in it, and was attempting to unravel it. Chatta had her wand out, facing him down like she was in a duel.

"You put that down right now or I'll zap you!" she growled, one clenched fist shaking in obvious threat.

Didi's ears went flat in dejection, and he clutched the afghan even tighter. "Diiiiiiiii," he said plaintively.

I thought this time might come, and I'd come prepared. Before leaving Del'Hain, I'd asked Trev'nor to come up with an elaborate braided puzzle for our winged friend. Trev'nor had taken great delight in devising a system of knots so complicated it would take weeks for Didi to unravel it all. I drew it out of my pocket with a smile of sheer anticipation. "Oh, Didi?" I sing-songed cheerfully.

Didi looked at me cautiously. "Di?"

"Trev'nor gave me a toy for you," I informed him, presenting the knot with both hands. "He said that it would be nearly impossible for you to unravel this."

The meuritta's bright eyes fastened onto the string in my hand like a starving man would eye a banquet. "Di!"

Knowing that I had a little under a second before I was pounced on, I started to put it back into my pocket. "Of course, if you want the afghan instead…"

"DI!" he wailed in protest.

"Trade?" I offered innocently.

He emphatically nodded, tossing the afghan to me without a second of hesitation. I caught it with my right hand, tossing him the toy with my left. He nimbly caught it, chittering happily.

Chatta relaxed when all of his attention was diverted to the knot in his hands. "When did you get that?" she asked in gratitude.

"Night before we left." I grinned at her. "I thought it might come in handy."

"Thank heavens you were thinking ahead." Her eyes went to the afghan in my hand. "Now, how to undo the damage…" She tapped her wand thoughtfully against her jaw for a moment, considering. Then she pointed it at the unraveled edge. "Repair."

In seconds, it re-weaved itself back into the original pattern. I studied it carefully, but it looked fine. "Good as new."

"Good," she said in relief.

I carefully put the afghan out of sight, just in case Didi couldn't resist having both toys.

We all turned toward the doorway when we heard the heavy tread of boots crossing the porch. The door opened, a rather heavyset man entering only to come to a stop when he saw us. He was dark, like a Hainian, but with vivid blue eyes. Those eyes lit up in recognition as they passed over the occupants of the room. "Y-you're…"

"Indeed, Aral," Raile drawled in amusement. "They came for a quick visit and to use the pool. May I formally introduce Captain De Xiaolang of the Red Hand and his team—Shield Garbracen, Hazard Harewood, Eagle Sevar, and Aletha Saboton. Then we have witch L-Chattamoinita Delheart, Captain Riicshaden of Chahir—" Aral's mouth dropped at that, apparently recognizing Shad's name "—and the one you've been looking for all this time: Magus Rhebengarthen. Garth, this is Aral Bender, Elemental Mage and Sallah's husband."

Aral looked like a feather could knock him over. His eyes fastened on me, like his wife's had, with joy and relief and incredulity.

I walked to him, fighting a smile, and offered my hand. "Well met, cousin."

He laughed as he accepted the handclasp. "I guess we are at that, several times removed! We never expected for you to actually come here. Sallah was making noises about tracking you down when the baby was born, and perhaps visiting your parents."

"They'd love that," I assured him. "We never knew that magic ran in the family. They thought I was an anomaly."

"You are," Chatta assured me brightly.

I shot her a glare, but it only bounced right off her innocent smile. I'd get her for that comment later.

Aral snorted, releasing my hand. "And where is my wife?"

"She went to fetch Don," Raile informed him.

"She'll be back in a moment then," he acknowledged. He turned to look at Shad, and there was child-like wonder in his face. "Captain Riicshaden, I'm very glad to see that you're out of that crystal."

"Thank you," Shad replied with twinkling eyes. "I'm very glad to be out of the crystal."

"I'm sure!" Aral responded, mouth curving up in a rueful manner. "But how did you survive so long in there? By the time that we started reviewing history, and putting the pieces together, it had already been a hundred years since you were put in there. We were sure it was too late."

"The crystal was tied directly to a ley line," I offered when Shad floundered. "It was sustaining itself."

Aral nodded. "I see. You pulled him out, then?"

"Yes."

"Amazing," he murmured to himself. "There are two walking legends in my living room."

"And a third on his way," Terran noted in amusement.

"Eh?" Aral frowned at him, puzzled.

"Terran," I warned.

"They have to know sometime," Terran pointed out in an oh-so-reasonable tone. "And you can trust everyone in this room. You know that."

That wasn't the problem. I'd kept this secret so long it felt like… like I was committing some major sin to let it be spoken aloud.

"Trust us with what?" Chatta was watching me closely, brow furrowed in a slight frown.

I was saved by Sallah's voice coming from the doorway. "Aral, you're home!" She was flushed from her quick walk and nearly bouncing in place from excitement. "Don!" she called impatiently through the door.

"I'm coming, you impatient woman, I'm coming!" a light tenor responded, heavily colored in exasperation. "You'd think that the end of the world was coming the way you're carrying on." Finally the speaker appeared. His voice matched his looks; he was tall, thin, with dark auburn hair and grey eyes. He took one look at the occupants of the room and his words dried up.

Raile introduced us all again. Don's eyes grew slightly bigger with each person, and when they reached me, I thought they were going to fall out of their sockets. "You're actually here…" he breathed.

"We are indeed," Xiaolang replied, lips twitching.

"What did you mean, about the third one coming?" Aral asked Terran in confusion. "You can't mean Don."

"I meant Garth's nreesce, Night," Terran corrected. "Or, as Night is properly known, Trivoxor."

Every magician in the room froze.

Aw rats, that did it! I lifted one hand to cover my eyes, fighting to remain still and not bolt for the outside. "Terran," I growled, "did you have to mention this now?"

Night chose this moment to stick his head through the door, so he could see me. "What's going on?"

"Terran decided to bust open the keg," I answered tersely.

"Wait." Chatta's eyes were bouncing between me and Night, watching us as if our eyebrows had just turned fluorescent green. "You're telling me that Night is Trivoxor? As in, the legendary nreesce that will choose the most powerful mage as his Rider?"

Night and I shared panicked looks.

"Um, I'm going back to mowing the lawn." He scurried backward, disappearing at lightning speed.

"Coward!" I yelled after him.

"Garth, what is this about?" Xiaolang's voice was deceptively mild.

I'd get Night for this later. Abandoning me to all of these questions…maybe I'd get Didi to braid fluorescent pink braids into his tail. I longingly eyed the door, but alas, there were three people blocking me from the entrance. Besides, Shad was faster than I was— so was Xiaolang, come to think of it. I'd never make it to freedom.

"Garth," Chatta warned in a dark tone, "don't even think about making a break for it."

Busted buckets, she knew me too well. I sighed, shoulders slumping. No choice, I'd have to come clean. "Night is the only son of Advent Eve, the mother of the Nreesce Race," I explained in a near monotone. "And, well…there's sort of a prophecy attached to him."

"Keep going," Shad encouraged, eyes suspicious.

I refused to look at anyone while I recited it, instead focusing my eyes on the floor under my feet. "The Mother shall give birth, and her son will be named Trivoxor. Blood shall be mixed with his coming; strangers shall seek him. A Rider shall be chosen. Great power shall be his, and all shall know his name. When Trivoxor has chosen a Rider, the Balance will be restored. The son will be named Trivoxor and blood will be mixed with his coming."

Shield let out a low whistle. "That's quite the prophecy, Garth."

"I don't remember part of that," Chatta frowned, obviously going over it again in her head.

"What I recited is the Coven Ordan version." I smiled humorlessly.

"That's how Terran knew," she breathed.

"Precisely," Terran agreed. "That's the other reason why we were on the mainland. We wanted to find Advent Eve, if she were still alive, and figure out if she'd had a son or not. And we also wanted to know who that son had chosen."

"With that prophecy, I can't blame you," Shad concurred. He leaned forward slightly, grinning like a demented elf. "Garth, tell me, how is it that you get into so many things? This goes beyond a gift for trouble; it's almost a curse."

"There's no 'almost,' it is a curse." I was resigned now. After all, the worst part was over. "All right, Terran, they know. Can we drop this subject now?"

Raile cleared his throat, drawing my attention to him. "Boy, you aren't what we expected. Don't you think anything of your reputation?"

"I certainly do, sir. It's annoying."

Raile blinked. Then he started laughing so hard that he nearly fell off his chair. "You'll do, Rhebengarthen. You'll do. Don, let's get these people to the pool. We have work to do!"

I had never in my life seen a scrying pool this large. It was housed in a huge building, and easily took up half the room. Even if all of us jumped into it, we'd still have plenty of room to swim around. As expected of a pool that size, the power it drew on was enormous. Three different ley lines fed directly into it that I could detect, and I wasn't a hundred percent sure that it was only those three.

All around the pool were plants and small trees, almost like an indoor garden. It was a beautiful place to be, and obviously someone's pet project.

Only Xiaolang, Chatta and I went with Don and Raile to this

place. The rest of them knew they were out of their depth, and chose to stay with Sallah and swap stories. So it was a small group that knelt near the pool's edge.

"I do have a map with the location of the boy mage marked," Don told us as he settled into a comfortable sitting position. "What else are we looking for?"

"Shad tells us that before the War, there might have been scrying pools all throughout Chahir," Xiaolang answered. "We believe that those pools might still exist, and are being used to detect magicians as they come into their power."

Don hissed in an angry breath. "Dark magic, he might be right. I hadn't considered how the magicians were being discovered." His eyes drifted to me, the wheels turning in his mind.

"They didn't find me that way, at first," I answered the silent query in his face. "It was only when I came back for my family that they discovered me. But they don't rely on magical accidents to betray the magician. They have something else that helps them find people."

"That explains it," he muttered to himself.

"Explains what?" Xiaolang inquired, eyes narrowing slightly.

"Here, I'll show you." Don shifted his attention completely to the pool. The clear reflection shifted, colors bleeding in until a picture started to come into focus. I didn't recognize the area, although it was obviously in Chahir, with flat grassland all around it. The building in the picture was old, crumbling in parts, but apparently still usable. It was made of dark grey stone, looking forbidding and cold. I didn't recognize the building either— but I knew the mark on the building.

Chatta and I both gasped in recognition. "Chatta, that's—!"

"The Watchman's Seal," she confirmed darkly.

Xiaolang let out a frustrated growl. "You two have lost me again. Watchman's Seal?"

"Not everyone has what it takes to be a witch, or a wizard. Sometimes their gifts are just too focused to take on most of the spellwork necessary to be a full-fledged magician," Chatta explained quickly. Her eyes never left the image in the Pool as she spoke. "For those people that have magic, but can't pass the exams, the Trasdee Evondit Orra assigns them particular tasks. This is a practice that's been done since magicians were formally trained."

"One of those tasks is to be a Watchman," I continued the explanation, as Chatta obviously wanted to think instead of talk.

"Those who were adept at scrying could become permanently assigned to a specific scrying pool. Their job was to watch the surrounding countryside, and alert the nearest magician of any problems."

Xiaolang nodded in understanding. "So that Watchman Seal means that there's a scrying pool inside the building."

"Yes." I rubbed my chin thoughtfully, trying to turn the problem around in my head and see if there was a solution. "Don, since you haven't shown us the pool itself, I'm assuming there are wards on the building?"

He gave me an odd look. "Of course. Can't you see that?"

"I don't see magic," I explained absently. "I can only feel it. Chatta, what kind of wards are they?"

"Entry wards, mainly, to keep people out. But there's a glamour on it as well." She shot Don an admiring look. "You're quite good to see the building, considering the strength of that glamour."

Don flushed slightly. "Um, thanks. But I'm afraid I can't see inside."

She waved this away. "It's enough to know where it is."

"She's right," Xiaolang concurred. "Do you know of any others?"

"A few," Don admitted. "I haven't been paying them a lot of attention, honestly. I've been mainly focused on people."

"Shift your focus, Don," Raile ordered quietly. "I think this is more important at the moment."

He nodded in grim agreement. "Yes, I think so, too. All right, someone grab a map and let's get to work."

It was no surprise to me when Xiaolang drew a map out of his pocket. I think he was born with a map in hand.

For the next several hours, we were all busy searching for those buildings with the Watchman Seal on it. We found several—some of them obviously still in use, others lying in ruin. We marked them all down. I wasn't surprised to see that each province had at least one, perhaps two or three, depending on the size.

Xiaolang marked the last one down on the map before raising his arms over his head and stretching. "Hmmm…owww!" He rubbed at his shoulders with a pained grimace. "How long have we been at this?"

"Too long," Chatta groaned, shifting to her feet like a crotchety old woman. "Don, is that all of them?"

"I think so, but we might have missed one or two." He spread his hands helplessly. "It's a big country, and we did the search pretty fast."

"Unfortunately, we can't take the time to slow down and do a proper search," Xiaolang sighed. "The best we can do is try to contact you again in a few weeks, and see if you've found any more."

Don nodded in understanding. "That's probably the best plan. You're staying tonight, aren't you?"

"That's the plan." Xiaolang folded his map back up, shooting me a look under his lashes. "And I think we'll be leaving late tomorrow morning."

I shook my head ruefully. "Surely I'm not that obvious?"

"You are," Chatta and Xiaolang said in stereo.

"...thanks," I replied sarcastically.

To no one's surprise, Sallah and Aral put us up for the night. Don took the Red Hand, as he had enough guest rooms to accommodate the team. The rest of us were in the brick two-story Aral and Sallah lived in. It was a night of stories, conversation, and good food, and, unfortunately, the threatened memory crystals. My attempt to snatch them and hide them somewhere was foiled by Shad's quick reflexes. He grabbed them before I could, and had Chatta put some kind of unbreakable barrier around me while he viewed the memory.

Brat!

I suffered through the resultant teasing with a long face, and distracted them with a different topic as soon as I could.

It was very late when we went to bed, but I found that I couldn't sleep. After an hour of tossing and turning, I gave up and made my way downstairs. But the walls of the house were a little too confining, so I kept going, winding up on the front porch of the house.

This really was a beautiful place. The sky was so clear I felt like I could reach out and capture a star in my hand. It was becoming a toss-up on where I wanted to retire—Q'atal or here.

I wasn't sure how long I'd stood there, lost in thought, when I heard the scuff of feet behind me. I turned to see Aral standing just outside the front door.

"Can't sleep?"

"Neither can you, apparently," I observed.

He moved to stand next to me, arms casually propped against the banister, as mine were. "My mind won't shut off," he admitted.

Welcome to my world.

"How many mages are in Hain, Garth?"

I had to stop a second and add them up in my head. There was me, of course, and Trev'nor, and Hevencoraan, and Rheijennaan. Remcarparoden hardly counted anymore, since he was stripped of all magical power. "Four, including me. Why?"

"We have six mages over here," he murmured, blindly staring off into space. "Did you know? The most mages this world has ever seen at once was twenty."

We had half that number, and we were still searching Chahir for magicians. There was no telling if that was all of them, either.

"Sallah and I have a theory. We believe that magic is only partially hereditary. I think there's other factors, too, that wake up magic in a person. Garth." He turned to look at me, eyes almost solid black in the dim lighting. "Which place has the most magicians?"

"Here," I answered slowly, trying to understand what point he was making.

"Why?"

"Because you have concentrated bloodlines of magic here?" I admit it, I was fishing.

"You do in Hain as well," he pointed out. "So why do we have the most magicians?"

Actually, he had a good point. There were many people with magic in their blood in Hain. So why weren't there more magicians there?

Long forgotten Jaunten blood surged to the front, giving me an insight I wouldn't have considered, if not for this conversation. Why had the Jaunten become Jaunten? What had changed their blood so that knowledge became a hereditary thing?

The only people that became Jaunten were from Jarrell, which was close to the Isle of Strae.

A place where a great deal of magic was worked.

My body tensed as my mind raced, putting the pieces together to form a fantastical picture. "Are you suggesting that the more magically enriched the environment, the stronger the possibility that magicians will appear?"

He gave an approving nod. "That's it exactly."

"Aral, I was not in a magically rich environment!"

He tsked me in a diabolically cheerful manner. "Are you sure?

What are the ley lines like under Tobadorage?"

Until he asked, I hadn't thought about it. "The last time I was there, they were…growing…"

"The War destroyed most of the natural ley lines in Chahir; either that or drained them. It's taken two hundred years for the damage to be repaired, and even now they're not like they were. Still, enough magic is in the ground again to influence magicians to appear." He spoiled this authoritative argument by adding, "Or so Sallah and I believe."

Something about this line of reasoning seemed to make far too much sense. "You might very well be right," I admitted slowly. "I haven't been paying a lot of attention to the ley lines in Chahir, as I don't dare do much magic over there. Still…" Another, more recent experience popped in my head. "I was in Q'atal a few days ago, putting up a barrier for them. There were so many ley lines under their feet I was amazed they didn't glow."

Aral froze, eyes widening in realization. "Aren't all Q'atalians empaths?"

I nodded in confirmation. "They have a touch of precognition, too. This supports your theory, doesn't it?"

"It certainly does," he breathed.

I thought about it some more, turning it in different angles. I frowned when I realized the gap. "The only problem I see with this theory is that it doesn't explain the people who aren't magicians, even when all the conditions are right."

"Well," he said comfortably, "how do you explain a child in a family full of musicians who is tone deaf?"

He had me there.

"All I'm saying is that when the conditions are right, the odds of a magician being born go up. When those conditions aren't met, then odds are against it."

"I can't argue against that." It seemed like a pretty solid theory to me.

"Changing the subject a little…I'm curious. What was it like to raise Trivoxor, nreesce of prophecy?"

I debated several ways to respond to that question before settling on, "Did I tell you that 'Night' is short for 'Nightmare?'"

Aral blinked, looking blank for a moment before bursting out laughing. "That rough, eh?"

I shook my head ruefully. "By the time that he was old enough to graze on grass, I swore to myself that I'd do something very nice for my mother to make up for having to deal with me as a child. I understand how much sacrifice that requires now."

He clapped me on the back, still chortling. "I guess I shouldn't have expected any different. A child of prophecy is still a child, after all."

I couldn't have said it better myself. "All right, my turn to ask a question. What is it like, being married to another mage?"

That dried up his laughter, replaced by a faint frown. "Annoying, actually."

My head cocked slightly. That wasn't the answer I was expecting. "How so?"

"Garth, you should know the answer to this," he chided. "Our magic doesn't lend itself well to everyday tasks. My life would be a lot easier if I'd married a witch."

Huh. Okay, he had a good point there.

"You'd be wise to marry your Chatta," he advised with a wink.

I held up a hand, halting that line of thought right there. "We're friends," I said firmly. I was getting very tired of defending this point.

"Friends make the best spouses," Aral agreed. I think he was deliberately missing my point.

I gave up. Anything else that I said would be misconstrued as well. Out of nowhere, a yawn appeared and nearly dislocated my jaw. "Um, sorry."

"It's been a long day, and we should have already been in bed." Aral stretched his arms over his head, sighing. "I think my mind's settled enough to sleep now. Yours?"

I nodded. "Yes. Good night, Aral."

"Night, Garth."

It was late morning when the edges of consciousness finally started to surface around my inert form. I could hear the birds singing outside the window, and farther away the pleasant sound of activity in the kitchen below. Mmm. It seemed like a nice day. Maybe I should get up?

The bed had a death grip on me, however, and stubbornly refused to release my uncomplaining body. Why, the blankets alone must have weighed more than Night after eating a case of peanut butter and biscuits. The sheets were as soft as I could ever remember in my life, and the pillow was singing a siren song in my ear. Okay, so maybe I'd lie in bed a while longer.

Unfortunately—or fortunately, it depended on your view—part of me disagreed with this decision. My nose rushed to my rescue when it detected the tantalizing aroma of breakfast wafting up the stairs. My stomach tipped the scales of victory with a feral growl, seconding the opinion that breakfast was a good idea. Groaning, I capitulated and heaved the blankets off with great regret.

I stumbled to the wash stand, and poured some water from the pitcher into the basin. The cold water was a shock to my system, but it helped me to regain some control over my lethargic body. I stood there for a moment, trying to remember what it was I needed to do next. A cool breeze coming from the open window cued me that I should probably put on some clothes. I found something suitably clean in my bag, and was amazed that I remembered how to put them on. Feeling more confident in my ability to traverse the stairs without making a spectacular entrance, I followed my nose down to breakfast.

Sallah and Chatta were busy cooking and talking. It was amazing to watch the two of them together. It was like a dance, one anticipating the other's needs and movements. I stood there several moments watching the two of them in deep conversation, like they had known each other all of their lives, before they even noticed me.

Chatta was the first to pick up on my less than chipper demeanor, and handed me a hot mug of something with a cheery, "Good morning, sleepy head. I can't believe I beat you up!"

I mumbled something incoherent back, and gave myself over to the steaming contents of the mug. Whatever was in there was like an elixir, and the fog clouding my brain began to thin and dissipate. I finally found my tongue and gave the women a proper greeting. "So how is everyone this morning?" I asked, with a little cotton still stuck to the roof of my mouth.

Chatta eyed me with the look of a person with revenge on her mind, for the countless mornings that I had gotten up first. Sometimes, the only way to get her moving was to be ruthless. (She never saw it that way, though.) She decided to be merciful this once, and just gave me a knowing pat on the shoulder. I would owe her big time in the future, when our roles were inevitably reversed again.

Sallah broke the silence with a solid, "Good morning, cousin, I see you enjoyed the bed."

I shrugged a bit sheepishly. "We have been traveling so much on our mission for King Guin that we spend a lot of time camping out. My aching body sure appreciated the comforts of a soft bed and a warm blanket."

Night stuck his head through the open back door, and studied me with smug satisfaction. "I thought I was going to have to come up those narrow stairs to save you from whatever evil force was holding you captive," he said with a gleam of mischief in his eye.

I eyed him back. "Not all of us are morning people."

"There's a wide margin between not being a morning person and sleeping through the morning," he retorted. "I've already had a bath and a thorough brushing, and I came up to see if there was any more of those delicious apples and carrots left." Somehow he always found his way to a bath and the goodies before I did! I was really going to have to look into that.

Don and Aral and Shad came in at that moment, so I didn't have time to properly explore that thought, but I promised myself I would later. Aral hugged Sallah and asked, "Is breakfast almost ready, or am I going to have to go and steal some carrots from Trivoxor?"

He was rewarded with a swat of a spoon that would have landed squarely on his head if he hadn't ducked. "You don't look any the worse for wear," Sallah observed. "I believe you are keeping pace with me, and I am eating for two."

Aral held his hand over his heart, as if she had scored a killing shot, and Don and Shad collapsed onto the bench next to me, helpless with laughter. When he had recovered enough air to re-inflate his lungs, Don added, "Oh, she got you good Aral! I never noticed until now how similar you two are looking lately."

"I think it is very touching that the two of you do everything together!" Shad added with innocent sincerity.

Aral projected a mock look of dejection on his face, but held out his plate with both hands. He didn't mind the teasing when it came to securing great quantities of his wife's amazing cooking. Mage or no mage, few people could rival Sallah in the kitchen. My stomach reasserted itself at that moment, and I held out my plate too. Shad reached from behind me and put his plate over mine. "Have some respect for your elders, Garth," he intoned in an aged voice.

I threw an elbow into his ribs, which he somehow managed to duck without moving his plate. The man was far too limber.

Our banter was finally silenced by the sounds of people playing a symphony on their plates with their silverware. I was midway through another helping when there was a loud knock. Raile stuck his head in the backdoor and called out, "Is there enough for one more?"

Sallah ushered him to the table with one hand, an impressive plate of food in the other.

"I'm an old man, Sallah, you know I can't eat as much as I used to," Raile protested in a modest tone.

"Thank the gods for that small blessing," Sallah chortled in reply. Raile gave a deep warble of a laugh, and set to the business of catching up with the rest of us.

The food and our appetites ran out about the same time. We all just sat there in quiet contentment, too full to move. Don was the first to break the silence. "That was a real masterpiece, Sallah!" he said patting his stomach. "If I don't watch it, I'm going to start looking like you too!"

Sallah blushed, and quickly added, "Chatta was a great help to me this morning. She gave me some of her family's recipes that were wonderful!"

Chatta grinned back in appreciation of the accolades, and gave a low bow. "It's been a long time since I've had such wonderful facilities to prepare a meal in. We always seem to be on the way to somewhere else, and a meal is anything that fits between two pieces of stale bread. By the way, Garth has a wonderful game he introduced us to. The last one touching their nose has to cook, or do the dishes."

She stood there smiling at me, with her index finger planted squarely on her nose, followed immediately by Shad, Raile, Aral and Sallah.

Don held up his hand, "Don't look at me, I have to go take care of some business."

My reflexes weren't awake enough to save me. It left just little old me to tackle a mountain of dishes. "I'm a victim of my own game," I lamented sorrowfully. The rest of them had a good laugh at my expense, and then jumped in and helped me get the kitchen back into shape before the next onslaught.

Chatta was manning a dish towel, and exhibited a particular talent for spotting the minute particles of food that occasionally slipped by me.

"Am I supposed to wipe off the things you miss?" she asked in an arch voice, scraping at a speck too small to be seen with her fingernail.

"You know," I observed to her seriously, "all of those people that believe me to be perfect have never seen me do dishes."

"Obviously."

"My reputation would take a hit if they did." That was a rather cheerful thought, although I wasn't sure how to manage it.

"I can spread the word around if you want me to," Chatta volunteered with a syrupy sweet tone. "The marvelous Advent Mage can't get a dish clean to save his life."

"Oh, no! Yet another unfounded rumor, circulating around about the Advent Mage! Well, you did point out yourself that fine control is not your strong suit." Shad smiled sweetly. He needed all of his legendary speed to duck the dripping missile that narrowly missed his earnest expression.

With the kitchen dragon slain, we all headed into the living room, and sprawled out on the chairs and couches. My chair was a cousin to the bed—it grabbed me instantly and persuaded my body to not move.

Shad moaned, "If I had to duck a fireball from an angry wizard right now, I'd be toast! I used to dream of food while I was locked in that crystal. None of my dreams ever came close to that meal. Thank you, my ladies!" Sallah and Chatta fairly glowed with the compliment. Shad always had a way with any woman in his vicinity.

As I sat there contemplating a midmorning power nap, I finally noticed that Raile was dressed in a grey robe, with red piping. "Are you going someplace special this morning, Raile?" I inquired, with a nod toward his robes.

"Not at all," he assured me with a negligent wave. "I thought you might enjoy a brief tour of the city before you have to leave. No telling when you might make it back to see us again!" he added with a knowing grin on his face.

"I'll have to check with Xiaolang," I replied. "He wants to get started back to Chahir as soon as possible to locate the new mage."

"I'm sure he won't mind a short delay. I'll send word that we won't be too long. He and the team can join us if they wish." I kept seeing a brief look pass over his aged face, but it was too quick for me to have any idea what it meant.

Chatta chimed in with a look of interest. "I'd love to see more of the city; what we have seen so far has been absolutely amazing. I can't wait to tell Professor O'danne about the glamour concealing the pillar under a 'floating city.'"

"I'm always up for a little exercise in the sun, especially with you, Beautiful," Shad said, adding his support to the idea. Shad and I were going to have to have a discussion about his pet name for Chatta. Very soon. And I wouldn't be playing fair, either.

"Well, I certainly would enjoy seeing more of the city," I admitted. "We spent most of the daylight yesterday scrying for possible Watchman Pools."

Aral and Sallah said they had something else they had to take care of, but they would try to catch up to us later. With a heave of effort, I managed to get out of the chair, into my boots, and out the door.

As Chatta, Shad, and I emerged from the house with Raile, Xiaolang was walking up to the steps. "I got word that you were going to be getting a better look at the city, so I thought I'd bring my map and tag along," Xiaolang offered in answer to my unspoken question. "To my knowledge, no outside map currently exists of Coven Ordan; this will be the first."

I nodded in agreement, but I had the oddest feeling that I was missing out on a part of the conversation. Raile broke my chain of thought with a well timed grin, and a hand extended in the direction of the street.

Night had finished the last of his apples, and fell into step with the rest of the tour group. Didi was sitting on a nearby fence post working to unravel the braid puzzle. He didn't even pause in fingering the strands of the cords when Chatta scooped him up and put him on her shoulder.

"I'm going to have to get Trev'nor to do a few more of those puzzles for me," she commented as she watched the engrossed meuritta. "It could come in real handy when I don't have time to keep a close eye on Didi."

With that, Didi looked up from his treasure and gave an indignant "Di!" before he went back to his labors. We all just laughed at his single minded devotion to the bright bobble in his tiny hands.

"Raile, how long after the Remnant Magicians arrived here in the valley did they start to build the city?" Chatta asked with obvious interest.

"Well, first we had to buy the rights to have this land from Bromany," he recalled reminiscently. "That took a few months. But once we managed it, we began to build almost immediately. We had been in chaos for so long, first with the escalating fighting, and then with the exile orders to Strae. In order to ensure that our heritage and genetic lines survived, we were forced to leave our friends and associates behind. It was as important to us as eating, to finally have a safe place to call home again," Raile concluded, with a sad faraway look in his eyes.

I was getting the feeling that this wasn't second hand knowledge. Raile spoke as a person that had actually been there—he had witnessed all of this first hand. Shad and I exchanged startled looks.

Shad watched the elderly wizard with a knowing gaze. "So you were there during the evacuation and the exodus? How is that possible? I was there in Jarrell, but I was frozen in a crystal with healing charms hung all over it. How have you managed to live so long?"

Raile looked over at Shad and smiled. "I was just a boy when we arrived here in the BankNoren of Ordan. I was assigned the task of preserving our records and memory crystals, since I was too young to have my powers awaken yet. I was given special augmenting spells to extend my life, to await the time of the restoration of The Balance."

I let out a low whistle of amazement. I'd heard stories of such spells done, of course. But to me they were just that—stories.

"It must have been difficult to watch all of your friends and relatives grow old and die," remarked Xiaolang with sympathetic eyes. "I understand what it is to sacrifice your personal ambitions for the good of your people. I feel like your years of self-denial and dedication to your goals are about to repay you, in ways you quite possibly can't imagine." Xiaolang gave Raile one of those long, penetrating Q'atalian looks that make my skin crawl. Raile returned his gaze unflinchingly, and slowly nodded in understanding.

"So where are we headed?" I asked, hoping to lighten the moment.

Chatta picked up on my intention and added, "We seem to be nearing the center of the city. What is that building in the distance?"

Raile didn't bother looking in the direction Chatta was pointing; he didn't need to, as he obviously knew the one she meant. "That is probably the most unique structure in all of Coven Ordan, and one of the oldest. Construction on it began shortly after we arrived here, and it served as a gathering place for both convocations and entertainment. It has been expanded over the years, to accommodate our growing population, but we have kept the original design the same." Raile smiled as he took in the full view of the building.

I had a very odd feeling about the edifice as we headed in its direction. There was something very familiar about it, but at the same time something extremely ancient and unknown. As we prepared to enter the building through a huge arched doorway, I suddenly felt a wave of vertigo pass through me, and I reached for the wall to stop myself from falling. Chatta grabbed for me, and helped me get my footing again.

"Are you alright?" she asked, her eyes clearly showing the worry she was feeling. I didn't answer right away, I was too occupied with the sensation I was getting from the wall.

Night eased in behind me and placed his head against my back. "What is it, Garth? Show me what you are feeling." I just bobbed my head, not daring to break my concentration. I tried to open up my thoughts to him, so he could understand what I was experiencing. Night turned to the others and said, "He's not in any trouble, just give him a moment."

The stone beneath my fingers was smooth to the touch, almost velvety, like a bar of expensive soap. I was surprised when I realized that it wasn't cold; quite the opposite, it was warm and almost soothing. It was white in color, with small veins of brown and silver running through it at random. There was also a glow to it, like it was radiating energy. The rock reminded me of opals, the way the facets caught sunlight and shined like liquid fire. As an Earth Mage, I was very familiar with every type of rock and stone you could imagine, but this one was a complete mystery to me.

I stretched out farther with my senses, trying to grasp the elusive thread that seemed so familiar to me, but remained just out of my reach. I strained to hear the faint melody playing on the ends of my nerves. What was it telling me? I was on the verge of giving up when the answer came to me like a bolt of thunder.

"Earth Mage magic, magic from my own family!" I looked around at the group huddled close to me, offering their silent support. "This rock is not native to Bromany; it is from the Isle of Strae. How is that possible? How did it get here?" I looked directly at Raile, suspecting he would know the answer to my question, if anyone did.

Raile was looking directly at me, but I had the uncomfortable feeling that he was seeing straight into my soul. He had a relieved look in his eyes, like someone who had just completed a very long journey. As I watched him and waited for an answer, tears formed in his faded blue eyes and rolled down his weathered cheek without shame.

"You are correct Garth; the stone is not of this place. It is indeed from the Isle of Strae, the site of that last great battle. There was such a massive quantity of magic thrown from both sides that it changed the very nature of the stone. It is like a monument, for all time, honoring the memory of who perished there." Raile paused, like he was trying to order his thoughts before continuing.

"It's still there, isn't it?" I asked with a dawning understanding.

Chatta realized what I meant, and narrowed her eyes in speculation. "The survivors must have crafted a spell to allow this last reminder of their colleagues and loved ones to literally be in two places at the same time. It is like a living connection to their past!" she gasped in disbelief.

"You are quite right, my dear," confirmed the ancient wizard, "but it is so much more than that. It is also a barometer of the future, like a sentinel keeping a lonely vigil over the healing process of the earth. It signaled the terrible end of one chapter of our history, and has waited patiently to herald the opening of a new one. The ley lines were ravaged and depleted in those last desperate weeks, before the end found the combatants. The land itself reeled from the massive volleys of energy. But when the warriors were gone, the earth alone remained to mourn them, and begin the healing process.

"The power that courses through the veins of the planet, in the form of ley lines, was altered and out of balance. The greatest area of damage occurred in Chahir, the heart of the Magic War. The earth is not an isolated entity, but is part of a greater whole. It needs the people who share its vast expanse, both magical and non-magical, to be complete. For the last two hundred years, with some help, it has been slowly and methodically repairing the horrific damage it incurred. You, Garth, represent the culmination of that healing. You are the first mage to come forth from that decimated environment. Your birth signifies the return of the balance between power and life. Life cannot exist without power, and power is pointless without life. You have broken the dam that has carefully been accumulating power over that trackless stretch of time, and now the energy of the earth is once again able to influence the emergence of magic in Chahir. Power and life once again share the earth together, supporting each other day by day.

"I have waited all of my life for this day," Raile whispered softly, as if the very mention of it might cause his victory to vanish. "We would be honored if you would attend our convocation, as we give thanks for the return of the Balance."

I turned to look at Night, Chatta, Xiaolang and Shad, my mind numb from all of the information rushing at me. Night extended his right foot forward, bowing so formally that he almost touched his hoof with his nose. He answered simply, "The honor would be ours. I wish my mother had lived to see this day; she would be grateful to know her destiny has been fulfilled. We have now come full circle."

Raile was still waiting for my response. Huskily I whispered, "I would be honored."

We turned and followed Raile through the archway, emerging from the tunnel into a huge open air amphitheater, crafted from the same stone as the entryway, apparently without seams. Looking over the sea of faces turned in our direction, it was easy to see that every resident of Coven Ordan was in attendance. They rose to their feet as we made our way down the causeway to the dais. There was a rainbow of colors surrounding us, signifying the different callings of each magician. They smiled and nodded, with their hands opened, as we passed. Sitting in the front row, in an obvious place of honor for their efforts to rescue magicians from Chahir, was the entire Red Hand Team. It would seem that I was the only one who hadn't known that there was going to be a party.

I felt like running for cover, but Night had me hemmed in on one side and Chatta on the other. She looked up at me, as if to say she understood, and took my hand in hers. "I don't think you will ever be comfortable with your role as the Advent Mage, but you wouldn't be the man I have grown to respect and love if you did." I had no good response to that. As I stood there with my mouth wide open, Chatta reached up on tip toes and gave me a kiss on the cheek, and an unmistakable look that meant I was staying. Period.

I don't recall the words Raile said at the gathering, I just kept thinking about the Rheben mage who had initiated the sentinel stone on the Isle of Strae, and the Rheben mage who completed the circle in Coven Ordan. Chatta was right, I would never be at ease with the title of Advent Mage, but I was honored and grateful for the role my family played in restoring the Balance. Now it was up to me to see that Vonlorisen, the doms of Chahir and the Star Order Priests, didn't destroy the painstaking progress of the past two centuries. That was a role I was determined to fill to the fullest possible extent.

Ignorance and fear was not going to win a second time.

CRYSTALS

Terran dropped us off in Chahir. Considering how much magic that raised, and that there were three known Watchman buildings nearby, we had to leave the area quickly. Xiaolang pushed us hard and fast until we were far away from the area, and when we stopped for the night, our camp was in a very sheltered area. From the road, we couldn't be seen. In fact, we probably wouldn't have found the place, if not for Didi scouting from the air.

During the course of the past two days, I hadn't had much chance to talk one-on-one with Chatta. I'd been a little worried that she would be upset I hadn't told her about Night, but aside from surprise, she hadn't shown any emotion to the news. That didn't fit with what I knew of her.

I was worried enough about it to force the issue a little. While we were eating dinner that night, I made sure to sit right next to her. I also made sure to not look in Xiaolang's direction. For the empath, I was probably sending off all sorts of silent signals of agitation and uneasiness.

While I ate, I kept one eye on her, trying to gauge her mood. Aside from tired, hungry, and a little cold, I couldn't tell what she was feeling. It wasn't until I had scrapped my plate clean before I worked up the nerve to say something. "You..."

She lowered her spoon, looking up at me curiously. "Yes?"

"You're not...upset with me?"

Her head cocked. "Just taking a blind guess here, but are you referring to the prophecy you kept secret from me?"

Maybe I shouldn't have brought this up... "Um, yes."

For several long seconds she was quiet, just looking at me. I became more and more tense with every moment. In fact, I was ready to just beg for forgiveness when she finally spoke.

"I'm not really…upset."

I brightened slightly. That was good. Maybe I wasn't in trouble.

"I understand why you didn't say anything," she continued in a deliberately calm tone. "You made a promise with Advent Eve, and that should be respected. I am a little irritated that you talked this over with Terran before you told me."

"He's the one that brought it up," I sighed wearily. "And I was trying my best to convince him not to tell the whole world. He had a different opinion, though."

She gave a very neutral "Hmmm."

No, she wasn't really upset with me at all. Good! I relaxed, and for the first time that day, started to just enjoy her company.

"Now that I know about the prophecy, could you explain parts of it to me?" She arched a challenging eyebrow at me.

If this was the only price to pay for keeping her in the dark, I'd pay it gladly. "What I understand, sure," I agreed readily. "We know that 'blood shall be mixed with his coming' is referring to me accidentally turning Night a Jaunten."

She perked up. "Of course! I should have realized that sooner. 'Strangers shall seek him' must mean the Remnant looking for him."

I hadn't thought about that, but she was right. "Well, at least them. Maybe others are looking for him as well, who knows? The part about 'All shall know his name' when talking about the Rider must refer to my ludicrous title." I couldn't help but groan at that last thought.

Laughing, she patted my arm sympathetically. "I've never seen someone who hates being the center of attention become so famous. It's truly ironic."

"An injustice is what it is," I muttered sourly under my breath.

"What about the rest of it?"

"We're mostly speculating on it," I admitted. "The wonderful thing about prophecies is that you're only sure what they mean after they've been fulfilled."

She nodded ruefully. "Too true." She pulled a lock of hair over her shoulder, idly twisting it in between her fingers. "And the bit about 'once Trivoxor has chosen a Rider, the Balance being restored' we've already had answered."

"At least, I hope that's the full answer," I muttered.

"I wonder why that sentence was cut out of our version," she mused.

"Sloppy copying job on someone's part?" I offered. I'd certainly skipped words or sentences copying things before.

"That could be it," she agreed. "Or maybe it was deliberate?"

I hadn't really thought about it that far. "But to what purpose?"

"I can't think of a reason." She frowned, fingers halting in their motions. "It just seems very...odd to me that such an important sentence was left out."

Yes, it was odd. But dwelling on the possibility wouldn't do us any good either. "Let's not borrow trouble, shall we?"

"You're right." Even though she verbally agreed, the frown didn't leave her face.

"So where is he?" Xiaolang asked in exasperation.

"I'm not entirely sure," I answered slowly.

We'd found the town where Don had spotted the young mage easily enough, but neither Chatta nor I could find the boy. We'd spent the better part of the day looking around the whole area without any success. There was only one place left that we hadn't searched.

Surrounding the village on all sides was a huge mountain range called the Badden Range. It was typical of Chahiran mountains in that it was sparsely populated with short, scraggly trees and pale rock. But there was something about it that was weird.

Mountains had power in them, of course, that was to be expected. Normally, I could feel mountains miles away. And yet, even though I was practically on top of this one, I could barely feel a thing. "Chatta? Is there a glamour on that mountain?"

She stared at it, a frown of concentration wrinkling her forehead. "Actually, there is," she said in surprise. "Now why would you put a glamour on a mountain?"

"Good question," I murmured, perplexed.

"Maybe because there's something there you want to hide?" Aletha offered thoughtfully.

"That's the only thing that makes sense," Shield concurred.

It did, in a sense. But putting a glamour on a whole mountain just to hide something seemed a little excessive to me. Whatever was being hidden, it was either very large or very important. A knot of unease started winding its way around my stomach.

"Talk to me, Garth," Xiaolang ordered. He was watching Chatta and me intently, waiting for our reactions.

"It's a very strong glamour." I stalled, not sure what else to say.

Xiaolang groaned, looking up as if praying for patience. "Yes, I caught that. How much can you sense past that glamour?"

"I can barely tell there is a mountain there." I shrugged helplessly, spreading my hands out. "Forget about me seeing past it. Chatta?"

"I'm like you, I can barely see the mountain," she sighed. "One thing I can tell you, though, that spell is old. Very old."

"How old is old?" Shad asked.

"Ancient. Older than you, Cezza."

"That's pretty old all right," he acknowledged dryly. "Love you too, Beautiful."

"Will getting closer help?" Eagle wanted to know. "Or do we dare get too close when we don't know what lies ahead of us?"

We all looked expectantly at Xiaolang, waiting for orders. For a long moment, he stared at the mountain, as if mentally weighing the pros and cons. "I don't think we have any choice," he stated finally. "The boy's location must be in those mountains. Just stay on your toes. I don't fancy getting tangled up in some ancient trap."

I seconded that motion.

It was with wary caution that we made our way deeper into the hills. I strained my magical sense as far as possible, but only got limited results for my efforts. We were nearly at the base of the mountain when I realized something. "The glamour has to be tied to a ley line to have lasted this long," I noted to Chatta quietly.

She nodded in grim agreement. "And whatever it's hiding has to be huge—otherwise, why try to hide an entire mountain?"

"And knowing our luck, it's potentially dangerous," I sighed.

"Now, now," Shad cautioned cheerfully, "let's not borrow trouble."

A thought occurred to me, and I raised my voice so that it could reach to the front of the group where Xiaolang was riding. "Can I put up shields?"

He turned in his saddle to look at me. "What?"

"Can I put up shields?" I repeated. "That glamour is so large and powerful that it would mask anything I did. It should be safe enough, right?"

He blinked. "What, did my brain not wake up this morning? Go ahead, Garth. Can you make them large enough to cover the entire group?"

"Easy," I assured him. I raised my full shields, extending them to cover the group.

There were exclamations and jerks of surprise as the shield came down. I was puzzled about this reaction until Aletha said, "I can actually see them!"

Ah. Well, their surprise was understandable. After all, Chatta's shields you couldn't see at all.

Hazard extended a curious hand toward it.

"I wouldn't do that, Hazy," Shad warned sharply before I could even get my mouth open.

Hazard jerked back looking rather guilty, like a child caught with his hand hovering over something breakable. "Does that disrupt the shields?"

"No, but it'll knock you flat." Shad shot me a look, seeking my confirmation.

I nodded in agreement. "The last person that touched my shields got thrown back into a building and knocked unconscious."

Hazard clutched his hand closer to his chest, looking faintly alarmed. "I think I'll keep my hands to myself."

"Wise of you," Shad drawled.

I couldn't leave it alone. Curiosity wouldn't let me. "Shad, how did you know?"

He assumed a lofty expression. "You forget. I was alive when magic was freely used."

Aletha was fighting a smile by the looks of it, and losing. "Translation: Personal Experience."

"Gorgeous, you're blowing my cover," Shad complained with a mock-pitiful expression. Aletha just grinned at him.

"I didn't expect them to look like this, though," Eagle observed, tilting his head to look above him. "It glows green."

"Actually, this is very similar to the barrier he put up around Q'atal," Shad told him. "Only, of course, that one was much larger."

I shrugged in wry agreement. "All shields are very similar in nature to each other. It's how you put them up, and how you maintain them, that makes the most difference."

"So why can we not touch these shields, but people could pass through the shield you put up around Q'atal?" Xiaolang frowned in obvious puzzlement.

"Um..." I rubbed the back of my neck, trying to think of a good way to explain this. "Intent?"

Chatta, wonderful woman that she was, came to my rescue. "Shields that we put up around places—wards, we call them—are made so that people can pass through them safely. Our only intention when putting the spell into place is to keep certain people out. Personal shields like these, however, aren't meant to be as flexible. Actually, they have several layers to them. The one you can see is the weapons shield. But there are two others in there that you can't see—one against magic, and one against power backlashes."

Something visibly clicked for Xiaolang. "That's why you wanted the shield! To protect us from any magical attacks."

That was what I liked about him. He was quick on the uptake. I nodded. "Just a precaution."

"It's also why it hurts if you touch the shield," Chatta offered. "There's too much magic for a normal person to handle."

"Although, Xiaolang might be able to handle it," I speculated. After all, the Q'atalian children had been able to sense it when they jumped in and out of the barrier. Q'atalians might have enough magic to deal with a mage's personal shields.

Xiaolang held up a hand. "Forgive me, but I have no desire to test that theory out."

"Chicken!" Shad teased.

"I'm not a masochist," Xiaolang growled back. With a glare at Shad—which bounced right off, having no effect whatsoever—he directed another question to me. "So when will we be close enough to see past the glamour?"

I spread my hands helplessly. "That depends where the source of the spell is."

"And that could be anywhere," Chatta moaned.

Xiaolang cast a concerned look toward the sky. "We don't have much daylight left. How safe can it be to stay on this mountain tonight?"

"Very safe, if you let me put up wards around our campsite," Chatta told him.

His eyes were solemn and wary as he looked around us. "I think you'd better do just that."

It was a cold, quiet camp that night. We all felt uneasy on the mountain, as we had no idea what might appear and get us. We all spent one hour on watch, despite the wards that Chatta had cast around us.

Hayate was by far the warmest out of the group, with the blanket that Chatta made him. It had taken her a while, but she had finally figured out how to attach a non-traceable heating charm to it. That being the case, everyone wanted to sleep next to him. People were down to drawing lots to see who could sleep with Hayate when Chatta lost all patience and spent the next half-hour attaching charms to everyone's blankets.

Still, even with it, I woke up feeling chilled. I looked up at the clear sky and gave a resigned sigh.

Winter had set into Chahir.

Busted buckets!

I dressed very warmly that morning, anticipating that I would be rather cold the rest of the day. I truly envied Night and Didi for their fur coats.

Chatta had pity on a shivering Hayate that morning and cast a general heating charm over him so he wouldn't absolutely freeze. For her generosity, he rubbed his head against her chest and kept saying, "Nice witch, nice witch."

She was amused by this grateful affection, and patted him on the head. "You tell me when that wears off, and I'll renew it, all right?"

"Will," Hayate promised with an emphatic nod.

Xiaolang gave her a grateful smile even as he waved a general hand in the air. "Let's load up, people. I want off this chilly mountain."

We all pretty much agreed with that and broke camp with alacrity.

As the morning progressed, we ventured farther into the mountains. It was steep climbing, with little to no trail to follow. I had a shield up over us again, but Xiaolang didn't want us working too much magic—he was afraid of attracting attention. Considering some of the traps magicians were famous for, before the War, I didn't blame him.

The trail—if one could call such an inconsistent, narrow switchback a trail—led us farther up near the top of the mountain. In the shadow of these giant peaks, the land was made of dark blues and purples more than browns and greys. Vegetation of any sort was scarce, only scraggly weeds and twisted trees surviving in random patches.

It was probably near high noon when I realized that the magic I was feeling had changed. "Xiaolang?" I called to the head of the group. When he twisted to look at me, I continued, "The magic source has gotten much stronger. I think we're within a stone's throw of it."

He sat up straighter, looking around in greater curiosity. "I don't see anything."

"Neither do I," Chatta muttered. "There are too many rocks in the way, I think."

Xiaolang waved me sharply forward. "Garth, you be point. I think you have a better idea of where we're going than anyone else."

People shifted their horses aside so that Night could move through.

We pressed forward once more, only far more cautiously. I think everyone assumed by this point that there was some sort of incredibly destructive weapon hidden somewhere in these mountains.

Then again, they were soldiers. That was probably why they assumed such a thing.

We rounded a bend, which opened up into a dry ravine. And that was where I felt it the strongest.

"There!" Chatta and I exclaimed, nearly simultaneously, and pointed toward what looked like blank rock face.

"You sure about that, now?" Shad drawled, eyes sparkling.

"Chatta, smack him for me, will you?" I requested mildly. "You're closer than I am."

Shad ducked before she could hit him, chuckling like some drunken gnome.

"All right, we found it," Xiaolang said, eyeing the spot we had pointed out with the same caution a man would use facing a hungry wolf. "Now what?"

I rubbed at my chin thoughtfully, turning over possibilities. "I don't think it wise to leave it behind us," I finally stated. "We don't know what that glamour is hiding."

"What do you suggest?" Eagle leaned forward in his saddle, resting crossed arms on the pommel. "Can you break the glamour?"

Good question. Could I? "Not sure," I admitted. "Chatta?"

"I'm not sure I can either." She cocked her head, studying it through narrow eyes. "But you know, I think it's tied directly into the mountain. And…I think it's only surface deep."

I blinked. "So, it only appears to be solid rock? We could just walk through it?"

"I think so," she repeated dubiously. "Didi?"

The meuritta straightened from his perch on her shoulders, ears cocked inquisitively. "Di?"

"Can you check that theory for us? Cautiously," she added firmly.

He nodded in serious understanding. "Di." Using Chatta as a launching pad, he threw himself into the air, wings snapping out.

I quickly took my shields down before he ran into them. "Didi!" I yelled at him in exasperation. "Do you want to be fried?! Don't get into contact with my shields!"

He chattered back, dismissing my concern with a casual wave of the hands.

"I could wish stronger survival instincts on him," Chatta sighed in resignation.

We all watched with baited breath as Didi landed in front of the glamour shielded area. He crept forward, nose extended out as far as he could reach. Then he got close enough to go past the glamour, and his nose "disappeared."

I watched intently as his head followed his nose, and then the rest of his body. Taut seconds ticked past, feeling like eons passing. Five minutes later he shot back out of the glamour. He flew back to Chatta, chittering in excitement, nearly vibrating with urgency.

"Is it safe?" she asked, extending her arms to catch him.

He nodded emphatically. "Di!"

The tension evaporated with his assurance. Well, at least it wasn't like we were walking into a trap of some sort.

"What was in there?" Chatta inquired.

In answer, Didi lifted his paw and handed her a crystal, nearly the length of a finger. She frowned as she accepted it, but as soon as she touched it, her eyes flew wide. "Garth, this is a memory crystal!"

My head snapped around to stare at the mountain. "There are

memory crystals hidden in there?!" I felt my mouth go dry. That glamour was old, old enough to be there since before the War. And if the glamour was put there to hide those crystals…then that meant the crystals might contain information lost during the War. "We have to go in there," I whispered hoarsely.

Chatta nodded in fervent agreement. "Who knows what information is in there? Xiaolang, we can't just ignore this."

"I agree." He frowned at the rock, however, looking vaguely disturbed. "I don't like walking into the area blind, though. Any way to drop that glamour?"

Breaking glamours was, needless to say, not my strong point. I looked at Chatta. "Can you?"

"It's so old…" she muttered in a doubtful tone. "It would take me a while."

"I could break it."

My eyes dropped down to Night's head in astonishment. "What?"

"I'm a Breaker, remember?" He tilted his head to give me an amused glance. "I can break anything when I hit it. That includes spells, if they're tied to a certain place."

Actually, I had forgotten that.

"Well, Xiaolang?"

"Go for it," the captain encouraged with an expansive gesture.

Night trotted up, me still on his back, and eyed the rock for a moment. "Is this the strongest point?"

I focused on the area. "Just about."

"Here goes. Hang on."

I clung to the saddle as he reared back on his hind legs. With a snort, he slammed his front hooves against what appeared to be solid stone.

The spell shattered, the force of it hitting us so hard that it nearly ripped the air right out of my lungs. Night continued his descent onto solid ground, jarring me in the saddle with the hard landing. My teeth rattled in my head, and I slumped a bit, trying to get my breath back.

"You okay, Night?"

"Whew! Next time we do this, put up some sort of shield for backlashes."

"I can't do that and have you break something at the same time," I refuted.

"Well, we've got to come up with something. My ears are ringing."

"Mine too," I groaned. The next time I saw Sallah and Aral, I'd ask them their opinion on this. Maybe there was a way to adapt the shield.

"You two all right?" Hazard called.

"Yeah, mostly," I answered. Aside from my ears ringing and the headache brewing behind my eyes, I was just dandy.

I forgot about my minor aches and pains when I looked at what was right in front of our noses.

A wide entrance opened up in the mountain, extending a few feet before mushrooming out into a huge cavern. Just from this angle, I could see rows upon rows of boxes filled with every possible size and color of crystal imaginable. There was more, too—ancient bon'a'lons, shields, pictures, books. It was a veritable treasure trove for a magician.

"Chatta, come here!" I waved her forward impatiently. "You won't believe what's in here!"

She trotted her horse over to my side, only to rein to a halt as she got a good look inside. "Great...good...magic..."

"It'll take three or four wagons just to get it all out of there," I whispered breathlessly.

"And that's just what we can see." She shook her head, eyes so wide they nearly consumed her face. "What if the cavern goes back farther?"

I found the idea nearly impossible to fathom. I wanted to hop down and go exploring immediately, but the Jaunten blood in me knew better than to do that. "Any booby traps you can detect?"

"Nary a one," she denied.

I hadn't felt anything either, but there was so much magic in that cave I didn't really trust my senses at the moment.

I slid off Night's back, and as soon Chatta and I were clear of our mounts, we put up our personal shields, just in case. We exchanged glances and step by cautious step, we entered the cave. I tried to keep my eyes off the objects stored there, and instead measure how big the cave was. I wasn't sure if it was a relief or a disappointment that the cave didn't extend much farther. It would take a lot of time and effort getting everything out of here, so I was glad there wasn't mountains more out of sight. But still...despite all the effort it would take, I couldn't help but feel that it would be well worth it in trade off. Who knew how much information was in here already that had been lost for two centuries?

"Garth."

I turned to look at Chatta. She was kneeling near the entrance to the cave, staring at something. I walked back to her, following her gaze.

There, on the ground, was a pile of blankets, a cloak, and what looked like a small cachet of food.

"Someone's been here recently," I said, startled at the realization.

"Someone short," Chatta agreed, eyes minutely studying everything around the nest of blankets. "See? There's the imprint of a foot right here."

I followed her pointing finger. In the loose dirt of the floor, there was the impression of a heel and bare toes. "That's too small to belong to an adult," I observed. My Jaunten blood surged to the fore again, providing me with answers to what I was seeing. "That's a child's foot." I knelt down, studying it at closer range. "Recent. Perhaps within the past two days."

"Your Jaunten side told you that, didn't it?" she guessed.

"Yes."

She sighed in envy. "I wish I were a Jaunten sometimes."

I shook my head, smiling slightly. "I like you better with dark hair."

"Thanks. I think."

Xiaolang appeared in that moment. He let out a low whistle, head turning so that he could see everything. "Wow. There's a lot here."

I gestured him closer, pointing to the footprint. He lowered himself to rest on his haunches, eyes combing the area. "A child has been here in the past two days or so."

Chatta let out an irritated breath. "How do you two do that?"

He winked at her. "Mad skill."

She glared at him for that. "All right, Captain Obvious, then answer this question for me. What kind of child can see past a glamour of this strength and find this place?"

He blinked. "The boy mage. Of course!"

"Bing, bing! Give the man a cookie." She grinned at him unrepentantly.

"That's why we couldn't find him anywhere near the village," Xiaolang groaned in realization, running both hands roughly over his hair. "It's because he's been hiding in here!"

"At least part of the time," I agreed. "Now if we can just figure out where he is now…"

Xiaolang nodded, rubbing at his temples. "All right, change of plans. Chatta, I'm going to leave Hazard, Eagle and Shield with you. They'll help you pack this place up and get it ready for transport. Garth, we're going to track that boy down while they're working here."

"Right." Maybe with the glamour down, I'd actually be able to sense things again.

HAYDEN

The thing about Xiaolang's orders, I'd discovered, was that they were deceptively easy on the surface. They always sound simple.

They were not.

Find the boy mage, for instance. Simple enough order, right? Considering my abilities, and that the (insanely powerful) glamour of the mountain was gone, it should have been a snap to find the boy and grab him.

Actually, finding him wasn't difficult. I barely had to move. The difficulty came from the company he was keeping.

I led Xiaolang, Shad and Aletha down the mountain and around a bend. The boy was just around the next curve in the trail, still out of physical sight, but well within my senses, when I heard voices.

"—just let me go check," a young, high tenor was pleading.

"Not till you finish here, boy. This ain't near enough jewels to do any real bargaining with." The voice was gruff, influenced by rough drink and a poor lifestyle.

I held up a hand, halting everyone in their tracks. Xiaolang pulled up close to me and murmured quietly, "Is the boy mage the one talking?"

"Yes," I whispered back. "But who's the man with him?"

"He's no friend of the boy's." Xiaolang looked…angry. His eyes were narrowed, and had about as much warmth as naked steel.

"Empathy tell you that?" I hazarded a guess.

Xiaolang gave a short nod. "We need to intervene. Now."

"But there's something wrong," the boy was protesting in near-panic. "I can see everything again! Other people will be able to see it, too. I need to go look!"

"You're not going anywhere until you finish, boy!"

I came in sight of the two at that point. The man grabbed my attention first. I'd never seen a filthier individual—not even beggars on the streets looked that bad. Heck, Reschkeenen, when we'd first found him, looked like the Prince of Cleanliness in comparison. The only clean thing about this man was his cloudy blue eyes that glared up at me.

"Who are you?" he demanded belligerently.

I ignored him and looked at the boy. He was slender, half-starved, with an oversized tunic hanging off his shoulders. He was staring at me with eyes so wide they were in danger of falling out of his head. "H-h-he's a-a-a..."

The man gave the boy a sharp glance. "A what?!"

"A mage," I answered with quiet menace. "To be precise, I am Rhebengarthen, an Earth Mage."

Mr. Filthy sneered, obviously not believing me. "And whatcha doin' here? You ain't no kin of the boy's. He ain't got folks."

And you're taking advantage of that, aren't you, you filthy cockroach? Just beyond the man, I could see a handful of unpolished stones—gems, actually. It was pretty clear what was going on here. The man had somehow stumbled onto the fact that the boy could, with his magical powers, create precious stones. As an Elemental Mage, even untrained, it would be child's play for him.

From behind me, there was the sound of Shad's sword leaving its sheath. "Why don't I deal with Stinky, here, and you deal with the kid, Garth?"

"Deal." I headed for the boy, trusting Shad to guard my back, and Xiaolang and Aletha to give me a warning if something went wrong.

The boy, at my approach, scrambled backwards a few steps.

Surprised, I stopped. I'd never had this reaction before from a magician, not once they knew what I was. Even Reschkeenen, as terrified as he was, had only given a token protest.

Shad was dealing with the man, but the boy's eyes never wavered from me, even when his smelly acquaintance started loudly squawking. I wasn't sure what to do to win the boy's trust.

Busted buckets, where's Chatta when I needed her?

I sank to one knee, holding both of my arms well away from my sides, to prove that I didn't have a weapon in my hands. "Sorry. Am I scaring you?"

He didn't give any indication one way or the other, just watched me with those alarmed eyes.

"Let me properly introduce myself, all right? I'm Rhebengarthen, an Earth Mage dispatched from King Guin of Hain. King Guin's given me orders to rescue any magician in Chahir and help them safely into Hain, so they can be trained. The people behind me have the same task."

From behind me, there was an outraged bellow. "Get off me, you sword humping idiot!"

I glanced over my shoulder. Shad had Mr. Stinky pinned to the ground, face squashed into the dirt, both arms pinned behind his back at a highly uncomfortable angle.

"Now, now, no talking back to your elders," Shad contradicted in a pleasant tone. His mouth was smiling, but the eyes… A part of my mind catalogued that look for future reference. So that was what Shad looked like when he was really mad.

Mr. Stinky couldn't see Shad's eyes, so he didn't know that his survival depended on remaining still. He started squirming again, and cursing in a foul streak.

Shad grabbed a handful of dirty hair and yanked, pressing the exposed windpipe against a sharp edge of rock. The cursing became hoarse.

"If you continue to use such foul language, I'll only press harder," Shad warned in a deceptively cheerful voice.

"Shad," Xiaolang drawled in a relaxed manner, "I request that you do let the prisoner breathe."

Shad shot him a thoughtful glance. "You know, I was made captain before you. Technically, I outrank you."

Xiaolang met him look for look. He didn't say anything, and he didn't need to. The expression on his face said volumes.

"…Oh, all right, fine." Shad let up a little.

Mr. Stinky drew in a few ragged breaths, but wisely didn't push Shad again. Apparently he was quite attached to his air.

This little side show had been entertaining, but hardly helpful. I had lost my connection with the kid. He was becoming more upset, more involved in what Shad was doing with that reeking globe of flesh. I don't think he was even really listening to me.

What to say to get his attention? He'd been trying to head up into the mountains when we approached—he'd been worried because he could "see" it clearly. Maybe if I said something about that… I cleared my throat, catching his attention again. "We're the ones that broke the glamour hiding the mountain."

"Actually," Night corrected dryly, "I'm the one that did it."

"Close enough," I muttered to him.

I had the boy's complete attention now. "How?" he asked in a thread-bare voice.

With a casual shrug I answered, "It wasn't difficult." It just made your head ring for ten minutes.

Something flashed across his face, and he became wary again, shrinking a little farther from me. "…Don't believe you."

He had to know by looking at me, and Night, and Xiaolang, that we weren't normal. What had he been told, that would so thoroughly encourage him to scorn other magicians? Being raised in Chahir was surely part of his attitude, but it went deeper than normal.

"Allow me to prove it, young magus." Without taking my eyes from him, I raised a wall of clay and stone behind us, completely blocking the narrow passage we had just come through.

"Garth, give us some warning!" Aletha growled in exasperation.

Oops. Maybe I should have looked first…nah, she was all right. She was irritated, not in pain, so she hadn't been accidentally hit with something. Besides, I didn't dare look away from the boy.

For several long moments, the kid just looked at the wall that was now blocking him. Then he started shaking, long tremors that traveled from head to toe. "Take it down…take it down…take it down, TAKE IT DOWN!"

I grabbed him as he started rushing past me, holding him by the shoulders. It was like holding onto a skeleton—the child was all skin and bones. "I can take it down," I assured him in a calm, level voice. His eyes shot up, locking onto mine. "I can take it down," I repeated, as he seemed to need the reassurance. "But I won't, until I'm sure you believe me."

He stumbled back a pace, and I let him go without a fight. Wetting dry lips, he let his head hang, peering up at me through dirty bangs. "I believe you."

As easily as I constructed the wall, I deconstructed it, letting the clay and stone fall back into their original places.

"The—" he cut himself short, biting his lip in blatant uncertainty.

"The cave where all the crystals are stored is fine." It was a shot in the dark what he was worried about, but instinct said that was the right thing to say.

"You found that?" he squeaked.

"Of course. That's what the glamour was meant to hide. I'm sure you've figured that out by now."

He gave a hesitant nod.

I thought I had gained enough of the boy's trust now to ask this question. "What is your name?"

"Hayden."

Uh-oh. No family name? I gave him a half-bow from where I still knelt on the ground. "Thank you for the gift of your name, Hayden."

He looked surprised—no, stunned—at the civility. Had no one ever given this child a polite greeting?

His eyes darted uncertainly to the man that Shad still had pinned to the ground.

"That's Captain Riicshaden," I continued the introductions as if it were normal. "Behind him is Captain De Xiaolang of the Red Hand, and Aletha Saboton, also of the Red Hand." I gentled my voice even more. "Hayden, this man was using your magic, wasn't he? To make jewels."

The boy gave me a very hesitant nod.

"That was very wrong of him." It was probably the man's greed that had saved the boy's life, though. "Was he right in what he said, about you not having a family?"

"They're gone," Hayden whispered.

Poor kid. I shook my head, strangling the urge to break something, or rant about life's injustices. Not even having a family name in Chahir was like an automatic condemnation. You were considered a vagabond, a criminal, just on that fact alone. After all, decent people had family. I could imagine what this poor kid had gone through because of that prejudice.

"We're here to rescue you, to take you into Hain so that you can be trained in your powers."

He peered up at me doubtfully. "You're...taking me into Hain?"

My knee was killing me, but I didn't dare stand up. It was important that I could look him eye to eye. I instinctively knew that. "Yes. There's a school there, called the Academy for All Magic. I was trained there. They'll train you, too, so that you can use magic freely."

His wary expression didn't fade.

"Hayden," I made my voice as gentle as possible, "I can swear to you that if you go with me now, you'll never have to fear for your life again. Not like you do here. You won't want for anything—not food, not shelter, nothing." Inspiration hit. "In fact, if you're nervous about living with Hainians, my parents live in Del'Hain. You can stay with them until you finish your training."

Bright hope exploded over his face. "Will...will you give me your name?"

That wasn't quite what I'd meant, but I didn't have the heart to say so. This child was so desperate for a family to call his own it felt like someone was twisting a knife in my chest watching him. "Yes, if that's what you want."

"Promise?"

"Promise," I said firmly.

"Do you give your word?" he insisted.

I hadn't been called upon to give an oral oath in quite some time. It was legally binding in Chahir—it wouldn't exactly hold the same weight in Hain. Still, he was asking for my word, on my family's name, and no matter where I was the importance of that would never change. I extended my hand. "My word as a Rheben."

He accepted my hand, and every worry, every fear, every trace of anxiety just melted out of his face.

A bit of a mischievous impulse seized me and I said in a teasing voice, "In fact...I swear upon the little toe of my legless teddy bear."

He blinked, and then grinned, revealing two missing teeth. "Well, I swear upon the tail of my second brother's dead hamster that I'll go back with you."

Not to be outdone, I had to continue. "Well I swear upon the egg of my mother's dancing hen that—"

"Okay, boys, stop right there," Xiaolang ordered in amusement. "You're confusing an already addled mind."

"Kill joy," I accused.

"You can continue with the ridiculous promises later," he promised, eyes sparkling. "But we need to get moving now, unless you want to spend another night freezing on the top of this mountain?"

I considered that quite seriously. For about a tenth of a second. "You win."

"I normally do," he drawled.

"What will we do with Stinky?" Aletha inquired idly.

Xiaolang turned thoughtful eyes on the pinned man. "Nothing."

We all gave him an incredulous stare.

"What matters to this man more than anything is money," Xiaolang explained patiently. "And we are about to take away his only lucrative income. No punishment that we can devise can top that."

Put like that, I saw his point.

Shad didn't entirely agree, judging from the frown on his face. From his pocket, he took a length of strong twine and with deft motions tied Stinky's hands behind his back.

"What are you doing?!" Stinky demanded irately, tugging at his hands. "Your captain just said to leave me alone!"

"You're still breathing, aren't you?" Shad responded caustically. "But this is just to make sure that you don't do anything stupid tonight. It will take you a while to get your hands free."

"You can't leave me on the mountain like this!"

"I'm sure you can make it down to the village with your hands tied." Shad's smile had a feral edge to it. "Or at least, if you want to survive, you'd better make it down to the village."

I'd often wondered how Shad had become such an infamous captain during the war. He was such a happy-go-lucky kind of man, that I couldn't see him making serious decisions that decided the fate of men's lives.

I could see it now. All too clearly.

Xiaolang watched this without a word of protest. In fact, I think he even agreed with Shad.

I turned to Hayden, and encouraged him to climb up behind me on Night's back. While I had him in close proximity, I decided to ask a few questions. "How old are you, Hayden?" I was thinking about ten, but I could be off.

"I'm twelve."

I gave him a doubtful look. "Really?"

He sighed, as if this reaction didn't surprise him. "I'm small," he admitted bitterly.

At that, I had to chuckle. "I understand, Hayden. I was smaller than everyone else for years, too. In fact, it's only in the past two years that I started catching up." I heaved a rueful shrug. "And even now, I'm still shorter than most of the men around me."

"Are mages shorter than normal people?" He sounded distinctly worried by this idea.

"You can't blame this on magic, kid," I refuted. "It's all genetics."

"Is there magic that can make us grow?"

That stumped me. I hadn't even thought about it. "You'll have to ask Chatta. I'm not sure."

"Who's Chatta?"

"My friend," I explained. "Her full name is Witch L-Chattamoinita Delheart, but everyone calls her Chatta. She's up at the cave right now, packing everything up."

"She's packing up the cave?"

I cast him a sharp, enquiring look over my shoulder, but he was more interested than alarmed. Maybe he didn't realize what was really in that cave. Maybe it had only been a place of refuge for him. "Yes. There's information in there that has been lost for centuries. We want to take it with us."

"Good." Satisfied, he finally relaxed behind me.

I had a pretty fair idea how Chatta would react when she finally laid eyes on our boy mage. I had it pretty much pegged. As soon as we arrived back at the cave, Chatta stepped out to greet us, took one look at Hayden, and went into Mother Hen Mode.

I knew better than to interfere with a woman's mothering instincts. I just traded off with her—I handed Hayden over into her capable hands, and took over her job of packing the cave up.

I was elbow deep in a box when Shad drifted up to my side. He started helping, packing everything into a neater pattern in some of the boxes Chatta had conjured.

"You knew she'd react this way, didn't you?"

I shrugged, not looking at him. "She has strong mothering instincts." I could wish that the boxes were a little smaller. Fully packed, and they became rather heavy.

"I can't figure out," Shad ventured slowly, "if you simply know Chatta very well, or if it's women in general."

I shot him an amused look. "Half of my Jaunten ancestors were women."

"You know, that explains a lot."

"I thought it might."

Xiaolang's head popped into the cave. "How's it going in here?"

"Most of the work is done," I told him. "They did a lot while we were gone. I think we can finish up soon." Seeing that we were largely alone—Hazard, Eagle and Shield were toward the back of the cave—I lowered my voice and asked, "Is this the boy you were talking about?"

Xiaolang shook his head in frustration. "Not the right feel. He's heavy, but…no. Just the wrong boy."

Shad perked up, eyes darting between the two of us. "What's this?"

"I had a flash of precognition while we were visiting Garth's family," Xiaolang explained quietly. "There's a boy we're going to rescue out of Chahir that's very important—stranger yet, it's just as important that Trev'nor meet that boy."

Shad let out a low whistle. "That's…pretty specific. Is that all you saw?"

Xiaolang let out a growl. "Unfortunately, yes. Precognition isn't my strong suit, to my everlasting frustration. But I'll be able to recognize the boy when we meet him, if nothing else. We'll stumble across him eventually." Letting out a sigh, he waved the subject away with a casual flick of the hand. "Now. How much longer until everything is packed up?"

"An hour?" I offered hesitantly.

He nodded, taking everything in with his eyes. I knew that look on his face—he was mentally calculating, thinking, planning. "We're not going to be able to take this back down, not even if I went and scrounged up a wagon somewhere. The trail is too narrow and steep. And I know that you want to drop the boy off properly with your parents, considering the promises that you've made."

I saw where he was going with this. "You want me to use the earth transportation spell, and drop off everything in Hain, don't you?"

"You're quick," he approved. "We'll keep Chatta so that we can continue the search. Take a day and see everything properly settled."

I gave him a casual salute. "Yes, Captain."

Hayden wasn't bothered in the least by my earth transportation spell. It might have been because he mentally connected being in the earth with being safe—that cave had been his refuge for several years. But it might also have been because he was an Elemental Mage with a strong pull toward the earth elements. Either way, he was excited and peppered me with a hundred questions on the ride in.

The kid looked a lot better now. Chatta had used some sort of cleaning spells on him, and he fairly shone. His hair was already grown out to his shoulders, and considering he was a mage, we hadn't thought it wise to cut it. Chatta had pulled it back, instead. It had been the only practical solution, but…well, Hayden had very fair hair. Sometimes, when I looked at him, it felt like I was seeing my reflection—a shorter and younger, reflection, I grant you.

Also traveling with us were the mounds of boxes holding crystals, artifacts, weapons, and other relics from the cave. That would be my second order of business.

And then there was Night. Unhappy about being in the earth, and moody in general.

I debated on which to go to first—palace, academy, or home. I couldn't very well dump all of these boxes at my parent's house for long, so home was out. I wasn't about to drop Hayden into En-Nelle of Tain's hands without Guin knowing, either—I'd never get the kid back again.

Palace it was.

I did take a moment to drop the boxes temporarily off in my rooms. It barely fit, but I wasn't willing to leave that kind of valuable knowledge out in the open. And no one disturbed my rooms in the palace when I was out.

Then I wasn't quite sure how to go about everything. "Night, do you want to come with me?"

"I can, if you wish. But I thought it might be wiser to go warn your parents about Hayden."

Ah. Probably a good idea. "Do that. I'll go speak with Guin. I might have to talk with En-Nelle of Tain, too, I'm not sure. It'll probably be two or three hours before I can meet up with you."

"Yes, probably so."

I gathered up Hayden and we went searching for King Guin.

Once again, he wasn't in any of the places I expected to find him. Not in his personal study, not at court, not even in the kitchens, where I had found him last time. I finally tracked him down in the library.

Guin was busy researching something, stacks of books on the table next to him. I had to give this to the man—he knew how to work. I cleared my throat slightly to catch his attention.

With a start, his head whipped around, eyes going wide. "Garth! This is a surprise; you just left a week ago. I didn't expect you back so soon." His gaze dropped to the boy standing at my side. "And who's this?"

"This is Hayden, an Elemental Mage. Hayden, this is Guin Braehorn, King of Hain."

Hayden gulped, looking like he wasn't sure whether to hide behind me or bolt for the door. "Ah, um…thank you for the gift of your name."

Guin lit up like a little boy that knew where the candy was stashed. "It's a pleasure to meet you, Magus Hayden. I mean that. Another Elemental Mage, eh?"

Hayden blinked at this. Sheer delight exploded over his face. "There's another one?!"

"Yes, Rheijennaan is her name. I'm sure you'll meet her later. How old are you, Hayden?"

Hayden drew himself up proudly. "I'm twelve, sir."

"Twelve, eh? Then you're not quite old enough to enter the Academy." He hummed to himself, rubbing at his chin thoughtfully.

I could tell he was scheming something, and hastily interrupted before he could get any notions permanently lodged in his head. "I gave my word to Hayden that he could be adopted into my family, sire."

Guin shot me a look. "You have a habit of adopting people, Garth."

"It's my parent's influence," I admitted. "My mother would adopt the world if she could figure out how to do it. But Hayden has no family—not even in name. I swore to him that if he would come back with me, I would give him my name." As an afterthought I added, "Besides, he's going to need to live with someone that can understand him. He has no idea how to speak Hainish."

Guin's forehead crinkled at this thin reasoning. There were plenty of Jaunten couples that would be willing to adopt Hayden, and they wouldn't have any problem understanding him whatsoever. "Very well, Garth. I will honor your sworn word."

I released a breath I hadn't realized I'd been holding. "Thank you, sire."

"Hayden, you are a lucky young man. Garth's family is the best of people, and is sure to welcome you. I will visit later this week to see that you are properly settled in with your new family."

I made a mental note to warn my mother about that. Having a king drop in for a social call unannounced would surely give her heart failure.

"Before I take Hayden over there, sire, I should tell you what else we discovered."

Guin slowly went taut in his chair. "Another mage?"

I shook my head. "No. Almost better, really. There was a cave that Hayden used as his…well, safehaven I guess is a good way to put it. Anyway, inside the cave were mounds of memory crystals, and books, and weapons, and almost everything else you can imagine." Guin looked suitably impressed by this, but I relished adding, "It all dates to before the Magic War."

A beggar being given a bag of gold could not have been more ecstatic than Guin in that moment. "Are you sure?" he demanded, nearly bouncing in his seat.

"Positive," I assured him firmly. "Chatta took a quick peek inside one of them. We crated it all up, and I brought it all back with me."

Guin licked dry lips. "How much is there?" he asked hoarsely.

"It fills my sitting room."

I seriously thought he was going to faint. "That much?"

I loved surprising Guin like this. It wasn't easy to do; it took luck, skill, and timing. I didn't pull it off often. That was why I enjoyed it so much when I did. "Who do you want me to give it to?"

Guin gave an audible sigh of regret. "I suppose by rights it belongs to the Trasdee Evondit Orra." He thought about it a moment and ordered, "Trade all of that for the right to keep Hayden."

Now that was sneaky. "With pleasure, sire."

"How did your meeting with the Coven Ordan go?"

For several minutes I filled Guin in on our visit. He was as surprised about my lineage as I had been—yet another thing I needed to inform my family of—and was darkly satisfied with the confirmation of the Watchman Pools.

"Can you turn off the pools?" Guin was thinking so hard, I think smoke was coming out of his ears.

"I'm not really sure that's a wise idea," I admitted uneasily. "Ley lines are a very complicated thing. If you move one, or shut one off, a dozen are affected. Chahir is just now beginning to regain its original strength—I'm deathly afraid that tampering anything will destroy or damage that growth."

"Surely there's a way…" he trailed off.

"I need to ask some very pointed questions of the experts on pools. Neither Chatta nor I know enough to make any plans at this point."

"Go speak with the Sojavel Ra Institute," Guin advised. "That's the main research facility for magic in Hain. If anyone will know the answer to your questions, it will be them."

I hadn't realized we had a research facility for magic. But now that he brought it up, it made all kinds of sense for there to be one. "Shouldn't I be taking the 'treasure load' to them as well?" Surely they were the most capable hands to receive all that knowledge.

"The Trasdee Evondit Orra will probably order just that," Guin admitted. "But run the idea past them first."

"Understood."

Guin extended a hand to Hayden. After an uncertain beat, Hayden slipped his hand into that large, adult handshake. "I will see you later, Hayden," Guin promised in a low voice. "And if there is anything that you need, don't hesitate to call upon me."

Hayden was definitely overwhelmed. Guin had that effect on people, sometimes. "T-thank you," he managed.

Guin nodded and released him before returning his attention to me. "See him settled before you do anything with your treasure load."

I bowed in agreement.

"Oh, Garth." The king grinned at me slyly, as if paying me back for my revelation about the cache from the cave. "Perhaps when you have finished briefing the Council, you should swing by and pick up Trev'nor, before heading home. He was so disappointed when I had to tell him you were leaving on your last jaunt. I'm sure he will be excited to meet his new brother."

Trev'nor! I mentally slapped myself on the back of the head twice. He would go crazy when he met Hayden, another brother and a fellow mage to boot! Trev'nor spoke Chahirese, and was picking up the Hainian language and customs fast. Besides, his not-exactly-subtle brand of affection and friendship was just what Hayden needed. I had no doubts that he and Hayden would be inseparable in no time, despite the difference in their ages.

"Yes, Your Majesty." I grinned back at him in return. I should have known I wouldn't be able to hold an edge on Guin for long. With that the king gave us a farewell wave, picked up the cookie he had been hiding under the cover of his book, and went back to his research. I smiled to myself, shook my head, and reached for the door handle. Some things never changed.

I took Hayden with me to the Trasdee Evondit Orra. The first five minutes were civil. They talked to Hayden, put him to the triangle test, and confirmed that, yes, he was an Elemental Mage. Unusually, he was a well-rounded Elemental Mage, with equal capabilities in each element and no special affinity for one in particular. To be able to turn any element to his will was an amazing feat. When he was fully trained, the boy would be a force to reckon with.

Everyone in the council spent a few moments oohing and ahhing over this development, delighted by such a rare talent.

It went downhill from there.

En-Nelle of Tain, as usual, was the problem. Her voice was sharp and irate, squawking like a bat trapped in full sunlight. "Magus Rhebengarthen, you do not have the authority to make decisions about the futures of mages!"

I settled into a parade rest, just looking at her. "Lady En-Nelle, Hayden is not old enough to attend the Academy yet anyway. He is more advanced at this stage than most, but by no means is he ready to actively use magic. You have no use for him at this point. What possible harm can come from him being adopted into my family?"

O'danne started chuckling, which earned him a dark glare from En-Nelle. "Garth, my boy, I think Chatta is rubbing off on you. That was quite blunt."

It was rather undiplomatic in tone. "I gave this boy my word that he would be adopted by my parents," I said in a soft tone. Everyone in the room abruptly shut up and tensed, staring at me in surprise. "I will not allow my honor to be forsworn because of ridiculous pride. Hayden doesn't understand Hainish, or have any idea how to cope with this culture. He needs a grounding, something he understands, until he can come to terms with his magic and this country. En-Nelle of Tain, surely you can comprehend that."

"I suggest listening to him, Nellie," Doss suggested in a firm tone. "Garth knows from personal experience what the transition is like. Besides—" he gave me a subtle wink "—I don't care to make an enemy of the Advent Mage."

That ludicrous title again.

I decided it was time to switch tactics. "Besides, I thought you would be more interested in the items we found in the cave."

That got her undivided attention. "What items?"

I described the find in casual terms. Each person assembled in the council chamber hung on to my every word, as avid as a starving man watching a steaming plate of food. When I finished, I think En-Nelle was actually drooling.

"Where is it now?" she asked eagerly.

"Oh, I brought it with me," I assured her casually. "It's in Hain."

That didn't exactly answer the question, and she knew it. She frowned thoughtfully at the boy standing so quiet and nervous at my side.

"All I want is Hayden," I said with calm emphasis. "I'll happily deliver everything else wherever you want it."

Her greed did her in. One untrained mage couldn't compete with the knowledge I had hidden in my sitting parlor. She quickly backtracked. "Rhebengarthen, you do have a point about the young mage. Feel free to make any arrangements you feel necessary. But he will attend the Academy as soon as he turns fourteen."

That firm tone didn't even make a dent with me. "Of course, Lady En-Nelle. Where would you like me to put the memory crystals and such?"

"Bring them here, for now. Are you returning immediately to Chahir?"

"No, I'm staying overnight."

"Then come again tomorrow morning. I want to examine everything first. If there's too much for us to handle here, I will have you take it to the Sojavel Ra Institute."

Guin had certainly called that one. I bowed in agreement, and ushered Hayden out the door.

Hayden hadn't understood a word of that discussion, so I had to recap it for him as we went back to the palace. It took bare minutes to transport the lot of it back to the Academy. The Trasdee Evondit Orra fell on the crates like ravaging wolves. I quickly escaped before any fur could start flying, taking Hayden to safety with me.

I explained to Hayden about Trev'nor, and how he came to be living in Del Hain, on the brief hop over to his home. We surfaced on the street, just outside his yard, where he was playing with a ball. When he saw me, he let out a shriek of delight, and made an impossible leap over the fence into my arms.

"Garth!" he screamed into my ear, as he hugged life out of me. "I didn't know you were coming home!"

When I finally managed to get enough air to get my words out I replied, "It was a surprise. I've brought you a new brother!" With that, he scanned quickly over my shoulder and spotted Hayden. Trev'nor immediately let go of my neck and dropped to the ground. Using his most polite manners he bowed and introduced himself. "I am Trev'nor," he solemnly intoned, in perfect Chahirese.

Hayden's eyes went wide as he took in his new brother, and stammered, "Thank you for the gift of your name. I am Hayden."

With the formal introductions over, Trev'nor launched himself into Hayden's arms, and Hayden returned his embrace like his life depended upon it. I had known that Trev'nor would respond like this—maybe it was the Tonkawacon influence, but he just adopted everyone around him. At this moment, such complete acceptance was exactly what Hayden needed.

Trev'nor pulled back and started asking a million questions of his new brother, which Hayden tried to answer just as quickly. Tension bled from his face and shoulders as Hayden realized that Trev'nor honestly thought of him as a brother now. The most beautiful, breathtaking smile softened his face.

I just stood there with tears standing in my eyes, thanking the gods for the gift of family.

My parent's house looked as it had last time, only slightly livelier. I had a suspicion that everyone was home this time, unlike last time. When I opened the door, I called in, "I'm here!"

"Garth!" Asla was the first to appear, running toward me.

I caught her in a quick hug, pleased to see how energetic she looked. The last time I'd seen her, she was still recovering from her daughter's birth. It had taken a few months for Asla to really come to grips with what almost happened to her and her son, Aral. Not every woman had to face being turned in by their own husband to be burned at the stake.

But, being adopted into the family truly helped her. She was much livelier now, laughing and smiling more easily. It did my heart good to see it. Healing was possible, given enough time, support, love and patience.

She drew back, smiling brilliantly up at me. "I never expected to see you back so soon! Or...are you back?"

"Only overnight," I answered. "Is Night here?"

"I was out when he visited," she admitted. "He took Da out for some kind of shopping that Mom insisted on." Asla reached down and gave Trev'nor a bear hug and added, turning to Hayden, "This must be the young mage." She dropped down to Hayden's level, expression curious but friendly.

"Hayden, this is my sister Asla," I introduced. "Asla, this is Hayden. He is an Elemental Mage." For Hayden's benefit, Trev'nor leaned over and whispered into his ear, "Hayden, Asla is an adopted sister, too!"

He perked up at this, looking very interested.

Asla nodded in confirmation. "Yes, I am. I understand that you will soon be my adopted brother, too. Is that right, Hayden?"

Ah, so my parents had agreed. I hadn't expected anything different, but it was nice to have that confirmed.

Hayden was torn between smiling and crying, I think. "Yes, I am," he whispered with a thick voice.

Asla just smiled at him. "Then, welcome to the family."

"Thank you." There were definitely tears standing in his eyes.

"Garth!" my mother exclaimed, appearing from upstairs. "There you are; it's about time. Where's my new son?"

Yes, that was my mother all right. I hadn't been kidding when I'd told Guin that she would adopt the whole world if she could. "Mom, this is Hayden. Hayden, your new mother, Rhebenjaylanan."

Hayden didn't get a chance to say one word. Mom just kind of swooped in on him, lifting him up in a hug. His eyes popped open wide, and he froze a little. Almost gingerly, he raised his hands up to hug her back. Mom didn't let go until he relaxed, which was exactly what Hayden needed. He was starved for any kind of physical affection.

"Welcome home, Rhebenhaydenen," she whispered into his hair.

That did it. Hayden couldn't hold the tears back anymore; they just streamed down his face. Mom didn't seem to care that he was soaking her shoulder, she just held on and murmured some sort of soothing monologue.

As I stood and watched, Trev'nor slid his hand into mine, and grinned up at me with his most beguiling smile. "I think he's gonna' like it here," Trev'nor assured me. It was moments like this that reminded me just how proud I was to be in this family.

Aral burst in through the back door, stumbling to a halt just inside and taking in this scene. "What's going on? Garth, you're home!"

I bent down and caught him as he tackled me. "Oof! Aral, did you grow again?"

"I'm going to grow as tall as you," he said proudly.

"Aim higher than that, kid," I advised. "Try for Braeden's height, and you might get somewhere. Come meet your new...uncle." As Asla's brother, Hayden would, I guess, technically be Aral's uncle.

Hayden drew back, drying tears away with his sleeve.

Aral looked down, studying this new boy with a slight frown.

"He's an Elemental Mage from Chahir," I continued, setting him on his feet. "Hayden, this is Asla's son, Aral. Aral, this is Hayden."

"He's not old enough to be an uncle," Aral muttered.

Hayden seemed unable to decide about this point of family relationship, looking back and forth from Aral to Trev'nor.

"Well, think of him as an older brother, then," Asla advised in amusement.

Mom was more focused on practical matters. "Hayden, Trev'nor, Aral, are you hungry?"

"Yes!" the three boys sang out as one voice.

She rolled her eyes in mock horror. "Garth, I believe hunger is the universal constant in all boys! You come right back to the kitchen, and we'll fix you boys something to eat," Mom told the trio of starving birds. She took Hayden by the hand and started towing him behind her, with Trev'nor and Aral trotting happily along in their wake.

"I'm still a boy and I'm hungry, too!" I called after her plaintively.

She shot me an exasperated look. "Garth, I assume at this point that you can cook for yourself."

"I get no love around here," I muttered under my breath.

Asla laughed, linking her arm through mine, and started for the kitchen. "Come on, brother, I'll cook you something."

"Asla, have I ever mentioned how glad I am you're in the family?"

That made her laugh even harder.

I didn't bother worrying about Hayden from that point on. Between Asla and Mom, the kid was ambushed with all sorts of motherly attention. He ate every ounce of it up.

Trev'nor and Aral sat on either side of me, demanding an update on what I had been doing with the team in Chahir. I somehow managed to eat and answer questions at the same time, although the process slowed me down considerably.

Da showed up just as I finished off my plate, Night on his heels. I greeted them with, "It's about time you two showed up."

"And who was it that took three hours to get here?" Night inquired dryly.

"I had more to do," I pointed out righteously. "What kept you?"

"We went to buy a bed and some furniture for the boy," Da answered. He sank into the chair next to Hayden, looking him over. Hayden looked back just as frankly, but with a hint of nervousness. "So. I'm Rhebenardenen."

Belatedly, I continued the introduction. "Hayden, this is your new father. Da, Hayden."

Da dropped a hand on Hayden's head, smiling warmly. "Welcome to the family, son."

Hayden was a hair's breadth from crying again, but managed to hold the tears back. "Thank you."

"I trust that the two of you can manage to raise him and help him adapt to Hain?" I asked of my parents. "He'll need to be ready for the Academy in two years."

"We raised you, didn't we?" Da responded with an arch look. "We'll manage, Garth."

"I know. Why do you think I brought him here?" I lifted myself to my feet, looking toward the back door. "I assume that all the furniture is out there?"

"Sure is," Da agreed.

"Well, let's get it in, then."

"Garth, are you sure you have time for that?" Mom asked in worry. "You've been here so long already. Don't you have tasks that need to be done?"

"Not until tomorrow morning," I assured her. "I have leave to stay here tonight." Remembering all the things that I had to tell them, I smirked. "And believe me it's going to take all night to catch you up."

Everyone frowned at me. "What is that supposed to mean?" Asla inquired suspiciously.

"Let's get some furniture in before it rains," I suggested mildly. "I'll tell you when we have everything settled."

Without waiting, I ducked out the door. People were grumbling behind me about my bad conversational habits. I grinned, knowing they couldn't see the expression.

Teasing people was so much fun.

TRUTH

I went with Asla to the Academy the next morning. She was continuing her education, studying to be a witch. I understood from my mother that she was making incredible progress.

"I still can't believe it," she mumbled under her breath as we walked.

I spared her a glance. Early morning traffic on the streets of Del'Hain could be hazardous to one's health—I didn't dare take my eyes away for long. I'd get run over. "Believe what?"

"That the Rhebens have a history of magic."

"Ah, that."

"And that there are two of them still living in Bromany!"

"That was the part that threw me for a loop," I admitted. "They're really nice people, though." I was fairly sure they'd meet them eventually. Sallah seemed determined to meet all of us.

We reached the Academy gates and she hesitated. "I won't see you for a while, will I?"

I shrugged, palms spread. "Asla, nothing about this job is predictable. It might be a while, it might not."

"Well, in case it is…" She threw her arms around me and hugged me tightly. "Be careful."

I returned the embrace. "I will. And good luck studying."

With a last smile, she turned and hurried off to her morning class. "Garth!"

Kartal? I turned toward the hail. Sure enough, the wizard was coming toward me at a fast walk, looking…pleased? I never thought Kartal would be happy to see me. "Hello," I greeted pleasantly.

"I thought I'd have to go to your place to get you. You saved me a trip." He stopped a foot away. No, distance hadn't fudged his expression—he actually was pleased to see me. "I spoke with En-Nelle of Tain a few moments ago. She wants you to take everything to Sojavel Ra Institute."

That didn't surprise me. "All right. Is it in the same place I left it?"

"They didn't move it much," he assured me. "Also, King Guin said that you had questions to pose to the Institute?"

"Yes."

"But you've never been there, have you?"

"I didn't even know it existed until yesterday," I admitted wryly.

"Guin thought you would need a guide." He rolled his eyes. "Somehow, I got appointed to the task. I'm also tasked with getting everything to the right people."

I was actually glad to see him at this point. Heaven knew I wouldn't have a clue on where to go, or who to talk to. "I'm glad Guin sent you, then."

"Will this take long?"

"Where is the Sojavel Ra Institute?"

"Down near the Hobendon Peninsula." Kartal couldn't quite hide a smile as he said this.

The Hobendon Peninsula?! It seemed like ages ago, but it was only last year that I'd met Kartal in that region, both of us assigned to fix the flooding of the Komot River. "Now that's irony."

"Truly," he agreed.

"In that case, it might take an hour or so. By Earth Path, at least." I eyed him sideways, not sure if he'd agree to that.

"Good, I want this over with." With an imperious gesture, he motioned for me to follow him.

Some things just never changed. I took a moment to pray for patience, and followed the arrogant wizard.

I thought the Earth Path actually made Kartal nervous, but he wouldn't admit to that. He hid it well, except for his eyes. They kept darting around, as if he were waiting for the earth to start collapsing in on him.

I took pity on him and sped up, getting there quicker than the hour I'd estimated earlier.

We were nearly there when Kartal demanded, "How do you navigate doing this? You don't even know where it is!"

As long as I had been doing this, no one had asked me that

question. I actually had to think before answering, trying to formulate it in words. "Well…it's actually a mixture of things."

"Which are?" he demanded impatiently.

"I can sense all of the surrounding area when I'm in the earth like this," I explained slowly. "Rivers, mountains, lakes…I can sense it all. That gives me landmarks to work off of."

"Doesn't that ever get confusing? Don't you get confused about which direction you're going?"

"No."

"How?" he insisted.

"Because every patch of earth feels different than the rest. I can't mix up one area for another."

"Feels different?" he repeated dubiously. "Explain."

I searched for the words, but couldn't come up with a way to do it. "Kartal, I can't explain. I just know."

"Nonsense, there has to be some way to explain it."

I shook my head, losing my patience with his bullheadedness. "How do you explain the difference between blue and green?"

He was quick to open his mouth, but he paused. After a long moment he darkly muttered, "All right, I see your point."

"I just know," I told him. "I can't be any clearer than that. But also, I can feel people. If I'm traveling to a specific person, it's easy to pinpoint where they're standing. And this institute building is full of magicians—all I have to do to locate the place is find the most concentrated area of magicians."

"That's rather clever," Kartal admitted grudgingly.

This reaction amused me. Did he think I was all brawn and no brain? Actually, knowing Kartal, that was scarily possible.

I let the matter lie, focusing on getting to the Institute itself. I tried to come up in an area with few people, but the surface was pretty packed.

And as usual, when we rose out of the ground, I gave nearly everyone in sight heart failure.

I winced at this reaction. "Didn't anyone warn them that we were coming?"

It was a largely rhetorical question, but Kartal answered it anyway. "Apparently not." He turned and cast a thick shield over the crates. "Leave it there, for now. Let's go find the right people to take care of it."

That sounded fine, but, "Why the shield?"

"Researchers are insatiably curious."

I had to hurry to keep up with his quick stride as he went right through the half-panicked crowd.

Sojavel Ra Institute was a rather pretty place. The building was large and white, with huge arched doorways and covered walkways. It had a rather quiet, relaxing air to it.

We entered the main doors, Kartal confidently leading the way. The inside didn't quite match the outside—it was cluttered with all sorts of doohickeys and whatchamacallits, men and women of all ages wandering around with books and papers and artifacts in their hands. I took quick peeks into the rooms as we passed them. Some of these people were so engrossed in their work an explosion could happen right next to them and they'd barely notice it.

I was nearly past one door when my ears caught something.

"—telling you that Rhebengarthen is—"

My name? I skidded to a halt and backtracked. In this room, there were four men sitting around a square table. Or at least, I assumed it was a table underneath the thick stack of parchments, graphs, books, and maps.

All of the doors in this building had these little plaques on them, telling what was being researched in the room. I glanced at the plaque on this door.

Advent Mage Study.

I swayed where I stood, eyes glued to the plaque. They were studying me?!

"Garth, what's the hold up?" Kartal demanded, coming close enough to haul me along.

I couldn't say a word. I was just too stunned. I pointed instead.

Kartal took one look at the plaque and his mouth formed a silent "O" of surprise.

"You didn't know about this, did you?" I asked past a dry mouth.

"No idea," he admitted.

"You there!" One of the researchers, a portly man with greying hair, stood up to face us. "What are you gaping at?"

I was caught completely flat footed. I hardly felt like introducing myself, not to this group. I improvised with, "Ah, um, I was wondering why you're researching the Advent Mage?"

"That's obvious! If we can figure out how he gained the powers of a mage, we can influence more mages to be born." He drew himself up proudly. "We have several hard facts to draw from. Indeed, we're making tremendous progress."

"Progress!" one of his colleagues scoffed. "Bah! I'm telling you, magic comes from blood."

"Impossible," the portly man in front of me snapped. "Magical bloodlines are all extinct in Chahir at this point."

"Actually, he's partly correct," I offered. "Magical inheritance is part of it. But there are other factors, too."

"And what would you know about this, young man?" the aging scholar demanded arrogantly. "This is the Advent Mage we're speaking of! No one alive is certain on how he gained his power."

Looking at him, the word blockhead came to mind. If ever there was a mind blocked from new knowledge, it was this one. And because of that, there was nothing I could do. I smiled slightly, nodded, and walked away.

Kartal had to jog to catch up with me, catching my sleeve as he did. "Why didn't you say who you are?" he hissed near my ear. "He's completely wrong! They all are!"

A mischievous impulse seized me, and I looked at him in innocent surprise. "But Kartal, these are scholars. Experts in their field. There's no possible way they're wrong."

"Of course they are!" he protested in exasperation. "And we both know it!"

"But they have facts!" I teased, fighting a smile. "They have pictures, data, charts, graphs!"

"Will you please be serious?" he growled.

"I've met people like them before," I told him quietly, my amusement fading. "They're the kind of people that will argue that up is down, just to argue. You can't teach them anything."

"And so you won't try to straighten them out?"

"Too much hassle," I denied with a shrug. "They believe they know everything. That's a dangerous belief, but once a person gets to that point, nothing but the most drastic circumstances will convince them otherwise."

"They certainly don't know much about you," he grumbled under his breath. "I mean, they couldn't even recognize you on sight."

"Doesn't say much about their collective wisdom, does it?"

Fortunately for us, the people that Kartal took me to were not like those scholars. Lyra Doddridge was thin, neat, and very friendly. I dropped all formalities with her instantly. Her colleague was Adam Fawcett, a near-sighted man who looked like he dressed in the dark. With one arm tied behind his back. Still, he seemed nice as well.

"Well, this is amazing!" he exclaimed once the introductions were out of the way. "The Advent Mage, here."

I winced at the title. So help me, if I ever figured out who'd spread that stupid, thrice-begotten title around....

"I came to ask a few questions," I quickly said, diverting the subject. "What can you tell me about turning a scrying pool off?"

"I assume you mean a permanent pool?" Lyra's dark eyes were bright with curiosity.

"Yes, tied to a ley line."

"Hmmm." Lyra exchanged looks with Adam. "What do you think, Adam?"

"How old exactly is the pool? Usually the magician that made the pool can take it down easily."

I didn't want to hear that. "They're over two hundred years old. At least." I wasn't exactly sure on their age, but I knew they existed before the Magic War.

Their faces fell. "That long?" Adam muttered in dark contemplation. "Unless the ley line supporting it dries up, I can't think of a way to turn it off."

"Emptying the pool of water?" I suggested desperately.

Lyra shook her head immediately. "When a scrying spell is put on water, it holds the water in stasis. It can't be changed or removed."

Interesting. I hadn't known that.

Adam eyed me in speculation. "Moving the ley line would work too. Surely you considered that."

"Too dangerous," I responded with a firm shake of the head. "Moving one ley line would be easy. But no ley line is alone—it's always connected with a dozen others. It would be like pulling a string loose in the middle of a tapestry—the whole thing would unravel and knot."

They winced at this mental picture.

"Then the only thing you can really do is put a capstone over the pool." Lyra spread her hands in a helpless gesture. "That won't really turn the pool off, but it will buy you some time."

"In an emergency situation, that is definitely something to keep in mind," I acknowledged slowly, thinking that suggestion through. "But for a permanent fix, for what we have in mind, that doesn't really help." It would only buy us time, and limited quantities of it. Worse, it would tip off the government of what we were doing, and that we had the magical expertise to know what we were looking at.

"I'm sorry," Lyra sighed. "We haven't been much help."

"On the contrary," I assured her sincerely, "you've told me what the limitations are. That helps, trust me. Otherwise I would be randomly stumbling around in the dark, guessing, and probably messing everything up."

Adam had the most peculiar smile on his face. "Magus…you aren't anything like your reputation."

"My reputation," I groaned, "is a gross exaggeration."

"Yes, I'm beginning to see that." That funny smile widened a notch. "Tell me, have you heard that there is a department in this building that studies you?"

I felt my face heat up. Kartal tried to cover up a laugh with a fake cough, and didn't do a very good job of it. I resisted the urge to punch him. "Um, yes. I, ah, ran across them earlier."

"They must have loved talking with you!" Lyra exclaimed with innocent naiveté. "I'm surprised they let you go so you could talk with us."

Kartal lost it completely at that point. He was nearly doubled over, howling with laughter. This time I did punch him, straight in the arm. "Shut up!" I growled at him.

It didn't even faze him. He only slowed down enough to get out the words, "They didn't…even…recognize…him!"

Lyra and Adam gave me incredulous looks. I shrugged sheepishly. "I saw the plaque and went in to talk to them. They wouldn't even hear what I had to say. Like Kartal said, they didn't recognize me."

"Oh dear." Lyra lifted a hand to her mouth, eyes going wide.

Adam started laughing, deep guffaws that shook his whole frame. "Oh…oh…oh! I've got to rub this in! The Advent Mage, right in front of their noses, and they didn't even know it!"

There were times when I really wished I was a wizard. This was

one of those times. If I'd had the ability, I would have happily turned
Kartal and Adam into toads.

We were halfway down the hallway, heading for the outside, when
Kartal flung up a hand, stopping me.

"Garth, I think we should go back."

I gave him a blank look. "Back to Adam and Lyra?"

"No, no, no." He shot me an exasperated frown. "To that room
with the Advent Mage study group."

I didn't trust that smile on his face. It reminded me eerily of Didi
when he was contemplating mischief. "Why?" I asked cautiously.

"Garth, think about this for a minute. This institute is world-
renown for giving answers to magical questions. If those idiots come
up with some sort of reasonable-sounding explanation for why mages
exist, and how to create more of them, a lot of people are going to
believe them. It'll start an avalanche of mistakes."

He had a definite point there.

"You're the only person in this world with a prayer of derailing
them," he pressed on persuasively. "They'll listen to the Advent Mage,
once they know who he is. That's obvious."

As logical and reasonable as all of this was, it didn't match that
impish gleam in the man's eyes. "In other words, you really want to rub
in the fact that they didn't recognize me on sight. Not to mention you
feel the need to take them down a few rungs."

His smile was not at all nice. A cat waiting to pounce on a helpless
mouse couldn't compete with his expression. "Well, that too."

"Uh-huh." Knew it. Still, despite his devious intentions, I couldn't
deny the validity of the original argument. "Are you sure that it will do
any good? As I said before, they strike me as people who just love to
argue."

"With each other they love to argue," he corrected. "But they can't
argue with you. You're the expert on mages at this point. No one can
refute that you're the expert on yourself. Not much, anyway. Besides,
all things considered, wouldn't you like to try?"

I wasn't entirely sure I bought this, but there was a part of me that wanted to see if he were right. Besides, this was one of those rare occurrences when I could really enjoy rubbing my outlandish reputation in a little. I'd be a fool to pass up the opportunity. "Well, why not?"

"Ha!" He bounced in glee, grinning.

Nothing made Kartal happier than the opportunity to razz someone. Maybe his enthusiasm was infectious—I was kind of looking forward to the opportunity as well. Knocking something arrogant down is a deep delight of the blood.

I let Kartal lead the way back to that room. Nothing had changed much since we'd left it—four grouchy men were still gathered around the disorganized table, and they were still arguing with each other.

Kartal paused in the doorway, wolfish smile well concealed behind a bland expression. Clearing his throat, he waited until he had their attention. "Gentlemen, I feel the need to introduce myself. I am Roarke Kartal, wizard."

One of the men perked up instantly. "The same Wizard Kartal that was with the Advent Mage during the Hobendon Peninsula flooding?"

They were familiar with my taskings, at least. They weren't completely shooting in the dark.

Kartal flashed his most charming smile. "Indeed."

"Finally, an eye witness!" the portly wizard cried. He pounced on Kartal and dragged him to an open seat. "I'm Audax Vertas, wizard. You simply must come and tell us what you know."

"Oh it will be my delight, I assure you." Kartal's grin widened a notch.

Seeing that this was going to take a while, I put my shoulders to the wall and relaxed, settling in for what promised to be quite the show. Kartal has quite the tongue on him—as good as any lawyer's. I fully expected for him to wrap these men up in theory-logical knots.

Quick introductions were made all around. The man with wispy hair was Wizard Toplady, the one with the seemingly perpetual frown was Wizard Stott, and the combative wizard was Coles. Since I was being very quiet and still, not drawing any attention to myself, they forgot I was even in the room, and Kartal didn't introduce me. From the quick grin he flashed me, this was done on purpose.

Drama queen.

They fell into a discussion of magical bloodlines in exhaustive detail. I lost them about three sentences in, as I had no idea about any Hainian bloodlines. For that matter, I had no idea of Chahiran bloodlines, outside of my own. This was (thankfully) interrupted after a few minutes by Cole.

"Never mind the Hainian bloodlines," he growled, flapping his hands. "Those obviously don't apply to Chahir. In fact, I'm not sure that any bloodlines apply to Chahir, considering how most of them have surely been stamped out by now. What I want to know is why now? It's been two hundred years since we've seen a mage, until Rhebengarthen. Then after he appears, we get four more!"

"Five," Kartal corrected. "Another Elemental Mage was brought into Del'Hain yesterday."

There was a briefly stunned silence as they digested that.

"Five in two years..." Toplady mused, pulling at one ear in an absent fashion. "Almost unheard of, according to the histories. And all from Chahir. Why?"

"You can't assume that only Chahir can breed mages." Kartal smiled when he got four challenging stares. "Think about it—the young Earth Mage, Trev'nor, is an unknown. We have no idea what nationality he is. He doesn't look Hainian, but he could be from the Empire of Sol."

I'd never thought about where Trev'nor came from—but Kartal was right, he obviously wasn't Hainish. Actually...he rather looked like he could hail from Chahir with his fair coloring....I was diverted from the thought before I could trace it to its logical end by the argument at the table.

"There's never been mages from Sol before!" Stott objected.

"We didn't get mages from Chahir for two hundred years either," Coles pointed out. "We've never gotten a mage from Hain. There's a first time for everything. You've met Trev'nor, Wizard Kartal?"

"Oh yes. I was with Garth when we discovered the boy."

"Then the report that Trev'nor was initially raised by Tonkawacons is true?"

"Completely true," Kartal confirmed. His eyes were alight with amusement—he was truly enjoying himself.

"But there's no history of magic in Sol!" Stott reiterated, nearly wailing. "It doesn't make any sense!"

"It doesn't make any sense for Hain, who is so rich with magic, not to have mages, either," Cole snapped at him.

"Let's focus on one problem at a time," Toplady suggested. "Wizard

Kartal, you've spent considerable time with the Advent Mage. Did he have any theories about how his mage abilities came about?"

"Why yes, I believe he does know how," Kartal responded blandly. Turning, he looked at me, as innocent as a cat with feathers sticking out of its mouth. "What was the theory again?"

Don't ask me how, but I managed not to smile or chortle like a demented idiot. It was very challenging, as Kartal's wicked amusement was tickling my funny bone badly. My face was hurting from the effort. Matching his tone, I responded, "There are three factors, actually. One of which is bloodlines—although it can skip several generations without showing—but it also takes a certain condition of the land, and the mage's proximity to ley lines' power."

Dead silence. I was the focus of many suspicious stares. I think, just judging from Cole's face, that he was beginning to piece together who I was. He was torn between delight and horrified realization.

Vertas frowned impressively, which rather made him look like a bulldog. "Just what did you say your name is?"

"I didn't." Completely deadpanned, I gave a polite bow. "I am Rhebengarthen."

I seriously thought Vertas was going to drop to the floor in a dead faint.

It took Stott three tries to get words out of his mouth. "You…are the Advent Mage."

Kartal started laughing, mirth rolling out of his chest in waves. Apparently he just couldn't hold it in any longer. Gasping for breath, he managed, "Yes, he is."

"And just for your information, I hate that title," I added wryly.

I don't think anyone quite knew how to respond to that. Taking pity on their obvious bafflement, I took an empty chair at the head of the table. "Now, gentlemen, if you truly want to know how mages are being born these days, I'll be happy to tell you. I have my information confirmed with the Remnant Mages, so I can assure you it's all accurate. Are you willing to listen to me this time?"

"We are indeed listening, Magus," Toplady assured me with humble sincerity.

I smiled at him, and started outlining the same theory—which I was pretty sure was more than just theory—that Aral and I had talked about on his front porch, only a week ago. Kartal just sat back, enjoying the show. I knew without asking that he'd rub this in for years. These wizards might never live this day down.

Well, that wasn't my problem. I just laid out magical theory as logically and concisely as I could. As I talked, I realized that these men were genuinely listening. Stott was even taking notes.

Well. Maybe they weren't blockheads after all.

After some polite goodbyes to the researchers, I went back to Del'Hain to pick up Night. I left Kartal there in Sojavel Ra. He had that huge pile of treasure to help sort through, after all.

I took a few minutes to properly say goodbye to all of the family and pick up a few items in town. As I ran around, I filled in Night on what had happened this morning. Have you ever seen a horse try to laugh and walk at the same time? It's a funny sight, let me tell you. I actually got quite the kick watching his reaction to the story.

I thought I'd score some major points and picked up two of Chatta's favorite treats. Night teased me about doing this, but I was good at ignoring him when I wanted to.

Doing all of this had eaten up the morning, and it was nearly noon when I was done. Night and I voted on eating lunch there in Del'Hain before traveling back to Chahir.

After a very filling lunch of squinch and meat pie, I made sure all of my packages were on Night's back. Satisfied, I took us down into the Earth Path.

As usual, it was warm and quiet inside the earth. I let it flow over me, soothing away all the minor tensions flooding my body.

"You really do like it down here, don't you?"

"It's very relaxing," I answered contentedly, eyes shut.

"Aren't you worried about hitting something?"

"Not really."

He grumbled, but didn't reply. I decided it was better to just change the subject. "How is Hayden really?" I asked Night. I wasn't sure if the kid was putting on a good face when I was around.

"Ecstatic. There's a part of him, though, that thinks this is all too good to be true. He never says anything, but his eyes…"

I nodded in understanding. I'd expected something like that.

"Time will erase that worry."

"I wish we could bring good news back with us."

"Chatta was actually afraid this was the answer. She's quite good with pools, really. We just both hoped that the experts knew something she didn't."

"So what are we going to do?"

"Good question," I sighed. "I haven't the foggiest notion. We might end up just working around the pools, as we did before."

"I foresee a lot of glamour spells in our future."

That statement troubled me. Glamour spells were hard to hold for any length of time. They took quite a bit of concentration. And you couldn't hold them while you were asleep. For Chatta to cast a glamour over all of us, well, that would drain her quickly. I didn't exactly agree with Night.

I saw very limited magic being used in our immediate future.

CAUSE AND EFFECT

I didn't take the Earth Path directly to where the team was. That would have been like painting a target on all of our backs. Instead, I went back to what Shad had dubbed "the treasure cave" and stopped there. Then I pulled out a glamour amulet for both Night and I, and put them on. They would last five hours before breaking down; that should give us enough time to lose anyone that might be tracking us by scrying pool.

Once we were off the mountain, Night fell into a ground-eating lope. I settled back in the saddle, only keeping a cursory eye on where we were going. Riding a nreesce was so much better than riding a horse—I could just point him in the right direction and turn him loose.

"Garth, who do you think the boy is? The one that Xiaolang had that premonition about."

I rubbed my chin thoughtfully. "Honestly, I have no idea. The kid's got to be pretty important, if he's going to change Chahiran policy."

"One of the dom's sons or something?"

"Or something," I agreed, arrested by this idea. "Some of the doms have a lot of power and influence."

"I hope we find the boy soon. I'm getting kind of tired of being away from home so much."

I patted his neck in sympathy. "Yeah, I'm with you on that one." It wasn't just that I missed being able to see my family and friends on a regular basis, although that was a large part of it. I was also envisioning just how much work was piling up for me. Supposedly Kartal was handling a large portion of it, but still....

Owing Kartal favors would make anyone nervous.

"When this is over, let's buy a house," Night suggested in a burst of enthusiasm.

Where in blue blazes had that come from? "Not that I'm complaining, but why are you suggesting that now?"

"We're too handy for Guin," he explained with a slight timbre of irritation in his voice. "We're too convenient. Whenever something goes wrong, he thinks of us first because he knows that it'll be easy to lay hands on us quickly."

I followed this closely, mind spinning. "So if we were not in easy reach, say in our own house outside of the city…then he might stop calling on us so much?"

"I think so."

For about three seconds, I seriously considered what he was saying. "You know, Night, I'm feeling the sudden urge to go buy a house."

"I thought you'd see it my way." He sounded very smug.

"You're a devious person, Night, and I'm proud to know you."

He chuckled wickedly.

The rest of the trip, we discussed what exactly we wanted in our new house, making a list as the miles passed beneath our feet.

It took a day of hard travel, but I finally caught up with the team just outside of Netchdor in Farless Province. Xiaolang had told me to meet them there before I left—Farless was one of those provinces that were willing to enforce Guin's terms. It also possessed a permanent pool. For the experimentation that we wanted to do, this was one of the safest places to tinker.

The pool was largely abandoned, not a soul living within thirty miles of it. Everyone had camped just outside the building where the pool was housed, looking rather well established—apparently they had been here for a day or so, waiting for me. I waved as I came in. "Hey!"

"Garth!" Chatta leapt to her feet, abandoning whatever it was that she was cooking over the fire, and sprinted for me.

I quickly dropped out of the saddle, barely catching her when she threw herself at me. For a purely selfish moment, I hugged her tight enough to make ribs squeak. She laughed, tightening her hold on me in return.

The moment was completely ruined when Night poked me in the ribs with his nose, throwing me off balance. I nearly fell over, which would have been bad because I would've taken Chatta with me. Catching myself, I turned a dark glare on him. "And just what was that for?"

"You're taking up my hugging time too," he informed me with an equally dark glare.

That sent Chatta off into an extended giggle fit. Releasing me, she went to hug my bratty nreesce. "Now, Night, you know that I'd never neglect you."

Sighing in contentment, he rubbed his head against her back, tail swishing happily back and forth.

I watched this with narrowed eyes, plotting different methods of revenge. He's normally a deep sleeper....

Xiaolang saved Night from impending doom by joining the welcoming party. "So how was the trip?"

Shaking off visions of pranks dancing in my head, I smoothed my face out. "Good. My parents adopted Hayden—when I left, the kid was being smothered with attention and loving every minute of it." He was sure to feel overwhelmed soon. It wasn't just parents he had suddenly inherited, but four brothers, two sisters, a niece and a nephew—a veritable wealth of relations.

"Knowing your family, I hadn't expected anything different." A smile crinkled the corners of his eyes. "And our treasure?"

"Delivered to the Sojavel Ra Institute. The place is full of magical experts; they'll figure it all out. I took a moment while I was there and asked them about shutting off permanent pools."

That distracted Chatta from hugging Night, and she pulled away to look at me. "What did they say?"

"Pretty much what you said," I admitted with a weary sigh. "They thought moving the ley line or diverting the power would work. Other than that, our only option is putting some sort of capstone on it."

"I was afraid that might be the answer." She didn't look surprised, just resigned.

"I would like to take a few hours and really look the situation over." My eyes gravitated to the plain grey building where the pool was. "My first instinct on playing with ley lines is to say that it's too dangerous, but I might be wrong."

"It never hurts to double-check," Xiaolang agreed calmly. "But for tonight, rest. You've been very busy the past three days, and I don't want you making mistakes because of fatigue."

Not a bad idea. "I'll not argue."

"Speaking of making mistakes." Night gave me a pointed look. "Aren't you forgetting something?"

Forgetting something? Oh! "Busted buckets, I nearly forgot. Chatta, I picked up some of that sweet bread you like while I was in Del'Hain."

You'd think I'd just offered her a gourmet meal, complete with fine linens, silverware, candles, and music. The smile of unfeigned delight she wore put the suns to shame. "Strawberry?"

"Well, one strawberry, one melon."

Between one heartbeat the next, she darted in and pressed a kiss against my cheek. A slow flush burned its way across my face, and I swear that the place where her lips touched me made my skin tingle.

"You're the best friend in the world, Garth!" she exclaimed, nearly bouncing. "Which pocket is it in?"

I had to pull my scrambled wits together to answer her coherently. "Ah, right pocket, I think."

She darted around Night, happily rummaging in my saddlebags.

I just stood there and watched her with a dazed smile on my face. Shad sidled up to my side, eyes dancing. "Garth, you're blushing."

I threw an elbow at his ribs, which he dodged, the rat.

Why did I get the feeling that I was never going to live this down?

"You've got to tell them about the Advent Mage study group," Night encouraged with snicker.

Chatta paused with her treat in hand. "The what?"

I throttled down my own amusement, just thinking about her probable reaction—actually, the whole team was bound to be amused by this. "Let's sit down," I suggested. "This is a real doozy."

I decided it was safer all around for me to finish dinner while I told the story. I had this hunch that Chatta especially would be rolling on the ground with laughter, begging for mercy, by the time that I finished this story. So I picked up the spoon Chatta had abandoned, stirring the thick stew over the fire, and waited until everyone was sitting down before beginning.

Sitting was the safest position for them to be in, after all.

"So I had to take everything we found in the cave to the Sojavel Ra Institute," I started casually. "While I was in the building, I ran across a room that had a plate on it that read Advent Mage Study."

Everyone choked, torn between shock and laughter.

"Kartal and I had no idea there was such a study," I admitted. It was difficult to keep my face bland. "And as we stood there, just looking at that plate, one of the men in the room demanded to know what I was doing."

"Did he know who you were?" Hazard demanded.

I shook my head. "Not a clue."

"Wait, wait, wait." Chatta held up a hand, her expression incredulous. "The group that is supposed to be the authority on the Advent Mage couldn't recognize him on sight?"

"He really didn't even give me a chance to introduce myself either," I confirmed.

That set Chatta off into mad giggles. She had vast experience with the arrogance of wizards, after all. Hearing them make such colossal mistakes was very entertaining for her. "Please, please let me put this into a memory crystal."

I thought about that for a moment, but why not? The memory was a better way of showing them than my retelling of the story. "All right."

Chatta scrambled around for an empty memory crystal, casting the spell to open it up. I pulled the memory of my encounters with the Advent Mage group to the front of my mind, which Chatta captured effortlessly and stored in the crystal. She hit it with another spell to broadcast the memory so that everyone could see it play in their heads.

I sat back and watched their expressions, reliving the moment with them, and laughing about it all over again. When the memory was over, Chatta and Shad were hanging onto each other, laughing so hard they were having trouble breathing; Xiaolang had one hand over his eyes, errant chuckles escaping from his mouth; Eagle and Aletha were actually quoting their favorite lines to each other, chuckling dementedly; Shield kept rubbing at his lips to erase a smile, with limited success; Hazard was just rolling on the ground, arms wrapped around his middle and begging for mercy.

Watching them, I had this suspicion that this was one memory they were going to ask for an encore—probably as many times as Chatta was willing to cast the spell. Considering how entertained she was, it was going to be a while before she got tired of it.

If she ever did.

This might be a story that just never got old.

The next morning, I got up and bolted down a quick breakfast that Aletha cooked, and went to work.

This wasn't like the normal scrying that I usually engaged in. For one thing, scrying pools like this one have a seal on the bottom of the pool. Part of it is to moderate how much power seeps into it from the ley line, but part of it is to keep mages out. Don had actually warned me about this before we left Coven Ordan—no one wanted a mage accidentally popping into a pool by accident, so they sealed the bottom of it to prevent such a thing from happening. I'm sure this was an excellent precaution under normal circumstances.

But these weren't normal circumstances.

I slowly sank into the ground, senses heightened as much as I could do so. As soon as I got a good look at the ley lines under that pool, my heart sank.

This simply wasn't feasible.

I combed the entire area for nearly a hundred miles in every direction, but I still couldn't find a way to do this without tangling up ley lines past all redemption. Part of me was happy about this—an abundance of ley lines meant fertile soil—but for our purposes, it didn't help one iota.

"Garth, you've been down for an hour now."

Rats, had I really? I lost all track of time when I did this. With a mental sigh, I yanked back into my body.

And, as usual, I felt like I'd been thrown into an arctic pool. I was shivering so hard that I nearly bit my tongue. I really, really hated scrying.

"Garth?" Xiaolang knelt next to me, concern tightening the corners of his eyes. "Are you all right?"

"I h-hate sc-scrying," I chattered back through clenched teeth.

His head cocked at a slightly amused angle. "That didn't answer my question."

"He'll be fine in a few minutes," Chatta assured him. She wrapped a blanket snuggly around me, which did help warm me up.

Shield reached around her, handing me a steaming mug. "Hot tea."

My hands were stiff with cold, but I still managed to grab the mug with something like a death grip. "Bless you."

The first sip scalded my tongue and throat. The heat was delicious. I graduated from sips to gulps, feeling heat seep into frozen muscles. Oh, that was so much better.

"I'm sorry, Garth." Xiaolang was quiet, troubled, and his eyes were focused intently on the ground. "I didn't realize this was so difficult."

"The one part of magic I dislike," I admitted. "But don't worry about it. I know what's going on under our feet now."

"And?" Xiaolang prompted when I stalled.

"Too dangerous," I sighed. "That pool is sitting on a very strong ley line, and it's connected to two others that are equally strong."

"Only three?" Hazard obviously didn't see the problem.

"Three in the immediate area," I clarified. "And those three are connected to other ley lines. Picture—" I paused and tried to put what I had seen into a visual image he could understand. "Try to imagine this. The three ley lines are like three strings braided together. Can you remove one string without tangling the whole braid?"

He frowned, considering this. "I see what you mean."

Aletha was following this closely. "Is there anything we can do?"

"I can collapse the building on top of it. But they could dig it out again." I spread my hands in a helpless shrug. That was the best option I could offer, under the circumstances.

"And it will tip them off that someone with magical abilities is loose, and knows what the pools are," Xiaolang observed in a tired voice. "Too much danger, too little reward."

There was no condemnation in Xiaolang's voice or expression, but I still felt like I had failed, somehow. Like I hadn't met the expectations placed on me. "Sorry." I stared glumly into the mug.

Xiaolang sank onto his haunches. His hand grasped my shoulder, giving me a gentle shake. "Garth, this isn't your fault. None of this mess is your doing."

I grimaced. That didn't make me feel any better. "I know."

"Somehow, I heard a 'but' in there."

"But," I gave him a dry smile, "we both know how much easier this will be without those pools. I feel like…I'm failing all of you by not putting them out of commission."

"Garth." Chatta rolled her eyes heavenward, as if she was praying for patience. "We're not blaming you for that!"

I knew that. Intellectually, at least. But I still couldn't shake the feeling.

"It's not that you can't do it. It's that you won't do it."

I shifted to look at Shad, who was standing behind me. That statement had a wealth of understanding behind it.

Everyone was looking at him now, but it was Eagle that put the question out loud. "What do you mean?"

Shad's eyes never left mine as he explained. "By moving or tampering with a ley line, he risks destroying the land. As an Earth Mage, the idea is abhorrent. It would be a crime worse than murder, wouldn't it, Garth?"

I couldn't have explained it any better than that. "Yes."

New understanding dawned on their faces.

"Ah!" Xiaolang lit up, like a man who had just been handed an epiphany. "So that's the source of it. Hmmm." His eyes went vague, unfocused, as he thought on something the rest of us couldn't detect.

"Ignore him," Hazard advised good-naturedly. "He's gone into deep thinking mode."

"Well, what do we do now?" Aletha wondered. "Garth, do you need much time to recover?"

I waved this worry aside. "No, I'm practically fine now. We can move on if we need to."

"Assuming our illustrious leader snaps out of it…" Shield casually smacked Xiaolang in the back of the head.

"Ow!" Rubbing gingerly at the abused area, Xiaolang turned a dark glare on his first lieutenant. "What was that for?"

"Daydreaming," Shield drawled.

"You didn't have to hit me!" he complained in a near whine.

"Oh, but I did." Shield's smile was not at all nice. "I really, really did."

Xiaolang muttered something under his breath in Q'atalish. I was just as glad that I wasn't able to understand it. Eagle's understanding wince was enough to tell me that.

Hoping to divert a fight I asked, "So where to next?"

Still rubbing at his head, Xiaolang answered, "We go back to our original task. I think we should continue to head south, following the coastline for now. Are you sure you're up to moving right now, Garth?"

"I'm fine," I assured him.

Xiaolang nodded, accepting this. "Chatta, you used the pool earlier this morning. Did you see anything?"

She shrugged, her palms spread helplessly. "I found another Watchman's Pool, but I couldn't see inside. There's a very strong glamour over the building. I think I caught a hint of movement near it, though. There might be someone hiding out in that area."

"Then, people, let's move."

Once back on the road, I resumed searching. I focused more on it than I usually did, partly out of guilt, I admit. Despite my comrades' understanding attitudes, I still felt like I should have done more, somehow.

Chatta has a sixth sense for when I'm sliding into depressing thoughts. It's the only way I can explain why she knows when to come and poke me in the ribs.

I flinched and twisted to frown at her. "What?"

"Stop it," she ordered with a pointed look.

"Stop what?"

"Stop being needlessly guilty."

Easier said than done.

"I mean it, Garth."

What, she read minds now? I looked at her out of the corner of my eye. "How do you know I'm feeling guilty?"

"Because you get this little crease right—there," she pressed her fingertip between my eyebrows, "when you worry about something."

She had me there. I blew out a resigned breath. How did you argue with someone when they were right?

"Garth, remember what you always rant about when people call you the Advent Mage? You always say that you're not a demi-god— you can't do everything, or fix every problem. Remember?"

"That's not it," I refuted. She gave me a look that silently said oh really? "Well, that's not entirely it," I amended. "This is just the first problem that I've been given that I couldn't solve, somehow. The feeling…rankles."

She was trying not to smile, but one leaked past her guard despite her best efforts. "Surely you're not arrogant enough to believe that you can solve all the problems in the world?"

Put like that, and it seemed absurd. "Maybe I spent too much time around Kartal."

"Clearly."

I was about to make some sarcastic remark when I realized that there was someone approaching us. I frowned, turning in that direction. How very…odd.

"Garth?" Chatta looked the same direction I did, puzzled. "What are you looking at?"

"Someone's coming toward us."

"Magical, not magical?" she pressed, curious.

"I'm not entirely…sure," I responded slowly. "They don't even really feel human."

"Not human?" she parroted in surprise.

Apparently her response was loud enough for Xiaolang to hear, because he turned Hayate about and came alongside Night. "What's this?"

"Someone is coming in our direction, someone strange," I explained absently. "They don't feel like anything else I've ever felt."

"Animal, perhaps?" he suggested, looking very intrigued.

That suggestion struck me as wrong, although I couldn't give a rational explanation as to why it was wrong. "No…definitely a sentient being. It has more…awareness to it." That was as close as I could get to describing what I felt.

Xiaolang's eyes narrowed in concentration. He normally wore that look when he was actively using his empathy. His range wasn't that far—somewhere under a mile, or so he told me—but whatever was heading toward us was probably close enough for him to sense at this point.

"You're right, that's definitely a sentient creature." He relaxed after a moment. Far from satisfied, he was even more interested now. "Everyone stop!" he called.

The team came to an abrupt halt, people twisting to look at the captain.

"Garth, I'm getting the impression that whatever that creature is, he's coming to talk to you. I think he's also a bit shy, so we're going to back up a few feet and give you some space."

I nodded, playing along for now. "Did you get any hint of his intentions?"

"Not really. But he doesn't harbor any ill-will, so it should be safe enough to approach him."

Well, that was reassuring. Somewhat. I slid off Night's back and approached the side of the road. We were in the middle of the Flats—a thousand or so acres of grassland that dominated this providence—so the grass was waist high. It was difficult to see anyone or anything until you were practically on top of it.

I had the strangest sense of déjà vu, like I'd done this before—only instead of waiting for a person to come to me, I had gone to them.

The memory hit me hard, for a moment throwing me back two years into the past. This was like when I had found Elis dying in that no-man's land. I could almost taste the smell of blood, and feel the heat of twin suns beating down on me. Adrenaline flooded my system as that long day and night flashed through my mind, when I was being hunted by Manookin and his gang.

"Garth?" Xiaolang's voice was sharp with anxiety.

Shaking my head, I pushed the memory back into the recesses of my head, sealing it away again. That was not one of my more pleasant memories. "Sorry."

"Just a flashback," Night reassured them quietly. "This place strongly reminds him of the time he was turned Jaunten."

And the manhunt I had lived through afterwards.

Xiaolang was not entirely appeased. "We'll talk on this later."

"I second that." Chatta's voice was firm.

We didn't have time to say much else. A moment later, our visitor arrived.

As soon as he cleared the grass, I felt nearly faint with disbelief. A Gardener?!

None of the Solians knew what he was; I could tell by the puzzled sounds they were making. Chatta and Night however, froze in recognition.

Most people regarded Gardeners as a myth, or some sort of backcountry superstition. We barely covered them at the Academy. They were reputed to be a race that understood the earth and its underlying power in ways that no human could possibly match. There were some people that claimed that this world would cease to properly function without their influence. I thought that a bit far-fetched, personally.

Some of what I had learned was correct—at least, this one matched the descriptions. He was barely five feet tall with skin so pale it was nearly snow white. His eyes were larger than normal, a shockingly deep blue with no pupil. He didn't really have hair, more like the fine down of a swan that flowed to his shoulders. He looked unworldly, and strangely beautiful.

After a second of gaping, I kicked myself into action. With a very polite bow, I introduced myself. "I am Rhebengarthen, an Earth Mage from Hain."

He smiled—which strangely made him look like a mischievous child—and extended a hand to me.

Hesitantly, I reached out to take that hand.

And the world as I knew it exploded into a riot of sensations.

Feelings, images, thoughts—all of it was passed on in one lump package. I vaguely felt the impact as my knees hit the dirt, but that wasn't important enough to distract me from trying to unravel everything jumbling in my head. His hand—thankfully—only held mine for a moment. As soon as he stopped touching me, the tidal wave of pure information stopped.

It was only then that I realized Chatta was grasping both of my shoulders, and Night was hovering on my other side.

"Garth?" Chatta was definitely alarmed.

"What was that?" Night demanded. He sounded a little dazed. But as a telepath, I'm sure he was picking up on what I had just experienced.

"I'm okay, I'm okay," I muttered in hasty reassurance, my eyes never leaving the Gardener. My mind was unraveling all of the information it had just been handed. In the…impressions I guess you would call it…I had the sense of time passing. A lot of time passing. And the land being changed, many people working to restore the land from the damage it had taken; of ley lines being reconnected, and energy flowing properly again.

Several things clicked into place. "Of course," I breathed in realization.

"Garth, will you please explain?" Chatta was about one second from shaking answers out of me.

"I always thought it strange that certain parts of Chahir had recovered faster than others. I put it down as simply that it hadn't been as damaged during the war as other places. But that's not necessarily true. The Gardeners have been working all of this time, going from place to place, restoring the land." I abruptly laughed, delighted to finally have an answer to a question that had always alluded me.

"We truly appreciate it," I told the Gardner earnestly. "I didn't dare attempt such a thing on my own—I was afraid of messing everything up trying."

He smiled at me again, sincerely pleased by my response. He reached out his hand once more.

Knowing a little better what to expect, I cautiously touched him, mentally bracing myself for impact as I did so.

The impression this time was briefer, though, and not as convoluted—an image of myself near the Netchdor Pool. There was a layer of curiosity in the picture.

"Yes, I was there," I confirmed when he released me. "Those pools are being used to track down people with magical abilities. We wanted to know if we could shut them off, to prevent them from being used against us."

His head cocked, puzzled.

I shrugged helplessly. "I know I didn't do anything—I couldn't turn the pool off without either tampering or shutting off the ley lines. I didn't dare do either. That would cause too much damage to the land."

He reached out this time, touching my cheek with gentle fingertips, almost like a caress.

This time, there was the picture of other Gardeners working, but now they were around buildings that housed pools. The ley lines under the ground were being moved, their power diverted into other lines.

My eyes went huge as I processed this. "Would you do that? Truly?"

He nodded firmly. His fingers pressed a little harder against my skin. Clear as a bell, I heard: *You helped preserve our work. We shall help with yours.*

I nearly went limp with relief. "Thank you. I can't tell you how much that will help."

That seemed to amuse him. *But we do know. We can feel you as well as you feel us, Balancer.*

Balancer?

From the back of my head, a well worn memory surfaced. When

Trivoxor has chosen a Rider, the Balance will be restored.

Raile had talked about the Balance also, not two weeks ago in Coven Ordan. I gaped in amazement. "How did you know that was me?"

He trilled softly, and the sound was so close to laughter that I couldn't mistake it for anything else. He gazed up into my eyes, and gave me one final fond pat, like a doting relative who had known me all of my life. I had the most eerie impression that he knew me personally, but I had absolutely no idea how.

He left one last impression to not worry about the pools any longer, and then he released my face.

With a bow of acknowledgement to me, he turned and melted back into the grass, disappearing in moments.

"Wow." Night sounded stunned.

I nodded in agreement. Wow just about covered it.

Shad pounced on me. "Will you please explain what just happened?"

I looked into that impatient face and wondered—exactly where do I begin?

After a few moments, I managed to get my mouth working coherently again. "That…was a Gardener."

"And those are?" Eagle prompted with a hint of impatience.

"Gardeners are a race of people that…well, I thought them more legend than anything until this moment. Some people claim they are the ultimate mages—that we human mages are only a shadow compared to them. They know more about the land, and the animals and plants on it, than we can ever begin to understand. They are the ones that restore a land when it is damaged. It is because of their efforts here that Chahir is starting to recover." I looked back to the spot that the Gardener had disappeared, feeling a little surreal and off-balance. "I can't begin to describe…there just aren't words…"

Night bailed me out. "They don't really talk with words. What they do is give you impressions, images, pictures, and scenes, in order to communicate."

"There are layers of emotions in there, too," Xiaolang observed in a slightly strained voice. "I felt that."

"Yes, there was," I agreed shakily. "Apparently they've been keeping an eye on us. He wanted to know what we were doing near Netchdor, at the pool."

"We caught that much," Aletha assured us. "I gathered that they're going to help?"

"They'll shut off the ley lines powering the pools," I confirmed. "They can do the job I can't—they truly understand how the land works, and will be able to change things without consequences. Compared to them, I'm an absolute novice. He told me not to worry about them."

"So they're on our side?" Eagle hazarded.

"…That's not quite right." I frowned, struggling to put into words something I instinctively knew. "He said that what I did helped with their work—preserving the land—and that because of that, they were willing to help me."

Chatta knew most of this already, and while she was interested, she was still fidgeting. "But what did you mean, when you asked that last question?"

I dragged my mind back to the present. "He called me Balancer."

Chatta's eyes went wide. "Oh."

"Yeah." I shook my head, pushing myself up to my feet. This was too much for my poor brain to handle. I felt like my thoughts were running in mad little circles, chasing each other, without any insight.

"So, we don't have to worry about the pools, eh?" Xiaolang was obviously cheered by this development. "Excellent. That will make all of this a bit easier. All right, everyone load back up. We're burning daylight."

I climbed back onto Night. It was a good thing I wasn't on a regular horse, because the rest of the day I was so busy thinking of prophecies, Gardeners, and pools that I didn't pay an ounce of attention as to where we were going.

HINTS

That couldn't possibly be right....

Fighting off a wave of incredulity, I double-checked. I went slowly, taking my time to make sure I had an accurate count.

Forty-one people. Fifteen were magical.

Not twenty miles to the east was a gathering of fifteen magicians. Fifteen.

A gathering such as this would not be unusual in Hain, but in Chahir? I just couldn't wrap my head around it.

After several false starts, I managed to get my mouth and brain working together again. "Xiaolang?"

He turned expectantly, hope vivid on his face. "Yes? Did you find one?"

"More than one," I answered weakly.

"Two? Three?" Something on my face—or maybe he was reading my emotions, who knew?—told him that something was up. "How many Garth?" he asked slowly, his eyes intent.

I had to swallow, twice, before I could force the answer out of my mouth. "Fifteen."

A small, petty part of me enjoyed everyone else's surprise. They nearly fell out of their saddles from the shock. By common consensus, they all turned their mounts to form a rough circle around me.

"Fifteen?!" Shad repeated, nearly choking. "In one place?!"

"Fifteen magicians," I refined, "forty-one people in all. Here's the really weird part—they're all gathered around the pool."

Chatta let out a low whistle. "Now that's unexpected."

No kidding.

Xiaolang nudged Hayate closer to me. "Can you give us anymore information? How many are witches, wizards, or mages?"

I shook my head, feeling helpless and frustrated. "They're too close together, too jumbled up. I can barely tell them apart. The majority are either wizards or witches, I can tell you that much. I think there's at least two mages as well, but don't quote me on that one."

"Fifteen," Xiaolang repeated thoughtfully, exchanging a look with Shield. He looked a little concerned, which was understandable. The most we had ever rescued at one time was three, and that had been a little challenging.

Fifteen would be a nightmare.

And it could well be more than fifteen. No ordinary Chahiran citizen would move to a scrying pool without some very good reasons. Following their magically gifted family member would be one of those reasons. If they were willing to move there, then they would likely move to Hain as well to keep their families together.

"Probably more than just the fifteen," Shad murmured, mind a thousand miles away.

"I think so, too," I sighed. "We're not talking fifteen, but probably forty-one."

Xiaolang went from worried to overwhelmed. "Quite. And I think we better be very careful how we approach them. They'll be on the defensive."

Chatta shook her head in disagreement, mouth set in a grim line. "We're not going to be able to just walk up there, not unless they want us to."

Aletha blinked. "Why?"

Shad, Night, and I all groaned in realization more or less at the same time. Chatta shot us a grimace, partly in agreement, partly in understanding.

"What?" Aletha demanded.

"They're sitting right on top of a permanent pool. It takes no knowledge to use it. Anyone can look at it. Worse—for us—if you don't focus a pool, it shows the immediate surroundings by default."

Xiaolang pinched the bridge of his nose, looking like he was developing a headache. "How much of the surrounding area can they see?"

"It depends on the strength of the ley line supporting it," Chatta answered with a slight frown. "If the ley line is weak, perhaps thirty miles or so. If it's strong…perhaps a hundred."

"Garth, we're about twenty miles away, aren't we?"

I wasn't surprised Xiaolang made that assumption. He knew my range, after all. I just nodded in confirmation.

"So they already know we're here." Hazard sighed, looking distinctly unhappy about the situation.

"But won't they realize we're not the bad guys?" Eagle was looking at me when he asked this. "I mean, these pools tell you when people have magic, don't they? Won't it be obvious that we have a witch and a mage in the group?"

"That's not going to help, in this case." Xiaolang's headache was contagious—I felt one coming on myself.

"Why?" Eagle persisted.

"The Star Order actually has a type of magic as well," Chatta explained in a dead voice. "It's part of the reason why they can detect other magicians. From the outside, we can be mistaken as a Star Order hit squad."

"We're not dressed like them," Aletha pointed out.

"They're in the habit of trying to dress inconspicuously," I stated tiredly. "To them, we'll look like a typical squad; two Star Priests, and a squad of soldiers. The only part of our group that might cause some confusion is Hayate and Didi—everything else will conform to Star Order tactics. Regardless, they're not going to risk it and let us get too close, not without putting up a whale of a fight."

An aggravated groan swept through the group.

Xiaolang pulled himself together, turning Hayate back around. "Let's at least get closer. We're going to have to think of a way to prove our good intentions."

We stopped that night about five miles away from the Hapt-den-War Pool and made camp. It was actually a fairly nice area, a shallow depression in between short rolling hills, with a small stream nearby. We were largely sheltered from the wind and curious eyes. It was a good place to stay.

That was good, considering that we'd probably be here a few days.

I'd like to say that during the day of riding one of us came up with some brilliant plan on how to approach these people, but we didn't. Aletha and Shad—the two sneaks—put their heads together for hours, but couldn't think of a good way to approach without putting people's backs up. They consulted a lot with Chatta, trying to gain an idea of the magical end of things. Not one of them looked pleased by the conclusions they were drawing.

If only the area we were in wasn't so desolate. We were still in the Flats, barely. There wasn't any decent cover out here for miles around. Even some shrubby trees here or there would have helped tremendously.

We all gave up and just focused on setting up camp that night. I managed to trick Aletha into cooking again, so we had something decent for dinner that night. (I might have to watch my back, though. She was rather peeved at me, and that's a dangerous woman to have on one's bad side.) Xiaolang set up a watch, with Hazard taking the first hour.

I rolled out my bedding next to Chatta's. I'd never say this—she'd scalp me if I did—but I was worried about her. I'm pretty difficult to get up in the mornings, but Chatta's darn near impossible. If we were suddenly attacked in the middle of the night, odds were she'd sleep right through it. If something did attack us, I wanted to be close enough to throw up a shield around us both.

I had my eyes closed, and was just beginning to doze off when she dropped into her bedroll.

"Garth?"

"Hmmm?" I responded, feeling much too lazy to use actual words.

"About what happened yesterday…."

That was such an open-ended line I had to wonder what she meant. Yesterday I had come face-to-face with a legend, an actual Gardener. Yesterday I had discovered that I wasn't the expert on earth magic that I thought I was. A lot had happened yesterday. "Which part?"

"About that flashback Night said you had."

Ah. That part. I knew Xiaolang said we'd talk about that, but it hadn't been brought up since then, so I assumed the matter dropped. Looked like I was wrong. This might be somewhat important. I rolled up onto one elbow so that I could look at her. "Yes?"

"You've told me the story, or the bare bones of it, once before." She was sitting cross-legged, a faint line of worry tightening her forehead. "Now that I think about it, you sort of glossed over the part where you found Elis, and when you were made Jaunten. Was it...bad?"

"I'm not sure how to answer that," I responded almost ruefully. "Becoming Jaunten itself isn't painful—just a huge shock to your body. You feel a little...hyperaware, I guess, for several hours afterwards. I didn't really mind that. I still don't. It saved my life, what Elis did, and it's given me incredible knowledge to draw upon ever since. Life would have been much more difficult for me if I weren't a Jaunten."

The solemn set to her eyes didn't change. "Garth, I saw your face in that moment. Whatever memory had you locked up, it wasn't pleasant."

I let out a pained breath. "No. It wasn't. The area yesterday looks a great deal like the land just outside of the Black Ridge Mountains, did you know that? It's all flat grassland. I've never liked areas that open. It's too...empty, too desolate."

A smile flicked across her face, there and gone in the next instant. "I know. You love cities."

"Yes." I smiled up at her, remembering different times that she had laughed at my enthusiasm for being in a crowded city. My smile faded as I remember what I was telling her. "When I left the mountains, heading into the grassland, I was already uncomfortable. And then I smelled something—like rust and salt, and realized it was fresh blood. That just made my unease worse, and put me more on edge. But I went looking for the source, not wanting some wounded animal, half-crazed with pain, attacking me from behind. And then I saw Elis." My eyes screwed shut at the memory.

She took my free hand in one of hers, squeezing gently. "I'm sorry. Am I making this worse, by making you talk about it?"

I shook my head, not sure what to do in this circumstance. "I've never told anyone the details, not like this. Most people heard the story I told you. It's strange, I know, to be so attached to a man I knew for barely a day."

"He changed your world," she whispered in soft understanding. "What's difficult to understand about that?"

I squeezed her hand, feeling comforted. She understood. I'd never been able to convince other people, outside of the Jaunten, why I felt so indebted to Elis.

She gently let me off the hook. "So it was the area we were in that brought the memory back so strongly?"

I nodded gratefully. "Yes, that's it exactly. For a moment, I felt like

I was back in that grassland, looking for something that was possibly dangerous. It's odd, isn't it, how memories ambush you. I haven't relived that moment for nearly a year."

"Did Elis ever have any family?" she asked suddenly.

"A brother, actually. I met him—Jems is his name—at one point, and shared a few hours by exchanging stories. He's a good man, like Elis was." Talking with him had actually given me a better idea of what Elis had been like. I'd been afraid at first that it would be awkward, but Jems had been too easy of a man to like.

Chatta released my hand and relaxed back on her bedroll, curling up comfortably on her side. "Have you ever thought about turning other Earth Mages Jaunten? They'd know everything you know. It would give them a huge advantage."

"Trev'nor is still pestering me about that," I admitted. "And if he still wants to ten years from now, I'll probably give in. But really, I haven't thought much about it."

"But all of that knowledge and experience just lost…" She sounded faintly horrified at the idea.

"It won't be," I pointed out, fighting a smile. "Assuming I can convince some daring woman to marry me, all of my children will be born with Jaunten blood."

She had clearly not considered that. "Oh! That's true, isn't it?"

"And even if that doesn't happen, Hevenreien, Cora's brother, carries my Jaunten inheritance."

"Yes, but he's not quite the same. A mage would have to constantly badger him with questions."

I couldn't argue with that. "Why this sudden curiosity about Jaunten?"

"I just realized that I don't understand that part of you at all. Most of the time, you act like your Jaunten blood doesn't impact you."

"Some of the time, that's true," I allowed. "None of my Jaunten ancestors knew anything about magic. But you'll notice that I've never used a map."

She blinked. "You're right, you haven't. Jaunten knowledge?"

"With all of my ancestors combined, there isn't a cranny in all of Hain that I can't recognize on sight."

"Now that's handy," she observed enviously.

She had no idea. Before I'd become a Jaunten, I was notorious for getting lost.

Didi appeared from the air, landing with a soft thump near Chatta's hip. With a wide yawn that nearly dislocated his jaw, he snuggled in against Chatta's chest. Eyes closed, he chittered in sleepy pleasure.

I stifled a yawn myself. "I think he has the right idea."

Chatta nodded, eyes already falling closed. "Garth…thanks for telling me." The words came out a little slurred.

Smiling, I relaxed and let comforting darkness swallow me whole.

Mmm. Peanut butter. That sounded so good…

Last time I'd had to chase Night around the backyard for it, as Mom only made one batch, and the brat wouldn't share.

Eyes still closed, I shifted a little on the rocky ground. I didn't need to take a peek to know that it was very late at night, and nowhere near my turn to take the watch. Shifting some more, I tried to go back to sleep. It did no good, of course. I was hungry now.

Grumbling, I woke up a little more. I hated food dreams. I always woke up starving from them.

Mom had packed a jar of peanut butter for me right before I left. Unless Night had somehow pleaded/blackmailed/threatened someone into feeding it to him, it should still be there. Maybe I'd be able to sleep some more if I had some.

I was sitting up before I realized that I could hear Night's voice in the back of my head.

"Mmmm. Thick and creamy. So good! As good as Jaylan's…"

That brat! Had he somehow convinced whoever it was on watch to feed him MY peanut butter when I wasn't looking?!

My brain cycled that one through, and then realized that wasn't right. He'd said "as good as Jaylan's." So if it wasn't my mother's peanut butter, whose was it?

"Just one more cracker…no wait, don't make me stretch my neck for it. I'm too far from camp as it is."

What was that idiot doing? Trying to broadcast my mind I asked, Night, what are you doing?

"Um." Don't ask me how, but I could almost feel the guilty wince in that monosyllable.

Where are you getting the peanut butter from? I tried not to sound darkly suspicious, but I was.

"Um...we have a visitor?"

We have a what? Blinking, I tried to wake up enough to think. A visitor? From where?

"I believe that she's from the pool. She hasn't said much about that, but she's definitely a Life Mage. She feels just like Hevencoraan."

Great magic! Bring her into camp, then! I want to talk to her.

"About that...I've tried! She can't believe that I'm talking to her; she keeps thinking it's her imagination or something. I've been trying to make friends with her so she'll come back to camp with me."

How? I inquired dryly. By letting her feed you peanut butter?

"It's all for a good cause," he pointed out righteously.

Cause my left eyeball! I made my mental voice as dry as possible. How noble of you to sacrifice yourself for our sakes, Night. And how is your plan progressing?

"I think it's going to take at least three more crackers of peanut butter."

I groaned, letting my head thump against my knees.

"No, wait, don't go that direction!"

Alarmed, I sat back up. Night, what's going on?

"She keeps drawing me away from the camp. Come on, miss, not that way? We really need to go back..."

Night, she's obviously not comfortable being so close to our camp. Just plant your feet and refuse to move. I'll be there in a second.

"But she's got another cracker just slathered in peanut butter!"

Don't move, I ordered sternly.

"I can just stretch my neck out a little further..."

I groaned. He wasn't listening to me at all. Kicking off my blankets, I tugged on my boots quickly. Night, where are you?

"Head toward the pool, you'll run into me."

I was nearly outside of the fire's light when a shadow detached itself from the ground. My heart leaped in my chest before I realized that it was Shad. "Oh, it's you."

"Yeah. Night's been out there for a while. Do you know what he's doing?"

"Being bribed," I growled.

He blinked. "I'm sorry, what?"

I grabbed Shad as I moved. "Just come on, and try to look nonthreatening."

"Um, they're really not evil…"

Night, what are you talking about?

"She keeps telling me that I'm a beautiful stallion—which she's right about—" I rolled my eyes at the smug tone "—but she also says that she's going to save me from 'those evil men' if I would just follow her."

The 'evil men' being us?

"Probably. Like I said, she's really not listening to me. Mmm. Yum!"

Night will you PLEASE focus?!

"But it's good peanut butter!"

I was going to kill him when I got my hands on him.

"Garth, considering what she said, I don't think it's wise to come any closer."

I flung out a hand, stopping both Shad and I in our tracks. Why not?

"Well, she thinks you guys are the bad guys. If you show up now, it's just going to spook her."

You say that like you have an idea in mind.

"Of course I do. I'll go back with her, and talk to the people at the pool."

I groaned, heading falling back to look at the starlit sky.

"What?" Shad demanded. "Will you please tell me what's going on?"

"Apparently there's a young Life Mage that lives up at the pool," I explained in a rapid undertone. "She's come down to try and steal Night away. I doubt she knows what he really is—every time Night tries to talk to her, she thinks it's her imagination." The girl must have quite the imagination. "She must be quite charming. Night thinks it's a wonderful idea to go back with her." I rolled my eyes.

"Like a spy behind enemy lines?" Shad was about a hair's breadth from bursting out laughing.

"Something along those lines." I made my mental voice as firm as possible. Night, you're not going back with her. Get that notion right out of your head.

"Seriously, Garth, I think this will work."

You're only saying that because you want more peanut butter!

"She's a sweet girl," Night defended himself, "and it's not like I'll be in any danger."

I took in a deep breath, and tried to remain calm and reasonable. Night, listen very closely. This girl is a Life Mage. If she doesn't believe that it's you talking, no one else up there is likely to. They'll think it's some Star Order trick. Believe me, I know how deep the paranoia about the Star Order runs in this country. It's only gotten worse since I left two years ago.

"Can't I at least try?" he asked plaintively.

We DO have our own peanut butter, you know.

"Yes, but you won't feed it to me!"

I buried my face in my hands. Sometimes Night was so mature and reasonable, that I forgot he was still a teenager. Or at least, I forgot until he did something like this and reminded me. Tomorrow morning, I promise to feed you half the jar. Just don't, whatever you do, walk off with a perfect stranger?

"How about the whole jar?"

I'll have Didi braid pink ribbons through your hair if you don't come back right this instant, I threatened.

"Garth, I'm dying from suspense here!" Shad complained.

"I'm arguing with a teenage Nreesce with a death wish," I half-growled.

"Ah. Judging from your expression…are you losing?"

"Badly."

Shad had the bad taste to snicker.

"Uh-oh. Garth, you better get here quick. She just pulled out a halter."

Aw rats! Duck it! I ordered quickly.

"I'm trying to!"

"Shad, run!" I took off as I said this, pelting around the curve of the hill.

"What's going on?" Shad demanded at my elbow.

"She's got a halter she's trying to put on Night."

"And how hard is he trying to avoid that halter?" Shad wanted to know, a demented grin tugging at his mouth.

"Peanut butter, halter…peanut butter, halter…Garth, how close are you?"

Night, if you're thinking about accepting that bribe, think again. You know the second you take it she's going to get that halter on you.

"But you're close enough to rescue me, right?"

NIGHT!

"It's a perfectly reasonable question!"

No, it is NOT!

"…Oops."

I just groaned.

Shad gave me a quick glance. "He got caught, didn't he?"

"Sounds like it," I sighed.

Fortunately, we were close. We came up another shallow depression, and nearly stumbled right into Night. He was standing there with a sheepish look on his face, a halter half-buckled on him.

Standing at his head was a slim girl with waist-length hair. I couldn't tell much about her, considering the wan lighting of the moon, but she was definitely a Life Mage.

She took one panicked look at us, dropped the halter, and bolted.

"No, wait!" I called uselessly after her. "Busted buckets." She was fast, maybe faster than me. "Shad, after her!"

I'd never met anyone that could outrun Shad. He was on her trail before I could get the words out of my mouth, grass moving noisily under his feet as he moved.

In seconds, he caught her arm. "Wait, we're not here to hurt anyone—"

I knew, intellectually, that a Life Mage can do more than communicate or sense all life forms. They can mimic them, too. But I'd never seen that in action. It was certainly quick! One minute Shad had a hold on a girl's arm, the next, she was gone.

"Where'd she go?" I looked around in panic.

"The cat!" Shad yelled, pointing off to the right. "Catch the cat!"

She'd turned herself into a cat?! I took off in pursuit, trying to watch the motion of the grass. The grass was too thick and tall to see a cat, but she was sure to disturb the grass as she moved, and that would help us figure out where she was.

Shad and I pelted all out, searching for her at frantic speed. Shad dove and nearly caught her once, but she sped out of his hands at the last second.

Maybe she got tired of being chased. Or maybe she was just scared and acting on the defensive. All I know was, one second I was chasing a small house cat, the next, she had turned into this black, ferocious looking panther. With a roar, she spun on her hind legs, and charged.

"Whoa!" Out of sheer survival instinct, I did an about face and started running the other direction. I snagged Shad as I ran, throwing up a shield around us as soon as I was close enough.

She skidded to a stop, pacing just outside of the shield, snarling at us in rage.

"We're not enemies!" I shouted in exasperation. "Will you calm down and listen?"

Xiaolang appeared out of nowhere, boots unlaced and a sword in hand. "What is going on out here?!"

Shad pointed at the panther. "Xiaolang, catch her!"

Our illustrious captain took a good look at the huge cat facing us and he demanded incredulously, "Catch that? Are you crazy? No way!"

"But—!" I couldn't get the explanation out fast enough. Once she realized that Xiaolang was armed, she took off again, disappearing quickly into the thick cover of darkness. I could have found her again, of course. My eyes might be useless, but I could still sense her. But there was no way I could catch her.

And I wasn't sure, now that I'd calmed down some, whether that was the best approach anyway.

"Too late," Shad sighed.

Xiaolang raked a frustrated hand through his disheveled hair. "Will someone please explain what is going on?"

I glared at my nreesce. "We have a traitor in our midst."

Night gave me an offended look. "I am not!"

"And who was bonding over peanut butter?" Shad's expression was a little too innocent.

"I was making friends with her!"

Xiaolang sank his head into his free hand. "This is going to be good, I can see it now. All right, back to camp. You can fill me in there."

TACTICS

My hand clenched around my mug as once again, female laughter rang in the air. I didn't mind that they were enjoying themselves. Truly. It was always nice to see pretty women laughing.

But did it have to be at my expense?

"…And then she turns into a cat…" Aletha gasped, tears of mirth streaming down her cheeks.

"And Super Soldier over here couldn't catch her," Chatta added with a look at Shad.

"Neither could the all-powerful Advent Mage," Shad drawled in return. He wasn't upset—Shad's twisted sense of humor still thought the whole situation last night was hilarious. Seeing the girls laugh about it just upped the level of entertainment for him.

"…and then she turns into a panther…" Despite the fact that Aletha and Chatta had already gone over this story three times, they both cracked up again.

"And Garth automatically runs from her!" Chatta had an arm wrapped around her waist, gasping. "Oh—stop, stop, it's too much!"

Aletha had either no pity, or was too amused to stop now. "Night, come tell us what his face looked like."

I shot a glare at my nreesce. "Do and die."

Night's eyes darted between me and Chatta, and I didn't need to be a telepath to know that he was tempted to tell the girls all about last night despite how I felt about the matter.

"Oh, better!" Chatta had this expression on her face that I didn't trust. Every time I'd seen that particular look, mischief followed. "Night, come here. We'll make a memory crystal of last night."

Oh no. No, no, no, no, no! Have last night as a crystal memory, so that everyone in the world (or in Chatta's reach, same difference) would know about it? Over my dead body. The glare I gave Night could melt steel when he took a step forward. "Night, if you take one more step, I will ban you from peanut butter for LIFE."

Night froze in mid-step. "Seriously?" His eyes were wide with alarm.

"Now, Garth." Chatta was smirking at me.

I gave her the most menacing glare possible. "I can't stop you from laughing about last night, but if you think that I'm going to sit idly by and watch you spread that memory around, you've been eating too many mushrooms."

She blinked at me, all innocent naiveté. "But they're such good mushrooms! They make me see pretty colors."

Two could play this game. "Seriously, you'd better stop. You're starting to glow."

"I'm a witch, I'm supposed to glow!"

"A neon green?"

Chatta, as she normally does, fell to insults when she started losing. "Vertically challenged pipsqueak."

"Mother of a fat drunken pig," I retorted immediately.

"Ha! Shrunken freak of nature!"

"At least I'm not vertically challenged!"

"Obviously I need to teach you more insults!"

"Why? Mine's fine—it's short and simple, rather like you."

"Oooh, first blood." Shad was watching us with unholy glee.

Chatta gave him a glare that could have frozen a man on the spot. "Garth, how about a temporary truce?"

"In order to beat up on Shad?" I eyed him thoughtfully. He had been the one to tell the story to the girls, which had started this whole thing. Yeah, I could be decently mad at him. "You're on."

"Excellent," she purred. She drew her wand from her sleeve in a particularly sinister manner.

Shad didn't look as nearly as worried as he should. "Now, now, let's not be hasty. We're all friends, aren't we?"

"We'll leave you breathing," I promised with a feral smile.

Xiaolang cleared his throat, effectively capturing our attention. Even though he was only half-dressed (still without jacket and boots), and was sitting on his bedroll, he still somehow radiated authority. "May I remind you that we're barely five miles away from a very nervous group of magicians? No fooling around."

"Killjoy," Chatta accused him.

I nodded in quick support of this opinion.

"Ah, c'mon, C2!" Shad sounded like a whiny three-year-old. "I can take 'em. Having them both out for my blood makes for a really good workout."

Xiaolang rolled his eyes. "Why must I be the adult here? And what's this C2 nonsense?"

"I was made a captain long before you were," Shad explained with a shrug. "So you're Captain Number Two—or C2, for short."

Xiaolang rolled his eyes, either in a sign of exasperation, or to pray for patience, I wasn't sure. "Shad, you have the most convoluted mind I've ever known."

"Why, thank you, C2!"

"That wasn't a compliment."

"You want to try beating some sense into me?" Shad nearly sparkled at the notion.

"No!" Xiaolang growled in irritation.

Shad slumped, crestfallen. "I can't pick a fight with anyone this morning. You're all a bunch of old women."

Xiaolang had no sympathy. "You'll live, Shad."

Grumbling, he slunk off away from the camp, picking up his sword as he went.

"He's not good at waiting, is he?" Shield observed in amusement as he watched Shad stalk away.

"That's only part of the problem," Xiaolang muttered under his breath.

I waited for him to explain that cryptic comment, but he focused on putting his boots on, not saying another word on the subject.

Once Chatta got over her amusement, that mind of hers started to analyze the situation. "But how did she know how to switch forms like that?" I think the question was largely rhetorical, but she was still looking at me in confusion.

"That part didn't make sense to me either," I confessed. "Cora was telling me that it took practice switching forms. And she had to be shown how to do it." Thank heavens the Remnant Mages had shown up, especially Hay-el D'Auch. Without her, Cora would have really struggled.

"Hmmm." It wasn't quite a sound of agreement, just one of deep contemplation. Then she straightened abruptly, snapping her fingers. "Storage."

She'd lost me. "I'm sorry, what?"

"When the Watchmen Pools were actually in use, they were used as more than just magical watchtowers," she explained rapidly. "They served as way stations for magicians, too, if needed. And things were stored there as well."

My eyes went a bit wide as the full implications sank in. "So there could very possibly be magical artifacts in that building?"

"More than just that, but books, and parchments, and memory crystals, and weapons, and who knows what else!" she disagreed.

Xiaolang looked up from his boots, joining the conversation. "So you're suggesting that this Life Mage could have self-taught herself using these books?"

"Assuming they're there? Yes, it's a definite possibility."

"I think that's exactly what happened," I offered slowly, running last night's events back through my mind. "It would explain the gaps in her knowledge. Not recognizing what Night was, for instance. Not knowing by looking at me what I am. My shield should have been a dead giveaway."

Xiaolang looked pained. "So you're telling me that we have fifteen half-trained, self-taught magicians up there who are feeling defensive? Lovely. Thanks so much for sharing."

"It wouldn't do any of us any good if we went in blind-folded to the possibilities," Chatta pointed out with ruthless logic.

Our poor captain pinched the bridge of his nose, groaning. "This just makes a difficult situation worse."

Chatta gave him a sympathetic smile. "Sorry. Maybe we're wrong."

"No," he sighed. "I'm not that lucky. Besides, that theory fits too neatly to not have some element of truth in it."

I was afraid he was right. "So how are we going to approach this?"

"We'll try being polite, first."

Sometimes, polite doesn't work.

Xiaolang thought it a bit much to bring all of us—it would send off the wrong signals. So he just took me and Shad with him. We got within two miles of the pool, and explosions came out of nowhere.

It was such a strange mix of attacks—bolts of fire, rocks zipping at dangerously high speeds, raw magic that could char bone. They were all lethal attacks, certainly, but not normal; none of the ordinary attack methods that a wizard or witch would use in battle. (And considering how many times I'd sparred with Kartal and Chatta, I could recognize those spells instantly.)

We'd been forced to hastily retreat. Shad was all for pressing forward—he hadn't had any difficulty evading the attacks—but Xiaolang held back. We didn't want to hurt these people, our future allies. And it would take some serious damage at this point to get them to stop.

I shielded us as we went back to the camp, not quite trusting that we were out of their range yet.

"Phew, that was fun!" Shad was nearly bouncing as he walked, eyes sparkling. "Can I do that again tomorrow?"

"No," Xiaolang ordered in amusement. "You're likely to get carried away."

"But I haven't been up against a challenge like that for nearly two hundred years! I wouldn't hurt anybody. Please?"

"No."

"Kill joy."

"But I'll have you and Aletha try to sneak in tonight."

Shad's face nearly split with a demented grin. "All right! Now we're talking."

"Just those two?" I objected. There were, after all, forty-one people up there.

"If it comes to a matter of sheer numbers, then we've already lost," Xiaolang answered patiently. "And these two are my experts at infiltration."

"I like sneaky," Shad supported this with a fervent nod. "Sneaky is fun."

He was getting waaaay too into this. "At least remember not to get caught near the pool," I said, suddenly remembering that there was a shield under it. "I can't break through the seal without some serious consequences."

Shad didn't look as daunted by this warning as he should have been. "What kind of consequences?"

"The building collapsing on top of your head, for instance."

"Ahhh. That wouldn't feel too good."

"It would ruin your whole day," I agreed dryly.

"Garth, do me a favor? Don't rescue me."

I snorted. He was going to eat those words later.

No matter how powerful a pool might be, it still had limits. If you were hiding in a city, for instance, the magician using the pool would be hard pressed to pick one person out of a crowd. Same idea applies to forests, and twisty mountain passes. Permanent pools are built to oversee a wide range of land all at once, which is very handy—but it's hard to focus on smaller details. Only a truly gifted wizard or witch can coax a close-up view from a pool, which was what made Don's work so impressive back in Coven Ordan.

The problem was we weren't sure just how good the magicians up there were when it came to using that pool. How much of us could they really see, or were we little better than small figurines for them?

Chatta, Xiaolang and I gathered well away from the fire that night, giving Aletha and Shad some last minute tips before they went skulking.

"If their pool is truly on the default setting like we think it is then they won't be able to see you," Chatta assured them for the second time. "All they'll see is pitch blackness, except for our campfire. You shouldn't have any trouble."

"Go slow," Xiaolang cautioned. "They might have some automatic defenses in place that we don't know about. After all, they've been here for a while—there's no telling what they've done."

"Yes, Da," Shad replied sweetly.

"Oh, get out of here," Xiaolang shot in exasperation. "And don't get caught!"

With a casual salute, the pair slunk off into the darkness. There was only a sliver of moonlight to see by, which hopefully would help them. With nothing else to do, we went back to the fire. The wind had a definite nip to it, which didn't surprise me, as we were quickly heading for winter. Fall was nearly over now. Hayate was huddling under his charmed blanket, and the look he gave Xiaolang was downright pitiful.

"Cold," he mourned.

"I know, we all are," Xiaolang sighed. "Garth, how cold does it get in Chahir?"

"Pretty cold," I admitted. "Especially up here, since we're so far to the north. I've heard that it gets cold enough up here to freeze a man's hand to wood."

Hazard especially was giving me an appalled look. He hated the cold almost as much as Hayate. "That's ridiculous! What do people do up here during the winter?"

"Stay inside," I answered dryly.

"This part of Chahir is infamous for its ice storms," Eagle added. He looked slightly troubled, as if he were just now remembering this information. "They can blow in within hours, and the ice lasts for days at a time."

I nodded confirmation. "I had an aunt that lived up here with her husband. After about ten years, she got sick of it and dragged her family back south, where it was warmer."

Xiaolang hummed thoughtfully. "What are the possibilities that people would try to leave Chahir in the dead of winter?"

I hesitated, thinking that question over. When I answered, I was confident in my opinion. "Slim to none, weighing more to the none side. It becomes far too dangerous to travel in winter. It's like a death sentence to travel more than a mile or so outside of the home. Even the garrisoned troops don't move. If anyone's abilities did wake up during winter, they wouldn't dare try to escape before spring."

"Death sentence, eh? Even for us?"

"Especially for us." My voice was grim.

"Because we don't have guaranteed shelter," Chatta murmured in understanding.

"Or a guaranteed food supply," Shield grumbled.

Xiaolang's eyes narrowed in contemplation. "I see. How long do you think it will be before winter really sets in?"

"Another month, at most." Ruefully, I added, "I wish we'd had this conversation three days ago before we met up with the Gardener. He would have known the exact answer to that question."

Even though Xiaolang couldn't possibly see it, his head turned in the direction of the pool. "Then this could very well be the last group that we rescue for the year. We don't dare move around during winter."

"No," I agreed.

"That might be a good thing," Xiaolang reflected.

"Why, because we're all a little haggard and threadbare?" Shield held up a sock and stuck a finger through the hole in the toe.

"Partly." Xiaolang grinned at him. "And we're all tired. This is very nerve-wracking work. Tired men make mistakes. We all need a little rest and relaxation."

From the east, there was a sudden explosion of magic and light. I jerked up to my feet automatically, scanning the area. "Rats. I think they were just discovered."

"I can't see," Chatta complained under her breath. "They're too far out."

"How far?" Xiaolang demanded, coming to stand at my side.

"About two miles..." I answered slowly. "In fact, pretty close to where we were caught yesterday."

He groaned. "That answers that question—they have permanent armaments in place."

Another explosion of light flashed brilliantly on the horizon, this one further in. I swore under my breath. "Chatta, did you see that?"

"Yes, and I recognize the spell," she replied grimly. "And there's no way that spell can be altered for some sort of defense. A person has to cast that one."

"Long distance?" Xiaolang guessed.

"Oh yes." Her mouth quirked in one corner in a humorless smile. "This also answers another of our questions. They can use that pool."

I realized what she meant, and felt like banging my head against something hard in sheer frustration. "Of course."

Xiaolang looked at us, slightly puzzled.

"They have to do something to the pool to influence the image to lighten," Chatta explained in a morose tone. "That takes a bit of practice, to see at night. They're better at manipulation than we gave them credit for."

"Half-trained magicians," Xiaolang grumbled under his breath. "Guardians deliver us."

Shad and Aletha came running up a few minutes later, both a little breathless and something the worse for wear. Shad had a scratch on one thigh, and Aletha looked like she had been scorched by an open flame—nothing serious, but I think if she hadn't reacted quickly enough, it could very well have been serious.

"Sorry, C2, but mission failed." Shad probably meant to sound contrite, but was too high on adrenaline to be convincing. "But man, was that fun!"

"Speak for yourself." Aletha was definitely put out with the evening. "Those idiots scorched my hair. Just look at this!" She waved the tip of her braid in the air—and I saw what she meant. At least an inch or so was melted.

"I'll fix it," Chatta soothed. "Just come over here, where there's enough light for me to see by."

The girls went over to the fire, talking with animated gestures as they went.

Xiaolang looked like he was ready to join me with the head bashing. "So did we learn anything tonight, or was it a complete waste of time and effort?"

"Oh, they can definitely see us," Shad assured him. "At first it was just the ground fortifications. Those are even more challenging than going against a wizard or a witch—the spells just came up out of the ground. You either dodged 'em or you were toast. But after Gorgeous and I got past those, they started flinging spells at us from the roof. And then we ran into the second line of defense. We couldn't watch both ground and air at the same time, so we decided to retreat."

"We barely made it back out alive," Aletha grumbled.

"Second line of defense, eh?" Xiaolang rubbed his chin thoughtfully. "That speaks of military expertise. Actually, the whole set up reminds me of military experience."

"They could have someone with a soldier's background up there," I pointed out. "We have no idea what these people used to do before they moved."

Xiaolang didn't seem to appreciate this thought. "I hate planning with little information." With a sigh, he turned back toward us. "All right, let's get some sleep. And I expect someone to think of something brilliant by tomorrow morning. Otherwise, we're doing this the hard way."

THE HARD WAY

I was shaken awake the next morning by an urgent hand. "Garth? Garth! Wake up."

Shad sounded worried, which didn't say good things to my still half-asleep mind. Shad was never really worried about anything. By the time that Shad grew concerned about something, everyone else was running for cover. My eyes snapped open and I sat up abruptly, looking around me in growing panic. We weren't under sudden attack were we?

No…the camp was still this morning, most people still sleeping. The sole exceptions were Shad and Xiaolang, who were both kneeling next to my bedroll. "What?" My mouth felt like it was made of glue and wool, making it difficult to speak.

Xiaolang's words were so quick that it took a second for half of them to sink in. "Shad thought of something. Before, we thought that the Star Order was finding magical people through the pools, but that isn't always the case—it can't be. Three of the pools are abandoned. So if the Star Order isn't finding people by the pools in those provinces, then how are they finding them?"

I stared at him, brain so fuzzy that only half of that question made any sense. Taut seconds ticked by while I tried to think logically, but the only thing my brain could come up with was, "Tea. I need hot tea."

Shad rolled his eyes. "Why is it that both of our magical experts are impossible to wake up in the morning?"

I groaned, covering my eyes with one hand. "Why can't you come up with the complicated questions after I've had breakfast?"

Xiaolang chuckled slightly at our banter, but being the nice man he was, got up and fetched me a cup of hot tea.

It was comfortably hot, not scalding, so I chugged it down. "Now, say that one more time. Slowly."

Shad started speaking, giving me the gist of the problem again. While the heat spread through me, waking me up a little, I tried to think their question through. We'd assumed that the pools must be how the Star Order was tracking down all of the magicians in Chahir. And that was true, to a point—but in Coven Ordan, Don had pointed out three pools that were abandoned. Obviously in those provinces, the Star Order had to use some other method than the pools to detect magicians. The triangle was one way, of course, but you had to be practically on top of a person before that would register anything.

"I'm not an authority on how Star Order magic works," I said slowly, thinking out loud. "No one is, outside of that Order. They keep their magic a closely guarded secret. But they could have their own version of scrying pools, or something that works along the same lines. In fact, for them to be effective, they'd have to have something along those principles."

"So it wouldn't be farfetched to assume that they could see what we're doing here?"

I stared at Shad, horror blossoming like poison in my chest. "Great good magic," I rasped, "they could very well do just that. Worse, they probably are. With all of the magic that's been thrown around the past three days, we might as well have set off fireworks to announce what we are doing."

Xiaolang raised his fingertips to rub at both temples. "I was afraid that would be the answer. Trevesa. All right, we're going to need to make some rapid decisions here. How big of a force will they send to deal with us?"

"The Star Order really isn't that big." I was thinking rapidly, pulling together everything I had learned about them and the little I knew from Jaunten knowledge. "They depend on the government to support them. They're not going to have a lot of people to draw from. Still, I would expect about twenty or so from the Star Order and about a hundred garrison troops."

Xiaolang blanched. "That's overkill, isn't it? There are barely fifty of us."

"They don't take anything for granted." My mouth set in a grim line. "I could very well be underestimating it. They're known for trying to overwhelm their opponent on two-to-one or three-to-one odds."

A deep frown was etched into Shad's forehead. "Didn't your father say that when you were caught in Tobadorage a squadron of twenty men was sent to capture you?"

"Yes."

"Twenty against six," Xiaolang said softly. "Overwhelming odds, indeed. Were any of them part of the Star Order?"

"No. I'm not sure why," I reflected thoughtfully. This wasn't something I had considered before. The Star Order usually populated the cities more than the country, just for the simple fact that it took more people in the city to keep track of such a dense population.

Xiaolang was already moving on, thinking ahead. "Regardless, we need to start planning for the worst. We've already been here three days. I wouldn't be surprised to see them start arriving today, or early tomorrow."

I couldn't disagree with that analysis. The nearest city was only about forty miles away. It would take a day to get people organized to move, and awhile to get here. We were actually lucky that they hadn't descended on us earlier. "The foot soldiers won't prove any problem for me to deal with. I can wipe out most of them in a few minutes. But the Star Order…." My hands clenched on my mug as dark suppositions whirled in my head. "Their magic is very strange. I've only witnessed it once, and it wasn't like anything else I've ever seen or heard of. I'm not quite sure how to combat it, Xiaolang." And I didn't want Chatta anywhere near it.

"I'm not quite as worried about that as you are." Xiaolang flashed Shad a tight, feral smile. "After all, I have an expert who can get past magical attacks. Even the Star Order is susceptible to a foot of steel."

Shad sparkled like a child let loose in a candy store. "Now there's a thought. Maybe I can get some fun after all."

"I thought you'd like that." Xiaolang's smile widened for a moment. "My main concern is the people at the pool. They've proven that they can defend themselves, but against expertise and that number of opponents? They wouldn't really last against us for long, if we went all out. It's only our hesitation in hurting anyone that has let them hold up this long."

I couldn't disagree with that analysis. "I can put up a barrier around it," I offered.

"Something like what you did around Q'atal?" Xiaolang perked up, intrigued by the idea.

"Yes, something like that."

"This won't exhaust you, will it?"

Considering how I had collapsed when I last did this, I suppose the question and concern was valid. "No, not at all. This will be much smaller, just around the pool itself. It will take minutes to set up, and hardly any energy on my part."

Xiaolang thought about it for a moment before nodding firmly. "Do it now. Shad, wake everyone else up. We need to make some contingency plans."

Shad had far too much fun waking everyone up. He pounced on people, bouncing on their stomachs, messing with their hair—he pinched Hazard's nose shut so he couldn't breathe, which had the large man flailing awake in instinctive panic. By the time everyone was semi-conscious, they were all ready to kill him.

Me, I just sat back and enjoyed the show.

I had a twisted sense of humor—I'd never claimed otherwise.

Taking pity on my friends, I cooked breakfast that morning. Hot food put everyone in a slightly better mood, and by the time they were done eating, Shad's imminent death had been downgraded to mere dismembering.

Considering the high caliber of soldiers and magicians out for his blood, I thought Shad looked a bit too calm. But then, it was Shad. The world would have to be on the verge of cracking open before he started to really worry.

We were down to scraping the bottom of our plates when Xiaolang cleared his throat, calling our attention to him. "All right, now that we're all here in body and mind," Xiaolang cast everyone a dry smile, "let's start thinking. Garth, can you give us a warning when the Star Order is coming?"

I paused, carefully phrasing my reply. "I can feel anyone from the Star Order from a distance, yes. I won't be able to give you a very accurate account of how many soldiers are with them. Or how well they're armed."

That definitely gave Xiaolang food for thought. "Hm. Chatta?"

"I'll have to do a scrying, of course, but I can show you exactly what we're up against."

"In that case, you search."

She gave him a casual salute. "On it, Captain."

"For the rest of you, our plans are still going to be shaky at this point, as we have little idea of what the enemy will react like. But I think we'd better start doing some contingency planning. Garth is going to put a barrier up around the pool to keep any unwanted visitors out."

An unbidden thought popped up in the back of my head. "I'm going to need to send them some sort of message. Otherwise, if they start hurtling magical attacks at that barrier, it's going to bounce right back at them."

Chatta smacked her forehead with the palm of her hand. "Argh, you're right!"

"Not to mention they might have a heart attack if this glowing dome suddenly drops over them," Shad observed in sarcastic humor.

That was another valid thought. "Right. Didi, I'm going to write a letter to them. Do you think you can dive through and deliver it?"

"Di!" Didi drew himself up in a cocky manner.

Chatta was studying her flying friend with clear worry written all over her face. "I'm not sure about this, Garth. I mean, he's small and quick, but...they have some formidable spells over there."

"Have you got a better idea?"

"Actually...I might." She tugged a free lock of hair in and out of her fingers, obviously thinking. "We've been shown they have an excellent command of that pool, right?"

"Right," I agreed, wondering where she was going with this.

"And they're just as obviously keeping a very close eye on us."

I made a noise of agreement, encouraging her to go on.

"So why do we need to go all the way there to give them a message? Why can't I just scrawl something in large, glowing letters here, so they can read it?"

How was it that it's always the simple answers that evade me? Was my brain defective somehow? "I like it. Xiaolang?"

"Make the letters at least a foot long, so they can easily read them," he ordered. "And run it by me before you write anything down."

"Right." I rummaged in my pack until I found my hereto-unused map making supplies. Pulling a piece of paper free, and a pen, I set to it. Chatta looked over my shoulder, offering suggestions and corrections. After a few minutes of concentration and work, it came out to read like this:

To the people at the pool:

We are a team of magicians and soldiers from Hain, tasked by King Guin to rescue anyone with magical abilities in Chahir. We are aware that there are fifteen magicians at the pool now, and wish to help bring you safely out of Chahir and into Hain.

Right now, we suspect that the Star Order knows about you, and will be coming here soon. Either today or early tomorrow, we think. To protect you, we will put a protective barrier around the pool. This barrier will not allow anyone inside that means to harm you. The Star Order cannot directly attack you with the barrier in place. However, do NOT cast magical attacks through the barrier. They will reflect back on you. The barrier is meant to deflect magical attacks of all sorts.

"Anything else I should add?" I asked her.

"Hmm…I don't think so. Xiaolang?" she called.

Xiaolang broke off the conversation he was having with Hazard and crossed to us. I handed him the paper, watching as he read it through quickly. "That's good enough," he finally pronounced. "But put it into Chahirese."

I blinked, and then realized that I had automatically written it in Hainish. I hadn't even thought about it. Granted, I had been speaking Hainish a great deal over the past two years, but still. Habit was a wonderful thing. "Right. Chatta, if you'll do the honors?"

"Um…re-write it in Chahirese first?" She gave me a sheepish smile. "I don't always spell everything right."

As I had coached her more in being able to speak the language fluently than being able to read it this didn't surprise me. I took it back from Xiaolang and rewrote it quickly.

When I was done, Chatta went off to the side, far away from the camp to have enough room. Writing that much with one foot long lettering was going to take up a lot of space.

Against the thick grass of the flatlands, glowing letters of blue light danced, highly visible. It actually looked sort of neat. Magic was absolutely brilliant sometimes.

All of the soldiers had their heads together, talking strategy and plans, which I would have very little to do with. My weapons were generally big rocks, after all. Oh, and sand. Sand was my friend. It's wonderfully easy to manipulate. That considered, I drifted over to Night, who was (unsuccessfully) attempting to open the last jar of peanut butter with his teeth.

"How long should we wait for them to read this before I go put up that barrier?"

He raised his head, eyeing me thoughtfully. "Ten minutes? Long enough for it to sink in, but not so long that they try to stop you."

That sounded about right. I was glad that I didn't have to get any closer to that pool to raise the barrier. Trying to dodge attacks and do complicated magic was a sure way to get scorched.

"Garth, I'm begging here. Please, please, open this."

I slanted him an evil look out of the corner of my eyes. "You ate a whole jar. That one is mine."

"But I'll need my energy soon!" he wheedled. "Please?"

It was true that we'd be going home soon, and I'd get more peanut butter then. And it was also true that he carried me everywhere, and he'd need the extra energy later.

But busted buckets, I didn't want to share.

Night lifted one hoof, eyeing it thoughtfully, and then turned that same look on the jar. I just knew that he was considering breaking the jar open to get what he wanted. That pretty much decided me. "Okay, okay, just don't bust it open!" I said hastily, waving him down. "And you can't have all of it, just half."

He was so glad to get some that he agreed readily to this. I dug out some crackers—thankfully not smashed too badly—and started feeding him peanut butter. Sighing in pure bliss, Night flicked his tail and let his eyes droop, crunching away contentedly.

I watched him, exasperated and smiling. He really was a peanut butter addict. I never should have fed him the stuff.

"Okay, all done!" Chatta bounced over, snitched a cracker, and dipped it into peanut butter before I could stop her.

"Hey, that's mine!" Night straightened in alarm. You'd think she'd just tried to steal his firstborn child or something.

"Don't be selfish, Night," she returned easily, happily munching through her snack.

I fed him another cracker to stop more wails of protest. "Now all we need to do is wait a few minutes."

"That's all you need to do," Chatta corrected, "I get to do a scrying and see if I can't find any Star Order Priests lurking about."

"Yeah, have fun with that."

Wrinkling her nose in aggravation, she went to fetch a canteen. "Garth, I don't have a bowl handy for this. We used it for dinner last night. Make one for me, would you?"

"Sure." That wasn't a difficult thing to do. "How big do you want it?"

She ran her wand thoughtfully along the edge of her chin. "About two feet across?"

"Okay." I focused on a clear spot, off to the side of the camp, raising hard bedrock up to the surface. When it was clear of grass, I melted it enough to change the shape, forming a shallow bowl two feet in diameter. "Like that?"

"Perfect, thanks." She settled near it, pouring water in carefully.

While I was waiting, I fed Night one more cracker. He tried to get two more, but he'd already eaten half the jar, and I wasn't encouraging his habit to eat like a pig. With the jar safely stowed away, I figured that it would behoove me to put a saddle and bridle on him. We might not have enough time to get ready later.

Judging that I'd waited long enough, I walked a few feet away from camp, just to put all of the distractions behind me. Barriers were tricky things to deal with—I'd only done it wrong once. The furniture hadn't survived the experience. From that point on, I'd been very careful to pay attention to what I was doing.

Still, this wasn't as difficult as the barrier that I had put up around Q'atal. I doubt anything could top that. I tapped into one of the more powerful ley lines to sustain it. I had debated with myself about whether I wanted this barrier to collapse soon or not—but then I thought, why not make it last longer? It would keep a powerful tool out of the Star Order's hands. Besides, I wasn't sure how many attacks that barrier was going to have to repel. Making it weak on purpose sounded like a recipe for disaster.

I raised it up all at once, forming a solid, perfect dome over the building. Even though it was smaller, it still required effort on my part. I was breathing a little hard, sweat dewing my skin by the time it was up and finished.

Eagle drifted up to stand beside me. "That didn't take you long at all," he observed. He sounded a bit bemused.

"It never does." It just usually requires a lot more energy.

"Do all of your barrier glow green like this?"

I hadn't thought about that until he asked. "I suppose they do at that." I rubbed the back of my neck, thinking about it, but I couldn't recall even one barrier that hadn't glowed.

"Huh."

We waited a long moment, neither one of us speaking.

"Garth, I can't tell at this distance—have they attacked the barrier?"

"Not that I can tell." I focused, trying to really pinpoint everyone at the pool. "I...think...they're all inside the building." I wasn't a hundred percent sure of that, but the strongest feeling of magic was inside the building itself, and I didn't detect anything outside of it. "I hope they heed my warning and don't attack it."

"How bad would it be?"

"Depends on what spell they use," I admitted. "It could be minor or major, depending on what they do." Seeing that hadn't alleviated his concern, I coached into terms he was familiar with. "It's like the difference between a pebble and a boulder. If you throw a pebble at a wall, and it bounces back at you, it doesn't hurt you much. But if you throw a boulder..."

He grimaced. "Let's hope they don't throw anything."

"I'm good with that."

Behind us, Chatta hissed, sounding like an enraged cat. "Xiaolang, they're coming!"

The Ascalon captain moved so quickly he almost seemed to teleport to her side. "Where?"

"Maybe thirty miles to the south of us? They're just outside of Praison."

"That's twenty-five miles," Xiaolang corrected, brows drawing together. "How many?"

There was taut silence as they both counted the soldiers in the scrying pool. The rest of us waited with baited breath, waiting for that answer.

"I counted eighty soldiers, forty Star Order Priests," Xiaolang said in a painfully calm tone. "You?"

"The same," Chatta agreed faintly. "They're moving at a pretty good clip."

"They don't want us to disappear before they can capture us," Shield noted in dark confidence. "And they probably know that winter's going to set in soon—they want this situation resolved before they're caught out in the elements."

Xiaolang nodded, agreeing with his lieutenant's observations.

Shad came over to lean against Chatta's other side, peering at the image in the water. "Beautiful, to your eyes, do any of them glow?"

Chatta frowned up at him. "They all glow."

I groaned when I realized what that meant. "They're all connected to each other, is that what you're seeing?"

She didn't take her eyes off the scried image. "That's what it looks like. The magical aura over them is blood red. It seems to be in some form of personal shield, too."

"If you're right, this is going to get tricky." Shad turned on his heels to face Xiaolang. "I only fought with a group of Star Order Priests once and it wasn't fun. When they link up like that, those shields of theirs are nearly impossible to break through."

Xiaolang groaned, rubbing at his temples with both hands. "Good news, people, I want good news."

"I can break the shields," Night offered. "After all, shields are easy for me to break through."

Chatta turned a look on Night that was so intense she nearly went cross-eyed. "I wonder why…it's true that I've never seen anything withstand a Breaker's power."

I thought I saw where she was headed with this line of thought. "If you can figure out how it works, can you duplicate it?"

"I certainly hope so." She frowned at Night's hooves.

"Before you get sidetracked with that, I need a little more intel." Xiaolang pulled her attention back to the scrying. "These personal shields, can you get around them?"

"I don't know." I couldn't help but frown slightly. "Star Order magic is strange. Very strange. I'm not sure how to combat it and I don't know enough about it to predict their capabilities. They use blood magic, that I know, and they can borrow power from other people to augment their own, but that's about all I'm sure on. This link up of theirs is a typical tactic to share power and give the whole group strength."

Shield was following this explanation closely. "So wouldn't that mean that someone in that group is the focal point?"

"That's how it worked in my day." Shad looked at Chatta for confirmation. "Do you see anyone that looks more powerful than the others?"

"That red aura is blurring everything," she sighed in exasperation, "I'm having a hard time making out details."

"If we could just figure out who the focal point is, then we can take him down, and the rest will be easy pickings." Xiaolang caught my eyes and held them. "Can you discern who it is?"

"It might take me a while to shift through everyone, but I should be able to," I answered slowly.

"Xiaolang?" Chatta was studying her scrying pool as we talked. She had the strangest look on her face, as if she had run smack into a wall she hadn't realized existed. "I think...I think the soldiers have a sort of personal shield on them."

Xiaolang spun on his heels, surprise and wariness playing across his face. "I'm assuming that you don't mean the conventional metal shields?"

"Right. Magical shields. Granted, those shields are attached to the metal shields, but still...these people are not going to be easy to fight."

Xiaolang started muttering darkly under his breath. It was in Q'atalish, so I didn't understand what he was saying. I was just as glad that was the case.

"Can you give us some sort of protective spell too?" Aletha inquired hopefully.

Chatta blinked. "Now there's a thought. Hmmm. I can think of a spell or two that will work, with some modification. Give me a few minutes to work it out."

Xiaolang stopped muttering. "Well, that evens the odds. Some."

"Why are we even worrying about this?" Shad objected. "Garth, can't you deal with these soldiers the same way you dealt with the ones in Tobadorage?"

"I'm not sure," I admitted. "Normally, I'd say of course I can. But there are forty Star Order Priests over there, Shad. Even a mage's power is going to find that many attackers challenging. And those shields...they probably protect against any kind of magical attack as well. Chatta, am I right?"

She spread her hands helplessly. "I think so, yes. Their magic looks strange, of course, but I can't guarantee that you're wrong."

Shad let loose an irritated growl.

"I'm perfectly willing to try, though," I assured everyone. "Chatta and I might be wrong—we're only guessing, after all."

"Do try, just don't overextend yourself," Xiaolang ordered. "Chatta, how fast are they moving?"

"I expect them to be here about noon," she admitted.

"Alright." Our captain blew out a breath, turning to look at the pool. "I think that they are going to head straight there, despite the barrier. We need to start fortifying that area. Garth, I know that barrier of yours is supposed to keep everyone out, but I don't like all of these uncertainties of yours. Worst case scenario, let's assume they can somehow get through the barrier and prepare some contingency plans." Xiaolang looked around the group, meeting each person's eyes for a moment. "I know we're outnumbered, but we're not beaten. Let's start working on things to even the odds."

DESPERATE GROUND

Xiaolang's predictions were right on target. The Star Order went straight for the pool as if they were a homing pigeon.

We'd spent most of the morning doing everything we could to prepare for the battle ahead. The team had put their heads together and worked out the best defenses for the area. Chatta and I had taken their ideas and put in ground fortifications and traps, all around the area of the pool. I'd actually raised the pool a little, making it higher ground. In a loose circle, I'd made the ground rocky, difficult to scale so that people could only approach from one side. Outside of this edged ring of rocks were various pits, spots of quicksand, and entrapping spells. No one was going to sneak up from behind us.

I'd done most of the fortifications and ground defenses, leaving Chatta free to study how Night's Breaker ability worked. She'd come away after an hour or so and started testing theories out. It'd taken three solid hours of hard work and muttering on her part before she devised a spell that worked like a Breaker's power. Whether it would work against the Star Order Priests' shields…well, we could only pray that it did.

Now we were all standing inside the barrier, watching them come. The air was cool, and there was a slight layer of frost that crunched underneath our boots, but I didn't feel the it. Adrenaline was pulsing through my system.

We had perhaps five minutes before contact with the enemy. As much as I'd sparred with people, and done weapons training, this was the first time I'd gone all out against enemy soldiers. In the fight to come, I might have to kill these people to protect myself. That wasn't a thought I enjoyed.

Chatta stood at my side, her wand out and ready. There was a hard, distant look in her eyes, and she was a little paler than usual.

I wanted to be right next to her, protecting her in the battle to come, but there was no guarantee that I'd be able to do that.

Xiaolang glanced back at me, smile twisted but still reassuring.

"Xiaolang says to tell you not to worry about her," Night said quietly in the back of my head. "He'll watch out for her when you have to go for the priests."

That let me breathe a little better. Xiaolang was like a force of nature when he fought. I couldn't envision anything getting past his defense.

Especially not with Chatta's protective spells enhancing his abilities.

Chatta had taken a rain-repellant spell and a strengthening spell (meant for broken bones or something of that nature) and blended them. Now everyone on the team had reinforced bones and skin. Arrows and blades wouldn't exactly bounce off of them, but they'd leave only minor scratches. It was the same idea as wearing metal armor, only without the bulky weight.

Reminded, I called her attention to me. "Chatta?"

She looked up, head slanting to one side in silent question.

"You did write that spell down somewhere, didn't you?"

"No, why?"

"It's brilliant," I said honestly. "I think you need to share it with other people when we get home."

For a brief moment a genuine smile flashed over her face. "I'll remember it, don't worry."

"Good." I didn't have time to talk about anything else. I had another task given to me after this morning's strategy session, something that I had to do quickly if it were to be effective.

The enemy was well within my range now. It was time to test just how much those shields of theirs protected them from. I turned the ground underneath their feet into a softer, looser soil and tried to suck them into the ground. Unlike the time I had tried this on the Tobadorage City Guard all of those months ago, this time it didn't work. The soil couldn't get a good grasp on anyone. It slithered right off the shields. I growled when I realized why – the magic in the dirt was being repulsed, so the ground in turn was repulsed. Frustrated, I let the earth become solid again.

"Sorry," I apologized to everyone.

Shield clapped a hand on my shoulder. "You tried. We had a feeling it might not work."

I grimaced a smile in acknowledgement but didn't let myself dwell on it. There were other things that I needed to worry about now. Over flat grassland like this, a person could see a long distance away. We could watch the main force as it moved toward the pool pretty clearly. For several moments, what I was seeing just confused me. There were these long, wooden machines being hauled along, with swarms of soldiers all over them. What were those?

Shad hissed beside me in recognition. "Catapults!"

Uh-oh.

Xiaolang's brows furrowed as he studied the catapults. "Garth, that barrier of yours—will it protect against catapults?"

"No," I groaned in realization. "It will only think of a boulder as a rock—no matter how fast it's moving."

"Can you do something about that?"

I thought about it for a moment. Then the obvious answer occurred to me. Even long distance—if I could think of only a mile as long distance—earth and stone was my domain. I could manipulate it however I wished. "Yes."

"Then do it."

When the first boulders were launched into the air, I caught them with my magic, halting them in their tracks to just let them hang suspended in mid-air. I couldn't hear actual words, of course, but even a mile away I could hear the shouts of dismay. That just warmed my heart.

In fact…chuckling to myself evilly, I molded the boulders into large heart-shaped pieces of stone.

Then I dropped them on their catapults, smashing them to smithereens.

"I think you enjoyed that too much," Shad noted with a smile.

I couldn't quite wipe the evil smile off my face. "Shad, you have no room to talk."

The troops heading for us were only a quarter of a mile away now, too close to safely ignore. Their catapults were gone, destroyed. But I had acted to stop them, which would suggest a weakness to their minds—would they figure out how to exploit that weakness?

Although I wasn't sure how they could. There was just this

tightness in the pit of my stomach, an uneasy feeling that something was going to go wrong very soon. I found it impossible to ignore.

If I had somehow missed it with my magical sense, then the bright flair against the barrier would have told me. Angry, red sparks flew up from the barrier as it was penetrated.

"Dark magic!" I swore. It was those thrice-cursed shields that were allowing them inside the barrier. As I watched, several of them put the shields smack against the barrier, then they levered them up over their heads, walking underneath and clearing the barrier easily.

I made a mental promise to myself to figure out how they did that later.

Right now, I had to get them out of here.

There was a column of soldiers and priests stacked about a dozen people deep, three people wide, with shields overlapping in some sort of attack formation—or so it looked like.

My bon'a'lon snapped out in my free hand, extending to full length with a soft click and chime of metal. Night danced impatiently at my side, his hooves sounding a staccato against the hard packed earth. He and Shad struck out at the same time, hitting the first wave of soldiers that came near.

In the next moment chaos descended.

Every person on the team engaged with the soldiers, their movements quick and lethally efficient. Chatta fired off her spell left and right, undoing the magical shields attached to the soldiers, giving us that needed edge to get past that impenetrable defense and defeat the enemy.

I desperately wanted to join in the fray but didn't. I had a different task. I had to trust Shad and Night to watch my back while I searched for that one person who maintained the link.

The noise within the barrier was deafening, full of the clash of metal on metal, screams of pain, the softer thumps of people crashing to the ground. It took several moments for me to block it all out. Focus, I told myself over and over, focus on the feel of the magic. Ignore everything else. After several moments of intense concentration, I managed to do it.

The link the Star Order Priests was maintaining was incredibly intricate. I couldn't follow the pattern. It weaved in and out, feeding off the owner like some sort of twisted parasite, drawing power off the people around it. Just touching it with my senses was making my stomach do queasy twists.

Wait, what was that? That wasn't linked to any person nearby. I latched onto a thread of power and started following it. It twisted and meandered, tapping into at least three people's shields, but finally dead ended into one person.

No…that wasn't quite right. It was attached to one person and they were drawing it from some other outside source that was hovering just outside of my senses. I mentally took a step back and looked at the bigger picture and realized that person was holding dozens of lines just like the one I'd found, all of them coming in from that outside source.

The realization of what I was sensing smacked me in the middle of the eyes. He had a whole group of people he was drawing power from long distance. And he, in turn, was feeding that power to everyone around him.

My eyes snapped open. "Shad, Night, I found him!"

"Good." Shad executed a harsh swing of his sword, hitting his opponent with the flat of the blade on the chin, effectively knocking him unconscious. "Go!"

I didn't aim for anyone in particular—I didn't need to. They were so clustered together that even if I had just struck out blindly, I would have hit someone. I spun the bon'a'lon in my hands and started carving a path forward.

Those shields were fancy and formidable, but they didn't do much good now that Chatta had robbed them of their magical barriers. I injured perhaps ten or fifteen men before the front ranks realized what was going on and turned to face me.

Shad shot ahead of me, engaging the men who were heading in my direction. "Garth, forget them and go!"

I saw sense in that order as soon as he said it. I was the only one that knew where the key priest was. As soon as he was defeated, this would end very quickly. Still, I couldn't just cut a straight path as Shad wanted me to. I was pressed in on all sides by soldiers, priests, and spells being shot around my head. Shad was just as boxed in as I was. In fact, the only person who had breathing room was Night, who was breaking people's shields left and right. In desperation, I shoved my way to his side and threw myself onto his back.

"Night, go!" I had to yell to be heard over the din of voices, clashes of metal, and the shouting orders.

Night reared slightly, lashing out and hitting two shields at once—I wasn't too surprised to see them instantly shatter. The men behind the shields flew backwards, nursing—I was sure—broken arms.

Night reared again, letting out a noise that reminded me eerily of a battle cry. Using teeth and hooves, he fought his way through the Star Order soldiers.

On his back, I sent the bon'a'lon whistling through the air, striking at anyone trying to harm us.

For a moment, an insanely clear moment, I felt like I was in harmony with all of those mages two centuries ago. Night might be terribly young for his position, but he was fighting like the trained war horse and magician's mount he was born to be—he was protecting me, as he was destined to do.

And I was fighting just as zealously to protect him.

With an equine scream of rage, he burst through the last of the resistance, and into the first rank of priests.

The Star Order Priests weren't difficult to pick out. They were in the silver robes of their Order, looking faintly sinister to my eye. When they registered I was nearby, they turned to face me.

I threw up every shield I had, protecting us—or so I hoped. Their magic had already defeated mine once. I wasn't confident of anything anymore. I was grateful when the attacks from the pool ceased firing in my area, focusing more on just the priests in front. At least I wouldn't have to dodge their attacks and the priests'.

Now that I was close enough, and without any sort of distractions— enemy soldiers breaking through my impenetrable barrier were very distracting—I had to refocus to find the priest I needed to take down.

"Garth, where?" Night demanded of me impatiently as he lashed out with his back hooves.

I didn't want to speak and risk biting my tongue because of his wild bucking, so I sent a mental picture of the one that we needed to reach.

"Got it. Hold on." Night was barely able to take two steps when the nearest Star Order Priest took the staff in his hands and gave an expert swing at my barrier.

I hissed in pain as the power on my shields overloaded, sending a backlash powerful enough to singe my nerves. Shrieking hinges, but that hurt! He swung at me again, and this time I dodged backwards, not letting my shields just take the brunt of the blow like I usually did.

I didn't want that staff to touch my shields at all.

"Garth, why are you dodging?"

"Back up!" I ordered with a hint of panic. "That staff is covered with blood magic; it can actually penetrate my shields!"

Night didn't back up like I expected him to. He reared instead, his front hooves flashing and striking the staff whistling near us. The priest yelped in panic when his staff broke, and then his eyes rolled up in his head as he simply dropped to the ground.

I stared in amazement. Fortunately, some part of my mind was still thinking logically and came up with an explanation. In order for blood magic to work, it had to be linked to a human being—in other words, for the staff to have any power, it had to be connected to the blood of the user. When Night struck out at them, he not only broke the shield but also whatever linked magic they were using in connection with those shields.

A hungry smile took over my face. "Night, break their weapons!"

"Working on it." He twisted so sharply that I was wrenched sideways in a squeak of leather.

Shad appeared out of thin air next to us, commandeering a stirrup from me and hanging on to the pommel with a white knuckled grip.

"Chatta's put a charm on my weapon that has Night's breaking ability!" he shouted over the din. "If you can get me to the priest, I can get through his shields!"

Now when had she figured out how to do that? I shook my head to clear away the thought. Later, I'd ask later. I twisted in the saddle again, taking an absent swing with the bon'a'lon at a priest that dared to get closer, searching for the priest…ah, there! I pointed to him. "The priest not interested in fighting. The one with the fancy trim on his robe, who's just standing around watching. That's the keystone." I grabbed Shad's arm to keep him from flying when Night did another one of his bucking attacks. "If I put you on the ground and vault you into his direction, can you manage?" I asked rapidly.

Shad gave me a sharp nod. "Do it!"

He dropped from his perch, knees bent slightly as he landed. As soon as he touched earth, I sent a sharp pulse up through the ground, vaulting him in the sky a good five feet. He didn't flail as I half expected, but instead tucked into his chest a little and flipped, coming down toward the priest with targeted precision.

I lost all sight of him as priests swarmed me.

It was completely against my training to release all of my shields. Still, they were doing more harm than good at this point. Every time that a priest hit them, it sent a wave of power at me, which bloody well hurt. I couldn't afford to be injured or distracted, not when there was that many of them. I trusted in my weapons training and my instincts instead, fighting with the bon'a'lon alone.

Night had not been idle while I was fighting. In fact, he had taken out two more. It became a blur of staffs, and faces, and those strange silver robes. I could feel the blood pounding in my ears, the sweat trickling over my skin and down my back, the ache in my arms from the force and speed I demanded from them. None of my training had prepared me for this.

But I wasn't going to lose to them. Not ever.

Night let out another war cry, and his back legs lashed out behind him. Over the sound of wood cracking, and the moans of pain from the priests, I heard Shad yell.

A staff came whistling at me again, and I had to catch it or be hit in the face. I bent a little over Night's back, sending the bon'a'lon up and around, unarming him and hitting him squarely on the side of the face. He stumbled to the ground, crying out in pain.

Night broke the staff before I could reach it, snorting in satisfaction. I think he enjoys breaking things. Silly nreesce.

Shaking my head, I looked up, guarding for the next attack. Three more priests were heading for me, the promise of grim death in their faces. I snarled in response. They weren't going to take me down.

From the opposite end of the barrier, I heard an anguished cry. Startled, I jerked around, searching for the source. Shad? Surely not! Shad was a much better fighter than me. If I could defend myself, then he shouldn't have any problem.

Unless a priest had somehow used blood magic to get around his guard....

I didn't like that kernel of doubt one iota. "Shad?" I yelled in panic.

The three priests in front of me abruptly jerked to a stop, the most astonished surprise scrawled on their faces. And then they stumbled forward, like they were on some sort of taut rope that had been suddenly cut.

"Got him!" Shad's voice rang out jubilantly.

I had a brief moment to indulge in a wave of relief. In the next instant, a powerful spell whipped through the air, striking every shield within sight and shattering them completely. I blinked, somewhat surprised at the ferocity of the attack. I recognized Chatta's magic easily, after so much time sparring and working with her. For her to do a spell like this, someone must have given her enough time to do an elaborate incantation.

With their personal shields broken, their main source of power gone, and most of their weapons shattered at their feet, the priests around me looked terrified. They backed away slowly, the ones closer to the entrance actually turning to run. Some ran forward, toward the still fighting soldiers.

"Stop them!" Xiaolang yelled in desperation. "They're stealing power from the soldiers!"

I could feel my blood run cold as I realized what he meant. The priests, desperate for power, were trying to drain the soldier's of their life force to augment them. But a normal man doesn't have the power that a magician does—a drain like that would kill him. I whirled around, sensing the priests that were working active magic, and grabbed them ruthlessly with tentacles of stone. Without no finesse, I dragged them away from their intended victims and roughly gathered them into one mass in front of me.

Three more joined from the opposite side, bound by magical tethers that I recognized as Chatta's handiwork. As she rounded up that side, I reached for the ones trying to escape, scooping them all up in a wave of the earth and pitching them into the group as well. I didn't dare let anyone escape.

As soon as we had all of the soldiers and priests in one area—all of the living ones, anyway—I dropped a barrier around them. They were able to penetrate my barriers when they had powerful blood shields around them, but they couldn't do it now.

Shad sauntered toward me, glancing at the injured enemy as he skirted the outside of my latest barrier, rubbing at his chin idly. "Are they secure in there?"

"Perfectly," I assured him. "Was the key priest hard to get to?"

Shad gave me a rougish grin. "He was ridiculously easy to defeat."

I laughed, clapping his shoulder. "Shad, you're so modest!"

"Hey, you brought me along for my fighting abilities, remember?" He mock pouted at me. "It's not all just looks and charm."

I rolled my eyes. "What charm?"

"Oh, now that was low."

"Save the banter for later," Night advised. "Someone is coming out of the pool."

Huh? My head snapped around. Night was right, there was someone coming cautiously out of the building. He had a crystal in one hand, which I assumed he knew a little of how to use. I found it interesting that he wasn't the typical Chahiran—his hair was a thick chestnut in color, and his skin was a more swarthy tan.

The team gathered around me as he approached. I took a second to do a quick inventory. It looked like Xiaolang had a nasty gash along one arm, which someone had hastily bandaged, and there were some obvious bruises forming on everyone but for the most part we were alright. I let out a breath of relief. Thank the Guardians we hadn't lost anyone in this frantic battle.

I turned my eyes back on the man as he stopped directly in front of me, eyes wary but not condemning. We regarded each other without a word, the silence taut and almost thrumming between us.

"If you defeated the Star Order Priests," he finally stated, "then you must be our allies. Who are you?"

"Did you read the letter?" I asked cautiously.

A rueful smile flitted over his face, almost too fast to see. "A blind man couldn't miss that letter. We know where you come from, and what purpose you are here for. But who are you?"

A reasonable question. "I am Rhebengarthen, an Earth Mage."

His breath hissed in between his teeth. Recognition was clear in his eyes. "You're of the Rhebens!"

Um…hmm. Why did he recognize my family name? "Yes, I am."

He relaxed noticeably, even smiling. "We found records in the building that listed the known mages before the war. There was three of the Rheben line." Thoughtfully he added, "All of them were Earth Mages, actually."

"It's hereditary," I admitted. "With me are Captain Riicshaden of Jarrell—" he definitely recognized that name, and his eyes flew to Shad, looking a little astonished "—and my nreesce, Night."

If Shad surprised him, Night flabbergasted him. "So that's what a nreesce looks like…" He shook his head. "Forgive me, Master Night, we heard only rumors of what a nreesce was. We did not recognize you."

"Yes, I know." Night winked at him. "You make really good peanut butter up here."

A startled laugh burst from his mouth. "So it was you! Jillian was telling me that she almost had a stallion bribed away."

"I assume that Jillian is the Life Mage?" I inquired politely.

"Yes. Um, you can tell?" That unnerved him a little.

"Yes," I confirmed dryly. "The same way that I can tell you're a wizard." Oh he was definitely surprised by that. "Do I glow brown and green to you?"

His eyes narrowed. "Actually…yes."

"You're seeing my magic," I explained patiently. "Most magicians see magic. I'm one of the few exceptions. I can only feel it."

"Oh." That took a moment for him to fully absorb. Then he blinked back into the present. "And who are your companions?"

I turned and introduced everyone. He responded politely to every person. "I am sorry, I'm being very rude. I am Nihuishen. Just call me Huish, everyone does."

"Thank you for the gift of your name."

"Will you come in?" Huish invited, a hand extending toward the building behind him. "I think, all things considered, you have the right to."

I hit the spell on the bon'a'lon, putting it up on my belt. "We would be very pleased to come up, Huish."

HOMEWARD BOUND

I'd never been inside a Watchmen Building, obviously, but it wasn't at all what I'd pictured. It wasn't open and airy, like Don's pool, but the hallways were narrow and made of dark stone. And there were lots of boxes, bags, and the like strewn in neat piles to one side. The building wasn't very large, and it was easy to see that a lot of people were crammed in here—their effects were spilling out of the cracks.

The whole team was walking behind me, looking a little sweat-soaked, tired, and grubby. But we were all definitely relieved to be actually invited inside. We had taken a moment to do one more precaution before coming inside. Chatta had cast a heavy sleep spell on all of our captives, just in case the priests decided to try something else to get out of my barrier. We had a good eight hours to think of what to do with them.

"Huish, how did all of these people gather here?" Xiaolang was honestly curious. This puzzle had been driving him crazy for days.

"That's actually my doing," he admitted. "When the Star Order Priests first came for me, I ran and managed to hide from them here. They never even looked for me here. I thought it made a really good hiding place, and then I found the scrying pool. It took me a few months to figure out how to use it, and then I started seeing other people that were doing magical things, or were being pursued by the Star Order, and I just couldn't ignore them."

The courage and sheer gumption of this man astounded me. It wasn't enough that he was hunted by the Star Order—he had pushed it over the edge by actually helping out other magicians! I felt respect for him raise another notch.

"It could not have been easy to find fifteen magicians, and bring them and their families here," I commented.

Huish gave me a penetrating look, his quick walk slowing a little. "You said that you can feel magic. You can feel all of us?"

"If I'm close enough," I admitted easily. I found it intriguing that he hadn't figured out that people who glow had magic. Or maybe he had attributed some other reason for it? When this was all over, I was definitely going to sit down and talk to the man. And then I started to slow, too, as I started to detect something I hadn't felt three days ago. It felt very familiar. Oddly familiar. In fact, if I hadn't known better, I would have said it was a Jaunten.

But that was impossible. There was only one other person with Jaunten blood in Chahir.

Huish turned and nodded toward someone coming from a different hallway. "Aiden, come meet the Red Hand and two magicians from Hain."

It took only a moment for me to recognize him. That was a face that I couldn't ever forget.

His hair was different, of course. Being made into a Jaunten always turned a person's hair white. I hadn't expected anything different. He'd seriously aged since the last time I'd seen him, looking to be in his late thirties instead of late twenties. His grey eyes went wide when they saw me, and for a split second he looked terrified.

"You." Without any conscious direction on my part, my bon'a'lon leaped into my hand and out to full extension. With a hiss and click, the blades snapped out, one of them hovering inches away from my enemy's throat.

Huish went rigid with surprise. "What are you doing?!"

Dolanaidenen flung out a hand to stop him in his tracks. His eyes were sad, almost defeated as he stared at me. "You cursed me that day, Magus. Is that not enough?"

"That was before I knew she was pregnant, you filthy whoreson!" I snarled back.

I would swear that he hadn't known that until I told him. The surprise on his face was too genuine to fake. "I didn't know," he whispered.

"What difference does that make? You were ready to sacrifice your three-year-old son!" I spat out, reliving the horror I had felt that day. To my dismay, Dolanaidenen bowed his head in shame, and slowly sank to his knees there in front of me, waiting patiently for his destiny to embrace him.

Chatta laid a restraining hand on my arm. "Garth, who is he?"

"Asla's ex-husband."

"Ah. I see." There were layers of anger under those words. The restraining hand on my arm dropped. I took that as tacit permission from her to continue.

"Perhaps she understands, Garth, but we don't." Xiaolang sounded calm, but there was this ring of authority that stopped me in my tracks.

"Not that it's not entertaining," Shad assured me with irreverent humor. "I didn't know you could get angry. You're normally such a relaxed fellow."

"It's not a good thing, believe me," Aletha muttered to him anxiously. "Buildings tend to be demolished when Garth loses his temper."

I didn't break everything when I got angry, Aletha....

"Garth?" Xiaolang prompted, not entirely patiently.

I'd never told anyone this story, and I didn't want to now. After a moment of wrestling with myself, I gritted out through clenched teeth, "When Guin was still negotiating with Vonlorisen, I had the task of rescuing anyone nearby with magical abilities. At one point, I rescued a young mother and her three-year-old son from being burned at the stake. The person who turned them in was the woman's husband." It took another deep breath before I was calm enough to finish the story. "At the time, I thought it a befitting punishment to turn that man into a Jaunten—effectively showing him how stupid his beliefs were, and painting a target on his back at the same time. That was before—" my hands tightened on the bon'a'lon "—I knew that Asla was three months pregnant."

"And why are you feeling so protective of that woman?" Xiaolang was carefully neutral.

"Asla became a Rheben six months ago." I figured that was explanation enough. I wasn't protecting some random stranger, I was protecting my sister. That changed things.

Dolanaidenen hissed in a shocked breath. "You married her?!"

How did he jump to that asinine conclusion? "No, we adopted her."

He didn't lose his surprise, but he did become rather confused.

"So you're the mage that turned him." Huish scanned me from head to foot, expression pensive.

That phrase had a great deal of understanding in it. My eyes cut to him. "You know the story?"

"Aiden told it to me before we let him in here. I had reservations at first, but he's worked as hard as anyone to protect the people here. And his knowledge has been invaluable. What you did, Magus, gave us an ally."

I didn't want to hear that. I was all wound up, and I wanted someone to pound on. Huish's words just took away my target.

Shad drifted up to my side, eyebrows cocked at an amused angle. "We had a saying in the service, Garth. 'A weapon is something that makes your enemy change his mind.' I think you've already changed this man, and for the better. That—" he jerked his chin to indicate the bon'a'lon "—would be overkill."

I was getting outmaneuvered on this one. "Xiaolang, is he sincere?"

The Q'atalian was fighting a smile, no doubt sensing that I was on the verge of caving in. "Yes."

Rats. With a desolate sigh, I shut the bon'a'lon off, putting it back to its normal size. "Oh all right, you win." I sounded like a petulant five-year-old, but I couldn't help that. And I wasn't completely sold on Donalaidenen's supposed change of heart either. Maybe I was just prejudiced, I don't know. If I wasn't ten layers of angry at the man, I might have a better perspective on the situation.

Dolanaidenen licked dry lips, eyes darting nervously to the weapon still in my hand. "What... The baby. Was it also...?"

I could guess what he meant to ask. I just scowled back, not willing to give him any more information than he had.

"I wouldn't push that question," Xiaolang advised, not entirely without some sympathy. "Aletha's right on this score—buildings tend to be demolished when Garth loses his temper. Fortunately for us, he's normally quite calm."

I sighed, rolling my eyes heavenward. "Once, only once did I have a fight where buildings got hit. And that was because I was fighting another mage! Why is everyone insisting on painting me as some sort of out-of-control natural disaster?"

"Because that's the only time we've seen you that mad?" Aletha offered.

"You can't assume something from only seeing it once!" I protested. "And I fixed everything afterwards," I added as an afterthought.

"No, really, he doesn't destroy buildings normally," Chatta came to my defense. "The time before that, he just punched Kartal."

I ran that through my head. "Um, Chatta…that didn't really help."

Xiaolang snickered behind one hand. Everyone else just outright laughed.

It took the rest of the day to get everyone packed up and ready to go. The team scattered throughout the building, helping to organize people. Chatta and I focused on the storeroom Huish pointed us to. As she had guessed, the room was full of weapons, crystals, a few wands, and books—lots of books.

Including something I'd only heard about—Magician's Indexes.

At one point, before the world turned topsy-turvy, Chahir kept a running index of all the magicians. There were two reasons for this; one, to give the common citizens a way to prove whether a magician was what he said he was, or just a charlatan; and two, to give the government a way to keep track of all of the magicians in Chahir with a list of their abilities. Anyone could pick up a copy, as long as they had the need and the proper payment for it.

When I found the first one, I just held it for several seconds, my mind unable to wrap around the concept that one of these had actually survived the purging after the Magic War. And then I croaked, "Chatta, look at this!"

She looked up from her own stack of books and craned her neck around my shoulder to see what I was pointing at. I knew when the full realization of what I was holding hit her—her jaw dropped. "That's an Index!"

"I know," I answered, stroking the binding reverently. "Can you believe it? No wonder Huish recognized my family name! He had this as a reference."

"The knowledge of family bloodlines for Chahir in that book alone," she breathed, shaking her head, "it's indescribable. Even the Remnant doesn't have a full copy, just what they could remember."

I wrapped the book carefully and put it into a crate. "We need to get this to the Trasdee Evondit Orra as quickly as possible."

"No kidding." Chatta marked the crate with a spell to where we could find it easily later. "There is the oddest collection of things in here. I found two books on defensive spells alone."

That certainly explained a lot of things.

"What do you think about Donalaidenen coming with us?"

I glanced at her face, but she was so neutral in expression and voice that I couldn't tell what she thought of it. "Maybe he really has repented for what he's done—Xiaolang thinks so. I'm still too angry with the man to be objective. As long as he stays away from Asla and her children, I frankly don't care where he is."

A small, amused smile quirked her mouth up. "You really don't hold grudges, do you?"

"Not typically, no."

We spent the whole time packing pointing things out to each other. As large as the room was, it didn't take long to get everything ready to transport. We were a good team; we had worked together so often that we just knew how the other would move.

Xiaolang found us just as Chatta was finishing marking the last crate. "Ah, I see we're done already. I think I have everyone ready to move now. Garth, we're putting them all outside, well away from all the soldiers. I think we should be ready in a half hour or so to leave."

I nodded in acknowledgement. "Speaking of which, what do you want me to do with all of those soldiers and priests?"

Xiaolang's forehead wrinkled as he thought about it for a long moment. "Just release them from their stone shackles and leave them here. I don't hold with killing unarmed men."

I had half-expected this answer, and just nodded. "Fine." I was planning on having a little chat with them first, though.

"Chatta, do you need a help with those boxes?" Xiaolang inquired.

"No, I've put a transportation spell on them," she answered with a winsome smile. "They're ready to move when I say so."

Xiaolang had seen enough of her magic to where he could just accept this with a nod. "Then let's finish cleaning up so we can go to Hain."

The soldiers were stripped of equipment, supplies, and weapons—

considering that it was Shad that was in charge of that duty, they
were lucky to not be stripped right down to their underwear. Then I
cheerfully transported them a good two miles away, just in case they
had any ideas of running for help. Shad watched, a demented smile on
his face.

Not one person dared to complain.

With that expression on his face, Shad could be pretty scary.

While Shad was doing that, I created graves for the soldiers that
had fallen and buried them. Chatta had one soldier tell her the name
of dead and she erected quick gravestones. We didn't want the families
of these men to forever wonder where their sons or husbands were
buried. It was an unpleasant task and I was relieved when it was done.

Once the soldiers were gone, I focused on the Star Order Priests.
They were a sad lot now, with all of their weapons broken. Even those
fancy robes of theirs were dirty and ripped.

I stood there studying them for several moments. Xiaolang joined
me, staring at them as well. "So, what do we do with them?"

"I don't know," I sighed heavily, feeling a headache brewing. "We
can't just turn them loose."

"No, they'll just go right back to committing the same atrocities,"
Xiaolang agreed grimly. "At the same time, I don't hold with killing
captives."

I didn't either, but I was afraid that turning them loose would be
a greater evil. Their future victims would not appreciate our restraint.
If only they didn't have this twisted magic in their bodies…magic. I
frowned slightly as I thought that through a little more. "Without their
magic, they would lose most of their power. If they cannot be priests of
the Star Order, they lose their sanction to hurt and hunt people."

Xiaolang looked intrigued by this thought. "You think we can turn
them over to the Coven Ordan, have them stripped of their magic, and
then it would be safe to turn them loose."

"Can you think of a reason why that wouldn't work?"

"No," he responded slowly, clearly still thinking, "I think it's a
good plan. I assume you can use the pool to call them."

"Yes, that would—" my words dried up as my senses registered
that we had a visitor. I nearly tripped, I spun around so fast.

Standing calmly, just inside of my main barrier, was a Gardener.
He was different than the one I had met before. A little taller, eyes
a trifle darker. He approached me in a no-nonsense stride, hand

extended.

I sank to one knee, watching his approach in confusion. Where had he come from, and why? I gently took hold of the hand he extended.

"We will take these men from you," he informed me and for once there was no other images interwoven with the words, although I detected a trace of barely restrained anger. "We are not pleased with the harm they have caused. We will teach them what they have done wrong."

I almost felt pity for the priests in that moment. I cannot imagine what teaching methods a Gardener might employ, but I would think that they are very methodical instructors. The priests would understand thoroughly just how wrong their actions were, which would be hard to bear.

"We would be glad for you to take them," I responded carefully. "We were worried about what to do with them."

At this, he smiled slightly, and I knew then that the anger was not directed at me, but them. "Then release them." He paused, looking around him carefully, and his eyes narrowed slightly in displeasure. "This land does not look right."

"I'll fix it," I promised hastily. I did not want a Gardener mad at me. "This was just temporary, to help us fight them."

He nodded in approval. "I trust you to do so, Balancer." He released my hand then and gave a pointed look at the captive priests.

I removed the barrier and stood again. With a small wave of his hand, he gathered up all of the priests and disappeared into the earth in the next instant.

"Well." Xiaolang cleared his throat slightly, expression rather stunned. "That was...unexpected. I take it that the Gardeners know what to do with them?"

"He said they were going to teach them what they had done was wrong," I explained. "He's not happy with what they were doing."

"Or with what you did here," Xiaolang observed, eyes twinkling in dry amusement. "I caught that much."

"Er...yes." I winced at that and started right then and there to start dismantling all of the fortifications I had just built that morning.

Xiaolang chuckled slightly as the land started smoothing out again into the plains they were meant to be. "You're relieved, aren't you, that the Gardeners are going to rehabilitate them."

I shrugged slightly in response. "I want to believe that men can redeem themselves. I wanted to give them the opportunity to do just that."

"That's why you just turned Asla's ex-husband Jaunten, isn't it?" His eyes were shrewd, perhaps a tad amused. "You wanted him to redeem himself as well."

Huh. I hadn't thought of it that way before—I just thought it poetic justice to paint the man with the same brush his wife and son had been painted. But maybe Xiaolang was right. "Perhaps."

"Has anyone told you, Garth, that you're just a nice man?"

I suppressed a smile. "Only when they want something from me."

Shad approached, watching as I took away the ring of rocks and put it all back where it was supposed to be. "Cleaning up? And where's our captives?"

I let Xiaolang fill him in as I focused on doing a good job of cleaning up. Like I said, I didn't want a Gardener mad at me. It took longer to fix everything than it had to create it all, but life is normally like that. By the time I was done, Xiaolang had disappeared somewhere and only Shad was still there.

"Looks like we were never here," he commented in approval.

"Thanks." It was only then that I realized Shad had not voiced any plans for the next three or four months. "So what will you do over the winter?" I asked.

"Xiaolang has invited me to come up with him," Shad answered easily. "He wants me to teach people up there my techniques for dealing with magicians. He claims it can be applied to any opponent. Beating up on raw recruits for the next four months sounds fun to me."

Those poor recruits. Shad was nearly bouncing with glee just thinking about it. It was better that he was up there causing mischief, though, than in Hain pestering me. A bored Shad was just as dangerous as a bored Didi—I didn't want either one in my vicinity.

"Garth!" Xiaolang called from near the pool. "Aren't you ready to go yet?"

"Coming!" I yelled back. I had to suppress the urge to run back to the group. I was eager to go home.

Despite my warnings to everyone, some people just couldn't handle traveling by Earth Path. After consulting with Xiaolang about it, he used his empathy to calm everyone that was panicking, holding them in something like an empathic trance until I could get them to De'Hain.

With all of the people, horses, crates, bags, and the like, we took up a pretty good area. The only place that I could think of to come up above ground that could hold all of us was the main courtyard to the palace. Well, Guin needed to know about all of them anyway, right? This was just killing two birds with one stone.

I brought all of us up, pretending not to hear all of the sighs of relief behind me. After being in water and traveling, I could at least empathize now with how everyone else viewed traveling in the earth.

There were the usual shrieks of surprise from everyone aboveground as we came up. I just eyed them wearily. Seriously, when were they going to get used to this? I'd been using this method and popping in and out of the palace for nearly two years. One would think, judging from their reactions, that they'd never seen me do this before.

By some stroke of good luck, Val Haben was in the courtyard when we came up. I'd never seen Haben startled, and for a moment I enjoyed the sheer dumbfounded, jaw-dropped surprise on his face as he took in all of the people behind me. "Garth…" he said slowly. "I see you've been busy."

"Only fifteen out of all of these are magicians," Chatta piped up, waylaying his assumptions before they could get truly grounded.

Haben managed to get his jaw back into its socket and nodded. His eyes couldn't stop roving over the people waiting behind me. "That's still very impressive. Wait one moment. I'll get some Jaunten to help sort everyone out."

Huish maneuvered up to stand next to me as Haben scurried off. "Who was that? He sort of…glowed…a little. Like Aiden."

This surprised me. "Jaunten glow to you?"

"Jaunten?" he repeated in surprise. "That man was a Jaunten?"

"The Head of the Jaunten, actually. Val Haben."

"Oh." He blinked, processing this. "Yes, there was a faint hint of red around him. I suppose that's the magical influence on his blood."

"Yes, that's exactly what it is," Chatta confirmed. "While you're here, the Jaunten will help you settle in and adapt to Hain."

Huish nodded, acknowledging this. "Magus, what about you?"

"I'll do whatever I can to help all of you as well," I confirmed. "But I can only do that during these winter months, while we wait for the winter storms to pass. Then my priority will be rescuing people out of Chahir again. I'm sure you can understand that."

A small smile tweaked Huish's mouth. "Yes. I can understand that."

Which reminded me. I turned to Xiaolang, waving a hand to catch his attention. "Xiaolang, do you and the Red Hand want a lift up to Ascalon? I'll take you up, if you want to avoid all the snow and cold weather."

His eyes lit up. "Would you? I'd appreciate it."

Aletha groaned. "I'd almost prefer the snow. How long will this trip take, Garth?"

I paused and thought about it, distances and magic balancing in my head. "Um, three or four hours? That's a rough estimation on my part, as I've never actually tried to go that far on the Earth Path."

She winced. "That long, eh?"

Eagle slung a friendly arm around her shoulder. "Think about it this way, Aletha. Which would you rather do, sleep outside for two weeks in freezing temperatures, or put up with a confined space for four hours?"

Aletha considered that quite seriously for about three seconds. "Okay, Earth Path wins."

"Wise of you," Eagle murmured with a wicked smile.

Haben must have notified Guin, because the King of Hain appeared out of a side door. "Well, I see that Haben wasn't exaggerating. Captain Xiaolang, you have set a new record with this group."

"I can take no credit for it," Xiaolang answered ruefully. "It is this man that is responsible for bringing everyone together." He turned and caught Huish's elbow, dragging him forward. He switched to Chahirese in order to make the introductions. "Huish, this is Guin Braehorn, King of Hain."

Hearing this, Huish gulped nervously and went stiff with panic.

Xiaolang ignored the reaction and kept going. "Your Majesty, this is Nihuishen, the appointed leader of this group."

Guin, no surprise, walked right up and made a proper bow to Huish. "Thank you for the gift of your name, Nihuishen. And I'm honestly delighted to see you and your people. Would you properly introduce me to all of them?"

Huish was definitely overwhelmed, but after a moment pulled himself together. Squaring his shoulders, he answered in a reasonably calm tone, "Of course, Your Majesty."

I watched in approval as my adopted king greeted each person individually. This was why I respected the man—he truly cared about each person in his kingdom. It was so easy to serve a man that had every person's welfare in mind.

As Guin walked around talking to people, Chatta leaned in and murmured, "So, what are you going to do for the next four or five months?"

"I have vacation time coming, and I'm using it," I stated firmly. "Every other time I've tried to take a break, some emergency has popped up to stop me. This time, I don't care what happens, I'm taking a break."

Chatta snickered. "Isn't that what you said last time?"

"I mean it this time." My chin jutted out obstinately.

"You said that too," Night drawled.

I ignored him. "Besides, I want to buy a house while we're here."

Night perked up. "I'd almost forgotten about that."

"What house?" Chatta had her head cocked slightly in question.

"Garth!" Guin called over the crowd. "I need you to go and tell the Trasdee Evondit Orra about the influx of magicians they're going to get soon. And after that, go talk to Haben and see what he's doing to arrange temporary housing for these people. And after you do that, help me sort everyone out. When that's done, you need to—"

I listened to the growing list of tasks in horror. Guin didn't expect me to do all of that today, did he?

Maybe I needed to go visit Small Rider, or something. Obviously, if Night and I were to get our vacation, we needed to be elsewhere.

EPILOGUE

Surely, surely he was mistaken.

Vonlorisen stood just inside the doorway, facing the palace gardens. Normally this place brought a sense of peace to him. Its carefully tended foliage, beautiful flowers, and ancient trees created a sense of tranquility that anyone could appreciate.

Today, his favorite garden did nothing to soothe him.

His eyes were fixed on a small boy of six, who was currently playing in the garden under the watchful eyes of his nurse. After an hour of playing, his clothes were a little dirty and mussed, blond hair escaping the neat combing to creep into his eyes. He didn't look like a prince, sitting there so happily in the dirt—only like a little boy.

Surely, surely he was wrong.

The boy noticed him and waved cheerfully. "Granda!"

Vonlorisen waved back, half smiling. "Are you behaving yourself, Nolan?"

The boy launched himself from a sitting position to his feet with an easy bounce, running happily to his grandfather. "I'm being good!" he assured him as he ran. Once close enough, he grabbed Vonlorisen's hand and started tugging at him impatiently. "Come see, Granda."

Vonlorisen had been incapable of saying no to his grandson ever since the child had been born. This time was no exception. He allowed himself to be led further into the garden, past the stone pathways, and into the thick shadows of the trees.

"Here she is!" Nolan beamed up at him, eyes sparkling. "I told you there would be six, didn't I?"

Vonlorisen's eyes followed his grandson's pointing finger. There, comfortably ensconced in a shallow box, was a black and white cat, lying on her side. At her belly were six nursing kittens of varying hues, obviously recently born as their eyes weren't open yet.

A sick dread filled the King of Chahir's stomach. This wasn't the first time this had happened. Nolan had predicted weeks ago that the mother cat would bear six kittens. Before that, he had gravely informed his grandfather that his favorite horse was sick to his stomach—a fact confirmed later that night by the head groomsman. Vonlorisen would have been able to ignore or rationalize such incidents if they just didn't happen so frequently. And it was more than these astounding predictions; the boy could talk to the animals too! He'd seen his grandson stroll right up to vicious warhorses without an ounce of fear, pat them on the noses, and speak to them as if they were a human being. And those ferocious, war-trained beasts would whicker happily and nuzzle back against that small hand, completely in the boy's thrall.

"Granda, what's wrong?" Nolan frowned, growing upset at the older man's lingering silence.

He couldn't keep ignoring this. Whispers were already traveling all through the palace, insinuations about the prince's true nature. It had progressed past the point where he could pretend that nothing was wrong. And the Star Order…they were no longer simply whispering behind his back. Vonlorisen dropped to his knees, putting his eyes level with the boy's. "Nolan, how did you know?"

The boy shrugged, bewildered by the question. "I could feel them. Can't you do that, Granda?"

Vonlorisen shook his head, throat constricting. That was the one answer he had been dreading to hear. "No, my boy, I can't feel what you do. And I can't talk to animals like you do."

Nolan blinked, bemused by this knowledge. "Why can I do it, when no one else can?"

"I don't know," he whispered hoarsely.

"Is it bad, Granda?" Nolan was too young to really understand how his country worked, but he could see that his grandfather was obviously upset.

He hesitated, unsure on how to answer that question. Sidestepping the issue, he asked instead, "Do you think it's bad, Nolan?"

Nolan gave a bewildered shake of the head. "Why would it be bad? This doesn't hurt anyone. I can help. I can see things other people don't. And the animals can tell me how to help them. That can't be bad, can it, Granda?"

Vonlorisen looked into that innocent, trusting face and found that he could not say Yes, it's bad. Don't you realize what you are? There was no way that his grandson, his only grandson, was guilty of all of the accusations the Star Order heaped upon people with magical abilities. He was a child, curse it. An innocent child.

Similar words, from nearly nine months ago, came back to him. "In Del'Hain, there is a five-year-old mage like myself," the young Earth Mage had declared. "Do you suspect him of such unholy practices? This is not some unnatural power, but a gift—as other people are born with gifts. You do not suspect people gifted with musical or artistic ability to be servants of some dark purpose! Why then should people with magical gifts be under such harsh suspicion?"

Was that mage right?

"Granda?"

Vonlorisen looked into the eyes of his grandson, and for the first time in his life, started questioning everything he thought he believed.

That wasn't where he let the matter rest. He couldn't just accept it that easily. Late into the night, when most of the palace was retiring, he went into the family archives. He went back two hundred years in the records, and started tracing his way through the family tree from there.

It took hours, and several generations before he found what he was looking for. Dread nearly choked him as he read the inconspicuous line.

Vonresken, Life Mage. After Founding 26-102.

"My great-great-great grandfather was a Life Mage," he breathed, eyes closing in pain.

For a long, long time, the King of Chahir sat in the dark, staring at that one line entry. The single light from the candle on the desk was on the verge of flickering out when he rose stiffly to his feet, walking toward the front of the archives. A wizened little man sat waiting for him, twisting his hands together in agitated motions.

"Ti—" Vonlorisen had to clear his throat before he could speak. Taking a deep breath, he tried again. "Tittles. Summon Saroya and have him meet me here."

Tittles stiffened, understandably alarmed. Having the Head of the Special Forces summoned in the dead of the night (to the archives of all places!) did not speak of good and happy things. "Yes, sire!"

Vonlorisen watched the ancient archivist scurry out and prayed that he was making the right decision.

ABOUT THE AUTHOR

Honor Raconteur grew up all over the United States and to this day is confused about where she's actually from. She wrote her first book at five years old and hasn't looked back since. Her interests vary from rescuing dogs, to studying languages, to arguing with her characters. On good days, she wins the argument.

Since her debut in September 2011, Honor has released almost 30 books, mostly of the fantasy genre. She writes full time from the comfort of her home office, in her pajamas, while munching on chocolate. She has no intention of stopping anytime soon and will probably continue until something comes along to stop her.

Her website can be found here: http://www.honorraconteur.com, or if you wish to speak directly with the author, visit her on Facebook.

Made in the USA
San Bernardino, CA
26 January 2020